Over three hundred missiles *lunged* towards Battle Group Seven-One at an acceleration the Alliance targeting computers had never been programmed to handle. What should have been a thirty-second closing period was now *ten*.

Dozens of missiles died to lasers and positron beams—but it should have been *hundreds*. Where nothing should have made it through the outer perimeter, over a hundred missiles broke through and charged the Battle Group.

A dozen simply...blew up. The upgrade clearly hadn't been designed into the missiles, it had to be a software kludge the missiles' hardware couldn't always handle. It showed in their AI, too. Missiles went off course, lured by ECM, or just plain *missed* without any apparent effort on the Alliance's part.

But not all, and even *Manticore* and the logistics transports' missile defenses engaged in the last-minute desperate attempt to survive as the starships maneuvered and fighters dived at the closing weapons.

They almost stopped them all.

Gravitas took the first hit, the strike cruiser the biggest ship in the battle group. The Imperial cruiser *leapt* through space as the gigaton warhead went off bare meters from her hull, her icon flashing bright orange on Mira's display as her computers tried to assess the damage.

Two more missiles hit starfighters head-on, collisions the tiny ships could not survive.

The last pair collided with the logistics transport *Venture* and detonated, vaporizing the unarmored transport in a massive blast of antimatter fire that took eighteen hundred souls with it.

Second Edition November 2016

Battle Group Avalon 2016 Glynn Stewart

Illustration © Tom Edwards

TomEdwardsDesign.com

ISBN-13: 978-1-988035-11-6

ISBN-10: 1-988035-11-2

Printed in the United States of America

BATTLE GROUP AVALON

GLYNN STEWART

CHAPTER 1

Alizon System
12:11 February 20, 2736 Earth Standard Meridian Date/Time
DSC-078 Avalon, *Bridge*

Captain Kyle Roberts, commanding officer of the deep space carrier *Avalon*, watched his bridge with calm anticipation. His newly promoted executive officer didn't know him as well as some of the other officers did, but the Captain could tell that James Anderson knew *something* was up with his massive redheaded Captain.

Anderson was reacting exactly as a good XO should when his Captain was up to something, Kyle noted, slowly and unobtrusively going around the bridge to check in on the crew at each station. The big supercarrier was currently in orbit around the recently liberated world of Alizon, and the bridge's Bravo shift could easily be taking the current calm for granted.

The Fleet Commander was less unobtrusive than he likely *thought* he was, but that was a lesson that Kyle would provide gently once the current exercise was over. War upended many of the conventions of peace, and many of the officers in Alliance Battle Group Seventeen were new to their ranks or, like Fleet Commander Anderson, arguably too junior for the roles they held.

"Sir!" a young—*far* too young—voice suddenly shouted in the bridge. "We have Alcubierre emergences—multiple ships!"

"How many contacts?" Anderson snapped, visibly dropping into his old tactical officer role before restraining himself and allowing his replacement, Lieutenant Commander Jessica Xue, to continue her report.

"We are refining and confirming with the system net," the black-haired woman told her seniors. "I have eight contacts, all in the twelve-million-ton range. We'll resolve volume as they get closer."

"Older ships," the XO murmured aloud.

"Any radio IFF or Q-Com arrival alerts?" Kyle asked Xue directly. Friendly ships would normally send an alert ahead via the quantum entanglement communicators available on any starship.

"Negative, sir," she replied crisply. A moment later, the flashing questionable contacts on the tactical plot turned to bright red. "Flag has designated them as potential hostiles, Bogies One through Eight."

"Any orders from the Admiral?" he asked, turning to the communication officer on duty.

"Negative, sir."

"Vice Commodore Stanford is running the CSP with two squadrons of Falcons, sir," Anderson pointed out. "Shall I have him set up for a scouting intercept and take the ship to battle stations?"

Kyle smiled. *Avalon*'s Commander, Air Group *should* have known better, but it would work. "They're still several hours from anything but extreme missile range, Commander," he said quietly. "Send the CAG out for a high-speed scouting pass. You can bring the ship to Condition Two, but I think battle stations aren't needed yet."

The absolutely *filthy* look Commander James Anderson gave his Captain in response to that order told Kyle his XO had finally worked it out. Like a good soldier, though, the pale Commander, as redheaded as his Captain, shook his head to clear his thoughts and dropped into his neural link to give the orders.

12:20 February 20, 2736 ESMDT
SFG-001 Actual—Falcon-C type command starfighter

Vice Commodore Michael Stanford, Commander, Air Group of the space carrier *Avalon* and commanding officer of Starfighter Group Zero Zero One, knew *exactly* what sneaky-rat game was being played.

Since that sneaky rat wore admiral's stars, however, the CAG had smiled, saluted, and promptly rewritten the schedule to put himself in charge of the sixteen starfighters and forty-seven other people in the two squadrons making up today's Carrier Space Patrol. Just in case.

"All right people, we have eight unknowns coming in a slow trajectory, and the Old Man wants us to make a sweep and see who they are," he told them. "We're going to play it nice and careful, and that makes that sweep at half a million klicks and as high a delta-v as we can turn between here and there. We are *not*—I repeat, *not*—going to try and take on eight starships with sixteen starfighters. You get me, ladies and gentlemen?"

A series of acknowledgements came back and the Vice Commodore smiled grimly. He might have his suspicions about this whole affair, but either way, his people were going to put on a good show and come back alive.

"One point six light-minutes and counting, people," he told them. "Go."

Any sense of acceleration would have suggested imminent failure of the six-thousand-ton starfighter's mass manipulators, but Michael Stanford was linked into his Falcon's computers via his own neural inputs. In a very real sense, the pilot *was* the little ship.

And he accelerated toward the potential enemy at five hundred times the gravity of humanity's ancient home.

#

Forty-five minutes later, Michael's squadrons were pushing six and a half percent of lightspeed relative to their targets and watching as the starships spread out into an anti-fighter formation. The formation was a bog-standard one, used by every force that had encountered starfighters repeatedly, that cleared everyone's lines of fire.

No clue *there* as to the strangers' identity. Sensor reports from his fighters were filtering back in, combining to give him a somewhat more detailed image of the ships. All eight were roughly the same mass and cubage, the roughly twelve million tons and thirty million cubic meters of the capital ships of a decade and more ago.

"Everyone go full active with sensors at our closest approach," he ordered. "Radar, lidar, light them up and give me targeting solutions we can feed the Battle Group missiles."

His starfighters carried blocks of quantum-entangled particles linked back to a switchboard facility in the Castle system. Since *Avalon* carried almost identical blocks, any message they sent via the quantum-entanglement communicators would reach her in fractions of a second, the longest delay being the length of the fiber-optic cables back home. Data Stanford fed Battle Group Seventeen could be used for immediate missile launches.

Normally, this kind of scouting was the job of automated probes, which was part of why the CAG figured his people *had* to have smelt the rat by now.

"Pulsing sensors...*now*," his engineer reported. The starfighter shivered slightly as it unleashed enough energy to strip paint at close range, and Russell waited patiently for the beams to hit their targets and rebound.

His fighters were four seconds past their closest approach as the data came in and the computers began to crunch it. The Vice Commodore ran over it with a practiced eye. Two battleships, two carriers, four cruisers...no fighters launched except a defensive patrol—yet.

Then his computer pinged happily and dropped class identifiers onto every ship on the display. The carriers were both *Ursine*-class and the battleships were *Hammer*-class. *Both* of which were fifteen-year-old Castle Federation designs.

The cruisers were a mix, one *Last Stand*–class battlecruiser—another Federation ship—accompanied two *Fearless*-class Star Kingdom of Phoenix ships and a single *Rameses*-class Coraline Imperium strike cruiser.

Every last one of the eight warships was a starship of a member state of the Alliance of Free Stars, and as Michael watched, IFF and Q-Com arrival codes suddenly began transmitting. His computer happily changed all of the icons to green in front of his mental "eyes" and tagged each ship in turn with its name and hull number.

With a grunt, the Vice Commodore opened a direct link to Captain Roberts.

"They're friendlies, Captain," he said in a gracefully calm voice. "Looks like the *Horus* and a few friends from home."

"That's good to hear," Roberts replied, his voice far too level for the stunt he'd just pulled on his crew and fighters. "It's always nice to have friends this close to the front."

"You realize we fooled absolutely *no one,* right?"

13:10 February 20, 2736 ESMDT
DSC-078 Avalon, *Bridge*

Kyle grinned as he received Vice Commodore Stanford's...*eloquent* description of the other man's opinion of the trick Admiral Alstairs and her Captains had agreed to pull. He took a moment to check that it *was* a direct, private link—there was a *lot* he'd put up with from the older hands and his senior officers in private—and then let the Commodore vent. In four languages.

He hadn't even known Stanford *spoke* French.

"You should have at least told *me*, sir," Anderson said quietly from next to his command chair. "As the exec, I should be aware of exercises like this."

Kyle raised an eyebrow at the younger man and gestured him closer. Activating the privacy screen around his chair, he rotated to meet Anderson's eyes.

"James, you were included on the memo Admiral Alstairs sent out," he pointed out calmly. "All of the captains and XOs were. I know we get a *lot* of email, even sitting in orbit like this, and even with neural implants, it takes time to go through it all. But"—he raised a finger—"it's your job to be on top of things. You should be bringing plans like that to my attention, not the other way around."

Anderson looked embarrassed.

"With Solace gone, I've been playing catch-up since I took over," he admitted. "My mail has not been near the top of my priorities."

"I understand that," Kyle told him. "And *I* should have realized you were that under water and backstopped you without you asking.

Honestly, I'm glad we saw this *now*, not when a *Commonwealth* battle group came out of Alcubierre."

A light flashed on his console, informing him that the Admiral was sending out an all-ships message.

"We'll resume this," he promised Anderson. "We *both* clearly still have some work to do!"

He dropped the privacy shield and looked over at the com officer.

"Put the Admiral in the 'tank, Lieutenant Carter," he ordered.

Rear Admiral Miriam Alstairs' image appeared in the middle of the bridge's main holographic display tank. Every officer in the room was linked into the computers via neural implants, but the Castle Federation Space Navy had long ago realized that a visual display was the best way to be sure *everyone* saw it.

"Ladies, gentlemen, as I'm sure you're now aware," she noted with a wicked grin that looked...incongruous... on the slim and graying older woman, "our reinforcements have arrived. I am inviting all captains, executive officers, and CAGs to report aboard *Camerone* for a working dinner this evening.

"I have our orders from Alliance High Command," Alstairs told them, "and I want all of your impressions of them—new captains and old alike. Nineteen hundred hours ESMDT, people. Undress uniforms—like I said, this is a working dinner."

The image faded, and Kyle glanced over at his XO.

"Arrange a shuttle, James," he ordered. "It seems we and Stanford are invited to the Admiral's party."

19:00 February 20, 2736 ESMDT
BC-129 Camerone, *Deck Two Officers' Lounge*

Captain Mira Solace, commander of the battlecruiser *Camerone*, was distracted to the Void and back again. She'd had several days' notice of the Rear Admiral's intent to host all of her newly expanded force's senior officers, but it was also the first time she'd held *complete* responsibility for such an event.

Everything needed to go off *perfectly*. So far, it seemed to be going well. The two Imperial Lord Captains—Hendrick Anders from *Gravitas* and the newly arrived Ingolf Benn from *Rameses*—had been first to arrive. Their XOs and CAGs had found the buffet, but Anders and Benn formed a perfectly matched glowering pair of blond giants in one corner.

Anders had mellowed since the early days of Battle Group Seventeen. That seemed to have brought him down, roughly, to the new Captain's level of discontent with a Federation officer being in charge of the force.

As she scanned the room, six officers, all women, four in the dark-blue tailed jackets of the Royal Phoenix Navy and two in the dark burgundy jackets of the Royal Phoenix Space Force, entered. The senior officers of *Indomitable* and *Courageous*—fully half of the Royal Navy's reserve ships—looked uniformly young. Like the Federation, it seemed that the Star Kingdom of Phoenix had dug deep into its junior ranks to find worthwhile officers for its re-commissioned reserve.

Admiral Alstairs was waiting for the Phoenix officers, cheerfully greeting each of them in turn as Mira matched their faces to the records in her implant, and then glanced past them to where her XO was guiding in a group of Federation officers from the new ships.

When the flag captain turned her attention back to the Admiral, the older woman was gone. Mira had a spasm of panic, glancing around for her boss, when a gentle hand fell on her shoulder.

"Breathe, Captain," Miriam Alstairs told her softly. "You've done a good job, and your people have the matter in hand. Nothing is going to fall apart if you have a glass of wine and appetizer while the guests arrive. It is, after all, *my* party, not yours."

"Yes, sir," Mira said automatically, and Alstairs chuckled at her.

"Mira, *Avalon*'s officers have just arrived," the Admiral pointed out. "I am no fan, I must remind you, of impropriety—and I think it would be *most* improper if you didn't sneak your boyfriend into a side corridor for a solid kiss."

Mira flushed, turning to meet the Admiral's gaze—and realizing that Alstairs was wearing what was getting to be a *very* familiar wicked grin. She hadn't thought the Admiral was even *aware* of her relationship with Kyle.

"I'm neither that old nor that blind, Captain," Alstairs told her with a wink. "Shoo. Enjoy my party. Believe me that I'll have work for you later," she finished, suddenly entirely serious again. "This many senior brains in one room *definitely* has value to me."

CHAPTER 2

Kyle was looking for Mira Solace as soon as he and his senior officers entered the lounge. He promptly received a gentle elbow to the side from his CAG and glared over at Michael Stanford.

The wispy blond man met his glare levelly. All three men wore the same black jacket over shipsuit uniform, but Stanford's was piped in the blue of the Space Force instead of the two Navy officers' gold.

"Try not to be *obvious* you're in lovelorn-schoolboy mode, skipper," Stanford murmured. "It's embarrassing the ship."

A steward had just handed Commander Anderson a glass of wine, and the sound of his XO almost choking on the drink nearly made up for the low blow.

"And you wouldn't be as bad if Commander Mason was here?" he asked genteelly.

"Probably would," the CAG agreed cheerfully. "But Kelly is at the backend of nowhere fifty light-years from here, and *I'm* not the Captain and the national hero, Mister 'Stellar Fox.'"

Kyle regarded Stanford levelly for a long moment.

"I've been a bad influence on you," he concluded aloud.

"Sirs," Anderson hissed. "*Admiral.*"

Avalon's Captain was used to looking down at people. Miriam Alstairs didn't quite require him to visibly bend his head down, but the older officer was even shorter than Stanford.

"Rear Admiral." Kyle greeted her with a crisp salute, followed immediately by his subordinates. "*Avalon* party, reporting as ordered."

"It is good to see you understand the concept," Alstairs replied sweetly. "Welcome aboard *Camerone*. I look forward to hearing your... *unique* take on our orders after supper."

"I live to serve, Admiral Alstairs," the captain replied carefully. He *thought* she was teasing him, but he didn't know Miriam Alstairs all that well. It hadn't, after all, been *Kyle* who'd disobeyed orders and taken *Avalon* on a wild goose chase. That had been Battle Group Seventeen's previous commander—whose orders Kyle had obeyed without sufficient question.

"And now," Alstairs continued, "I intend to exercise my renowned powers of subtlety and slice off Commander Anderson and Commodore Stanford to discuss their impressions of the new *Templar*-type starfighters the Phoenix cruisers have brought us—leaving *you*, Captain Roberts, to the tender mercy of my flag captain."

While they'd been speaking, Mira Solace had arrived behind the Admiral. The smile she directed at Kyle was surprisingly shy for a woman he'd seen remain a black onyx statue while ships and worlds burned around them. He suspected his own expression was something similarly foolish.

"Chop, chop, boys," Admiral Alstairs told Kyle's two senior officers, then turned to the two lovers with a serious expression on her face. "You've got about five minutes of privacy, then dinner is starting. We'll be busy for a while after that, and I want *both* of your opinions on our orders. Use what time you have."

With that, she swept off with two overwhelmed-looking officers in tow. Solace kept smiling at Kyle and he felt his heart flip.

"This way," she said quietly, leading him out of the lounge into a side corridor.

#

Five minutes together wasn't nearly long enough for them to catch up, even after only a week completely apart. But it was enough for Mira to regain some of her equilibrium and reenter the now-crowded lounge with equanimity.

It was almost certain that *someone* in the crowd had noticed her and Captain Roberts entering together and drawn the correct conclusion. As far as she was concerned, they were *welcome* to it—there were no regulations being violated, so as long as they were moderately discreet, there was no problem.

They returned just in time, as Mira's chief steward promptly informed the gathered guests that dinner was served. *Camerone*'s captain had helped put together the menu, and she was eager to see it turned into reality.

The battlecruiser's staff of stewards had truly outdone themselves on the preparations as well. Once dinner was called, the folding barrier that had split the lounge in half slid out of the way to reveal five small six-person tables and one larger table for the Admiral herself. Each table was covered in a white tablecloth and already held steaming bowls of soup.

Avalon's officers, as befitted the staff of the Battle Group's former flagship, were seated at the larger table with the Admiral, her chief of staff, and *Camerone*'s senior officers. Politely unobtrusive stewards made sure that each of the officers ended up at the table designated for their ship.

Once everyone was seated, Admiral Alstairs stood and tapped a spoon against her wine glass to gather everyone's attention.

"Ladies, gentlemen, herms," she greeted them. "We have four Navies and Space Forces represented here tonight, each with their own traditional toasts and greetings for these affairs. Unlike most of you, I served in the last war—a very young, very junior officer then—but I remember the tradition we forged in the face of the enemy."

She raised her glass.

"Spacers of the free stars, I give you liberty and the Alliance!"

#

When the dinner was done and the food was cleared away, Kyle knew better than to let himself sink into a food coma. He might not have the high-powered link to his in-head computer he'd had as a starfighter pilot, but even the implant capabilities his injury had left him were enough to pick up the holographic display tank hidden under the white tablecloth.

Once again, Rear Admiral Alstairs rose and commanded everyone's attention. *Avalon*'s captain found the small woman's ability to do so impressive—*he* could dominate a room without much effort, but he was a good foot taller than Alstairs and twice as broad. Size wasn't everything, but it certainly *helped*.

"As those of you who've been paying attention have probably realized by now, you're not getting away without some work this evening," she told them all. "We have received our orders from Alliance High Command, and I intend to pick your collective brains on how best to achieve them.

"First, however, I have an announcement from Alliance High Command that affects you all," she continued. "We are, as of twelve hundred Earth Meridian today, no longer designated Battle Group Seventeen. With the addition of our reinforcements, we are now the eighth largest deployment of Alliance warships and have been appropriately re-designated.

"We are now Alliance Seventh Fleet," Rear Admiral Alstairs told her senior officers. "I have been informed that to avoid further disruption to our chain of command, I am to remain in command of Seventh Fleet for the immediate future. Admiralties being notoriously frugal, you can guess how much of a raise that came with."

Kyle joined in the collective chuckle that resulted.

"I have also been informed that we are intended to act as one of the Alliance's two main offensive forces until the rest of the reserve is online and fully refitted," she said, her voice surprisingly calm. "The other force, designated Fourth Fleet, has been tasked with retaking the systems that fell in the Commonwealth's most recent campaign. We, for our sin of being in one of the systems the Commonwealth took in their first attack, have a different objective."

The projector underneath the head table whirred to life, and a three-dimensional image of the section of space the Terran Commonwealth had designated the "Rimward Marches"—and the Alliance of Free Stars simply called "home."

The front ran through the middle of the map. On one side, the immense red sphere of the Terran Commonwealth, the largest star nation in human space—and one convinced that *all* human space should be part of itself. On the other side, the dozen different variations of green that marked the different polities that made up the Alliance of Free Stars.

"We are here," she noted. A single star in the middle of the three-dimensional display flashed green. Many of the stars around it were red, marked with green carats to note that they *had* been Alliance worlds. "Thanks to Captain Roberts"—she nodded to Kyle— "we retook Alizon from the Commonwealth. But the other five systems that the Commonwealth took in their first offensive remain in Terran hands.

"Seventh Fleet has been tasked with liberating those systems."

Kyle ignored the consternation in the rest of the room as he leaned in to study the display. It didn't include any detail on the estimated Commonwealth strength in each system, but the astrography itself laid out some of their priorities.

Alizon was the most "northern" system—galactic north being defined based on Earth's polar direction and a ninety-degree angle versus Sol's ecliptic plane—of the six taken in the first wave. Three of the other five were "beneath" Alizon, spread out almost equidistant along a line that had marked the old limits of the Alliance. Frihet sat in an almost mirror position to Alizon to the galactic south, and then Huī Xing was further coreward, once the closest Alliance system to the Commonwealth.

"As part of that tasking," Alstairs noted, "we are *not* expected to maintain the security of Alizon. The Alizon Star Guard had a carrier assigned to the fleet at Midori. With the Royal Phoenix Navy reinforcing that fleet with the rest of their reserve, Alliance High Command has agreed that the Star Guard should come home.

"They'll be bringing friends from Thorn and Sebring as well," she continued. "A three-ship task group, combined with the gunships and fortifications that have been brought in over the last month, should suffice to protect Alizon while Seventh Fleet kicks the Commonwealth off the *rest* of our worlds. They're scheduled to arrive in four days, at which point we are expected to commence offensive operations."

"It's going to take most of that to get our deflectors up to the new specs," Captain Christine Olivier of the Royal Phoenix Navy cruiser *Courageous* pointed out. "They did all the heavy lifting in the yards back home, but they sent all the reserve ships"—the green-eyed and dark-haired woman gestured around at the rest of the new crews— "out with a lot of parts and pieces still needing to be put in place."

Kyle nodded to himself, surprised they'd made even that much of a concession to getting the ships forward. The early months of the war had shown that ships with last-generation deflectors were *far* too vulnerable to high-power positron beams to be allowed in the line of battle. Facing an enemy with the same weapons, the older ships had *half* the effective range of a modern vessel. A mass refit program had been commenced, and High Command had ordered that no ship without modern defenses was to be allowed at the front.

"My information is that that should take roughly a week?" Alstairs asked Olivier.

"That's what my engineers are saying," Olivier agreed, glancing around at the other captains for confirmation. No one argued—but who would want to be the one telling the Admiral you'd take longer than everyone else?

"Good," the Admiral said. "I will delay our operations before I'll send out ships that aren't ready, people," she told them firmly. "Our intelligence on enemy strength is mixed but suggests that each of our old systems is currently defended by three capital ships, mostly older cruisers and carriers.

"My preference is to assume they have the same upgrades we have," she noted dryly. "While the geography suggests certain courses of action to me, I want to hear everyone's opinions."

Other holotanks lit up under each of the tables, mirroring the main table though not yet allowing access.

"We have one final mission objective that I haven't mentioned yet," the Admiral told them as everyone studied the tanks. A single red star without a green carat acquired a flashing gold carat. Kyle placed it immediately from his pre-war briefings and inhaled sharply as he waited for her to confirm his assessment.

"Once we have liberated the systems the Commonwealth has taken from us, our final mission objective is to assault the Commonwealth naval base at Via Somnia," she said flatly. "The intention, ladies and gentlemen, is both to neutralize a clear and present danger to Alliance systems—and to, for the first time *ever*, seize and occupy a Commonwealth star system."

CHAPTER 3

A plan was starting to come together around the room, most of the officers seeing the same astrography that Kyle had and using it to inform the suggested strategy. The main idea seemed to be to hit the first three systems, Cora, Frihet, and Hammerveldt, simultaneously—punch out most of the holding forces in the region before the Commonwealth even knew the Alliance was going on the offensive.

It definitely had appeal to Kyle. The most successful offensive the Alliance had launched to date had been almost an accident, triggered when Battle Group Seventeen's then-commander, Vice Admiral Tobin, had launched a revenge campaign for the bombardment of an Alliance world.

Tobin had disobeyed orders, lied to Kyle and his officers, betrayed the trusts given to him—and led *Avalon* to liberate Alizon and destroy four Commonwealth capital ships. His crimes had left him in a brig cell orbiting Alizon for now, but his victories would likely buy him a quiet discharge without prejudice.

Few of the other occupants of those brig cells would share that mercy. Tobin's chief of staff had turned out to be a spy and an assassin, and had used the authority of her position to organize an attempted *mutiny* against Kyle. Her deception meant most of the prisoners were only facing dishonorable discharge, with only her core conspirators and those guilty of murder facing major charges.

The plan taking shape around the room—apparently already code-named Operation Rising Star by Alliance High Command—would follow up on Tobin's unauthorized victories and kick the Commonwealth in the teeth. Given the availability of quantum-entanglement communications, the use of multiple dispersed and converging battle groups was possible, if risky. The op plan allowed them to back off at multiple points if they took too much damage or faced heavy resistance.

He *really* liked it. Flexible and aggressive, it was exactly the kind of counterattack the Alliance needed to launch—and from the pleased smile on Admiral Alstairs' face, it was the plan she'd had in mind from the beginning. By having her captains come up with it, she'd earned their buy-in without even trying, and potentially picked up a few key tricks and details she hadn't thought of.

Kyle was making mental notes of the tactic when a critical alert slammed into his implant. *Every* officer in the room stopped what they were doing—mid-action, mid-sentence—as a data dump from the Alizon Star Guard hit them.

The Guard was waiting on the return of its carrier to be a fully reconstituted force, but they'd taken over the logistics depot the Terrans had built in the system. From those resources and a few Q-probes borrowed from Seventh Fleet, they'd assembled a new system scanner net. A net that had now detected something.

"This is Star Guard Sensor Command," the speaker told everyone after the critical alerts had grabbed their mental attention. "We have Alcubierre-Stetson emergences at the three-light-minute mark. Eight signatures, four twenty-million-ton, four fifteen-million-ton. We are attempting to resolve details, but we have detected the launch of several hundred starfighters."

That was four modern and four last-generation—but still powerful—warships. More than enough firepower to punch Battle Group Seventeen out of existence...but nowhere *near* enough to challenge *Seventh Fleet*.

The room erupted around Kyle. Multiple officers were shouting often-contradictory suggestions at each other and the Admiral, and orders to their juniors.

"*Enough!*" Alstairs bellowed in a parade-ground voice to make any Marine drill sergeant happy. She waited for the tumult to quiet, then surveyed her people with severe eyes. Kyle was suddenly *very* glad he hadn't been one of the officers in near-panic.

"The Commonwealth has just made a critical error," she pointed out to them. "These ships are insufficient to defeat Seventh Fleet—*but* they *are* enough that the Terran commander may be willing to push her luck. Especially if she doesn't realize our older ships' deflectors have been upgraded." Her smile was *predatory*.

"I intend to take full advantage of that fact." The holotanks throughout the room now displayed the Alizon system. "Even if they launched a fighter attack immediately upon emergence, we have *time*, people. Get to your ships. Await my orders. Seventh Fleet *will* protect Alizon."

#

"Hold on a moment, Captain Roberts, Captain Solace," the Admiral said calmly as the room began to empty, gesturing for Kyle and Solace to remain in their seats. "The rest of you can go," she told the two CAGs and XOs. "Have *Avalon*'s shuttle ready to fly."

A moment later, the two captains were alone with Alstairs, who turned a level gaze on them.

"Mira, you're my flag captain; I need to know your thoughts," she said calmly. "Kyle, you have one of the most twisted minds I've met yet. I want your ideas."

Kyle gestured for Solace to speak while he organized his thoughts, studying the holotank.

"My main concern is the new ships," *Camerone*'s Captain said after a moment. "Their deflectors are upgraded from what they *were*, but they're still not up to the standard we want them at. They're in limbo—and more vulnerable than they'll be in a week."

"But their fighters are modern," Alstairs pointed out. "Only the battleships *need* to close inside their vulnerable range—and I don't think that's the battle we want to fight. We have seventh-gen fighters—and Intel says the Commonwealth *still* hasn't deployed one."

"I don't disagree, ma'am," Solace replied. "But I'd suggest we keep *Zheng He* up front, with the older ships behind her deflectors and those of the other new ships. Gets them into the fray but covers for their weaknesses."

Zheng He was the Renaissance Trade Factor battleship assigned to Seventh Fleet. Every bit as large and modern a unit as Kyle's *Avalon*, she was also far more optimized to take—and *deal*—direct damage than the carrier was. She had the heaviest deflectors in Seventh Fleet, and putting her out in front would help keep *everyone* alive.

"*Good* idea," Alstairs said sharply. "Thank you, Mira. Still feeling into this myself, remember." She turned to Kyle. "Well, Roberts? Any fancy tricks or deadly surprises?"

He laughed.

"Despite my reputation, ma'am, I know when those tricks are needed," he pointed out. "They're generally all-or-nothing affairs, and that's a risk we don't need to take today." He shrugged. "We have the bigger hammer. Let's hit them with it."

"With the older ships in the fleet, though, do we really?" Solace asked softly.

Kyle grinned.

"We *might* not," he agreed. "But the *Commonwealth* sure aren't going to think so if we head straight for them, are they?"

22:30 February 20, 2736 ESDMT
DSC-078 Avalon, *Bridge*

Theoretically, Kyle could command *Avalon* naked in his shower via his neural implants. Nonetheless, he heaved a sigh of relief as he made his way onto the supercarrier's bridge, Anderson two steps behind him.

"Status report," he snapped, glancing around the room to confirm his top crew was on duty. The bridge was a circular room, with screens showing high-level data of the ship's status surrounding the scattered consoles. Most of the work was done by implant, but it remained easiest to share data visually.

"Flag reports all ships at ready status," Xue replied crisply. "Our fighters are deployed; Vice Commodore Stanford is launching now and assuming command."

"And our Terran friends?"

"All eight ships are inbound toward Alizon orbit at two hundred gravities," the tactical officer informed him. "The Star Guard blew two Q-probes getting in close for IDs. They have them as two *Volcano*-class carriers, two *Saint*-class battleships, three older *Assassin*-class battlecruisers and a *Lexington*-class strike carrier." Each ship flashed both on the screen and in the tactical plot in Kyle's neural feed as she spoke. "They are holding back nine squadrons—ninety starfighters, looks like the Assassins' groups—and have launched the rest as a forward strike."

Kyle considered, running the numbers. That was five hundred and fifty starfighters, which could be a problem if...

"Any class ID on the starfighters?" he asked. "We're still looking at Scimitars?"

"Yes, sir," Xue confirmed. "No sign of upgrades or modifications, either. They're inbound at four hundred and fifty gravities. They launched missiles at roughly the same time—first salvos are still forty minutes out."

Capital ship missiles—and the Commonwealth's Stormwinds were almost *identical* to the Alliance's Jackhammer in capabilities— had stupendous total ranges but only twice the acceleration of a starfighter. He checked the plot and inhaled sharply as he saw the numbers.

Five salvos of one hundred and twenty-six missiles were inbound. Six hundred plus missiles was a number he was more familiar with seeing associated with the far smaller and inferior *fighter* missiles, not all-up Stormwinds.

Silently, he checked on the command network. He had been linked into it since arriving on *Avalon* several minutes before, but several of the other captains hadn't been. Finally, Lord Captain Bann of the *Horus* and his CAG clicked on.

"All of your ships have reported ready to my staff," Rear Admiral Alstairs immediately noted over the neural link. "If anyone is *not* prepared for battle, this is your last opportunity."

It would take a *brave* officer to retract the statement from their crew that their ship was ready for battle. If anyone *wasn't* ready, they weren't that brave, and the only answer to Alstairs' question was silence.

"Good," she continued crisply. "Vice Commodore Stanford, what is the status of our fighter wings?"

Even with the new ships, *Avalon*'s CAG was the senior starfighter officer in Seventh Fleet. Kyle had checked—both of the new *Ursine* carriers' CAGs had been promoted to Vice Commodore even more recently than Stanford.

The officers of the new ships were all like that. Kyle had been a Captain for mere months, and they *still* looked so new, they squeaked to him—despite every last one of them being older than him, their promotions were weeks old.

The Reserve had two thirds as many ships as the active Castle Federation Space Navy had before the war—manning them all was a strain on the Navy's personnel.

"All fighters are in the air and all squadrons are reporting in," Stanford replied, several moments delay obvious as he coordinated with his new subordinates. "We have one hundred forty-four Arrows from the Imperials, ninety-six Templars from the RPN, and five hundred and ninety-two Falcons. These bastards are so screwed it isn't even funny, ma'am."

"I want a CSP held back to cover us from their missiles, CAG," she ordered. "Your discretion—but I don't want those Scimitars getting anywhere near my fleet."

"Recommend we hold back the Arrows for fleet defense, ma'am," the CAG replied immediately. "The Falcons can take these bastards on their own, but I get the feeling our Phoenix friends will complain if we don't let them test their shiny new ships out."

"Then go demonstrate why the Commonwealth really does need a seventh-generation starfighter, Vice Commodore," Alstairs ordered. "All ships, forwarding you a formation now. *Zheng He*, I want your deflectors between the Terrans and our new ships. Everyone else, fall into place and move out after the starfighters."

"Request permission to engage with missiles," Captain Lora Aleppo, the *Zheng He*'s commander, asked. "If they're shooting at us, I'd like to return the favor."

"Agreed. All vessels, coordinate missile salvos with Captain Aleppo," the Admiral confirmed. "Let's be about it, people."

CHAPTER 4

Alizon System
23:00 February 20, 2736 Earth Standard Meridian Date/Time
SFG-001 Actual—Falcon-C type command starfighter

Michael Stanford spent the only "quiet" thirty minutes of the flight studying the statistics on the Royal Phoenix Space Force's new *Templar*-type starfighter. It was a smaller, lighter, spacecraft than his own Falcons, but still carried three missile launchers to the Falcon's four and a heavier positron lance. They were weaker on electronic warfare but closer than the Imperial Arrow had been.

Given that the Templar was a triangular wedge, similar to but narrower than a Falcon, with two missile launchers on one side and *one* on the other, he suspected she may have had a missile launcher pulled and replaced with EW gear late in the design process—after, for example, the early deployment of the *Arrow*-types demonstrated the value of the Falcon's electronic countermeasures.

Between his almost seven hundred starfighters, the space around his strike was an absolute *mess* of jamming. His own ships were communicating with each other by Q-Com and linked into Seventh Fleet's sensors and Q-probes, allowing them to see clearly, but the Terrans were going to have a problem localizing them as targets.

Of course, the six hundred plus missiles about to flash past his starfighter strike at over ten percent of the speed of light were equally difficult to see. Capital ship missiles had the mass and the power budget to devote to powerful electronic countermeasures and didn't need to worry about keeping their emitters intact for the long term.

"All right, people," Michael said calmly over the all-ships link. "Remember, every missile *we* blow to hell is a missile that Seventh Fleet doesn't have to worry about. One shot per salvo and then prep your missiles for our Scimitar friends. One full salvo and then lances."

As a starfighter pilot, the Vice Commodore was in the top half percent of the human population for his ability to interface with computers via neural implants. It was this ability, and a slew of supporting low-level artificial intelligences and drones, that allowed a crew of three to control an eight-thousand-ton spaceship wrapped around multiple zero point energy cells and antimatter rockets.

"Kayla, prep the missiles for the fighter intercept," he ordered Kayla Arnolds, his starfighter's fair-haired gunner. "I'll handle the positron lance for the missiles."

He barely had enough time to hear Lieutenant Arnolds' acknowledgement before the missile swarm was on them and the Falcon's single fifty-kiloton-per-second positron lance spun up.

The starfighter's power readings spiked as the zero point energy cell at the core of the lance spun up, electrons being pulled off into the ship's power grid while positrons fed into specially designed capacitors.

The weapon charged over about a third of a second, accumulating enough captured positrons to feed the beam—and then Michael released that energy into space. The Stormwinds were throwing out enough jamming that his computer was only throwing up probability zones for missile locations, so he aligned the lance with a spot where several zones overlapped and fired.

He slashed through space with a single three-second pulse of positrons and hit nothing. Even with almost seven hundred beams cutting through space, most of them missed—but not all. Dozens of massive fireballs lit up the Alizon system as containment failed on one-gigaton antimatter warheads—or on the missiles' antimatter fuel tanks.

Moments later, Michael's command starfighter trembled as it blasted through the expanding field of debris and radiation. The mass manipulators that compensated for acceleration reduced the turbulence, but it was still a rocky ride.

Then they were clear—and closing on the second wave of missiles. There was less time for the computers across the starfighter strike to resolve targets and calculate probability zones—leaving where to fire almost entirely up to instinct.

Instinct was why there were still humans aboard a starfighter—and while Michael Stanford almost certainly wasn't the *best* pilot in the seven hundred ships he led to war, he was definitely one of the *better* ones.

He let instinct take over, dodging and weaving through four more salvos of missiles. Twice, his slashing cuts through space caught a missile, detonating it in a blast of pure white fire and radiation as dozens of its brothers died around it.

Finally, they were through—and a good third of the missiles the Terrans had launched were gone. The remaining four hundred were the CSP's problem now—and Michael turned his attention to his strike.

"Report, did we lose anyone?" he demanded, skimming his tactical plot.

The Wing Commanders from *Avalon*'s group and *Camerone* reported first, knowing exactly what he'd want to know. The CAGs for the new ships took a moment to confirm with their own subordinates before responding to him, but thirty seconds after clearing the last missile salvo, he'd confirmed all six hundred and eighty-eight starfighters were intact and with him.

A few had radiation damage, lost sensors and such, but the Q-Com network linking the entire strike together could easily make up for that. They had seven minutes now before they were in missile range of the Terran fighters.

"All ships, prep one full salvo of missiles," he ordered. "We have them outnumbered and I want to save the birds for the capital ships. Take any that survive the salvo with lances." He glanced at the Templar's specifications again and came to an instant conclusion. "Phoenix ships, hold your lance fire until the Falcons are in range. Everything these guys see, Walkingstick'll know. Let's not tell him anything he hasn't learned yet, shall we?"

Chuckles answered him. Q-Coms worked both ways—the same tech that allowed a probe hanging sixty thousand kilometers away from the Commonwealth Task Force in Alizon to tell Seventh Fleet what the Terrans were doing in real time; also allowed Marshal James Walkingstick, the supreme commander of the Commonwealth offensive, to know exactly what was going on in the same timeframe.

Timers flashed up in Michael's mental displays. A little over four minutes to missile range—over four and a half million kilometers at this closing velocity. One hundred and fifty seconds for the missiles to reach their targets—and fifty seconds after that for the Falcons to reach lance range of any survivors.

The Commonwealth missiles would reach Seventh Fleet over a minute before any of that...

23:07 February 20, 2736 ESMDT
DSC-078 Avalon, *Bridge*

Avalon's bridge was quiet. Kyle's displays showed him half a dozen side conversations taking place via the neural links, but no one was speaking aloud as they watched the waves of missiles sweep in toward Seventh Fleet.

The starfighters had done better than he'd expected. Out of the six hundred and eighty missiles the Terrans had launched, only four hundred and eight had survived passing Seventh Fleet's starfighters. Even as the Stormwinds had blown past the fighter strike, the Arrows they'd kept with Seventh Fleet had opened fire with their own missiles in interceptor mode.

The Arrows' design had proven to have flaws in combat, especially compared to the Falcons with their far heavier electronic warfare capabilities, but they still carried six missile launchers apiece. For every Stormwind closing on the Alliance fleet, their defending starfighters flung two missiles back at them.

Space was filled with antimatter explosions as the missiles salvos intersected. This kind of head-on intercept was inefficient at best, but

GLYNN STEWART

it made for one *hell* of a show as collisions and proximity kills took out missile after missile.

With a practiced eye, Kyle realized that none of the first few waves were going to make it through the Imperial starfighters' defensive fire. The later waves would have to survive the newly created temporary belt of radiation and debris in their path, but some would still make it through.

"Target all lances and defensive lasers on missiles waves three through five," he ordered. "I'm taking any scratches on the hull out of your pay!"

The quiet dissolved into surprised chuckles, and *Avalon*'s Captain smiled to himself. The Commonwealth had *no* idea what kind of fight they'd picked.

23:11 February 20, 2736 ESMDT
SFG-001 Actual—Falcon-C type command starfighter

The Terrans were in range a fraction of a second before Michael's people, and the icons of the closing Scimitars vanished behind a solid wall of missile threat icons. Each of the four hundred and fifty Scimitars launched four Javelin starfighter missiles into space, sending eighteen hundred missiles blasting towards his people at a thousand gravities.

Even as Seventh Fleet's CAG noted the numbers and presence of the enemy missiles, the Vice Commodore felt his own ship tremble as Kayla Arnolds returned the favor. Four Starfire missiles launched from each of his Falcons, plus three from each Templar—sending over *twenty-six* hundred missiles back at the Terrans.

"Missile defenses online," Michael's engineer confirmed over their in-ship link. "Lasers cycling at one hundred and three percent designed efficiency, ECM emitters at full power."

The two massive formations of starfighters lunged at each other through space, their missiles closing the distance between them at twice the acceleration of the fastest starfighters. Emitters threw jamming and deceptive siren songs into space, luring missiles off-course or onto perfectly straight, easy-to-intercept, courses.

The Falcons and Templars did a far better job of confusing the missiles than the Scimitars did—but where the Alliance ships had launched a single salvo of missiles, the Commonwealth fighters launched three.

Michael left guiding his missiles in to his gunner and focused on keeping the starfighter alive. Even keeping a part of his mind on the big picture, most of his attention sucked down to the plain and simple task of "do not die".

A tsunami wave of explosions reached across space, the deaths of the incoming weapons only helping to hide the survivors. He spun the starfighter through a series of spiraling pirouettes to throw off the missiles, even as his engineer fired lasers again and again.

"We have kills!" Kayla announced. "Multiple impacts, my Gods— their *entire formation* looks like it's on *fire.*"

Even the complete annihilation of the Commonwealth fighter group wouldn't save the Alliance craft from the missiles already on their way. A second salvo burned in even as they neared positron lance range, and the jammers continued their song as the lasers reaped their harvest.

"Lance range in ten seconds," he snapped across the network. "Fire at two-twenty-five."

He spun his Falcon sideways, a burst of thrust added to by the force of the explosion he barely dodged. The doughty little ship took no serious damage—and they were in range.

Hundreds of positron lances flashed into space, beams of pure antimatter cutting across the distance between the two formations at nearly lightspeed...and missing. The range was right for the strength of electromagnet deflector fields the Scimitars were supposed to have, but...

"*Shit!*" someone bellowed on the command channel. "They've upgraded their deflectors!"

"Won't save them," Michael reminded his people. "Those Scimitars have crap for lances; sustain fire until you hit!"

Their intercept speed was almost eight percent of the speed of light. The conversation flashed through the neural links in fractions of a second—and the range kept dropping as they thought at each other.

Two seconds passed. The Templars, with their more powerful lances, started burning through. There were only a handful of Scimitars left, now scattering to try to evade the solid hammer of the Alliance formation—scattering in vain.

At one hundred eighty thousand kilometers, the Falcons finally found the range. Eight seconds later, Seventh Fleet's starfighters blasted past the wreckage of their enemies.

"Who's left?" Michael finally asked, able to breathe for a few minutes as they cleared. "Who did we lose?"

The answers came in faster this time—and were stunning. Four Falcons, all from the new carriers, and two Templars. The emergency pods on all six had managed to trigger, though that was no guarantee of survival in a high-radiation combat environment.

The Commonwealth fighters, upgraded or not, had been outnumbered and outclassed.

"Sir," Arnolds interjected. "I think we spooked them—their capital ships are turning!"

CHAPTER 5

Alizon System
23:15 February 20, 2736 Earth Standard Meridian Date/Time
DSC-078 Avalon, *Bridge*

Kyle breathed a sigh of relief that was probably audible across the entire bridge when the last missile died several thousand kilometers short of even the fighter screen. Capital ship missiles were *smart*, and even having been gutted by Stanford's people, one could have made it through—and one hit would cripple any ship in the fleet.

"Sir, Q-probes report the Commonwealth ships are turning," Xue announced. "Ninety-degree vector shift perpendicular to the ecliptic, pushing to emergency acceleration: two hundred and thirty gravities."

"I guess they decided they don't want to play our game," Kyle murmured, running the numbers. Two hundred and thirty gees was an *expensive* game for the older ships in the Commonwealth force. They could do it, but their standard acceleration was set as much by their fuel efficiency as anything else.

Thanks to the mass manipulators woven throughout the Terran ship, they could increase the mass of their exhaust, decrease the mass of the ship, and create gravity fields to compensate against those hundreds of gravities—but at a price. Right now, the older ships would be burning several minutes' worth of fuel for normal acceleration for every minute they ran the higher accel. But... He crunched the numbers and sighed.

"Xue, Anderson," he said quickly. "Check my math—when can they go to Alcubierre-Stetson?"

His XO and tactical officer ran through the same numbers he had and he compared all three results.

"Burning straight up like that, they're eleven light-seconds away from clear enough space," Anderson said aloud. "Call it...twenty-eight minutes."

"And our range when they jump to FTL is just under one point seven million klicks," Xue added. "Nobody—not even *Zheng He*—can hit them with lances at that distance."

A ping on the command channel tore Kyle's attention away from his staff.

"All ships, target the Commonwealth with capital missiles and open fire," Alstairs ordered. "Maximum rate of fire, ten salvos."

Among the many refits the Reserve ships had undergone before being sent to the front was updated missile launchers. All twelve of the ships in Seventh Fleet had the same twenty-two-second cycle time on their launchers. Another ten salvos would run the ammunition stocks down a lot...but Alizon *was* a logistics depot. They'd rushed supplies in to replace the Commonwealth missiles they couldn't safely use.

There was no guarantee they'd hit—the starfighters the Commonwealth had kept back had made short work of the earlier salvoes—but they'd also arrive *after* the starfighters had their own opportunity to engage.

The Terrans had made their turn in *perfect* time. It was down to the starfighters now—but there were ways to optimize that.

23:20 February 20, 2736 ESMDT
SFG-001 Actual—Falcon-C type command starfighter

Michael Stanford could run the same numbers the officers back on the capital ships were running. The starfighter strike could empty their missile magazines as they swept by—but the Terrans were closing up their formation. A lance strike would be...expensive.

"Adjust vectors," he finally ordered after several long moments of thought. "Maintain a minimum one-million-kilometer radius. We're not playing with lances today—not when we've got a three-million-klick missile range to play with."

If the Admiral wanted him to close to knife-fighting range, she would have told him so. A full missile dump at maximum range was going to give the Terrans a headache either way. And since the mission was to defend Alizon...they'd already won. It was just a question of putting the boot in.

"Michael, it's Roberts," a voice said calmly over a private channel. "We're launching a full spread of missiles. If you delay your launch to arrive alongside the Fleet's next salvo, I think that will make an impression."

"That's almost a thirteen-minute delay in launch," Michael noted. "We could soften them up for you."

"We're not getting them all either way, CAG," *Avalon*'s Captain reminded him. "If we hit them with three salvoes of a hundred and fifty capital ship missiles *plus* twenty-six hundred fighter missiles, that should soften them up for the follow-up salvos."

"Admiral on board?" the CAG asked.

"Just flipped her the numbers," Roberts replied. A moment later, another voice came on the channel.

"It makes sense to me, CAG," Admiral Alstairs told them both. "But it's down to you at this point; we're fifteen million kilometers behind you."

"I like it, ma'am," Michael Stanford admitted. "Let's bleed the bastards."

#

Michael explained the plan to his subordinates. Then explained it *again* when some of the more inexperienced ones didn't quite get the value. Just adding the capital ship missiles' jamming capabilities to the salvo would make their own lighter missiles significantly more effective.

Once everyone was on board, the Vice Commodore watched the missiles rapidly gaining from behind him. The Terrans had started firing missiles themselves, but the angle was such now that he had no chance to intercept them.

Demonstrably, however, Seventh Fleet could handle its own defense now. The Vice Commodore's job now was to see what damage they could do to the Commonwealth before they ran.

"All starfighters, stand by to fire first salvo on my mark," he ordered briskly. The computers promptly calculated the numbers for him—given the Fleet's missiles' higher base velocity, he needed to launch before they passed him to arrive at the same time.

"Mark," he snapped.

Six hundred and eighty-two starfighters launched missiles as one. Twenty-six hundred and thirty-four missiles blasted into space.

A minute later, another salvo followed.

The third salvo was weaker, as the command starfighters scattered through the formation gave up the last missile in each magazine for their more powerful computers and larger Q-Com arrays. It still added over twenty-five hundred missiles to the hundred and forty-seven fired by Seventh Fleet.

"That's it," Arnolds said quietly. "I'm relaying what telemetry we can send from the Q-probes, but now it's down to luck and how good their defenses are."

"Do what you can," he ordered her. "You won't be the only one."

Even as he watched the missiles go in, he gently adjusted his starfighter's course, curving the eight-thousand-ton spacecraft farther away from the fleeing Commonwealth ships.

"Burn, you sons of bitches," he snarled under his breath. He might *know* that the Commonwealth hadn't ordered the bombing of the Alliance world Kematian—hell, a Commonwealth warship had *stood aside* when *Avalon* had caught up with the ship that *had* bombed Kematian—but he could still blame them for starting the battle that had made him watch a world burn.

The Terran starfighters had fallen back to this side of the capital ships. They had to know their survival chances were slim, but defending the starships was their job. The purpose of a starfighter was, in the cold equations of war, to die so that the million-times-more-expensive starships lived.

And die those starfighters did.

Michael Stanford was well aware he hated the Commonwealth now, more than he ever had before. The massacre at Kematian had sunk into his soul over time and only made him *angrier*.

He still found himself mentally saluting as the Terran Carrier Space Patrol lunged out at the first, almost twenty-eight-hundred-strong missile salvo, launching their own missiles as they went. Ninety starfighters put three hundred and sixty missiles into space—four times in a single minute—and then opened fire with lasers and positron lances.

They died. None of the missiles in that salvo had been targeted on starfighters, but the AIs in the Jackhammers recognized the threat—and delegated the lesser Starfire missiles to deal with it. The Scimitars ripped a hole in the center of the first salvo—and none of them ever made it out.

But their sacrifice served its purpose. Less than a thousand missiles of the first salvo made it through, and they collided with the interlocked defenses of eight capital ships—spearheaded by the massive laser arrays of two of the Commonwealth's *Saint*-class battleships.

None of those missiles made it within a hundred thousand kilometers of the Commonwealth ships—but the second salvo had no starfighters to blunt it and was less than thirty seconds behind.

The explosions started almost half a million kilometers out, the lasers and positron lances reaching out at weapons whose only defenses were jamming and maneuverability. With almost a hundred and fifty capital ship missiles feeding the jamming and confusion, even the Saints' defenses were less effective than they could have been.

Missiles died in their hundreds, but hundreds more survived. A desperate salvo of their own missiles, fired at the last second, gutted much of the remaining salvo—but not enough.

Michael cheered in his starfighter's cockpit as missiles slammed home. The Saints were in the rear, and the massive twenty-million-ton battleships lurched as they took hits—but somehow, the monsters kept flying, kept firing.

Only a handful of missiles snuck past the two battleships. Two of the cruisers were hit, spinning and venting atmosphere—but still managing, incredibly, to keep pulling their emergency acceleration.

Then the *third* massive salvo arrived. The Saints, already damaged, already struggling to maintain their acceleration, couldn't stop them all. Michael *knew* they couldn't stop them all, and watched with bated breath.

Then the engines on one of the Saints blew. The damage and the strain were too much, and an antimatter reactor overloaded, gouging the ship and bringing its acceleration to a sharp halt.

Its ECM down, its defenses shattered, it was easy prey—and the missiles leapt on it. Even Michael, with telemetry feeds back from the missiles, couldn't be sure how many missiles had hit the monster warship. Even half a dozen would have been too many—and it was *dozens.*

Blinded by the battleship's death, not many missiles made it past her—and the remaining ships defended themselves with a will. Some might have hit home—it was hard to say in the chaos of the explosions—but none of the ships fell out of formation.

The rest of the salvos were smaller. Even made up entirely of Jackhammers, Michael had very little hope. Missiles died in their hundreds, each salvo creeping closer and closer, but none quite closing.

Until *another* engine blew. The *Lexington*-class carrier was the oldest ship in the task force, almost a pure carrier with a medium lance armament and *no* missiles. At the front of the formation, she'd avoided any damage at all.

But her engines couldn't take the strain. She'd been designed with a safety margin, but the ship was twelve years old. Maybe corners had been skipped along the way; maybe they had never figured they'd have to push her that hard for that long when they'd designed her safety margin.

It was irrelevant. As the final salvo closed in, two of the massive antimatter thruster nozzles accelerating her failed and fed reaction mass back into the positron capacitors. Untouched by the Alliance, the twelve-megaton carrier simply...came apart.

One of the Assassins ran headlong into the debris field. For a moment, that ship stopped accelerating—and the remaining missiles *lunged* at it.

The Commonwealth spacers stopped *almost* all of them. A single Jackhammer made it through—and collided with the older battlecruiser at almost ten percent of the speed of light. Half of the ship continued forward, spinning end over end through space. The back half simply... *vanished*.

"That was our last salvo," Arnolds said slowly. "Sir, they're evacuating the last cruiser—do we intervene?"

Before Michael could even reply, Admiral Alstairs came over an all-hands channel.

"Let them go," she ordered briskly. "The only thing any of us can do at this point is shoot lifeboats...and that is not a line I'm prepared to cross.

"Let them go."

CHAPTER 6

Alizon System
11:00 February 21, 2736 Earth Standard Meridian Date/Time
DSC-078 Avalon, *Captain's Breakout Room*

With the holoconferencing system engaged, the tiny breakout conference room attached to Kyle Roberts' office looked *huge*. He and Stanford sat at the physical table in the room, and the hologram tank slid out of the wall and showed the "virtual conference room" with all twelve Captains and nine CAGs of Seventh Fleet—plus Rear Admiral Miriam Alstairs and her Chief of Staff Luiz Fernandez.

"Ladies, gentlemen, herms," she greeted her senior officers.

The addition made Kyle blink and check—hermaphrodites were a relatively small minority in the Castle Federation, though larger in some other Alliance members. Captain Eden Mauve of the *Clawhammer* was apparently a herm—as, to his surprise, was Lord Captain Benn of the *Horus*. Mauve was a tall, androgynous officer, much the stereotype of the odd gender. *Benn* was the Imperial stereotype of the stocky blond warrior chieftain, which was admittedly less gender-specific than many of its members liked to present it.

"I've spent most of the morning conferring with Alliance High Command," Alstairs told them all. "Their conclusion is that Commonwealth Intelligence misestimated the arrival time of our reinforcements. We've apparently been playing games with information in our own systems, and Command's conclusion is that, pretty much Alliance-wide, our civilian sectors leak like a sieve."

She shook her head grimly.

"As I'm sure our new ship captains are aware, but I *wasn't* until this morning"—she nodded to the commanders of the reinforcements— "all of their departure messages to family and friends were delayed seventy-two hours.

"This meant that the Commonwealth commander thought you were three days later than you were, and was planning to defeat us in detail."

Kyle chuckled evilly, and he wasn't the only one. Walkingstick had sent enough ships to deal with either component of what was now Seventh Fleet, but he'd rolled the dice on catching them separately—and failed.

The real mistake had been the Terran commander on the scene not withdrawing, immediately, of course. A mistake that Walkingstick was probably explaining the cost of right now—assuming the officer in question had *lived*.

"That said, we also don't believe we're likely to see a new offensive against Alizon anytime soon," the Admiral told them. "We are clear to commence Operation Rising Star as soon as practically possible."

"Does that mean we can finish getting our deflectors upgraded?" Captain Mauve asked. "My *Clawhammer* will go toe-to-toe with anything you point us at, ma'am, but I'd like to at least have the same *range* as my enemies!"

"That's our first priority, yes," Alstairs confirmed. "It looks like you'll have even longer than expected—Command had asked us to remain in place until *Suncat* returns home. That should be a week."

"What about landing forces?" Lord Captain Anders of *Gravitas* asked. Kyle didn't like the man, but he definitely had a point—if they were expecting to liberate planets, they were going to need more troops than the Marines aboard their ships.

"That may be our biggest delay," the Admiral admitted. "We still expect to receive three Federation Marine Corps assault transports, but they appear to have been delayed..."

Kaber System
11:00 February 21, 2736 ESMDT
AT-032 Chimera *Landing Group, Assault Shuttle Four*

Lieutenant Major Edvard Hansen watched the tactical plot feeding into his neural implant in silence. Morrison Hab was *monstrous*, a twenty-kilometer-long O'Neill cylinder built by people who figured mass manipulators were too expensive for their space habitat.

When the pirates had shown up, they'd seized the main power facility at one end of the cylinder as their first step, then moved throughout. A new version of a very old dark side of humanity—most modern pirates kept the rape and murder to a minimum, but cleaning out several million people could make you very rich.

If no one caught you.

Unfortunately for the bastards who pulled the plan together—and *fortunately* for the citizens of Morrison Hab—the assault transports pulled together for the new Fleet the Alliance was assembling had just rendezvoused in a nearby system when the news came down.

The order to go free Morrison Hab had followed that news by *minutes.*

A Navy—Imperial, not Federation, sadly—cruiser had beat them here. The pirates had responded by setting charges in the power facility and warning they would blow the entire Hab—and its million-odd residents—to pieces if the Navy got any closer. The assault transports had snuck in on the other side of the star, and now *hundreds* of assault shuttles were making a ballistic approach to the big hab.

Kaber was a sparsely populated system—Morrison and the eight other habs like it were the only homes for humans in a system with no habitable worlds—so at least they didn't need to worry about local traffic. Just hitting *each other.*

Hansen checked the plot again. The lanky, raven-haired officer's unit—Bravo Company, Third Battalion, One Hundred Third Castle Federation Space Marine Bridge—was in the first wave, heading straight for the power facility. If they carried the day, a million people would live.

If they *messed up*, three entire brigades of Marines—twelve thousand or so soldiers, give or take—would die with those million people.

Lieutenant Major Hansen had been one of the Marines who'd boarded *Ansem Gulf* before the war, back when the Stellar Fox had just been a starfighter squadron commander—a squadron commander who'd saved Hansen's life and those of his brothers. He'd been one of the Marines who'd survived to board the pirated liner, and one of the people who'd cleaned up the bodies. He'd risk his own life—and every one of those twelve thousand of his siblings-in-arms—to prevent that happening on an even larger scale.

"Just *look* at those ships, sir," his senior NCO told him under his breath, bringing his mind back to the tactical plot. "Those two are just regular wrecks, but what is *that*?"

"That" looked like a regular merchant ship, except that they weren't concealing their energy signature and the signature looked more like a *cruiser* than a freighter.

"Intel says it's a Commonwealth Q-ship," Hansen told the Gunnery Sergeant. "They want it intact."

His man whistled.

"That's gonna be a tight one, sir."

"That's the Brigadier's problem," Bravo Company's commander replied. The 103rd Brigade had drawn that straw—and Brigadier George Hammond was leading his entire First Battalion on that strike himself. "*Our* problem is to make sure that we take that facility, or we *all* get to visit Heaven tonight."

The sergeant chuckled.

"You know what they say, sir... 'If the Navy and the Space Force...'" He started to trail off, but Hansen took up the poem himself—loudly enough for everyone in the shuttle to hear and join in.

"...ever look on Heaven's scenes, they'll find the streets are guarded, by Castle's *damned Marines!*"

The *entire company* had joined in by the last line, the men trapped in the suits of armor that were unpowered until they hit assault mode.

As they wrapped up the poem, Hansen *howled*—the keening wolf howl of a Castle Federation Marine about to go to war.

The shuttle echoed as his men joined in, and he smiled broadly as the *pilot* joined in—and then hit the thrusters.

As howls rang through the shuttle, the spacecraft lit up with a massive spike of energy and blasted forward at a thousand gravities.

The armor helmets slammed down, cutting off the noise, and Hansen's armor powered up.

The pirates were doomed.

Alizon System
11:10 February 21, 2736 ESMDT
DSC-078 Avalon, *Captain's Breakout Room*

"My understanding," Admiral Alstairs noted, "is that transports should be back on their way by tomorrow morning. From our perspective, the pirates couldn't have picked a better time to try and attack the Kaber system. We don't normally have much in place to protect them.

"Once the Marines have arrived, we are expected to launch Rising Star almost immediately," she concluded. "That still gives us a week and a half at minimum to get everything sorted on our side. Is that sufficient for everyone to get their deflectors up to full strength?"

The only response was nods from all of the new captains. Kyle was checking logistics as they were nodding. Alizon had enough missiles and other munitions to completely replenish Seventh Fleet, though not a lot more. Logistics this far away from the core Castle Federation and Coraline Imperium territories were more difficult than anyone liked.

There were enough replacement starfighters to get the fighter groups back up to strength, though he made a mental note to have Stanford touch base with the Imperial CAGs. Several of their starfighters had been destroyed stopping the final missile salvos, and not all of the escape pods had made it out. Alizon should be able to provide replacement crews...*if* the Imperials were willing to take them.

"We're going to be out on the end of a long supply line," Alstairs reminded everyone, as if reading his mind. "We can replenish fuel and missiles if we have time, but the demands of the offensive may not allow that. Watch your munitions use—positrons are cheaper than missile chassis."

Most of the capital ships would have the ability to manufacture replacement munitions, so long as they could extract raw resources from somewhere. Even reaction mass could be drained from an available gas giant. *Food* was harder, often the biggest limitation on the ships' endurance.

"If no one has further questions?" Alstairs glanced around the holographic "'room'.." "If not, we have a lot of details to sort out, even if the Marines seem to be giving us a bit more time."

CHAPTER 7

Kaber System
21:00 February 21, 2736 Earth Standard Meridian Date/Time
Morrison Hab Main Power Facility

Edvard Hansen leaned against the wall in what had been the main control center for the power facility, the helmet of his powered battle armor in his hands as he regarded Major Brahm, Third Battalion's XO, levelly.

"We're pulling out *already*?" he asked in disbelief. "Last download I had still showed pockets of resistance in the hab itself."

"We're Federation Marines, Edvard," Brahm replied calmly. "And Kaber is an Imperial protectorate, not a Federation one. While the Coraline Imperium is grateful for our assistance etcetera, etcetera—and don't get me wrong, Lord Captain Amelia Hermann was *very* grateful—*Renown*'s Imperial Marines should be able to take it from here. And we, as I doubt I need to remind you, Lieutenant Major, have somewhere else to be."

"Sir, yes, sir!" Edvard chorused flatly. "One of my men died to retake this plant. I'm not sure my company is going to be entirely happy to just...leave."

"We lost twenty-six people all told, son," the shaven-headed Major told him bluntly. "In trade, we saved one million, one hundred and twelve thousand, four hundred and ninety-two civilians and took just over four thousand pirates out of circulation. I'd hope your people would regard that as a win."

"They will, sir," Bravo Company's commander replied. "Eventually. But if we're on-station for less than twelve hours, it's hard for that to sink in."

"I know," Brahm admitted. "Once we're out of here and into Alcubierre, however, you are cleared to brief them on Rising Star. I suspect realizing we're going to be taking back the systems the Commonwealth invaded will help morale."

"It might," Edvard admitted. The fight for the power plant had been anticlimactic. Most of the pirates hadn't even had a chance to realize the Marines were coming, and the remainder had lacked weaponry able to penetrate the Marines' armor. His one trooper had died to a pirate shooting a power conduit instead of her.

Brahm sighed, looking at him levelly. Both of them still wore their armored suits and carried their helmets. Edvard was suddenly very aware of the smell of aging blood that filled the room—the original control team had died at their stations when the pirates had boarded, and the pirates had joined them not long ago.

"Never lost a man before, have you?" he asked. "But you were at the *Gulf*?"

"Not under my command," Edvard admitted. "We were...the lucky ones at *Ansem Gulf*. The second wave. Once Roberts had blasted the defenses clear, we had it easy."

The Major grunted, looking around the room as if to make sure they were alone.

"Right reaction," Brahm said slowly. "Right place, even. *Never* show it in front of the men. It hurts, son. And it should. But you can't let it get in the way of doing your damned job; do you get me, Lieutenant Major?"

"Yes, sir," Edvard replied. There was a little more conviction in his voice now, but not much more in his heart.

"We're at war now, Hansen," the XO reminded him. "We're about to be on the front lines, the very *tip* of the spear. That's where they send Marines."

"That's where they send Castle's *damned* Marines, sir," the younger man replied crisply. He *wanted* to be on those front lines. He'd had a cousin on Cora, an exchange student. So far as he knew, the girl was dead.

Brahm chuckled.

"Exactly," he agreed. "We share enough tech that most of the Alliance has the same gear we do. The Imperium and the Star Kingdom train as hard as we do. But they don't have our *heart*. Federation Marines are the tip for a reason. We earned it—but we also *asked* for it."

Edvard said nothing. There wasn't much for him to say.

"If it helps *you*, Lieutenant Major, you should know that we captured two of the pirate ships," the XO told him. "One of them is what we thought it was—a Commonwealth *Blackbeard*-class Q-ship. We took it, we keep it. Your men *don't* hear that, understand me? That we have that ship is now classified, and my understanding is that Command has *plans* for her.

"Plans our Marines' deaths made possible," Brahm concluded. "We don't always know the answers, son. We don't always know why we send our men to their deaths, and that's the nature of war. But we do our job. Can you?"

"Do the job, sir?" Edvard asked. "Yes, sir. We're Castle's damned Marines, after all."

22:30 February 21, 2736 ESMDT
AT-032 Chimera, *Bravo Company Barracks*

"Gunny," Edvard greeted his senior NCO quietly when he found Gunnery Sergeant Jonas Ramirez waiting for him outside his company barracks. Ramirez was a dark-skinned weasel of a man, wiry and fast, but also smart as a whip and honest as a rock. "How're the troops?"

"Grieving," Ramirez said shortly. "Maybe…half a dozen of them have lost a comrade-in-arms before."

Edvard looked at the door leading into the central bay for his Marines' barracks. It wasn't *that* thick of a door. He should have heard something from the other side, unless his Marines were being unusually quiet.

"It hurts," he agreed. "How're you doing, Gunny?"

"Millie was a good trooper, El-Maj," Ramirez replied. "Well liked. Even I am going to miss her."

The Lieutenant Major nodded and sighed slowly.

"Time to do the job," he half-whispered, and heard the Gunny chuckle.

"And this is why I'm a Gunny and you're the Lieutenant Major," Ramirez told him. "Right behind you, sir."

That cracked the last of Edvard's hesitance and he opened the door, marching into the center of the bay linking his Marines' berths. Four corridors spread out from that bay—three holding a platoon's squad bays, the fourth holding the headquarters section and the officers' quarters. The Federation Marines didn't believe in separating their officers and men much, though the officers' quarters *did* have another exit.

"*Atten-hut!*" Edvard bellowed, his implants projecting his voice and linking into the barracks' PA system. "Bravo Company Headquarters Section, front and center!"

Suddenly, his men were scrambling. As soon as *most* of the headquarters section's twenty men were close to position, the company commander continued the sequence.

"Alpha Platoon, fall in! Bravo Platoon, fall in! Charlie Platoon, fall in! Bravo Company—*attention!*"

As his men fell into ranks—the central bay held the lockers for their gear and acted as their briefing room and main pre-prep area for missions, it was big enough for all two hundred of his people—Edvard Hansen studied his Marines.

None were in uniform. About half were still in the skintight black bodysuits they wore under their armor. At least a third were at one stage or another of being drunk or stoned. Only combat implants and training were keeping them all upright and in something resembling attention.

"We lost one of our own today," Edvard told them. "You all know that. You're wondering if it was worth it—what could possibly have been worth Millicent Ivanovich's life?"

He stalked forward, eyeing the surprisingly neat formation and meeting many of his people's eyes directly.

"One million, one hundred and twelve thousand, four hundred and ninety-two civilians," he told them simply. "That's how many people are still alive aboard Morrison Hab today—alive, above all other reasons, because when Third Battalion of the One Oh Third was told to take that power facility before the pirates could blow it, *we did so*."

Spines straightened throughout the room and he knew he'd hit his mark.

"Lance Corporal Ivanovich was a Marine, ladies and gentlemen," he reminded them. "She volunteered, same as the rest of us. She put herself between the innocent and those who would do them harm—and she died protecting them.

"That's the job," he told them. "We are Castle Federation Marines, and you knew when you signed on that you were damned for a ten-year term."

That managed to get a few chuckles out of his people.

"Millie died doing the job," Edvard said. "A lot of us will before this is over. The reason we got rushed off of Morrison Hab is that Command needs us at the front—backstopping the Navy as they punch holes in Walkingstick's battle plans and *take back our systems*."

He surveyed his people again.

"Now, the Navy and the Space Force can blow starships to hell and seize the high orbitals, but we all know to take and hold ground, you need boots on it. We're going to be those boots. So, hold your heads high, Marines, because Command knows that we are the best they'd got—and they're sending us to where they need the best!"

Ramirez started the wolf howl from behind Edvard, but he wasn't sure that the officers and NCOs picked it up first. It took seconds before two *hundred* howls filled the barracks, and only Edvard's implants could save his hearing.

CHAPTER 8

Alizon System
08:00 February 28, 2736 Earth Standard Meridian Date/Time
DSC-078 Avalon, *Captain's Office*

"Hi, Dad!" Jacob Kerensky waved wildly into the recording camera. In theory, Kyle could communicate instantly with his family via the Q-Com network, but this close to the front, policy dictated otherwise. He could get around that—rank had its privileges, after all—but even now, his communication with his son was...awkward.

"We spent a whole class today on the war and the first carriers," the twelve-year-old boy continued excitedly. "I mean, we all *saw Avalon* last year, but, well, she looked a lot different before she got all shot up!"

Kyle winced. He'd exerted some of those privileges of rank to get Jacob's class right next to the old *Avalon* when she was being assessed for whether she would be scrapped. His nightmares happily reminded him of how the old ship, the very first space carrier of the new era, had acquired the holes and scars Jacob was talking about.

His son happily babbled on about school for another ten minutes, and Kyle marveled at the resiliency of youth. For the first eleven years of Jacob's life, Kyle had been completely absent. He had, quite literally, run away and joined the Space Force when he'd found out his girlfriend's implant had failed and she was unexpectedly pregnant.

She'd done well for herself, as he was reminded as Doctor Lisa Kerensky finally inserted herself into the feed.

"All right, Jacob," the lanky blond woman said with a smile. "You do realize your father covered all of this in the Academy, right?"

"Well…maybe, but it's *soo* cool!"

Kyle couldn't help but smile at Jacob's enthusiasm. The thought of his son following him into the military *terrified* him, but given the boy's current interests, it was seeming more and more likely.

"Go get ready for bed, dear," Doctor Kerensky told her son. "Your grandmother is coming by soon."

"You're going out with Dan again, aren't you?" Jacob asked. His words sounded more bitter than the smile on his face suggested.

"Go," the boy's mother answered. As the child disappeared, she dropped herself in front of the camera. She was more dressed up than usual, suggesting that Jacob's assessment was bang on.

"We're going to the Navy Annual Gala," she told Kyle. Her new boyfriend was Daniel Kellers—clearly "Dan" to their son—a Member of the Federation Assembly and, last Kyle had checked, a sitting member of the Committee on Military Appropriations. "Lots of men and women and jackasses in uniform. Your running off to join the military on me may have given me an inaccurately high opinion of soldiers."

In the privacy of his office without spectators, Kyle stuck his tongue out at her. No one had to know, after all.

Her smiled faded to something gentler, and she leaned forward.

"Rumor mill tells me you're seeing someone," she told him. He laughed again—in this case, the "rumor mill" was him saying so in his last message. "I'll confess to looking up her pictures. She's *gorgeous*."

He didn't think the edge in Lisa's voice was *jealousy*, per se. A warmer, less poisonous, cousin perhaps. Almost…happiness?

"Her *record* makes me think she can keep you in line, too," his ex continued with a grin. "Don't let this one get away, Kyle," she finished, suddenly serious. "I know you're not a scared eighteen-year-old anymore—but neither is she. She's more likely to chase you halfway across the galaxy and drag you back than I was!"

The image of Lisa Kerensky chasing his bus down the street brought a grin to his own face. He didn't think it would have worked out for either of them, but he wondered if it would have changed his mind.

Of course, so many other things would have changed. Who knew if someone else in his place would have done as well? *Ansem Gulf*, Battle of Tranquility, the pursuit of *Triumphant*...

"I know you can't tell me much from the front," Lisa concluded. "But message us. Let us know you're okay. And message your mother," she added with a grin. "I'll remind her to message you when she gets here."

The message faded to black and Kyle smiled to himself. It meant a *lot* to him that Lisa approved of Mira. It probably wouldn't have changed much if she didn't, he was honest enough with himself to admit that, but he was glad she did.

Time could heal only so much of the distance his duties and sins had put between them. For Jacob's sake, if nothing else.

With a sigh, Kyle turned back to his work. He could record his response later, and he had a lot of work to get through to justify taking the evening off—some enterprising soul had set up a full-scale restaurant on one of the new fighter bases in Alizon orbit, and Mira wanted to try it out.

11:00 February 28, 2736 ESMDT
BC-129 Camerone, *Bridge*

"Stand by for test fire," Fleet Commander Keira Rose, tactical officer of *Camerone*, announced.

"What's our position?" Mira asked, eyeing the battleship floating in the center of the tactical plot. She knew *roughly* where they were relative to *Clawhammer*, but this kind of test wasn't something they wanted to mess up.

"We are five hundred thousand, two hundred forty kilometers and one hundred and seventeen meters away from *Clawhammer*," Commander James Coles, her navigator, replied.

"That is a bit over three times the maximum effective range of our secondary battery against *Clawhammer*'s pre-refit," Commander Rose noted. "It should be *seven* times the effective range of a seventy-kiloton lance versus their upgraded deflectors."

"Yes, it should," Mira agreed. "However, since even a seventy-kiloton-a-second positron lance is still a beam of pure antimatter that could gut our friends on *Clawhammer*, let's do this by the book, shall we?"

Miriam Alstairs had not necessarily been *slack* as a Captain, but she and her bridge crew had worked together for three years. Mira Solace had inherited that crew, and while she knew they knew *each other* well enough to operate with less explicit discussion than "the book" called for, *she* didn't know them that well.

"Understood, ma'am," Rose apologized crisply. "I have secondary lance seventeen spun up, positron capacitors at sixty percent and rising. Targeting point Zeta, standing by to fire on your command."

"Point Zeta" appeared on the tactical plot in Mira's head as a highlighted white point, roughly fifty meters behind *Clawhammer*—close enough that the beam would intersect the battleship's electromagnetic deflectors, far enough away that if something went *very* wrong and *Clawhammer*'s deflectors failed, *Camerone* wouldn't gut the older warship.

With a thought, Mira dropped into the channel with *Clawhammer*.

"Captain Mauve," she greeted the battleship's androgynous commander. "We're ready for the test shot on our end, and the probes are in position to report the results. What's your status?"

"Every test so far shows all green, Captain Solace," Mauve replied. "You may proceed when ready."

Mira gave Mauve a firm nod and turned her attention back to Rose.

"Fire one three-second burst from secondary seventeen," she ordered.

"Three-second burst, aye. Firing."

The beam wasn't truly visible to the human eye, but *Camerone*'s computers drew it in as a bright white line emerging from the battlecruiser, crossing the almost half-million kilometers to *Clawhammer*—and clearly deflecting *well* away from the battleship.

"Yes!" Rose exclaimed, then quickly restrained herself, looking embarrassedly at her Captain.

Mira maintained her calm face, the expression she knew most of those who knew her called "the onyx statue" and levelly met the pale younger brunette's gaze. As the officer started to flush, she winked.

"I call that a successful test, Captain Mauve," she told *Clawhammer*'s captain. "How's the deflection vector look?"

"Right where it should be for the upgrade," Mauve replied. "We're lining *Sledgehammer* up for the second wave test. This should be a show."

Sledgehammer had started out several hours before, carefully aligning herself almost four *million* kilometers from the other battleship. Against the older deflectors, the battleship's one-megaton-a-second main lances could be deadly at over two million kilometers.

Nothing compared to the potential range of a fighter strike, but still demonstrative of why Command had refused to send forward any ship without modern deflectors. *Now* the battleships should have an effective range of almost a million kilometers—half what it would have been before.

"*Sledgehammer* has fired," Rose reported, and Mira turned her gaze back to the display.

The battleship was reporting the beam via Q-Com, and Q-probes along the route reported its travel in nearly real time. The beam traveled close enough to the speed of light to make the distinction irrelevant, but that still meant an almost thirteen-second transit time for a four-million-kilometer shot.

Mira caught herself holding her breath for the full time. The beam, drawn on her plot in bright white again, hit *Clawhammer*'s deflectors, running against the magnetic field around the ship and shifting away from the battleship by more than enough to protect it.

Then something went wrong. The deflectors collapsed, and the beam *snapped* back into its original line. There was nothing *Sledgehammer*'s crew could do, having already ceased fire over ten seconds earlier. Mira swallowed her held breath in horror as the massive beam swung back towards the *Clawhammer*—and finally, barely, cut out twelve meters from the hull.

Camerone's captain exhaled, took a deep breath, and exhaled again, looking helplessly over at Rose.

"What happened?" she asked.

"I'd say they overloaded something and blew the emitters," Rose said slowly.

"Captain Mauve, what's your status?" Mira asked, realizing she still had *Clawhammer*'s captain on the line.

"Shaken," the herm replied bluntly. "We took some fringe energy from the beam getting that close; should be repairable." Mauve gave a headshake. "Looks like we lost an entire primary power coupling. The deflectors appear to be fine; we just didn't check the new power demand versus some of the older parts."

Clawhammer's captain looked back at her people.

"We've got some more work to do here before we're ready for another full-power test," Mauve continued. "I need to get to it!"

15:00 February 28, 2736 ESMDT
BC-129 Camerone, *Flag Conference Room*

"What the *hell* happened?" Rear Admiral Miriam Alstairs snapped.

The Admiral's anger wasn't directed at a particular individual, but it was still enough to make all of the captains on the holoconference quail, including Mira herself.

"My people have been through the power coupling in detail now," Eden Mauve said quietly. "In all of the planning and rush to get the refit complete, not to mention sending us out here with half the parts on board to install ourselves, no one ever did more than a cursory check of the power demand of the upgraded deflectors.

"Given the energy density of a zero point energy system and our need for backups, most of our ships are overpowered for their needs. We had the power *supply* for the new systems," Mauve concluded, "but not necessarily the power *grid* for the new systems." The battleship captain shrugged. "Add in that some of the parts were in the last year of their life cycle and scheduled for replacement in the near future, and we had a recipe for a critical failure. Better found in testing than in battle."

The herm took nearly being vaporized by the accident far more in stride than Mira could have in the same place.

"And your damage?" Alstairs asked.

"Minimal," Mauve said crisply. "We can't bring up a Stetson field until we've replaced the emitters the energy bleed burnt out, but we should be able to go FTL inside forty-eight hours."

Without a Stetson stabilization field, a ship *could* generate an Alcubierre warp bubble. The crew would be almost instantly killed by the radiation compression inherent to the bubble, shortly followed by the ship vaporizing and the bubble imploding, but it *could* be done.

"That beam should never have come as close as it did, regardless," Urien Ainsley, *Sledgehammer*'s Captain, said quietly. "Across thirteen light-seconds, we're supposed to have a beam variance of under one hundred meters. The beam was over *two* hundred meters off-angle and fully coherent."

The brown bear of a man shook his head and met Mauve's gaze levelly.

"We're checking all of our main lance emitters for their calibration," he told her. "I've already confirmed there was a miscommunication on Lance Five that resulted in a missed calibration after the yard work. We fucked up, Eden," he said levelly. "I'm sorry."

Mira watched the Admiral glance from one Captain to the other and sigh.

"All right," she told them, her voice calmer now. "We've got time, so let's beat this till the horse stops bleeding. We're going to do a full fleet-wide reexamination of the power grids. I am *not* losing a ship to a power failure!

"Second, I want every lance in the fleet recalibrated."

Mira winced, along with the rest of the Captains. Examining *Camerone*'s power grid would be relatively painless, if not quick. It was a chore for bots by the dozen but didn't require very many people.

Regulations required a human set of eyes on the calibration statistics of a positron lance. Even the lightest lance fired a beam of pure antimatter that could devastate a planet relatively quickly. *Camerone* alone had one hundred and forty-four positron lances. Recalibrating them all would take *days*.

The starfighters weren't as big a deal. None of the little ships in the fleet were more than a year old—and recalibrating *their* lances was part of their regular post-flight maintenance.

"Our last update placed our Marine brigades four days out," the Admiral continued. "We should be able to complete the recalibration in three days. It's been a rough day for a lot of our people, so I suggest we let everyone off the hook tonight and get started in the morning."

Mira tried not to look *too* relieved as she glanced at Kyle Roberts' image in the holoconference. As the holotank slowly shut down, she realized she hadn't managed it, as both her XO and Admiral Alstairs were grinning at her.

21:00 February 28, 2736 ESMDT
Alizon Star Guard Orbit One, Commercial Concourse

There were enough shuttles flying back and forth between all of Seventh Fleet's ships and the main orbital platform of the Alizon Star Guard for Kyle to simply add himself as cargo to one of them. He wasn't entirely surprised that Orbit One had picked up a number of civilian entrepreneurs selling to Alizon's rapidly rebuilding self-defense forces—it had been built as a "civilian transfer station."

That "transfer station" had required less than two days' work to transform into a fully functioning starfighter base. Within two *weeks*, positron lances and missile launchers hidden on the surface had been brought up and mounted into preexisting slots.

Whoever had come up with the design had been both bold and brilliant. It had enabled Alizon to be reasonably safe even when Kyle's then-Admiral had dragged *Avalon* on a wild-goose chase, abandoning the system with a single Federation fighter wing and a pile of stolen and refitted Commonwealth starfighters for defense.

Since the station had passed Commonwealth inspection as civilian, however, it still had a large trade concourse in place. The empty stalls and restaurants spoke as much to the current disorganized state of Alizon's government and economy as much as anything else.

At some point, likely while the station was under construction and trying to fool the Terrans, someone had installed a water fountain at the end of the concourse and trees along the entire center line of the two-hundred-meter mall.

Mira was standing next to the fountain, but it took him a minute to recognize her. This was actually the first date they'd managed to pull together, and he'd never seen her out of uniform. She wore a long blue dress that offset her dark skin to perfection, and he found himself frozen in place for a long moment, just staring.

Finally shaking himself, he approached her with a smile.

"I didn't realize there was a dress code," he told her, gesturing down at the uniform *he* had worn.

"Kyle, do you even *own* something other than a uniform?" she asked with a chuckle.

"I think I have a suit somewhere," Kyle hedged. "It might not fit." He stepped back from their embrace, looking at her in awe. "You are beautiful."

"And you are a walking eyeball magnet in your uniform, so you're doing just fine," Mira replied. "Come on, the restaurant's this way."

She took his hand and led him towards one of the occupied stalls. A sign proudly announced it was the Third Charm restaurant, featuring 'traditional Tau Ceti cuisine'.

"What's Tau Ceti cuisine?" he asked as they approached the live human dressed in a dark burgundy suit at the front door.

"I have no idea," his lover replied cheerfully. "It's the only sit-down restaurant I could find that we could get to without commandeering shuttles for a date." She stepped up to the host. "Reservation for Solace."

The host, however, was looking directly at Kyle.

"Of course, ma'am," he said crisply. "If you could wait here a moment?"

The host was gone for several minutes and Kyle was wondering just what was going on when he reemerged, trailing a tall dark-skinned woman with a red tattooed dot between her eyes and a chef's hat. She almost met Kyle's own height, and as she approached him, she swept off the hat in a deep bow.

"Captain Roberts!" she greeted him. "We didn't know you were coming; we would have made extra preparations!"

Kyle swallowed awkwardly. "That's not necessary," he told her slowly.

"Alizon is free, thanks to you," the chef—and, he was guessing, owner—replied. "Come in, come in! Mukesh, the best wine in the house! Ninette, clear the high table! We have Captain Roberts in the house!" She swung on Kyle himself. "And do not think for *one moment* you are paying to eat in *my* restaurant, Captain!"

"Let it go, Kyle," Mira murmured in his ear. "I hadn't thought about this, but you *did* save their planet, after all."

He nodded his acceptance and followed the Third Charm's owner in. Mira was right next to him, her hand still warm in his and bringing a smile to his face.

They were promptly seated at a table near the kitchen but out of the way of traffic, on a slight dais with an incredible view of the restaurant. The Third Charm had been extremely carefully decorated, with circular tables and wire-framed chairs that wouldn't have looked out of place in an old movie's Paris café', matched with hand-woven tapestries depicting Hindu gods and scenes from Tau Ceti's colonization.

Looking at the menu, Kyle rapidly ended up relying on his implant for translation. It was technically in English but an odd dialect with a lot of French and Hindi words added in.

"So, looking at this," Mira told him, "Tau Ceti cuisine is what happens when a Frenchman marries an Indian woman and they're compromising on what to feed the children."

After poking at translations through their implants, they settled on the 'escargot rogan josh' for an appetizer and continued to peruse the menu.

"You know we're going to be in different battle groups," Mira said quietly after the waiters had moved on.

"It makes sense," he admitted. "Split the modern warships up, we're half again the volume and mass of the ships from the Reserve. *Avalon*'s our most powerful unit, too."

"It's going to be a busy few days with the recalibration now, too," she sighed. "You are *not* permitted to die on me, Kyle Roberts. Is that clear?"

"I wasn't planning on it," he chuckled. "The same is true for you, you know. I need to introduce you to my mother. And my son, for that matter," he admitted. "Apparently, his mother looked up your picture online. I'm told she approves."

It was Mira's turn to chuckle.

"You should have seen the twenty-two-minute-long loop of exclamation and shock my sister sent me back when I told her," she replied. "I'm not entirely sure she *breathed*."

Kyle smiled, but he also understood why she'd raised the topic.

"We probably won't manage to get together again before we move out," he acknowledged aloud. "We'll survive, though. Duty divides so many."

"It does," she nodded. "For *tonight*, however, I must point out that this station has more than one entrepreneur aboard—and one of them has opened what I'm told is a *very* nice hotel." Her hand sneaked across the table to settle on his. "Suffice to say I have a room booked and nearly ten hours before I need to be back on ship. Let's take what time we have."

He lifted his glass in a silent toast of agreement.

CHAPTER 9

"We have Alcubierre emergence signatures," Xue reported. "I have four signatures and they are on schedule for *Suncat* and her companions."

Kyle studied the emergence signatures on the screen. *Suncat* herself was a thirty-million-cubic-meter, twelve-million-ton carrier—effectively an *Ursine*-class ship like *Polar Bear* or *Grizzly* built under license. The two strike cruisers accompanying her—*Excelsior* of the Thorn Defense Force and *Voltaire* of the Sebring Space Navy—were home-built ships of a similar technological pedigree.

The fourth ship was a Federation vessel, a *Myth and Truth*–class mobile shipyard intended to bring those three ships up to the same specifications as the Reserve ships assigned to Seventh Fleet. The addition of the *Basilisk and Toad* had caused the delay in *Suncat's* arrival. No one had wanted one of the incalculably valuable mobile shipyards flying unescorted.

"Looks like we're the closest," Kyle observed. There was no point in calibrating Seventh Fleet's energy weapons without test-firing them, which required enough safety distance that the Fleet was spread out around the system. "Take us over to say hi and hail them for me."

His bridge team was used to his idiosyncrasies by now, and Maria Pendez, his chief navigator, started the ship moving even as the com officer linked *Avalon* to *Suncat*—via a quantum-entanglement switchboard in the Castle system.

"Welcome home, Captain Larue," Kyle said quietly as the channel opened, and the space-black face of the only surviving starship captain of the Alizon Star Guard appeared on his screen. "It's good to see you and *Suncat* where you belong."

"It's good to be back," Kojo Larue rumbled back at him. "And the welcome committee is fitting as well. I must thank you, Captain Roberts, for all you have done for my people—all that fate would not permit *me* to do." He clasped his hands together and bowed over them.

Kyle nodded, acknowledging the bow as non-awkwardly as he could. Captain Larue had been the senior officer of the Star Guard and able to do whatever he wanted with his ship. His ship had been desperately needed where it was, and would also have been insufficient against the defenses *Avalon* had encountered in the system.

"Rear Admiral Alstairs will want to speak with you as well," Kyle warned Larue. "So will President Ingolfson." There was, after all, no way the senior survivor of the Star Guard was going to stay a Captain longer than it took Alizon's president to find him and pin a set of Admiral's stars on him.

Larue's resigned expression suggested he'd made the same assessment Kyle had.

"Of course," he allowed. "Our presence, I hope, is sufficient to allow you to liberate other systems as you did mine, Captain Roberts?"

Kyle glanced around his bridge. Everyone here was cleared on Rising Star, though the intended launch date was still being kept somewhat quiet. Larue needed to know though

"Operating Rising Star will kick off as soon as our Marines arrive, Captain Larue," he told the other man. "We're going back and we're kicking the Commonwealth off our worlds."

"With you at the heart, I do not think they will know what hit them," the black giant on *Suncat*'s bridge said with a bright grin. "And other worlds will know the Stellar Fox as we do. We will speak before you leave, Captain Roberts, but may God go with you in all your travels."

Kyle *hated* that nickname, but somehow it was less offensive coming from Larue than the news media.

"May the Gods walk with you as well, Captain."

16:00 March 1, 2736 ESMDT
BC-129 Camerone, *Shuttle Landing Bay*

Mira Solace eyed the camera team she'd been ordered to allow on her ship more than slightly askance. She understood why the heavily jowled blond President next to her wanted this recorded, but she'd wanted to have her own public relations people do the recording.

The shuttle bay they stood in was hardly a *classified* portion of the battlecruiser, but she still didn't trust the news people not to screw up *something*.

But President Ingolfson had wanted this recorded and broadcast to all of Alizon, and Admiral Alstairs had signed off on it. Which left Captain Mira Solace standing with those two worthies and *Admiral* Kojo Larue, waiting for her boyfriend's shuttle to arrive.

With a band.

As the shuttle drifted slowly in to a safe landing, she wondered what he was making of it. All she'd been allowed to tell him when she'd asked him over was that they were having an in-person staff meeting with the Star Guard's new Admiral.

Nonetheless, the shuttle door opened as soon as the area had cooled down, and Kyle Roberts' massive frame was suddenly visible in that exit.

The band struck up as soon as they saw him, the spirited trumpets of "Alizon Triumphant" ringing across the shuttle bay as Kyle slowly stepped forward. He met Mira's gaze with an arched eyebrow, and she smiled. She suspected his opinion of Alizon's adulation of him, but he was taking it in stride.

Her opinion was that it had to be directed at either him or Vice Admiral Tobin, and since Tobin was in a *jail cell* awaiting shipment back to Castle, it landed on Kyle. Both Alizon and the Federation needed him to smile and take it.

Which was exactly what he proceeded to do. Carefully giving the camera crew his best profile, he walked down the carpet Ingolfson's people had laid on her shuttle bay deck and approached the Admirals and President.

"Ma'am." He greeted Alstairs with a crisp salute, then turned to the Alizonis. "Sirs." He saluted again. He gave Mira a firm nod, but she *hoped* the camera hadn't caught the softening of his eyes when he met her gaze.

"Captain Roberts," the Rear Admiral greeted him. "As I suspect you've guessed, there is more going on than a staff meeting. I don't believe you've actually met Kenneth Ingolfson, President of the Alizon Republic?"

"I have not," Kyle confirmed. His expression appeared bemused to Mira, but he shook the President's offered hand.

"Captain Roberts," Ingolfson said calmly. "I'm sure you have wondered at the lack of full gratitude from the government of the Alizon Republic. You saved our world, after all."

"You seemed busy," the big Captain demurred, and Mira caught at least one choked-off chuckle from the media contingent.

Maybe the reporters weren't *all* bad.

"The biggest constraint, Captain, was that we had neither an Admiral of the Star Guard nor a fully reconstituted Congress. In the absence of both, my options were limited as to how we could honor you—and those options did not appear appropriate.

"Now, however," the President continued, "Admiral Larue has returned to us and been properly promoted as the senior officer of the Alizon Star Guard. Now, with the permission of the current Provisional Government of the Alizon Republic, he has something for you."

Larue was a big man, matching Kyle in almost every dimension and with skin and hair black as deep space. He seemed more...intense than Kyle too, and Mira found him mildly unnerving.

"Captain Kyle Roberts," he said formally. "Kneel, please."

Kyle obeyed, taking a single knee on the carpet runner.

"By the authority vested in me by the people, the Republic and the government of Alizon, as senior officer of the Alizon Star Guard, I hereby bestow upon you the Diamond Nova of Honor."

Larue produced a gold medal on a black ribbon from a box the President handed him. Mira caught enough of a look to see the supernova carefully inlaid into the front in small diamond chips. In another context, it would probably be gaudy—but it was also Alizon's highest award for valor.

"Please accept the Nova both on your own behalf and on behalf of your crew and pilots who fought bravely and victoriously to free our system from the Terran occupation.

"While Alizon is free, your deeds will not be forgotten."

CHAPTER 10

Alizon System
18:00 March 1, 2736 Earth Standard Meridian Date/Time
BC-129 Camerone, *Flag Conference Room*

While Alizon's medal-awarding ceremonies were thankfully brief, by the time the President and his media people were done with Kyle, he felt like a wrung-out dishrag—and *then* discovered there actually *was* still an in-person captains' meeting taking place aboard *Camerone*.

The advantage to dating the flagship's captain was that he had somewhere to store the gaudy atrocity the Alizonis had given him and didn't have to *wear* the thing into the conference. He'd also stolen a shower and was feeling almost human when he sat down in the big conference room on the battlecruiser's flag deck.

It was a small gathering, just Rear Admiral Alstairs and her twelve warship captains. The room was big enough that they only occupied the bottom tier of the four-tier amphitheater-style space. Alstairs stood in the center, looking at each of her people in turn as they settled in to see what was going on.

"While *part* of this meeting was an excuse to get Captain Roberts where President Ingolfson could successfully ambush him," Alstairs admitted to a muted chorus of chuckles, "I also wanted to get us all together, face-to-face, at least one more time before we kick off Operation Rising Star."

Tired as he was, that got Kyle to straighten up and pay attention. The high-level plan for Rising Star had been bounced back and forth between the captains and Alstairs' staff for a while now, so all of the captains knew the plan. More detailed plans were dependent on which ships were assigned to which attacks.

"The plan for Rising Star calls for three battle groups of four ships each," Alstairs continued, as if listening to his thoughts. "We've all run through scenarios of which ships should go where, and we all know the intel on our target systems inside and out. We're down to details and assignments, and I've been buried in discussions with Alliance High Command on those assignments for the last two days."

With a wholly unnecessary gesture, Alstairs brought up an image of all twelve ships of Seventh Fleet in the holoprojection above her head.

"The biggest issue is that we have no O-Eight officers in Seventh Fleet except myself," she said bluntly. "Most of our captains, especially those in our latest reinforcements, are extremely junior. If we'd been organized properly, a force of this size would have an O-*Nine* in command, with at least two Rear Admirals for subordinate commands.

"But with the current rush of ships and flotillas across the Alliance, it seems no one had any Admirals to send us," Alstairs continued dryly. "Operation Peacock, Fourth Fleet's mission to liberate the systems the Commonwealth took in January, is currently being commanded by an Imperial *Vice* Admiral. Our highest flag officers are commanding the largest deployments—defensive formations, one and all.

"Which leaves us in a quandary I intend to solve in the finest of Federation traditions: by breveting people to ranks that don't exist," she told them with a chuckle. "Captain Roberts, Captain Aleppo: get up."

Kyle obeyed, eyeing the small woman with the pale skin and the shaved head who rose as well. Lora Aleppo was generally quiet, but when she spoke, the battleship captain was worth listening to.

"I am breveting you both to Force Commander," the Rear Admiral told them briskly. "And yes, before you ask, Lora, I'm aware the Trade Security Force has no such rank. It's not like it comes with a pay raise."

Kyle didn't even need to look around to know that he was getting a death glare from Lord Captain Anders. The Imperial Captain was senior to him by two years, and Ingolf Benn, the other Imperial Lord Captain, was a year senior to Kyle—the *only* one of the new ship captains senior to him.

The *other* seven captains, O-7s all, had been promoted since October of the previous year—making them all junior to Kyle despite his *five months* as Captain. Since Mira had been promoted to command *Camerone* only at the end of January, Aleppo and the two Imperial captains were the only captains actually senior to him.

"Ma'am, I feel it necessary to point out that there are several Captains here senior to Captain Roberts," Anders noted aloud, his Coraline drawl grating on Kyle's ears.

"And none commanding as powerful a warship," Alstairs told him. "*Avalon* will be the keystone of Battle Group Seven-Two. Neither *Gravitas* nor *Horus* is capable of fulfilling the same role."

With another gesture, she split the twelve ships into three groups of four.

"I will command Battle Group Seven-One, *Camerone*," she continued. "Seven-One will consist of *Camerone* herself, *Horus* and *Gravitas*, and *Grizzly*."

Kyle nodded to himself. *Grizzly* would provide the core of BG7.1's long-range striking power, with the three battlecruisers augmenting the older carrier's fighter group and providing the direct smashing power that *Grizzly* lacked. Assigning both of the Imperial ships to her own group also kept the problematic Captain Anders under the Admiral's own eye.

"Battle Group Seven-Two, Avalon, will be under Force Commander Roberts," Alstairs announced. "*Sledgehammer*, *Courageous* and *Indomitable* will support *Avalon*."

That gave Kyle a *lot* more direct firepower than he was used to, with the Phoenix ships augmenting *Avalon*'s own starfighter wings. Once they picked up their assault transport, Battle Group Avalon would be able to complete any mission they were given.

"Battle Group Seven-Three, *Zheng He* will be under Force Commander Aleppo," the Admiral finished. "Backing up *Zheng He* will be *Polar Bear*, *Clawhammer* and *Culloden*."

7.3 was a hammer to Kyle's mind. Two battleships, a carrier and a *Last Stand*-class battlecruiser? Less fighter strength than either of the other two groups, but *Zheng He* had the most powerful positron lances in Seventh Fleet. Commonwealth tactics called to close with Alliance forces, but anyone closing with Battle Group 7.3 was going to feel the pain.

"These assignments, for those of you wondering"—Alstairs very clearly *didn't* look at Anders—"have already been signed off on by High Command. Each Battle Group will pick up one of the three CFMC assault transports en route to Alizon for their ground forces.

"The Marines have provided an updated ETA, and High Command has signed off on the activation date based on that arrival time. As of twenty hundred hours this evening, Operating Rising Star is officially go in ninety-six hours.

"It's time for payback."

09:00 March 2, 2736 ESMDT
DSC-078 Avalon, *Main Conference Room*

Vice Commodore Michael Stanford had wondered when the name of *Indomitable*'s Commander, Air Group, had crossed his desk if the Sub-Colonel Sherry Wills commanding the battlecruiser's starfighters was the woman he knew.

He still wasn't mentally prepared to see the petite, curvy blond woman walk into the conference room along with the other five Royal Phoenix Navy and Space Force officers invited to the face-to-face meeting Force Commander Roberts had called of the new Battle Group *Avalon*'s officers.

Wills noticed him and gave him a lascivious wink, followed by a small, almost imperceptible, headshake. *She* clearly remembered the evening in the Phoenix system where her wing had bought *Avalon*'s fighter pilots drinks.

And everything that had followed it.

Of *course* his one-night stand was now one of his subordinates.

The Stars' sense of humor was far too vindictive for anything else to happen. It wasn't like there wasn't a copious supply of one-night stands from before when Kelly Mason—currently executive officer of a strike cruiser in the Federation's Home Fleet—had turned him into something resembling an honest man.

Thankfully, Stanford was sitting beside Kyle, so hopefully *Avalon*'s Captain hadn't noticed the interplay. He was going to be in enough trouble with his girlfriend without his *Captain* knowing what was going on.

"Now we're all here, let's get down to business," Roberts announced, bringing Michael's attention back to the moment instead of future problems.

"You all know the high parameters of Operation Rising Star," he continued, "but this briefing is to familiarize you with *our* portion of it."

The holotank over the conference table lit up with a three-dimensional model of a star system. It was an F-series star with eleven planets and an asteroid belt. The outer three planets were gas giants, the inner three chunks of rock burnt to a crisp. Planets four and five, as well as the asteroid belt between them, were in the Goldilocks zone. The rest were mostly-useless frozen balls of rock between the habitable worlds and the gas giants.

"The Cora system, people," Roberts concluded. "Two habitable planets. An asteroid belt with three major dwarf planetoids, easily terraformed given the application of Class One mass manipulators to create gravity. The system was colonized late; being a high-energy F-class star, it was missed in early scouting sweeps. The fifth planet, Montreal, is heavily inhabited, with a secondary colony on New Quebec, but the potential for a system almost as wealthy as Phoenix is there.

"The colony is owned and operated by a special-purpose corporate entity originally created on Terra itself but relocated to Montreal prior to the last war to be entirely independent of the Commonwealth. They were a member state of the Alliance but had only local-system defense forces that proved insufficient in the face of the Commonwealth invasion."

Michael shook his head as he regarded the system. A corporate colony like that, especially in a system with *five* potentially inhabitable worlds, stood to become *fabulously* wealthy—and evolve into a system government. The up-front investment was enormous, and Cora's owners-cum-government had decided not to add real warships to that investment.

Now the Commonwealth owned their investment.

"Current intelligence suggests that the Commonwealth has three ships in Cora," Roberts noted. "Their best guess is two cruisers and a battleship, but it may be three cruisers, two cruisers and a carrier, or just about any other variation you can think of. We're going to plan this out—and we're going to plan it out assuming that they've stuck three *Volcano* carriers in the systems."

"Force Commander," *Sledgehammer*'s Captain Ainsley interjected. "That seems a lot of metal for the Commonwealth to tie up in a system like this. Modern hulls, at that."

"I agree," Battle Group 7.2's commander said promptly. "I suspect we'll be looking at something more akin to three Assassins or ships of a similar vintage. But if we plan to tangle with Terra's finest, we'll be more than prepared to deal with their second rank, won't we?"

#

Michael wasn't surprised to find Sub-Colonel Wills waiting for him as the staff meeting dispersed.

"Walk with me," he half-ordered, half-suggested.

She fell in behind him, walking silently as they put some distance between themselves and the gathering of CAGs, Captains and XOs.

"I wanted to clear the air between us," she admitted after they were well out of sight. "I'm an incorrigible flirt, and I'll confess that I never expected to end up serving under you—but I need to be *very* clear: I don't sleep with my superior officers."

Michael couldn't help himself. Her concern was so *very* different from his own that it shocked a sharp bark of laughter from him, and he looked over at Wills with a smile.

"Putting aside the *long* list of regulations that would break," he said mildly, "it would also piss off both Force Commander Roberts *and* my girlfriend. Pissing off senior officers and strike cruiser XOs is not conducive to long-term survival."

He surprised a choke of laughter out of Wills, whose posture relaxed as she continued to walk alongside him.

"I don't chase taken men, either," she pointed out. "Damn, we were both worried about the wrong thing, weren't we?"

"Apparently," he agreed. "Let's leave the past in the past, shall we?" He offered her his hand.

She shook it with a smile.

"Agreed."

"Now," he continued as they approached his office, "tell me about the Templars. I'm going to need to know it inside and out, and the best way to find that out is to interrogate a pilot."

CHAPTER 11

Alizon System
12:00 March 4, 2736 Earth Standard Meridian Date/Time
AT-032 Chimera, *Bravo Company Commander's Office*

Edvard Hansen loved watching Alcubierre emergences. The lanky, dark-haired Lieutenant Major's office had a holoprojector, normally used for small-scale briefings, which he'd learned he could set up to project two-dimensional images along all of the walls.

On emergence into the Alizon system, he had the projector set up to show him a slightly compressed version of the view outside the ship. Toward the front of the ship, the universe was red-shifted into oblivion. This close to arrival, the normal star-bow was expanded to cover most of the front half of the warp bubble, but the gravitational anomalies creating the warp bubble reduced the light to an unclear mess of purple and red.

Behind them, the universe faded to a blue so dark as to be nearly black. Smears of blue and red reached across the space between the star-bow and star-wake, a section normally only lit by the captured radiation of an Alcubierre warp bubble.

Then, for an instant only barely perceptible to the human eye and mind, the bow and wake met in the middle. The ship slowed to the same pseudo-velocity it had started with in the Kaber system days before, and the four distinct whorls of the singularities conjured by *Chimera's* Class One mass manipulators were suddenly visible—and the whole bubble *popped*.

The eye caught shreds of color scattering away, but Edvard wasn't entirely sure that wasn't a trick of the mind. One moment, the ship was surrounded in the ethereal colors of the warp bubble, and the next only by empty space.

It was an awe-inspiring transition, and he never tired of it. Once it was over, sadly, he needed to return to the mundane drudgery of the paperwork he was running through—an assessment of what supplies Bravo Company needed from *Chimera*'s auto-fabricators. Mostly munitions, though one of his heavy-weapons people had taken a beating sufficient to require both new armor *and* a new weapon.

The task was unexciting enough, he didn't even check who was at his office door when the admittance chime sounded, and found himself shooting out of his chair to attention when Brigadier George Hammond stomped into his office.

"At ease, son," the stocky, balding, commander of the 103rd Brigade said crisply. "You did good work on Morrison; this ain't a come-to-Jesus meeting."

"Of course, Brigadier," Edvard said, slowly lowering himself back into his chair and gesturing for his CO to seat himself. "How can I help you, sir?"

He normally reported to his battalion's CO, Colonel Silje, or her exec, Major Brahm. Outside of full-brigade officer briefings, he'd met the Brigadier exactly once.

"We've arrived in the Alizon system," Hammond told him briskly. "You'll be getting a briefing packet on what the Navy has put together as Operation Rising Star. Key point for the moment is that Seventh Fleet is getting into three Battle Groups, and each of those Battle Groups is getting an assault transport."

"That makes sense, sir," the Lieutenant Major replied, hoping for some kind of clue as to why he had the *Brigadier* in his office.

"We've been assigned to Battle Group Seven-Two, Avalon," his superior told him. "Force Commander Roberts has invited myself and several senior officers aboard *Avalon* to discuss our next operation, and explicitly requested that *you* be included."

Edvard leaned back, confused for a long moment, until...*Avalon*.

"Kyle Roberts, sir? The Stellar Fox? Asked for *me*?"

"You served with him aboard *Alamo*, as I understand," Hammond noted. "You were both at *Ansem Gulf*, which I would call a...formative experience for you both."

"Makes sense, sir," Edvard repeated, flashes of memory of the hell that had been the inside of the pirated liner crossing his mind as he tried to conceal his wince.

The Brigadier's silent pause told Edvard that the older man understood *exactly* what had just happened. The older man was a mustang, commissioned from the ranks during the last days of the previous war. He'd seen the same kind of mess.

"I tend to bring promising junior officers along on this kind of trip in any case," Hammond noted. "After your performance on Morrison Hab, you were on my list anyway. We make Alizon orbit in three hours—be ready to transfer over to *Avalon* then.

"And, son, a piece of advice?"

"Yes, sir?"

"If Roberts is anything like most of the soldiers the media hangs a moniker like 'Stellar Fox' on," Hammond said with the calm of experience, "he *hates* the nickname."

15:30 March 4, 2736 EMDT
DSC-078 Avalon, *Captain's Office*

"Have a seat, Major," Kyle instructed Hansen as the Marine officer entered his office. "Peng Wa sends her regards."

"How is the gunny?" Hansen asked as he carefully took a seat. He felt unsurprisingly awkward at ending up in the office of the Battle Group commander.

Master Sergeant Peng Wa was the senior Marine noncommissioned officer aboard *Avalon*. It would fall to the woman to coordinate the inevitable interactions between NCOs of different units required to make the officers' plans actually work.

She'd also, due to the virtues of experience, ended up effectively in command of the second wave of Marines that had boarded *Ansem Gulf*, after the first wave, including the Major in command, had been killed.

"I owe her my life a few times more than before," Kyle observed. "She keeps *Avalon*'s Marines in check, and I try not to die on her. It's a solid working partnership."

Hansen dared a smile, still clearly unsure of what Kyle wanted.

"*Avalon* is that dangerous a posting, sir?" he asked.

"You'd be surprised," Kyle replied quietly. He couldn't say much more than that. The entire affair with what appeared to be a *domestically* employed assassin organizing a mutiny and attempting to kill him was classified—not least for the political disaster it could birth if it became public knowledge.

Hansen nodded, clearly aware there was more going on, then shrugged and went for the heart of the matter.

"Sir, I have to admit to being unsure why you wanted to speak to me," he asked.

"A few reasons," Kyle admitted. "I'll confess to feeling somewhat... proprietary of the Marines who survived *Ansem Gulf*. If the media is going to tell me I saved you all, I feel somewhat responsible for you."

"You *did* save us all, sir," Hansen told him. "The second wave didn't have enough delta-v to break off before entering range of the weapons the pirates had mounted on *Ansem Gulf*." The Marine shivered in memory. "Assault shuttles can't stand up to military mass drivers."

"I and about sixty other pilots and flight crew saved you," *Avalon*'s Captain replied. "But *Ansem Gulf* was a mess. That's why I wanted to talk to you, away from the other Marines."

"Sir?"

"I understand the Morrison Hub operation went very smoothly," Kyle noted.

"I lost one of my troopers, but yes," Hansen confirmed with a sigh. The loss of his people clearly bothered him.

"Outside of you and the Brigadier, no one in the One Oh Third has really seen how bad a boarding operation can get," Kyle reminded the Marine quietly. "They haven't seen the aftermath the way you and I have."

The whole conversation was bringing up unpleasant memories for them both, but Kyle *did* have a purpose here. He forged on.

"Given that, I want your take on the Marine part of the ops plan," he finished. "Where it can go wrong, as much as anything."

With a purpose finally laid in front of him, Hansen seemed more comfortable. He straightened and took on a thoughtful look—and the slightly glazed eyes of someone consulting implant data.

"The unknowns bother me the most," he admitted. "We have a pretty good idea of what the surface situation is, but it sounds like we have almost no intel on the orbitals. Surface positions will probably surrender once we're in orbit, but we have no guarantee of local support like you ended up with on Alizon.

"It also looks like we're not planning on staying in-system very long," Hansen continued. "As I read the op plan, we're only set to be in-system five days. That's not a lot of time to secure an entire planet with four thousand troops."

"Or to provide for the long-term security of the system," Kyle agreed. "My understanding is that once we've achieved all of Rising Star's objectives, Seventh Fleet is to act as a nodal defense force until the region can be secured. Dividing the Fleet up to provide the security for the systems we're freeing would undermine our ability to maintain the offensive. We're taking a risk, but Command thinks it's worth it."

He carefully didn't state his own opinion of it. He wanted to see what the Marine made of the plan.

"*If* the orbitals are easily secured, and Cora preserved intact ground forces the same way Alizon did, we can do it," Hansen admitted. "If any of the orbitals have heavy security presences or Cora has no ground troops to back us up, this could turn into a month-long slug-fest. It comes down to just how effective the Commonwealth occupation has been."

"And luck," Kyle agreed aloud "I hate depending on luck."

CHAPTER 12

Alizon System
20:00 March 5, 2736 Earth Standard Meridian Date/Time
DSC-078 Avalon, *Bridge*

Captain Kyle Roberts—it was taking him to adjust to his temporary rank in his own mind—watched his new Battle Group make its way out of the Alizon system. All told, he was now responsible for six ships— four warships, an assault transport, and a logistics freighter carrying a load of orbital defense platforms—and almost thirty thousand people.

Avalon, built with the newest and best technology in the galaxy, was the largest ship in the group by a significant margin. The freighter *Sunshine* was the second largest by volume, the key metric for the Stetson stabilization field, falling between the Reserve ships and the supercarrier in age.

"Confirm the safety radii for the Alcubierre jump," he ordered his Navigator.

Maria Pendez, the curvaceously attractive, dusky-skinned officer who flew *Avalon* and currently was providing navigation support to the entirety of Battle Group Seven-Two, smiled back at him. Exposure had rendered him mostly immune to the young woman's charms, but Kyle had no doubts as to why Pendez had *no* problems getting the male navigators of the other ships to cooperate with her.

"All ships are at ten thousand kilometers separation and on course for the Cora system," she confirmed. "We are outside all detectable gravitational interferences and prepared to warp space on your command."

Despite the differences in age and quality of the six ships, all of them had roughly the same Alcubierre drive. *Avalon*'s Class One mass manipulators were smaller and had better computer support and control than, say, *Sledgehammer*'s—but they contained the same amount of carefully manufactured and aligned exotic matter.

The smallest warp bubble humanity had ever managed to generate was approximately three thousand kilometers across and required four Class One mass manipulators—exotic matter–based devices that could create, manipulate or remove the types of bosons that gave the universe mass. Those mass manipulators were expensive—*Avalon*'s were a third of her price tag. *Sunshine*'s were fully *seventy percent* of the freighter's cost.

Keeping a ship *alive* inside a warp bubble, a compressed section of space that picked up every atom and molecule in its path as it traveled between stars, was an entirely different matter. Stetson stabilization fields were extraordinarily power-intensive and had massive feedback issues as you scaled them up, but the emitters themselves were cheap.

Every time the Stetson fields got a little more advanced, ships got bigger. Since the Alcubierre drive never changed its cost, warships were only ever built in one size: as big as possible.

Since said warships were a significant chunk of a star system's economy, they stayed in service even as newer, bigger ships were built. Hence the three older ships in BG 7.2 being barely two thirds of *Avalon*'s size—that was as large as Alliance could build them in the mid-twenty-seven-twenties.

"All ships, report readiness," Kyle ordered crisply, studying his fleet via his implant to confirm the separation. Being inside each other's warp bubbles wasn't *fatal*—it would just prevent either ship from actually forming the bubble, which would be both time-consuming and embarrassing.

Verbal and text confirmations drifted back from the other five ships and he leaned back in his chair, meeting Pendez's gaze.

"All ships, warp space at your discretion," he ordered, and made a "go ahead" gesture to Pendez.

GLYNN STEWART

She smiled, and his implant informed her she'd opened a channel to engineering.

"Commander Wong, can you confirm the status of the Class Ones, please?" she asked sweetly.

"We are at one hundred and one point two percent readiness," *Avalon*'s chief engineer replied, more than a little self-satisfaction clear in Senior Fleet Commander Alistair Wong's voice.

Pendez glanced at Kyle, as if expecting him to take over the process, but he simply smiled at her. Given the personnel assessment he'd sent in for the navigator, she was only a few months from finding herself in an executive officer slot somewhere. This was a simple evolution—and good practice for her.

"Initiating interior Stetson fields," she announced. Moments later, the screens that coated all four walls, the floor and the roof of the bridge were covered with a faint haze as the field of electromagnetic and gravitational energy settled around the ship.

"Interior field active," Pendez reported. "Exterior field on standby. Mass manipulators on standby."

Glancing back at Kyle again, she threw the virtual switch in her implant and brought up the Class Ones. Four sets of distortion appeared in the haze of the Stetson field, as *Avalon* generated the singularities necessary for her to outspeed light.

A second layer of haze fell between the carrier and the outside universe as the exterior stabilization field snapped into place. Exponentially weaker than the interior field, the exterior field required vastly more power—as it wrapped itself *around* the space the warp bubble would form in, protecting the outside universe from the energies *Avalon* was about to unleash.

"We have singularity formation," Pendez reported. "Exterior Stetson field is active, no containment issues. Initiating warp bubble...now."

Avalon's immense arrays of zero point cells flared to life, and the power feeding to the Class One manipulators increased a thousandfold. The distortions seemed to move, and the space beyond the carrier wavered in their influence for a long second.

Then a bright flash of blue light encapsulated the ship—mirrored by five other flashes that *barely* made it into their new pocket of reality— as Battle Group Avalon launched into interstellar space.

Operation Rising Star was officially under way.

CHAPTER 13

Deep Space, en route to Zahn system
22:30 March 5, 2736 Earth Standard Meridian Date/Time
BC-129 Camerone, *Bridge*

Captain Mira Solace wasn't quite alone on the bridge of her battlecruiser. Her Alpha shift had left an hour or so after they'd entered Alcubierre drive, and the Charlie shift was always a half-strength group, even before the reduced shifts generally seen while in FTL.

Camerone's bridge was currently home to one of her junior tactical officers, a junior navigator, and two experienced petty officers keeping a careful eye on both the larval officers and the battlecruiser's captain.

Mira was studying a display only she could see, laid over her vision by her neural implant, showing the positions of all of the nineteen ships under Admiral Alstairs authority. BG 7.2 and BG 7.3 both had a single freighter attached alongside their warships and assault transport, but Alstairs had attached two of the massive logistics vessels to her own command.

Only two and a bit hours into their FTL trip, the three groups of vessels were still close together. They had sixteen light-years to go, and would be accelerating at one light-year per day squared halfway there—and then decelerating at the same rate the rest of the way. Four days to each leg, eight days total to cross sixteen light-years.

The exact distances to Cora, Zahn and Hammerveldt varied, but all three were between fifteen and sixteen light-years from Alizon. Adjusting the exact accelerations would allow all three Battle

Groups to arrive simultaneously—and quantum-entanglement coms would allow them to be *sure* all of the ships were in place before attacking.

It was an aggressive plan, one Mira was surprised Alstairs had got Alliance High Command to sign off on. The early setbacks had led to a much more defensive attitude on the part of the Alliance—but perhaps the continued losses to Commonwealth raids had made a difference.

The Alliance was still ramping up its industry and recommissioning the Federation's Reserve. Mira suspected that there were losses even the flag captain of their second-largest offensive fleet didn't know about. A continuous acid drip of shattered ships and lost lives, slowly degrading the Alliance's ability to wage even a defensive war.

Perhaps High Command had realized that if they didn't turn that momentum around, the Commonwealth would win. Marshal Walkingstick had been charged with the annexation of the Rimward Marches—a region of space that coincided almost perfectly with the Alliance—and she doubted he'd planned to take them all in one sweep.

Mira shook her head. All evidence suggested that James Walkingstick was a superior strategist, but even he couldn't have planned for the back-and-forth bloodshed and slaughter the war had brought out so far. The Terrans might have taken six systems in the opening strikes of the war, but they'd assaulted *nine*. The losses at Tranquility alone had been mind-boggling—six starships destroyed when Roberts pulled the stunt that earned him the moniker Stellar Fox.

The attrition so far had been in the Commonwealth's favor, but not by much. Maybe a solid offensive now could truly turn the tide of the war.

Or maybe all they would do was wake up a half-sleeping giant with four starships for every one the Alliance had.

Deep Space, en route to Cora system
10:00 March 7, 2736 ESMDT
DSC-078 Avalon, *CAG's Office*

"I can't tell you too much," Michael Stanford told the camera in his office as he recorded his message for Kelly Mason. "Just the fact that we're on delayed coms probably tells you enough—we're at the front, we're on an op." He paused. There *really* wasn't much he could tell his girlfriend. As a fellow officer, she'd *get* it, but it still made it hard to fill even a short vid message with content.

"It's funny watching Kyle take on a multi-ship command," he finally continued. "I don't know how the man does it—if they kept promoting me the way they promote him, I'd be floating debris in one of the systems we've left behind us.

"Kyle would be the first to call it luck, though," Michael noted slowly. "All I know is this operation is right up his alley—and as usual when he gets to call the shots, they're going to be looking the completely wrong way when we punch them in the side of the head."

With a smile and a slight shake of his head, he intentionally turned his thoughts from work.

"I've traded a few messages with my mom," he told Kelly. "She told me to tell you that you have an open invite to dinner at home. With Dad gone and me in the Force, I think she gets a little lonely these days."

His mother was a specialist automation troubleshooter, sent all around Castle and its star system—and occasionally beyond—fixing the *odd* problems that arose when you lined up several hundred semi-sentient robots and told them to build things. His father had been a starfighter pilot in the last war, and come home to fly interplanetary transport ships. Their schedules had clearly converged enough for them to get married and have three children before James Stanford's transport ship had suffered a critical systems failure and been lost with all hands and passengers.

"Since you're assigned to Home Fleet, I know you can make it home," he continued. "My *mom*, however, does not, so if you don't feel up to meeting her without me, we can beg off. You two did seem to get along, though, and it would probably be good for her. Her work gets her to *meet* a lot of people, but I'm not sure if she gets to know any of them.

"Let me know," he finished. "I look forward to hearing from you again. I love you."

With near-perfect timing, his admittance chime sounded moments after he finished the message. His implant informed him that Wing Commander Russell Rokos was outside.

"Come in, Commander," he ordered, sending a mental signal to open the door.

"Commodore," Rokos greeted him, the burly pilot taking the proffered seat. "I've been studying the specs on those Templars the Phoenixes brought to the party, and I have some ideas on how we can make the best use of them alongside our own Falcons."

"I'm listening," Michael replied, leaning forward. All he'd had on the docket today was routine paperwork, so almost anything was more useful.

"With the heavier lance they're packing, they're better at killing starfighters than the Scimitar is," Rokos pointed out. The Commonwealth's latest-generation starfighter had been designed as a starfighter-killer, but its multiple lances were lighter weapons. The Scimitar was deadly at close range, but it had to survive to *get* there. "What I'm thinking is we sneak one of the Group's Q-probes in as close as we can, and use the missiles to try and pick out squadron leaders and so forth—and then have the Templars hit them as we close. They've got almost forty thousand kilometers' more range against the Scimitars than we do."

"And shattering their command and control at that point would throw their datanet out completely," Michael agreed. "On the other hand, picking out command nodes in a combat datanet is *hard*."

"I know," the junior officer acknowledged. "But I had a thought there, too..."

There was never truly a time when the ship's captain was off duty. In the age of neural implants and quantum-entanglement coms, Kyle could arguably command his carrier from the other side of the galaxy.

The necessary bandwidth was more than any but the most expensive Q-Com links could handle for even one person, the almost-inconceivable price tag the major barrier between humanity and remote-controlled missiles and starfighters.

Still, sitting in his office away from the quiet but intense activity of the supercarrier's bridge was as off-duty as the temporary Force Commander could get while conscious. Having never commanded a six-ship formation before, he was *stunned* by the amount of work inherent in just keeping on top of the status of his ships.

The downside to neural implants and Q-Coms was that he could easily keep track of *everything* going on on all six ships. It would rapidly drive him *insane*, but it was theoretically possible.

Fortunately, he'd commanded starfighter groups before he'd commanded a starship. He'd learned there to leave the individual squadrons to his junior officers, watch the high-level reports, and step in when his juniors told him they needed help—or, often enough, when said juniors' senior noncommissioned officers told him the officers needed help.

The ships' computers could give him very handy high-level synopses of the ships' status, and nine times out of ten, that was all he needed. His captains were junior enough that they would have issues, and he'd been quietly messaged a few times in the two days of the trip so far, but nothing dramatic had arisen.

FTL trips were quiet, and this one seemed even quieter than usual. There was a sense of anticipation around *Avalon* that made Kyle nervous—but then, the quiet times of the mission that had ended up liberating Alizon had been marked by attempts to assassinate him.

With a thought and a flick of his hand, he threw the summaries he was viewing on his implant onto the wallscreen of his office. Six ships filled the wall—the abbreviated arrowhead of *Avalon*, the slightly sharper spike of *Sledgehammer*, the two diamonds of the Phoenix warships and the spheres of the freighter and assault transport.

The plan for Cora was both tricky and straightforward. If it worked, he could pull the Commonwealth out of position and gut them with few or no losses—and in the worst case, Battle Group Seven-Two would face a straight slugging match with an edge in numbers and firepower.

The plan *after* they took the system worried him. Rising Star called for Seventh Fleet to leave the systems behind them defended only by the orbital platforms the logistics freighters carried. Until they attacked the naval base at Via Somnia, they would make no major commitment to *holding* the systems they were liberating.

It made sense—but it also dropped one hell of a risk on the systems they passed through. They could be setting up a situation where Cora could switch hands three or four times in the next few months—each side spending ships and blood to take the system every time, and the system's infrastructure taking more and more damage with each battle.

Some of the systems near the Commonwealth border had barely recovered from having that happen to them last time. Even a *victory* in Operation Rising Star could leave the worlds the Alliance had set out to save in even worse shape.

Neither the star maps nor the status reports on his ships showed him an answer. He hoped High Command had one, but all he could do right now was his job—take the fight to the enemy.

CHAPTER 14

Zahn System
23:00 March 13, 2736 Earth Standard Meridian Date/Time
BC-129 Camerone, *Bridge*

Mira caught herself holding her breath as the countdown ticked toward emergence in the Zahn system. Slowly, as quietly as possible, she exhaled—hoping none of her bridge crew caught her nervousness.

Emergence into a friendly system was a calm, stately affair. Information relayed from in-system sensors via Q-Com allowed the incoming ship to place their arrival point clear of the small orbital bodies no system—except perhaps Sol—had perfectly tracked, as well as the many small in-system ships that drove a star system's economy.

Assaulting a *hostile* system had none of those luxuries, plus the added danger of enemy warships and defenses. Intel placed three Commonwealth warships in the Zahn system, and while they were *probably* in orbit of the inhabited planet Zahn IV, they *could* be anywhere in the system.

And Captain Mira Solace had never commanded a warship through a hostile emergence before. None of the emergences *Avalon* had gone through with her as executive officer had suffered the slightest issue, but there was always a risk.

Then the star-bow and star-wake surrounding her converged and the warp bubble popped.

Emergence.

"We have entered the Zahn system," Fleet Commander James Coles reported. "We are approximately forty million kilometers from the planet Zahn and ten million kilometers above the ecliptic plan. Zero-zero ETA assuming no interruptions and Battle Group flank acceleration, two and a half hours."

"Thank you, Commander Cole," Mira told her navigator, and glanced around the bridge. As always, her neural implant overlaid the walls with the image of the empty space around them. Dispersing shreds of Cherenkov radiation lit up blue sparks in her vision as the computers dropped icons in to note the other six ships of Battle Group Seven-One, *Camerone*.

"Commander Rose," *Camerone*'s Captain continued, turning to her tactical officer, "do we have a bead on Commonwealth forces yet?"

"Still processing the light from across the system, but I'm not seeing anything," Fleet Commander Keira Rose replied. "I'm picking up fighter base platforms in orbit of the planet—I'm currently calling it four *Zion*-class fighter bases. They'd support two hundred starfighters." As Rose spoke, she threw an image onto the physical main viewscreen so everyone could see it. Zahn IV—most commonly simply called Zahn—was a dry but habitable world, with massive landmasses and oceans that were more brown than blue. Rose added icons in orbit of the planet, first the four two-hundred-meter disks of the launch platforms, then a scattering of smaller red icons amidst the orbital industry.

Zahn had never been a wealthy world, and its sparse orbital platforms showed it. The Terran fighter platforms were the largest stations in orbit, although there were two big civilian space stations that weren't *much* smaller.

The hundred and twenty missile launch platforms stood out amidst that lack of orbital clutter. Between them and the fighter platforms, it was a formidable defense, potentially capable of standing off a warship on its own.

A warship. Admiral Alstairs had brought *four* warships. Not to mention that in the absence of at least sublight guardships if not real warships, there was nothing stopping them from slowly removing the defensive platforms with long-range missile fire. The fighters and missiles would complicate it, but Mira could defeat the visible defenses with *Camerone* alone, given time.

"Are you seeing what I'm seeing, Captain?" Rear Admiral Alstairs asked Mira quietly via her implant.

"We haven't picked up any true warships, ma'am," Mira confirmed. "No guardships, either."

"The Commonwealth likely wouldn't have brought guardships with them," Alstairs noted, "but this makes the back of my neck itch."

A moment later, Alstairs came onto a broader channel linked to all of the Captains, XOs, and Tactical Officers.

"All right, people, it's looking like Walkingstick has left the door wide open—but I am not prepared to trust that. Let's get the starfighters into space in a defensive formation and make our course for Zahn. All transports, move to the center of the formation and stay out of the line of fire.

"Let's get some Q-probes out there, too," Alstairs ordered. "I want a full sweep of the system ASAP. If they've left the door open, I'm happy to kick it down and take over—but if this is a trap, I want to know before they kick *us* in the ass!"

#

An hour later, the Q-probes were sixty million kilometers away, continuing to transmit in real time, and Battle Group *Camerone* had a solid idea what was in that radius. The answer was: not much.

No warships in hiding. No guardships patrolling and keeping an eye on the civilian shipping in the system. Two squadrons' worth of starfighters scattered around the civilian spaceships in penny packets, now burning hard for Zahn orbit, and the defensive platforms slowly concentrating themselves on the side of the planet facing *Camerone*.

"All right," Alstairs said finally. "I'm still feeling paranoid, but it's looking like that's all it is. Vice Commodore Bachchan!"

"Yes, ma'am," that worthy replied. Vice Commodore Gopinatha Bachchan commanded the one hundred and twenty-eight Falcons aboard the *Ursine*-class deep space carrier *Grizzly*—making her the senior starfighter officer in BG 7.1 and therefore the battle group CAG.

"Hold two wings back—one each of Arrows and Falcons—as CSP and then take the rest of your ships forward," the Admiral ordered. "We'll be launching missiles momentarily as a first sweep, but the lion's share will fall on your people. Clear Zahn's skies for me, Vice Commodore."

"With pleasure," Bachchan confirmed. "I'll hold *Grizzly*'s Wing Three and *Gravitas*'s Wing Two in reserve. We'll be underway in two minutes."

No one objected—it was, after all, Bachchan's call. *Grizzly*'s Wing Three was a third understrength—an oddity of the *Ursine*-class carriers' design, and *Gravitas*'s smaller fighter wing meant *both* of her wings fielded only five squadrons.

That would leave nine squadrons—seventy-two starfighters—to back up the capital ships and protect the transports, while the majority of the ships—twelve squadrons from *Grizzly*, five from *Gravitas*, eight from *Horus* and six from *Camerone* for a total of almost two hundred and fifty seventh-generation starfighters—headed for Zahn.

"All capital ships," Alstairs continued, "target missile platforms one through seventeen and coordinate your salvos. Launch in sixty seconds."

Seventeen was not picked at random, Mira noted as she gestured for Rose to set up the strike. That would put two capital ship missiles on each platform. It was a test as much as anything else. Two missiles—even Jackhammers—*probably* wouldn't penetrate the platforms' defenses.

But they might. And every platform they blew up was one that wasn't firing back.

"Ma'am," Rose responded quietly. "They seem to be done waiting as well. I have missile launch from the orbital platforms. Scanners mark as three hundred sixty inbound. Estimated time to impact, twenty-seven minutes."

"Our missile flight time?" Mira asked quietly.

"Twenty-nine minutes, ma'am. We are accelerating toward them, which gives them an edge."

"Do we know what launchers or magazines they have?"

"Negative," Rose told her. "Best guess? Sixty-second cycle, thirty missile magazines. They can empty those platforms before we hit them back."

Alstairs had clearly either been running the same analysis or listening to Rose—probably listening to Rose.

"All ships, change target priorities," she said calmly. "The missile platforms will shoot themselves dry, but those fighter platforms have anti-fighter lances. Target Zion One and fire when ready."

#

All of the warships in Battle Group Seven-One had been designed to engage on approach to the enemy, especially with missiles. *Grizzly* and *Camerone* were Castle Federation designs, arrowheads in space with the vast majority of their weaponry pointed forward. The two Imperial warships were more of a flattened cigar, but had built even more flexibility into their launchers' firing angle, allowing all of their missiles to fire forward as well.

Once the order was given, all four ships fired simultaneously, launching thirty-four Jackhammer capital ship missiles into space. Twenty-four seconds later, a second salvo followed. Then a third.

The fourth targeted the second Zion platform. Two more followed at that launch base, then the target shifted again.

In a little under five minutes, Battle Group *Camerone* fired twelve salvos of thirty-four missiles apiece. Then they suspended fire, waiting and watching as the missile salvos and starfighters lunged towards each other.

The defending starfighters were coming out to meet Bachchan's people. They didn't have much of a choice—velocity was life in a starfighter engagement, and the Alliance craft were looking to whip past the defenses at over five percent of lightspeed.

Seconds turned into minutes and Mira set a series of timers inside her neural implants' overlay of her vision. The missiles would reach Seven-One's defensive perimeter first, followed by the starfighters ranging on each other. Then the Battle Group would face a salvo of missiles every minute until the platforms ran out or the starfighters killed them—unless they'd *under*estimated the platforms' magazines, about twenty-five minutes either way.

This was the point in the battle where even if someone came up with a clever trick, very little was going to change. Physics dominated the decision now—the fighters *could* run, but being *far* too small to mount Alcubierre-Stetson drives, they had nowhere to run to.

"I guess it's too much to hope that they'll surrender?" her XO, Bruce Notley, asked quietly. Notley was a solid sort, unassuming, quiet, and very efficient at dealing with the day-to-day demands of a warship.

"They'd have surrendered before they launched," Mira pointed out to him. "They've got enough launchers over there that could make *Camerone* sweat on her own, but against the battle group? Better spitting in a fire."

Sadly, determination and a will to push to the last weren't restricted to the good guys—and that was assuming you could get everyone to agree on who the good guys were! Most Commonwealthers she'd met in peacetime, soldiers or civilians, really did seem to think that bringing all of humanity under one government was a good thing—and hence, the soldiers fighting for it were the "good guys'."

"We're coming up on turnover," Coles reported. "Any update from the flag?"

Mira checked her all-Captains channel.

"Admiral," she queried. "Any change on turnover plans?"

There was a pause as Alstairs considered. Turnover—flipping the ships to reverse their acceleration—would point the starships' engines at the defenses, inherently making them more vulnerable. The starfighters were still on their way and missiles were still spitting into space—but the truth was that the Commonwealth forces were utterly outmatched.

"Make turnover on schedule," the Rear Admiral ordered. "You may maneuver as necessary to protect your ships at your discretion."

With twelve minutes to go to missile intercept, all six ships flipped and began reducing their velocity towards the planet—and the missiles.

Mira's implant timers shifted, showing that they'd now gained forty-five seconds until the missile salvos started coming in.

That meant the starfighters reached their weapons range first. The Terran ships fired first, two hundred Scimitars launching eight hundred missiles. Moments later, the Alliance ships replied—and the two hundred and forty-eight more advanced craft flung over fifteen hundred missiles back at the Scimitars.

The Scimitars fired a second salvo sixty seconds later. The Alliance fighters didn't respond—didn't *need* to respond. Then the fighters slipped from Mira's mind as the missiles closed the range on *Camerone* herself.

"Standby missile defenses," she ordered crisply. Twenty-seven Commonwealth salvos were in space, and the first was now seven hundred thousand kilometers away and looming. "Engage at will."

Lasers and positron lances began to fill the space around *Camerone*. Electronic emitters sang complex songs of temptation and jamming, confusing and beguiling missiles to their deaths. Four warships loosed the full power of their weaponry and computers against the smart—but not *that* smart—brains of the Stormwinds.

Then the missiles revealed at least *part* of why Zahn's defenders thought they stood a chance. At the five-hundred-thousand-kilometer mark, with only a handful of their number destroyed, their acceleration suddenly *doubled*.

Over three hundred missiles *lunged* towards Battle Group Seven-One at an acceleration the Alliance targeting computers had never been programmed to handle. What should have been a thirty-second closing period was now *ten*.

Dozens of missiles died to lasers and positron beams—but it should have been *hundreds*. Where nothing should have made it through the outer perimeter, over a hundred missiles broke through and charged the Battle Group.

A dozen simply...blew up. The upgrade clearly hadn't been designed into the missiles, it had to be a software kludge the missiles' hardware couldn't always handle. It showed in their AI, too. Missiles went off course, lured by ECM, or just plain *missed* without any apparent effort on the Alliance's part.

But not all, and even *Manticore* and the logistics transports' missile defenses engaged in the last-minute desperate attempt to survive as the starships maneuvered and fighters dived at the closing weapons.

They almost stopped them all.

Gravitas took the first hit, the strike cruiser the biggest ship in the battle group. The Imperial cruiser *leapt* through space as the gigaton warhead went off bare meters from her hull, her icon flashing bright orange on Mira's display as her computers tried to assess the damage.

Two more missiles hit starfighters head-on, collisions the tiny ships could not survive.

The last pair collided with the logistics transport *Venture* and detonated, vaporizing the unarmored transport in a massive blast of antimatter fire that took eighteen hundred souls with it.

#

"Update the targeting parameters for that sprint," Mira ordered, trying not to look at the explosion on the screen that *had* been a ten-million-ton freighter. "You have forty-five seconds," she said flatly, using her implant override to slice part of the tactical controls over to her own console.

"I'll take over ECM," she continued calmly. "Notley, start using our Jackhammers in counter mode."

Commander Rose ignored them both, her eyes closed as she ran through data in her implant, revising again and again as she adapted the defensive programming to handle a sudden doubling of acceleration. Figures and programs flickered back and forth between the tactical officers on the warships, each contributing their own pieces as the seconds ticked away.

Explosions lit up the space behind the incoming missiles as the starfighters starting lashing out at the missiles targeting *them*, the chaotic mess of the starfighter battle barely registering as Mira spun

Camerone's ECM emitters up to full strength and wove a dancing song of deception and lies across space.

Then the second wave of missiles hit the defensive perimeter, and they got to see how well the tactical officers had done—with thirty-odd thousand lives still hanging in the balance. Again, at the half-million-kilometer mark, the missiles doubled their acceleration.

Even more self-destructed this time. The thrusters weren't designed for that kind of throughput; the mass manipulators weren't designed to cushion the force... The ten-second terminal period burned as much fuel as an entire hour of regular flight.

Even losing a quarter of the missiles to systems failure, it was clearly worth it. Three hundred and sixty missiles, even capital ship missiles, shouldn't have even been a *challenge* to the defenses of four warships. Now Mira desperately tried to lure the missiles aside with jammers and decoys, Rose slashed away with lasers and positron lances that now *knew* how fast the missiles were accelerating, and Notley guided the capital ship missiles he'd launched onto intercept courses forty seconds before.

This time, the lances claimed over two hundred victims, their explosive deaths marking the advancing front of the missile wave. Many of the others looked like they were going to miss...and then the Jackhammers struck.

There were no direct head-to-head intercepts. Those were difficult to arrange and inefficient. The Jackhammers detonated their one-gigaton warheads between missiles or close to them. Missiles were only lightly shielded—an explosion inside of five kilometers could get a proximity kill.

Seventeen missiles survived—only to career off into deep space, their speed and Battle Group *Camerone*'s ECM befuddling their electronic brains.

"We're dialing them in," Rose reported. "That was lucky, but the next time won't need luck."

Almost as the tactical officer finished speaking, the Q-probes reported the arrival of their missiles in Zahn orbit. The four fighter platforms had been generously equipped with lasers and lances, but not generously enough against thirty-plus capital ship missiles arriving at eight percent of lightspeed.

They were almost enough—Zion One survived—but two near-misses stripped defenses and sensors from the platform. Twenty-four seconds later, a missile from the second salvo struck home, crippling that platform. The third salvo obliterated it.

Even as their launch platforms started to die, the tsunami of missiles from the Alliance starfighters slammed into their Commonwealth opponents. Against eight missiles apiece, the Scimitars didn't have the defenses or maneuverability to survive. Less than thirty fighters survived—and flew into the teeth of the Falcons' lances.

The third missile salvo still required missile intercepts, but none of the Terran missiles made it past that last line of defense.

With the fourth, Battle Group Seven-One had their enemy's measure—and the destruction of half of the orbital platforms had reduced their ability to adapt for the Alliance's defenses. Not one missile made it past the missile defense net, and Mira breathed a sigh of relief.

"Ma'am!" Notley suddenly snapped. "Q-probes are picking up a wideband transmission from the surviving platforms—they surrender."

"Order them to detonate their missiles," Alstairs ordered immediately. "Reduce acceleration on ours until we've confirm the self-destructs, then move them on to retrieval vectors."

"Their missiles are going up!" Rose reported. "Self-destructs propagating along at lightspeed. That was sent before they got our message, ma'am."

"Guess they figured that was as clear as it could get," Mira acknowledged. "Admiral? Your orders?"

"Maintain zero-zero course for Zahn," Alstairs replied. "Once we're in position to cover their approach, we'll send in Marines to secure the stations and try to contact the surface."

The implant communication channel was as much mental as vocal. It didn't *always* carry emotion or intent as well as face-to-face, but it was definitely better at it than text communication. The Rear Admiral sounded both relieved and pleased.

"Zahn is ours."

CHAPTER 15

Cora System
23:00 March 13, 2736 Earth Standard Meridian Date/Time
DSC-078 Avalon, *Bridge*

Avalon erupted into Cora space with the inevitable burst of blue Cherenkov radiation. Kyle had considered hiding behind the system's gas giants, but they were too far away from the habitable planets to be useful.

Instead, he'd emerged directly on the ecliptic, a full light-minute from Montreal—Cora V. And they'd emerged alone—despite being the biggest ship in the Battle Group, *Avalon* had the best acceleration curve. She was best able to handle any trouble that came her way—and best able to get *out* of it.

"Stanford, get your people out there," Kyle ordered. "Pendez, settle us into a nice, slow orbit. Let's not rush in until we see what we've got. Xue, make sure all of our data is feeding back to the rest of the Group. Let's see what we have."

The kilometer-and-a-half-long carrier arced in the general direction of Cora's two inhabited planets on a curve that would make her closest approach to Montreal just over six million kilometers. It wasn't an aggressive course, and Kyle didn't *need* it to be.

"What are we seeing?" he asked aloud, studying the tactical plot in his neural implant. The computers were already filtering out the civilian shipping, but he could see three true starships in orbit. Xue had the other layers of data; she would break down what they were and let him know.

"All right," Xue responded slowly. "Bogey three here"—the largest of the starships flashed orange— "is a logistics ship—similar to *Sunshine*. She appears to be in the process of deploying orbital fortifications—I'm reading *these*"—two disks in orbit and several dozen smaller satellites flashed darker orange— "as two *Zion*-class fighter bases and missile launch platforms. None of them are reading as operational yet, which leaves us with *these* as a threat."

The last two starships flashed bright red.

"Bogey One is a *Paramount*-class carrier," she continued. "*Old* ship, probably being used to supply birds to the *Zions*, but she's easily retrofitted with modern missiles and carries a hundred starfighters. Her friend is a bit more of a worry—I'm reading a *Hercules*-class battlecruiser."

"Oh *she's* going to be fun," Kyle murmured. A Hercules was functionally brand-new, a contemporary to the *Saint*-class battleships and *Volcano*-class carriers carrying the main weight of the Commonwealth's campaign against the Alliance.

"Unless the Zions have fighters aboard, and their energy signatures don't look like it, we're only looking at about a hundred and thirty starfighters," Xue concluded. "But that battlecruiser has almost as many missile launchers as our *Battle Group*. She's a sniper, and she can hurt *Avalon* bad."

"Well, let's see just what she does," *Avalon*'s Captain replied. "And get me a vector on that logistics transport if she tries to run—I *want* that ship."

"Yes, sir."

#

It was fully ten minutes before the Commonwealth finally moved, and Kyle was starting to wonder if he needed to start insulting people's mothers by radio to get a reaction out of the Terran ships. Finally, however, the Paramount's fighters formed up on the battlecruiser, and the Hercules burned out after *Avalon*.

"The fighters are sticking to the same acceleration at the Hercules," Xue reported. "Two hundred and thirty gravities—I estimate sixty-five minutes for the battlecruiser to make lance range."

"Any missiles yet?"

"Negative."

"Let's change that, shall we?" Kyle asked cheerfully. "Give me...five salvos on the Paramount. Stanford gets the Hercules; he needs a second one on his resume."

"You're just nervous because you almost died the last time we met one of them," the CAG replied. "Which, for the record, you are *not* permitted to try this time."

Chuckles ran around *Avalon*'s bridge as the first salvo of nine missiles blasted into space. The crew was feeling a little twitchy at hanging out there on their own, even if they all *knew* where the rest of the Battle group was.

"Is anyone except the Hercules moving?" he asked.

"Rabbits are running for the bushes," Xue replied. "Civilian shipping is burning away from us as fast as they can—they don't want to be caught up in this. That Paramount is staying in orbit, as is the freighter. They seem to think the Hercules can take care of us."

"Well, then, let's encourage them in that line of thought," Kyle said. "Once those missiles are on their way, turn us directly away from the Hercules and go to two hundred gees. Let's see if we can tempt them into a fighter strike."

A little over two minutes passed, every twenty-two seconds marked by another set of nine missiles launching into space. Kyle noted approvingly that Xue had given them a more complex course than a straight path to the carrier. By arcing them around the Hercules, she'd increased their flight time by several minutes but prevented the battlecruiser from defending the carrier.

Thirty minutes to impact either way.

"We have missile launch from the Hercules," Xue reported. "Twenty missiles inbound."

"We are turning to run now," Pendez announced. "Let their missiles choke on *that*."

"Enemy missile time to impact, thirty-five minutes and change," the tactical officer noted. "Our time to impact for first salvo, twenty-eight minutes and counting."

Kyle checked the numbers. It would now be over two and a half hours before the Hercules brought *Avalon* into range of her massive, megaton-a-second positron lances. Their missiles were going to be more of a headache, but with all two hundred and forty of his starfighters flying carrier defense, that was more of a minor pain than a real issue.

As far as the Commonwealth could tell, the situation was well in hand. Either *Avalon* would flee into Alcubierre and the system would be safe, or the Hercules would bring her to bay and rip apart the carrier and her fighters with its lances at close range.

He checked the Hercules' position and acceleration.

In a little over sixty minutes, the Terrans would learn not to take appearances at face value.

#

"Sir, we just received a warning notice from *Camerone*," Anderson told Kyle quietly. "The defenders at Zahn have added what looks like a software kludge to give their missiles a terminal sprint mode. Not sure that our friend out here has it, but...it gave their missile defense issues."

"Update our software for the possibility," he replied. "We've got time."

Anderson coughed his agreement, turning his attention back to the computers. Their own missiles were still fifteen minutes from the Paramount, which was maneuvering to both protect the transport ship and make sure none of the civilian space stations were in the line of fire.

The last was a consideration not every starship commander would have thought of, and Kyle mentally saluted the other carrier's captain. It wasn't going to *save* the Terran ship—the carrier could *probably* take the Jackhammer salvos, but it wouldn't take a lot of bad luck for it not to, and Kyle's plan for the Paramount had already been set in motion.

The Hercules' first salvo would reach *Avalon* four minutes later, followed by another twenty missiles every twenty-five seconds for almost four minutes. The battlecruiser had sent ten salvos their way, then ceased fire to see what happened.

Two hundred missiles, even arriving in sequence, were going to be a handful for the supercarrier and her fighters. A manageable handful, most likely, but a handful.

Kyle wasn't even bothering to send his own missiles back. Nine missiles a salvo into the teeth of a modern battlecruiser with a hundred and thirty starfighters flying escort? It would have been a waste of ammunition.

His starfighter wing was the only thing that could threaten the Hercules, though the hundred-odd Scimitars could blunt the worst of the strike if he sent Stanford in. Even with the Paramount's wing in play, though, he figured SFG-001 could *take* the ship.

Even with *Avalon* alone, he figured he could take the system. Separating the Hercules from anything the Paramount could do would be the first step in that, so he was content to run at less than his top speed and let the battlecruiser slowly catch up.

For now, he watched his missiles close with the enemy. The carrier accelerated into their teeth, then turned at the last minute and opened fire. Lasers and positron lances did their work, and his first salvo died well short of the Terran ship.

The second and third suffered the same fate, though they died closer to the Paramount than the third had.

Kyle wasn't sure what happened with the fourth salvo. The Q-probes were close, giving him near-real-time data, but it still wasn't clear. One moment, the Terran ship was sweeping the missiles from the sky—the next, an entire quadrant of the ship's lasers stopped firing.

The spray of fire that took out the last of the fourth salvo was clearly desperate, almost random—and took the remaining defenses out of position for the fifth and final salvo.

One missile made it through. A one-gigaton direct hit split the old ten-million-ton ship in two, her prow and stern spinning off into space from the vaporized void that had been her middle third.

"Damn," he said mildly. "I...didn't actually expect that to work."

"Well, I hope you *do* expect this to work," Michael Stanford told Roberts over the com. His five wings of forty-eight fighters apiece were feeling a little exposed, drifting a hundred thousand kilometers behind *Avalon*. "Because a lot of us are going to be in trouble if it doesn't."

"My faith in you is extensive, Vice Commodore," the Force Commander replied brightly. "And I know when to get out of the way. Good luck."

Michael grunted acknowledgement at Roberts, then switched to his fighter group's channel.

"Rokos, Bravo Wing front and center," he ordered. "Use your missiles, your lances, whatever you feel is needed. We'll cycle the center Wing when you run out of missiles."

"You just want me dead so you can take my bunk," Wing Commander Rokos replied. "You're not dumb enough to think you can get my wife."

"Your wife and Mason would both kill me," Michael agreed. "Stay alive, people. I hate writing letters home."

Even front and center wasn't *that* much more dangerous for Bravo Wing than anyone else. Most of what Michael was dropping on Rokos's wing was the lion's share of the antimissile fire.

Seconds ticked away and the missiles closed. Vice Commodore Michael Stanford, Commanding Office Starfighter Group Zero Zero One, counted the seconds and kilometers in his implant until...

"Weapons free," he snapped. "Take them down!"

Suiting actions to words, he lined the nose of his own command starfighter up on the probability zone where his computers said a missile would likely be and fired. The eight-thousand-ton spacecraft shivered as the beam flashed into space—and he cheered as he connected, blasting the missile into vapor.

With twelve times as many starfighters as missiles, the first salvo didn't so much fail as evaporate. Michael's fighters charged on, cutting into the second salvo with equally deadly efficiency.

Here and there, a missile managed to sneak past the starfighters—Stormwinds, like Jackhammers, were *incredibly* smart weapons.

A single missile, though—even two, which somehow sneaked past Michael's people on the seventh salvo—was no danger to *Avalon*'s defenses. Michael's fighters ripped two hundred missiles—the best a modern battlecruiser could throw—to pieces in the time it took the missiles to pass the fighters.

Some days, Michael *really* understood why the Federation Senate had stopped funding battleships. At least cruisers brought *some* starfighters to the party.

"We are swinging bare-assed in the breeze and still here, sir," Rokos reported crisply as the tenth salvo died. "What do we do now?"

"Wait and see what our Terran friend does," Michael replied. "Think he's going to throw more missiles?"

"No," Force Commander Roberts replied. "He's seen that's pointless—he's going to close the range, rip you guys apart with his lighter lances, and then blow *Avalon* to hell with his big guns."

"Oh. Are we going to let him do that?" Rokos asked, somewhat abashed.

Roberts laughed.

"Wait and see, Wing Commander. Wait and see."

00:00 March 14, 2736 ESMDT
DSC-078 Avalon, *Bridge*

Midnight.

Avalon and the rest of Seventh Fleet had known the battle was coming; the full crew had been rested and awake when they'd arrived in their target systems.

The Commonwealth ships hadn't had that luxury. Twenty-three hundred hours was an odd time, too. Most of the "day shift" crew would still be awake, not quite having passed out yet. Without warning, though, the night shift would be the only people fully awake and functional. There was a good chance that the Hercules' captain had been pulled out of bed.

Nonetheless, Kyle figured *someone* over there had to be wondering why *Avalon* was running. At this point, he could easily turn the carrier and her fighters around and go head-to-head with the battlecruiser. It would be a near-run thing, but he figured he could take the Hercules. The Terran captain probably figured she could take *Avalon*.

"You were wrong," Xue announced. "They're launching more missiles."

"They're not aimed at *Avalon*," Kyle guessed. "They're going to see if they can strip away our fighter cover—or at least force us to keep SFG One in space and run them out of missiles. Watch this lot," he ordered. "If they *have* the sprint mode that Admiral Alstairs saw, they'll use it on our fighters."

Again, the missiles blasted into space every twenty-six seconds. He didn't expect them to stop after ten salvos this time, either. The Hercules had well over a thousand missiles in her magazines, and killing Stanford's starfighters was her best chance at carrying this battle.

"Flight time is seventeen minutes, almost exactly," his tactical officer noted. "Passing on our telemetry to Vice Commodore Stanford."

Kyle nodded acknowledge of Xue's report, but he was focused on the updates from the Q-probes. The missiles weren't going to matter.

The twelfth salvo of the new attack blasted into space and then, *finally*, the Terran battlecruiser crossed the somewhat arbitrary line in space he'd drawn before they'd even arrived in system. *Avalon*'s 'flight' had pulled the battlecruiser past the carrier's arrival point. The Hercules was far enough away from everything that she could have gone into Alcubierre drive if she'd chosen to.

The battlecruiser's course hadn't been perfectly consistent the whole flight out. Even on a roughly straight line, she'd swooped, curved, spiraled, and barrel-rolled to render missile or long-range lance fire more difficult.

But her course had been *roughly* straight. Straight enough for a message sent twenty minutes ago via Q-Com to have predicted her position *now* within a ten-thousand-kilometer error.

In a brilliant flash of blue Cherenkov radiation, the battleship *Clawhammer* and the strike cruiser *Courageous* dropped out of warped space—barely twenty thousand kilometers from the Terran battlecruiser.

One hundred and sixty-six light positron lances—lighter on *Courageous* than on *Clawhammer*—blasted into the Terran starfighters the moment the warships emerged. Their own sensors hadn't resolved the static radiation from their departure; everything was targeted by data relayed from *Avalon*'s Q-probes. An extra thirty-six beams cut into space to make certain of the kills, and *every* Terran starfighter died in two seconds.

Their deaths were a sideshow as *Clawhammer* took half a second to orient herself and fired her main weapons. A dozen megaton-a-second heavy positron lances hit the *Hercules*-class battlecruiser amidships and *held*.

Courageous's dozen six-hundred-kiloton-a-second beams arrived fractions of a second later—and hit only vaporized metal.

CHAPTER 16

Cora System
00:10 March 14, 2736 Earth Standard Meridian Date/Time
AT-032 Chimera *Landing Group, Assault Shuttle Four*

Fully encased in the two-hundred-plus kilograms of carbon filament armor and servomotors that made up his combat armor, strapped into an assault shuttle locked into a launch tube of an assault transport "threading the needle" of the effect of a planet's gravity on the Alcubierre field, there was no way for Edvard to appreciate emergence as he preferred.

Fortunately, the armor also had the ability to block external sounds. Marine combat drops came in two varieties—emerging a long way away from the target and sending the shuttles in alone, often on long ballistic courses, to try to achieve stealth, or pushing the limit of how close a ship could emerge to a planet, to try to achieve surprise.

Edvard was familiar with the horrifying keening noise aboard a ship threading the needle. His command network told him a *lot* about his men's suits, and he could tell which of his men had the same experience by who had turned off their exterior audio pickups as soon as the announcement came down.

By now, five seconds into the hell-ride, *no one* in his company still had their exterior pickups turned on. The Lieutenant Major made a quick note in his computer system to make sure everyone had the pickups *back* on before they boarded their target.

The Bridge network was feeding the company commanders a full tactical plot of the Battle of Cora. It looked like the ambush had gone off *perfectly* and, as expected, the Commonwealth Navy freighter was making a run for it.

Whoever was in command of the logistics ship had done the math and set her course in the exact opposite direction of the Alliance warships. It was arguably the safest direction—certainly the only one where a freighter capable of accelerating at two hundred gravities could escape starfighters chasing her at five hundred gravities.

Sadly for the Terrans, it was also the most *predictable*.

"Emergence in ten," Brigadier Hammond's voice echoed through the command network. "No one has a *clue* how close we're actually going to be. Good luck."

Even without the audio pickups running, there were a thousand unpleasant sensations associated with the gravity harmonics from sustaining a warp field this close to a planet. None of Edvard's people were showing the symptoms, but previous experience told him roughly two to three percent of the people aboard *Chimera* were going to be nonfunctional.

Suddenly, all of those sensations *ceased*, and he knew they'd emerged even before the network updated.

"Go! Go! Go!" he snapped at the pilot, even *knowing* the order was redundant. His company's assault shuttle was fired into space before he'd finished speaking.

"We came out sixty thousand kay ahead of her," his pilot announced to the company after a moment. "Going full burn right for her; this is going to be a *rough* contact. Forty-five seconds to update your wills and insurance!"

Edvard's implant happily informed they would be impacting the freighter at over fifteen hundred *kilometers* per second—exceeding the official rated survivability of the assault shuttle by approximately fifty percent.

"I hope you know what you're doing," he murmured to the pilot.

"We're damned either way, El-Maj—so I'll see you in Hell!"

"Bravo Company!" Edvard bellowed across his company network. "Power your suits, set for maximum impact absorption. This is gonna hurt—but the Terrans don't stand a chance. Because *we're Castle's damned Marines!*"

The company network dissolved into a series of wolf howls, joined after a fraction of a second by a voice Edvard recognized as the pilot. Unlike most of the company, Edvard knew *exactly* what the pilot was doing at that second—and he'd have been screaming too!

Then the engines cut out and gravity shut off as every mass manipulator in the shuttle focused its energy on somehow allowing his two hundred Marines to survive the fist of God of a fifteen-hundred-kilometer-per-second impact.

#

A hiss and a warm sensation rushing through his body told Edvard his suit's medical suite had assessed the situation versus the priorities he'd loaded in as part of the mission—and proceeded to inject stimulants to wake him up from the acceleration-induced blackout.

"Bravo Company," he coughed out, then swallowed against his dry mouth and tried again. "Bravo Company—sound off!"

His platoon Lieutenants and squad Sergeants responded over the next several seconds, implants allowing them to check in on their people and reply at the speed of thought.

Even as his subordinates checked on their subordinates, Edvard brought up a mental display that updated him on the status of his entire company. Over eighty percent of his people had been injected with stimulants, but everyone was now on their feet.

Every second they lingered in the assault shuttle was a second the freighter's defenders had to get ready.

"Move, people!" he barked. "We've got a freighter full of goodies to take. Move! Move! Move!"

As his first squad piled out of the shuttle into the shattered corridor they'd connected with, the Lieutenant Major checked the command network. Third Battalion had made their landing perfectly, all five assault shuttles quite literally *embedded* in the big freighter as it continued to attempt to flee the system.

The other three battalions of the 103rd Brigade continued on their course for the planet. Fourth Battalion would hit the Zions and the missile platforms, while Second seized the major civilian space infrastructure.

First Battalion, as always, got the sharp end of the stick. *Those* Marines were headed for Trudeau City to take control of the planetary capital away from whatever Terrans were guarding it.

A flashing mental icon informed him that the Colonel was contacting him moments before her command override dropped Amanda Silje's voice into his head.

"Hansen, Bravo Company hit closest to the main engineering bay," she told him crisply. "So, that's your objective. I do *not* want this ship jumping to FTL with us aboard, do you read me?"

"Yes, ma'am," he confirmed. "We are moving out."

With a thought, his implant brought up the detailed floor plans of the freighter. They didn't know her name, but they recognized her type. Her builder was notorious for using the same plans for every ship—a small savings versus the cost of the ship itself, but he guessed pennies counted when you ran a civilian ship-builder in the Commonwealth.

He highlighted the engineering bays—sixty meters back of their contact point and three decks down—and flipped the plans to his entire company.

"This is the target, people," he told them. "And it's one the Terrans will know to defend—and we knocked on the door pretty loudly on the way in. If they've got Marines, we're going to see them."

Edvard and his headquarters followed his Second Platoon out, with the last sixty Marines trailing them. Gunnery Sergeant Jonas Ramirez was waiting for the company commander, standing next to the clear path the Marines had cut through the debris.

"They're going to have Marines, sir," he said quietly over a direct channel. "We're not talking pirates, sir. Terran Marines will have armor, entrenched positions... This could hurt, sir."

"There's a limited number of ways into engineering, Gunny," Edvard pointed out. The ship had been built as a fast transport instead of a naval auxiliary—hence the lack of weapons, which had made the landing somewhat easier—but security of the key components had still been in the designers' mind. There were two corridors that connected to Engineering. They connected on different levels and had twenty-meter clear stretches with no side corridors right where they entered the bay.

Ramirez was right. The Federation Marines were moving—and moving *fast*—but Edvard's best estimate put them three to five minutes from hitting the nearer of those corridors. Unless the defending Marines were incompetent—and the Terran Commonwealth Marine Corps had a reputation as anything *but*—those corridors were going to be deathtraps.

"You're thinking like we want this ship intact," his senior noncom pointed out. "So are they—but I thought we only wanted the cargo?"

Bravo Company's commander stopped in his tracks, physically looking at the faceless shell of carbon filament ceramics encasing the gunny.

"You have a suggestion, I take it?"

#

In the end, Edvard sent Third Platoon down those three decks, with orders to engage but to take no unnecessary risks. They rapidly ran into stiff resistance—even the single platoon playing decoy outnumbered the defenders, but the two ten-man squads of Terran Marines had been given the time to set up serious defenses.

Most Marine security teams had access to carbon-filament ceramic barricades that were semi-mobile. The Terrans had set up four of them in a leapfrogged pattern in the hall, covering them from most non-heavy weapons fire.

Even Third Platoon's heavy weapon section could have cleared the hall, but the cost would have been high. To take down twenty Marines could easily cost Edvard thirty or more—a price he'd been depressingly resigned to paying until Ramirez had made his suggestion.

"We ready?" he asked First Platoon's heavy weapons Sergeant.

"Yes, sir," that worthy, who doubled as a demolitions expert, replied. "Ready to rock and hole?"

"Fire in the hole, Sergeant," Edvard ordered.

A moment later, thunder echoed through the empty corridor of the freighter as the charges detonated around them, cutting a thirty-meter diameter circle free of the floor—and dropping it right into the *center* of engineering.

Edvard rode the loose plate down with his First Platoon. His implant coordinated with his suit computer, identifying armed targets and flagging them for his attention. A flashing warning drew his attention to the half-dozen armored Marines actually in the engineering bay, presumably the defenders' reserve.

He brought his rifle up, the high-powered smart weapon identifying the target, classifying the target and selecting the appropriate munition from its multiple magazines, and firing when he pressed the mental trigger.

A three-round burst of heavy tungsten penetrators flashed across the room, connecting and punching through the armor before detonating their explosive charges. Armored troops took a *lot* of killing, but that usually did the trick.

In the less than two seconds it had taken the Marines to fall the full fifteen-meter height of the freighter's engineering bay, all six of the Terran Marines died—as did the half-dozen techs carrying weapons as a support.

"*Drop your weapons,*" Edvard boomed through his suit's speakers. "*Drop your weapons and surrender!*"

First Platoon was moving fast. Surrendering techs were rapidly cuffed and Marines moved to trap the defending squads against the anvil of Third Platoon's decoy. Gunfire echoed in the chamber, accompanied by the distinctive *crack-crack* of penetrators going off inside armor.

"Hold fire," a suit-amplified voice bellowed as his Second Platoon and HQ section came crashing down behind him. "We're laying down arms; we surrender."

The Terrans had sent a thirty-man half-platoon to defend

Engineering. Sixteen lived long enough to lay down their arms. Forty-five techs had surrendered, eight had died—and the Alliance now controlled the freighter's engineering bay.

"Shut down the engines," Edvard ordered. "Sublight, FTL, everything. This ship isn't going anywhere *we* don't let it."

Watching his people get to work cuffing the crew and pulling the Terran Marines from their armor, Edvard shared a cold, satisfied smile with his Gunny.

Bravo Company hadn't lost a single trooper.

CHAPTER 17

Cora System
08:00 March 14, 2736 Earth Standard Meridian Date/Time
DSC-078 Avalon, *Captain's Office*

Battle Group Seven-Two, Avalon, was now in complete control of the Cora system. Brigadier Hammond's Marines had taken the Zions and their attendant missile platforms without losses—the launch platforms, which also functioned as the control centers for the missile satellites, hadn't been manned yet.

Since the freighter *Lougheed* had been taken intact by Hammond's Marines as well, Kyle was now in possession of another *eight* fighter platforms, over three hundred missile satellites, and the five hundred Scimitars for the Zions. *Lougheed* had also carried the necessary munitions for the satellites and starfighters, and even the crews for the platforms.

Those crews were going to be a problem. *Lougheed* herself only had a crew of five hundred, but adding in the starfighter crews and the launch platform personnel, she'd been carrying over three *thousand* people. Kyle had nowhere to put them—he was hoping Cora did.

"Brigadier," he greeted Hammond as the balding Marine opened the channel for the meeting he'd requested. "Congratulations on a job well done. I understand your losses were minimal?"

"Worst down here," Hammond grunted. The Brigadier had accompanied the battalion assaulting the surface, of course. "You'd think they'd know it was over once the warships were gone."

Chimera was designed to, among her other purposes, provide orbital fire support. Twice in the seven hours since Hammond's people had landed, they'd had to call down fire from heaven. The second time had been when the Brigadier had summoned the Marines to surrender, and their CO had refused.

The assault transport had localized the source of the refusal and dropped a ground-penetrating bunker-buster from orbit. One of a Marine commander's favorite weapons, the missile dove nearly five hundred meters below ground before detonating—minimal collateral damage, utter destruction to underground facilities.

The fact that they'd *located* the command center had probably been part of the decision of the senior surviving Marine—seventh in the defenders' chain of command, apparently—to surrender.

Without someone in orbit to protect them, the Marines on the surface were sitting ducks. Kyle had once had a front-row seat to what happened when the warheads in his own magazines were unleashed on a planet. Even refraining from that scale of devastation, *Chimera* alone could even the balance between Hammond's single brigade and the defenders' multiple divisions.

"Any contact from the local authorities?"

"We've linked up with the mayor of Trudeau City," Hammond replied. "The Terrans left the city's municipal level government intact—in exchange for which Mayor Musil happily handed us the location of their shiny new command center."

"Nothing from the planetary government?"

"It looks like the Cora Development Corp executives are just plain *gone*," the Brigadier said bluntly. "At a guess, they cleared off world as soon as the Terrans took out their defenses. Stars know the bastards would have had the money to disappear anywhere in the galaxy."

Kyle sighed. Without a functioning local government, he didn't have a lot of options for dumping thousands of prisoners on the surface.

"So, the only planetary structure left is the Terran occupation?" he asked.

"I'm digging, Force Commander," Hammond said calmly. "It looks like the Commonwealth was using a lot of the municipal- and regional-level structures and governments from the CDC, but...a lot of people are going to be twitchy about collaborators, since those people were working *with* the Terrans."

"I'll check in with Command, Brigadier," Kyle told him. "We're supposed to be moving on in three days. We'll see what they suggest."

"We're digging up enough local cops and Cora Defense Force troopers that I think we can keep *order*," Hammond told him. "But I suspect that the Development Corp might be dead."

"Don't cry too hard, Brigadier," the Force Commander said dryly. Hammond didn't sound at all displeased with the fate of the Cora Development Corporation. "It would have made our lives a *lot* easier to have a functioning government around here."

Zahn System
08:00 March 14, ESMDT
BC-129 Camerone, *Admiral's Office*

Premier Báirbre Mantovani had the distinct look of a woman who had, not that long before, likely been quite obese—and was now disturbingly skinny. The head of Zahn's system government looked sick, her skin hanging loosely on her frame and her blond hair streaked with gray. Her suit was clearly borrowed, her office had clearly recently been redecorated with explosives, and the fire in her eyes was bright and unbowed.

Simply the fact that Premier Mantovani was transmitting from *her* office in Zahn Governance Tower was the source of much of that fire. Battle Group Seven-One's Marines had hit the ground running, two of the three battalions in-system dropping on Cobra City even as the third collected surrenders in orbit.

In theory, the surrender of the orbital platforms included the surface command. In practice, the Terran Commonwealth Marine Corps were not used to surrendering.

By the time Brigadier Yoxall, commander of the 58th Marine Brigade, had taken Governance Tower from the top down and deployed roving units into the streets, Zahn Planetary Army units had started materializing from the *damnedest* places. Some of those Army units had been in civilian wear with just rifles—but others had appeared with tanks and full suits of powered combat armor.

Like Alizon, Zahn had apparently *listened* when Castle and Coraline had helped draft emergency plans for the system falling to the Commonwealth. Mantovani had clearly been living a more austere life than she'd been used to, but when the Alliance had returned, she'd been in a position to be back in charge within the day.

"Rear Admiral, Captain," Mantovani greeted them. "There are insufficient words for me to express my planet's gratitude for your arrival. With the orbital platforms intact, no effort on our part would have sufficed to liberate ourselves."

Mira left that for the Admiral to answer, covertly checking on Lord Captain Anders. The senior Imperial officer was linked into the conference as well. He looked...well, he looked as tired as everyone else in the Battle Group.

"The Alliance promised that we would protect you from the Commonwealth and liberate you if you fell," Alstairs said calmly. "We came as soon as we were able, though I warn you that we cannot stay long."

"I understand," Mantovani confirmed. "We are already relocating the Terran prisoners to secure island detention facilities. We possess personnel qualified to operate the surviving fighter platforms, though the modifications to fire our missiles will be time-consuming. We are only in possession of a single wing of starfighters, as well. What aid are you able to provide us?"

"Not as much as we'd planned," the Admiral admitted, "let alone as much as you might hope. Our mission calls for the liberation of multiple systems, and we lost one of the logistics transports attached to my command.

"I'm pleased we took the Terran platforms intact," she continued. "We can provide you four more defense platforms, our own *Citadel*-class, plus roughly two hundred Falcon starfighters and two hundred and fifty missile satellites. We cannot," Alstairs admitted, "provide you with crew for all of those. I have a cadre sufficient to provide a skeleton crew for the platforms and trainers for the starfighters. I'm afraid we can't spare more."

Mira ran down the numbers in her implant. That was half of the load of the freighter still with them. Seventh Fleet had been provided enough *extra* that the loss of one freighter meant they should still be able to set up defenses for each liberated system.

Without the fourth freighter's worth of defensive platforms, though, she wasn't sure if the plan to take and hold Via Somnia would still be viable. It was a system the Commonwealth would *have* to retake, and without the extra firepower of the defenses, Seventh Fleet could be in trouble holding it.

"Your offer is approximately what I was warned to expect," Mantovani replied calmly. "We will shortly reestablish quantum-entanglement communications with Alliance High Command as well. I fear we will only be a burden on the Alliance for the moment, but my people will do their utmost to turn that around."

"We will arrange for transfer of the defenses and missile stocks as soon as possible," Alstairs told her. "My people will contact yours—I am certain you have a lot to deal with, Premier."

"The first day returning to work is always...extraordinary," Zahn's elected leader said demurely. "We will talk more soon, Admiral."

The channel to the surface cut out and Alstairs turned to her flag captain and most senior captain.

"Anders, Solace. Your thoughts?"

"They have more people and ships than I expected," the Lord Captain admitted grudgingly. "If they can refit the Terran missile satellites, this world will have formidable defenses."

"But not enough to stand off a serious attack without starship support," Mira said quietly.

"Exactly," Anders agreed, to her surprise.

She'd half-expected him to disagree on principle. She needed to remember that, abrasive as the man could be, he was *competent*.

"These people will take time to train," he continued. "Time *we* cannot spare. Time in which they are vulnerable." He shrugged. "There is little strategic value to this system, Admiral. Liberating it has only made it a target to the Commonwealth—we have done them no favors here as we cannot afford to defend this system enough to *keep* it free."

"Not to mention, where were the warships?" Mira asked. "We found none. Seven-Two hit two, one of them *ancient*. Seven-Three saw *one*—a last-generation carrier. We were expecting three ships in *each* system, so we're missing *six* capital ships from what Intelligence expected to see.

"Ma'am, I somehow doubt those ships just disappeared. If we're not careful, we could see a nodal force we didn't expect rush back in and take these systems from underneath us."

"I agree," Alstairs said simply. "So does Alliance Intelligence. So, for that matter, does Alliance High Command. It just...doesn't matter."

"Doesn't *matter*?" Anders demanded. "We've marked these people as targets and are leaving them with insufficient defenses, and it doesn't *matter*?!"

Apparently, Anders had a soul. Mira had to approve.

"Captain, please," the Admiral told him. "We always knew that these systems were going to be vulnerable. Seventh Fleet is *not* a defensive formation; *holding* these systems is not our mandate.

"But if we complete Rising Star and punch out Via Somnia, they will be safe, as the Commonwealth will lack the logistical support for offensives along this entire section of the front. In this case, the best defense truly is a swift offense.

"So, let's be about it."

Cora System
20:00 March 14, 2736 ESMDT
DSC-078 Avalon, *Captain's Breakout Room*

The little conference room attached to Kyle's office was large enough for half a dozen people. With the wonders of holographic conferencing, it currently held over a dozen.

Anderson and Stanford were actually physically present in the room, his XO and CAG providing *Avalon*'s input. Brigadier Hammond and Mayor Musil were relaying in from Montreal's surface. *Sledgehammer*'s Captain

Urien Ainsley, *Indomitable*'s Captain Gervaise Albert and *Courageous*'s Captain Christine Olivier were all linked in from their ships.

While those five were linked in by Q-Com, they could theoretically have used radio as all of them were within orbit of Montreal with *Avalon*. The other members of the conference couldn't have—the closest was Admiral Alstairs in the Zahn system, six light-years away.

Fleet Admiral Meredith Blake, Chief of Naval Operations for the Federation, was in the Castle system, nearly *sixty* light-years away. Sky Marshal Octavian von Stenger, *the* man in charge of the Imperium's military, was even farther away—in Coraline, eighty light-years behind the front.

Those two represented roughly a third of the Alliance Joint Chiefs of Staff, also known as Alliance High Command. While the senior officers of the Star Kingdom of Phoenix and the Renaissance Trade Factor were *important*, the other two Chiefs of Staff—from single-system polities inevitably poorer than Phoenix—were nonentities. If Blake and von Stenger agreed to something, High Command would back it.

Terrifying as having one third of Alliance High Command sitting in on the conference, however, it was the last four participants in the conference that were making Kyle's palms sweat.

The first, a dark-haired woman in a plain black suit, was Leanne Summervale—the Prime Minister of the Star Kingdom of Phoenix.

The second was a balding herm, slightly pudgy with age, with the visible cybernetic advancements typical of those walking the transhuman path—Hanne Kovachev, Chairman of the Board of the Renaissance Trade Factor.

Senator Maria O'Connell of the planet Tuatha represented the Castle Federation. In general, the thirteen senators who ran the Federation were equal—if one of them committed the Federation to a task or stance, they spoke for the Federation.

Kyle had at least *met* O'Connell. The other two heads of state were of the Alliance's second-ranked powers; he could *adjust* to having them on the conference.

The last member of the conference, at the far end from Kyle as the software was arranging the conference, was a pale, dark-haired young man—a little younger than Kyle himself—clad in an unmarked black uniform and wearing a plain platinum circlet.

Queen Victoria II of the Star Kingdom acted *through* her Prime Minister, though most realized that her power was quite real.

John Erasmus Michael Albrecht von Coral, Imperator of the Coraline Imperium, Prince of Coraline, Duke of the High City, and a long list of other titles Kyle could not remember without using his implant memory, made no such pretenses. The Imperium's constitution hedged and limited his power, but there was no doubt who held the final authority over the second of the Alliance's first-rank nation-states.

This gathering of fourteen people, half of them Seventh Fleet officers, included enough political power to decide the fate of a world—which was *exactly* what they had gathered do.

"Do we have any information on what happened to the executives of the Cora Development Corporation?" the Imperator began. He might have been elected—for life—but he'd been raised to the job and it showed in his level speaking voice.

"We are looking into it," Blake responded instantly. "However, they did not arrive at an Alliance world and announce themselves."

"I know they boarded a ship and tried to flee," Mayor Musil, a squat man with watery eyes and thin grey hair, told the Imperator, his disgust clear in his voice. "I do not know what happened after that."

"We're digging into captured records," Hammond added. "It is distinctly possible that their ship was destroyed in the battle."

"And the shareholders?" von Coral asked.

"Approximately six million of record," Musil replied carefully. "Sixty percent were in the Commonwealth. My understanding is that Walkingstick ordered them paid out—at cents on the dollar—when he seized the system. Most of the remainder are on Cora. *We* were expected to be grateful to have been brought into Unity."

Kyle was pretty sure he knew where the Imperator was going with this, and it wasn't a place that the shareholders of the CDC were going to like. It was the only real choice the Alliance had, however.

"With the senior executives missing or dead, and the vast majority of shareholders already having foregone their rights, it does not appear that the Cora Development Corporation is a functioning entity at this point, does it?" the young man, ruler of twelve star systems, said in a deceptively mild voice.

The conference was silent for a long moment, then Mayor Musil—the senior surviving member of *any* government on Cora—sighed and nodded.

"You are correct," he admitted. "As a native-born son of this world, I am hardly *ecstatic* to see us in this position, but I cannot deny that our government is gone and the corporation operating it is no more."

"Without some structure on Cora, it will be difficult for Battle Group Seven-Two to move on with the rest of Rising Star," Kyle noted. "The situation on the surface remains fluid, making it a security risk."

"I agree," Summervale said. "Unfortunately, Mayor Musil, I think it will take too long for Cora to sort out a new government on its own. I feel the Alliance must step in."

"This is our world," Musil objected sharply. "We are not going to idly stand by while the Federation or Imperium simply takes over!"

"No one is suggesting anything of the sort," von Coral told him, the Imperator's calming baritone helping cover the fact that Kyle was pretty sure that had been *exactly* what the Imperator was thinking. Coraline expansionism, after all, had been why there had been enough warships in what was now the Alliance to stand off the initial Commonwealth assault.

"A more nuanced approach is called for," Senator O'Connell told the gathering. "It is clear that Cora is not currently capable of providing their own security. I believe, however, that Brigadier Hammond should be able to leave behind one of his battalions to assist in maintaining order. Admiral Alstairs?"

Kyle glanced at Seventh Fleet's CO, who looked thoughtful.

"Both Zahn and Hammerveldt are capable of maintaining order without our help," she finally admitted. "Leaving a battalion on Cora shouldn't compromise our ability to complete Rising Star."

"A new governing structure will need to be implemented on Cora," Kovachev announced, the Chairman's voice oddly flat. "That government will then be responsible for paying out the remaining shareholders fairly."

That clearly hadn't been included in anyone else's thought process, though it made sense. Kyle would also have been shocked, however, to discover that the Trade Factor's government *didn't* own shares in the CDC.

"In the interim, an Alliance-imposed martial law is only partially conducive to public order," the herm continued. "Some form of local interim government is required. I suggest the appointment of a local governor, someone recognizable to the populace."

"I agree," the Imperator confirmed. "My understanding is that Mayor Musil is the senior remaining member of the previous government—and his actions in enabling us to take the planet with minimal collateral damage have been well publicized."

The only person in the conference who seemed surprised by the suggestion was Johannes Musil himself. Kyle had figured out what was coming the moment Rear Admiral Alstairs had told him who was being invited to the meeting.

"It appears to be the best option," Senator O'Connell confirmed. "As part of the Alliance, we will keep Cora safe while Interim Governor Musil restores order and holds a new constitutional convention."

"I... I... I'm not sure that I'm the right person for the job," Musil replied.

"Perhaps, but you're the only person who can do it," Summervale told him calmly. "Your world needs you, Johannes Musil. The right guiding hand could see Cora emerge from this stronger and wiser, but even a few missteps at this stage could leave your world ruined."

The mayor was not a large man, but Kyle could see him straighten at the Phoenix Prime Minister's words. Musil was a politician. He had to *know* he was being played—if Kyle could see it, he was sure the Coran man could see it—but it worked anyway.

"We all do what we must," he finally said. "On behalf of my planet and myself, I accept."

CHAPTER 18

Cora System
10:00 March 17, 2736 Earth Standard Meridian Date/Time
Orbital Fighter Platform Zion-K265

"Pack it up, people," Edvard ordered Bravo Company. His Marines were scattered throughout the airless, lightless void of the *Zion*-class fighter platform, checking to make sure there weren't any unexpected holdouts from the Terrans.

Even with Navy sensors telling them the station was empty of life, it wasn't *quite* busywork—there were ways to conceal the heat signatures of humans, after all.

"The new Governor *finally* found some people to send up to take possession of his new orbital defenses," the Lieutenant Major continued. "And we, for those of you who didn't read even the part of the ops plan you were cleared for, are heading out-system in two hours. *Chimera* wants us back aboard."

Third Battalion had drawn the figurative short straw and was going to be staying on Montreal, guarding the new government and training a new planetary army from scratch. It was a necessary job, and one with a lot more public attention and friendly locals than the general run of chores the Castle Federation Marine Corps got assigned.

They were welcome to it. Edvard Hansen had signed up to fight pirates and the Commonwealth, and that was where he was going.

He wasn't surprised when Ramirez materialized next to his arm.

"We only got seventy percent of the station swept, sir," he said quietly over a direct channel. "We covered the most likely areas first, so we can be pretty sure the place is empty, but..."

"I know, Gunny," Edvard told him. "We could spend a week securing platforms and satellites, though, and still be only 'mostly sure' they were empty. The Corans will be fine."

"Still doesn't feel right, leaving them in the lurch like this," Ramirez admitted.

"Since we, ahem, accidentally rendered the Commonwealth freighter unable to generate a warp bubble, they're getting everything she had aboard," the Lieutenant Major pointed out. "That's a lot of firepower, Gunny. More than most systems have to keep themselves safe."

"And no starships," his NCO pointed out. "Void, sir, are they even going to be able to man those platforms and fighters? Most of the people they had trained to do that died defending this system the first time."

"Needs must when the Void pulls," Edvard said quietly. "This op always called for temporary defenses in the systems we liberated until further reinforcements were available from the Reserve or new construction. They were *supposed* to have plans to hide their military personnel if the Commonwealth took over, but..."

"The CDC didn't spend the money," Ramirez accepted sadly. "It still doesn't feel right, sir."

"Well, Gunny, if everything goes right, this place will be safe, and we'll give the Terrans a beating they won't forget. Get our people moving. I don't *think Chimera* will leave without us, but we are trying to get three Battle Groups to one place at the same time!"

DSC-078 Avalon, *Bridge*

"So, Maria, can we do it?" Kyle asked his navigator.

"*I* can do it," she noted calmly. "Assuming we break orbit anytime in the next three hours, I can get us to Frihet on time. But you are talking a simultaneous arrival for three separate forces, all engaged in relativistic—if low-tau—courses while sublight and then warping space beyond recognition while flying faster than light. To pull it off, *I* need to be good—but so do Rear Admiral Alstairs' navigator and Force Commander Aleppo's navigator."

"Both of whom you have been talking to all but constantly for three days," the Force Commander observed with a cheerful smile. "So, Maria, can we do it?"

"Sixty-forty," she admitted. "But even if someone's timing is off, we'll know at least a day in advance and the other two Battle Groups can adjust their deceleration to match whoever is falling behind. So, yes, sir, we can do it."

"Any major concerns?" he asked, suddenly more serious.

"No," she replied. "Everyone's A-S drives have been gone over with a fine-toothed comb, and we're not even pushing *Avalon*'s engines this time. Besides, is this degree of finesse even necessary, boss?"

"I don't know," Kyle admitted. Alliance Intelligence put the same three starships at Frihet that they'd expected at Cora, Zahn and Hammerveldt. Since there had only been three starships *between* those systems, he wasn't sure what to expect at Frihet. "If Intelligence is right this time, bringing everyone in should give us a four-to-one advantage. On the other hand, if the missing ships are at Frihet..."

"I guess we wouldn't want only one Battle Group showing up, then," Pendez agreed. She shrugged. "We're just waiting on the Marines to return aboard *Chimera*. Once Captain Langdon confirms the Brigadier's people are aboard, we can be on our way immediately."

"Let's stick to the schedule unless something comes up," Kyle instructed. "This is a simple enough evolution for the moment, so let's keep it that way."

"Yes, sir."

#

"Seven-Two is ready to go as soon as our Marines are aboard," Kyle reported to Alstairs from his office. It was a small conference via Q-Com with the three Battle Group commanders plus Alstairs' flag captain. "I don't expect to be leaving late, though Commander Pendez tells me we have an hour or so of leeway before it will be an issue."

"Seven-Three departed six hours ago," Aleppo advised him. The Trade Factor Force Commander's Battle Group had the farthest to go—twelve light-years to Seven-Two's eleven or Seven-One's ten. "We are on schedule for arrival."

"Seven-One will be ready to depart in approximately eight hours," Rear Admiral Alstairs confirmed once her subordinates had finished reporting. "So far, we are on schedule for Phase Two of Rising Star?"

"Fully," Kyle confirmed. "We were able to use the captured Terran freighter to provide orbital defenses to Cora. I suspect she was intended to provide defenses to several systems, which will give Cora a very solid defense network once they're all online."

"How long is that going to take?" the Admiral asked.

"Longer than I'd like," Kyle admitted with a sigh. "From what Governor Musil has learned so far, barely ten percent of the Cora Security Force personnel survived. He *has* found their records, however, and has people digging up every *ex*-member of the Force they can find. Enough experienced volunteers have come forward over the last few days that Musil believes they can have the two deployed platforms online—at least as missile control centers—by tomorrow evening Standard Meridian.

"Refitting the platforms with non-Commonwealth Q-Coms is going to be the biggest task," he continued, "and Seven-Two is out of reserve blocks of entangled particles. Nonetheless, Cora's new military may not have a *name*, but they will have a fully functioning defense network by the end of the week—one that is only going to grow stronger given time."

"But you have the Federation platforms aboard the logistics ship still?" Aleppo asked.

"Exactly," he confirmed. "None of those platforms or fighters are being deployed here—Governor Musil has accepted the logic."

"That will help make up for the loss of the *Venture* in terms of Rising Star," the Rear Admiral said grimly. "A lot is going to depend on what we encounter at Frihet," she continued. "If they've based a nodal force there, we could be looking at an even fight."

"I'm not a fan of those," Kyle noted. "But with all three groups arriving, I'm pretty sure we can make them leap the wrong way."

"Somehow, that you want them looking the wrong way when you punch them doesn't surprise me," Aleppo said dryly. "I'm glad you're on *my* side."

"We need more data to really play them," he replied. "In this case, we're probably best off going in fast and crushing them with overwhelming firepower. It all depends on whether their missing ships are there."

"It's unlikely that those ships are missing for a reason we'll like," Solace noted. She was being quiet, though Kyle certainly had been aware of her presence. "I would guess they've been pulled back for upgrades. There's a lot of things they could be refitting their old ships with that would make our life harder—modern deflectors, for example."

"I don't trust a position *Walkingstick* set up to be as weak as this appears," Admiral Alstairs agreed. "I'm also concerned about rumors they've been testing a seventh-generation starfighter—by now, they *have* to have realized the deficiencies of the Scimitar's design versus our new ships. Re-equipping their carriers and cruisers with a starfighter capable of going toe-to-toe with our Falcons will be a headache."

"Walkingstick thinks like I do, I believe," Kyle told his fellows. "So, my question is...where does he *want* us looking—and what are we missing?"

"I don't know," Alstairs said slowly. "We can hope he didn't see Rising Star coming—we've been pretty lackadaisical about attempting to reclaim our systems, after all. But if he did... Watch your backs, people," she ordered.

"We'll discuss our plans for Frihet in detail as we get closer. Review what we have on the system, and for now, let's assume that all six of our missing ships are there."

#

The Rear Admiral and Force Commander Aleppo dropped off the channel, leaving just Kyle and Mira on the conference. Given that everyone else in the Fleet was limited to recorded messages to their loved ones, stealing even a handful of minutes made Kyle feel guilty.

"If we cut this off early, the Admiral will tell me off again," Mira said immediately, heading off his guilt with the smile so few people saw. It transformed the elegant ebony statue of his former executive officer's work persona into a still-gorgeous but far more human woman.

"How are you holding up?" he asked quietly. *Camerone* was her first command, and one she'd been rushed into with little notice or preparation. While they'd taken advantage of her no longer being his subordinate quite quickly, he was also concerned about the demands on her.

"Alstairs built up a good team," she told him. "And, thankfully, she also knows when to get out of the way. Her people don't look to her for orders instead of me *most* of the time." She paused. "It's good. We don't do the easiest job in the galaxy, but with this team behind me, I'm doing okay."

"I saw the Zahn reports," Kyle replied. "I'd say you're doing better than okay!"

"I at least didn't hang my ship out to dry as bait!" she said. "What were you *thinking*?"

"That I was outside the gravity zone the whole time and could have backup in place in twelve minutes," he told her with a grin. "Compared to the crap I pulled at Barsoom, that was *nothing*—and pulling it off captured a star system in exchange for thirty-seven Marines."

His grin faded as he remembered that. Most of them had died on the surface, taking Trudeau City. Just because the casualties had been light to take an entire system didn't stop them being people with lives and memories that were now lost.

"How often can you play the odds like that, Kyle?" she asked. "Sooner or later, one of your stunts is going to blow up in your face."

"I know," he agreed. "That's why the Cora plan had fallbacks and cutouts, Mira. Barsoom...Tranquility...those were all-or-nothing stunts where I had no choice. The worst-case scenario in Cora was realizing the entire Battle Group was outgunned and going back into warp before we engaged anyone. I *like* those kinds of options."

She shook her head.

"Fair enough, I suppose," she allowed. "I believe I have mentioned that you're not allowed to get yourself killed in this war, right?"

"And the same applies to you, my dear," he reminded her. "I look forward to stealing some *actual* time together in Frihet."

"Hopefully, the Commonwealth won't impede that plan," Mira told him with a smile.

"Walkingstick would probably like to cut our time short," Kyle agreed. "But with all of Seventh Fleet, I don't think he'll succeed."

"Oh, he won't succeed," Mira replied, her smile widening into something more predatory. "But he's welcome to *try*."

CHAPTER 19

Deep Space, En Route to Frihet System
20:00 March 17, 2736 Earth Standard Meridian Date/Time
DSC-078 Avalon, *Main Flight Briefing Room*

"Vice Commodore, this is Rokos."

The voice of his Bravo Wing commander echoed in Michael Stanford's skull as he approached his office.

"What is it, Wing Commander?" *Avalon*'s CAG asked.

"We need you in the main briefing room," Rokos replied crisply. "We're having a...discipline problem and need higher authority."

Stanford cursed whatever Stars had made him the CAG. With two hundred and forty starfighters under his command, that meant he had seven hundred and twenty flight crew, plus roughly a thousand deck personnel.

The flight crews, in his experience, were prima donnas to a man, woman, and herm. By and large, the Flight Commanders handled their squadrons, but problems filtered up to the Wing Commanders on a regular basis—and, occasionally, the worst cases hit the Vice Commodore in charge of the Group.

"I'll be right there," he sighed.

"Thank you, sir," Rokos told him crisply.

It was late in the ship's 'day,' three quarters of the way through the Bravo shift and two hours away from changeover. Flight Country was dead. The current Combat Space Patrol was being run by starfighters from *Indomitable*, playing trainer to several squadrons of hastily refitted Scimitars in the hands of Coran ex-retirees.

·141·

He was surprised, as he approached the briefing room, not to hear any signs of commotion. If a Wing Commander felt they needed to call in the CAG, there was usually shouting when said CAG arrived.

Michael's sense of paranoia, finely honed in recent months after an assassination attempt by the same woman who'd tried to take out the Captain, finally triggered when he stepped into the main flight briefing room—a room the size of many school gymnasiums, designed to allow addresses to or social events for *every* one of his seven hundred-plus flight crew—to find the lights down.

The door slammed shut behind him before he could begin to retreat, and he was halfway into reaching for his weapon when the lights came back on—and his ears were suddenly assaulted by *over seven hundred voices* chorusing, "Happy birthday to you!"

Even if any of his people *could* sing, enough of them couldn't that it dissolved into an overwhelming cacophony, aided easily along the way by the two men in the front—one tall and huge, one short and wide— both of whom had the lungs for volume but couldn't carry a tune in a star freighter.

"I see," Michael replied as the sound finally died down, "that your 'discipline problem,' Commander Rokos, was your own willingness to ignore my standing order to ignore my birthday."

"Without question, sir!" Rokos replied in perfect cadet form. "No apologies, sir."

"If you aren't planning on scrubbing starfighters with a toothbrush tonight, there had better be cake," Michael intoned perilously, only to find his Captain laughing at him.

Massive as Force Commander Kyle Roberts was, it was hard to be *intimidated* by him when he was grinning and laughing like a teenager— something Michael suspected that Roberts cultivated intentionally.

"Please, Michael," Roberts told him. "*Of course* there's a cake."

Avalon's captain gestured imperiously, and a path opened through the crowd, allowing Senior Chief Petty Officer Olivia Kalers, his deck chief, to roll a munitions trolley across the briefing room. Kalers was a shaven-headed woman with a permanently sour expression, but she was *trying* to smile. Pride of place on the trolley was a one-twentieth-size model of a Falcon starfighter, made of cake.

The other worthy pushing the trolley was Master Chief Petty Officer Cardea Belmonte, *Avalon*'s bosun. Belmonte was a massive woman with short-cropped white hair, and she *was* smiling—one of the biggest grins Michael had ever seen on a human being.

"Happy thirty-ninth birthday, Vice Commodore," she told him. "We made you a cake!"

#

By the time most of his people had swung by, seized cake, and wished him a happy birthday, Michael was feeling utterly wrung out. It wasn't often that he dealt with this large a portion of the nearly two thousand people under his command on anything even resembling a one-on-one basis, and the process had consumed over two hours of his evening.

Finally, he managed to snag a second piece of cake for himself and find a *relatively* quiet corner—to find Roberts waiting there for him. With, almost inevitably, a beer.

"How do you *always* have beer?" he asked as he gratefully grabbed the—still cold! —bottle from his superior.

"Because I always stock up when we hit a planet," Roberts replied cheerfully. "This is from a microbrewery just outside Trudeau City. I was impressed, so I grabbed a few cases."

"Cases," Michael repeated. "How much of your mass allowance is beer, boss?"

"Thirty percent or so?" the Force Commander guessed. "The refrigeration units take up a bunch too. I don't *have* that much stuff, Michael—I've lived shipboard for eight years at this point."

Avalon's CAG studied the party, a warm feeling settling into his chest at the sheer amount of work his people had put into it.

"Last time I checked," he noted, "my subordinates don't have easy access to my birthday. Someone more senior than Rokos had to provide that."

"That was me," his boss confirmed cheerfully. "Though I will note that your people came to me. It seems *Hammond* knew your birthday and set all this in motion before he got med-evaced. Rokos didn't know the exact date, but he knew it had to be soon."

There was nothing Michael could really say to that. Master Chief Petty Officer Marshal Hammond, *Avalon*'s former deck chief, had been badly wounded in the attempt to kill Michael himself. As the CAG—who had lost his legs just above the knees in the Battle of Tranquility—knew, there wasn't much that required someone to be shipped planetside for medical treatment.

Hammond had spent his last few weeks aboard *Avalon* in a wheelchair, wrapped in a "cast" that had effectively replaced the functions of several of his organs. The kind of internal reconstruction the Chief had required wasn't possible out of even the big carrier's resources, and he'd been shipped all the way back to Castle to get the best care possible.

"How's he doing?" Roberts asked, clearly following Michael's thoughts.

"It's *Marshal*, sir," Michael replied with a chuckle. "From the last communication I had from him, he's spending half of his day in a tank full of nanites, and the other half complaining that the nanites make him *itch*."

"Do they?" the Force Commander asked.

"In my experience? Like Void, sir. Like Starless Void," Michael confirmed, shivering. "Was worth it to walk again for me—and without proper regen therapy, Hammond was looking at that life support chair for the rest of his life—but *Void*, did it itch."

"I'll keep that in mind next time I'm facing dramatic, life-threatening injury," Roberts replied cheerfully.

23:00 March 17, 2736 ESMDT
DSC-078 Avalon, CAG's Quarters

Like a carrier's Captain, a carrier's Commander, Air Group wasn't attached to any of the ship's three shifts. Michael's sleep schedule was variable at the best of times, but he was usually asleep by twenty-three hundred hours Standard.

When he finally managed to make it into his quarters, though, his implant happily informed him that he had a private Q-Com message waiting for him. His mother's birthday message had arrived that morning, which left only one likely candidate.

Tired as he was, he couldn't stop a silly smile as Kelly Mason's image appeared in his mind. With a thought, he transferred the message to his quarters' wallscreen and dropped down on the side of his bed to watch her message.

"Hey, lover," she greeted him. She looked tired—she'd only sent the message an hour before and her uniform was rumpled from long wear. "Happy birthday. Interstellar shipping is a *bitch*, so you'll get your present when you come home."

The voluptuous blond woman smiled, sending a shiver running through Michael's heart.

"That gives me time to think of what *to* get you," she added wickedly. "It's been a hectic month," she admitted. "After the attack when you guys left, they've got Home Fleet pulling system-wide patrols, making sure nobody sneaks up on the Yards. At least we don't have to worry about the Reserve anymore."

She didn't elaborate—Q-Com transmissions might be the most secure communication known to man, with zero chance of interception, but that didn't invalidate operational security—but Michael had seen the same reports. With the first wave of the Reserve deployed, the Castle System Reserve was in the yards now. Twenty ships at a time, four months to commission each wave—it would take almost another year to get the Alliance's eighty reserve starships deployed.

Hopefully by then, there'd be new-wave construction to deploy as well. *Avalon*, for example, was over *twice* the volume of the Reserve ships sent out to reinforce her. There was supposed to be an entire *generation* of warships to match her, but only a handful of the Sanctuaries had been completed before the war started.

"I'd be okay with the patrols," Mason continued, "if they didn't *also* insist on inspections to keep the Home Fleet to the 'standard expected of the Federation's last line of defense'. I'll never object to engineers checking over my ship's tech, but inspectors going over my people's uniforms and corridor cleanliness?"

She shuddered, and Michael doubted it was feigned. The Federation's Home Fleet was *notorious* for its spit and shine—suddenly, being on the front didn't sound so bad!

"Spent yesterday cleaning the ship from top to bottom and today playing nursemaid to a pair of idiots who might fall into a fusion reactor or something if left alone," she concluded. "And that was if they didn't irritate anyone enough to *help* them fall, for Christ's sake."

His smile tried to split his face. His girlfriend's concerns were very real—and very much the concerns of a fleet attached to an unlikely target. Walkingstick's people had launched one attack on the system, but the logistics of that kind of operation were a mess. If nothing else, once your Alcubierre speed crossed the ten-light-year-per-day mark, ships started to have a real chance of just, well, disappearing.

Compared to the fear of losing his people when they hit Frihet, they were seemingly minor. Roberts's tricks had got them through Cora without fighter losses, but that couldn't continue. Starfighters, after all, existed to die so starships didn't.

Mason reached out toward the camera as if to touch his face. "I miss you," she said quietly. "I did, for your information, manage to make time to have supper with your mother. We ended up talking grandkids."

Michael's girlfriend, the executive officer of a strike cruiser, chuckled—and then sighed wistfully.

"She actually volunteered to take care of them while we were on duty if we wanted to do an in vitro pregnancy," Kelly told him. "I'm... Honestly, Michael, I'm tempted. I don't think I'd be okay with leaving our child with even your mother, but the thought of a child..."

She shrugged, and Michael was surprised at his own reaction. A year ago, the thought of having a child with *anyone* would have sent him running for the hills. Now...

Like Kelly said, he was tempted. But he agreed that he'd want one of them to raise the kid, and, well...regardless of any specific terms or contracts, he knew they were both in for the duration.

"Too many issues, I think," she finally declared. "Something for us to think about, though—as an *us*."

Her smile suddenly turned wicked and her hands slid to the zipper of her uniform.

"Now that I've gone all mopey and maternal on you, I think I need to give you what birthday present I can," she told him with a lascivious wink.

CHAPTER 20

Deep Space, En Route to Frihet System
03:00 March 20, 2736 Earth Standard Meridian Date/Time
DSC-078 Avalon, *Bridge*

Most people aboard a starship who couldn't sleep and wanted to see the strange light effects of a warp bubble would go to one of the observation bubbles every ship had. *Most* people had no interest in seeing the warped void of the gap between star-bow and star-wake, as it was mildly unnerving on first exposure.

As the Captain of one of the Castle Federation's most modern supercarriers, however, Kyle Roberts could drop himself down in the command chair on the bridge and keep one eye on his Charlie shift while watching the twisted space surrounding his ship.

The only threat in FTL was the nature of the bubble itself. Every particle in the path of the warships was picked up by the warp in space—and often hyper-energized as well. An Alcubierre bubble was a very hostile place, the stabilization fields a fragile shield against radiation levels that would slag the carrier's hull and kill her crew.

An ability to track or engage ships under Alcubierre drive would be the kind of superweapon that could change the course of a war. Until reaching Frihet, *Avalon*'s crew was safe. They would drill, they would prepare, and when they arrived at their destination they would go to war.

A thought changed the images being fed directly to Kyle's optic nerve from the strange lights of the warp bubble to a tactical plot of the Frihet system.

The plan called for the three Battle Groups to arrive simultaneously, evenly spaced around the "north" half of the system. After that, it devolved into branching flowcharts, depending on what Commonwealth forces were present and how they responded.

Much like his plan at Cora, there were cutouts and backup plans. Seventh Fleet would remain outside the gravity well of the planet until they were certain of the Commonwealth's strength. Using their Alcubierre drives to concentrate their force—or even to flee, if necessary—was an option until they drove farther in-system.

Rising Star was going well. Its sister operation deeper into Alliance space, retaking the systems the Commonwealth had seized in their second offensive, was reporting success as well. Those battles were harder-fought from the reports he had seen, but Fourth Fleet was twice Seventh Fleet's size—and with more modern ships as well.

For the first time since the war had kicked off the previous September, the Alliance finally seemed to have turned the balance. With the boost of the ships deployed from the Reserve, it looked like they were pushing the Commonwealth back on all fronts.

His tactical plot dissolved into a strategic map, the Captain studying the three-dimensional chart of stars. If Rising Star and Peacock succeeded, the Commonwealth would have been kicked back to their original borders.

Ship numbers started attaching themselves to battles and he sighed. Even one of Seventh Fleet's Battle Group commanders wasn't getting enough data to be sure of losses, but his impression from the reports he'd read was that Peacock was being *expensive*. The Alliance's best were hammering headlong into the Commonwealth's best with attendant losses on both sides—losses the Commonwealth could afford better.

James Calvin Walkingstick had volunteered to be Marshal of the Rimward Marches, charged with annexing the Federation and its allies. Kyle doubted he'd done so without a plan—and he doubted the Alliance had thrown any significant wrenches into his engines.

So, every day it looked like they were winning, Kyle was going to keep looking for the sucker punch.

He just wished he could guess what it was going to be.

09:00 March 20, 2736 ESMDT
BC-129 Camerone, Captain's Office

"Morning reports, ma'am."

Mira nodded to Bruce Notley, her executive officer, and gestured the sparse, white-haired man to the chair opposite her. She hadn't looked up just *how* old Notley was, but she did know that he'd joined the Castle Federation Space Navy as a junior enlisted rating in the middle of the last war, worked his way up to Senior Chief, and then been talked into taking a commission.

His tour as XO on *Camerone* was the final checkmark in his file before they gave the old warhorse his own cruiser. Alstairs had been lucky to have him—and Mira, as a first-time Captain, regarded herself as about ten times as lucky.

"Anything I need to be aware of?" she asked, gestured at the datapad he'd dropped on her desk. The reports could be—and actually were—directly transmitted to her neural implant. But Notley and Alstairs had built this tradition when she was Captain, and in the very first of these meetings Notley had sprung on her, he'd drawn her attention to a gambling ring about to explode in Engineering.

It hadn't been in anyone's reports. Gambling was allowed aboard Federation ships so long as they followed rules, after all. In this case, however, the ring had basically set up a roving casino in her ship—and in a casino, the house always wins.

Notley had brought it to her attention, and *she'd* made sure the bosun and chief engineer were aware of it. The *Captain* was a level of artillery not regularly brought to the party, which got the ring quickly dealt with—which had probably saved at least one of its members' *lives*, as ill feelings had been growing.

"Nothing too major this time," her XO admitted. "Launcher Six is still down. Engineering assures me we'll have it back online by tomorrow, well before we reach Frihet. Otherwise, *Camerone* is prepared for action in all respects."

Those were the words any warship captain wanted to hear, and Mira leaned back, smiling.

"So far, so good, huh, Bruce?" she asked rhetorically. "Any thoughts on what to expect at Frihet?"

"Not sure, ma'am," he admitted. "I have to admit, I'm nervous. It's unusual for Intelligence to be as wrong as they were about the last three systems. I guess it's possible we'll run into all of the missing ships at Frihet."

"We can take them in that case," Mira pointed out. "We'll have twelve ships to their nine, and I'm betting their defensive ships are older, too."

"So is most of our fleet," Notley said quietly. "Even *Camerone* isn't our latest—there's, what, seven *Defender*-class battlecruisers in the Navy? The Conquerors are a few months from commissioning. The only modern sixty-million-cubic-meter-plus ships in Seventh Fleet are *Avalon* and *Zheng He*. With the Reserve, most of our ships are under forty million cubic meters and maybe twelve million tons. If we run into nine Volcanos or Saints, we might have them *outnumbered,* but they'll have us *outmassed* and outgunned."

Camerone's captain sighed.

"I know. That's not what Intelligence *thinks* we're facing, but they also thought the Terrans had a lot more ships around here," she admitted. "Peacock hasn't run into them—thank God, that's been a Pyrrhic-enough affair as it is—but they have to be somewhere."

"Not sure where, though, ma'am," Notley told her.

"That's my next meeting with the Admiral," Mira replied. "I'll be sure to ask Intel what's going on."

"Bluntly, Admiral, Captains, we have no idea where Walkingstick's defensive units are based," Captain Sansone Costa of the Renaissance Trade Security Force's Intelligence Branch, said flatly. "Our agents in the systems seized by the Commonwealth have limited access to the covert Q-Com arrays available to them, but none of our operatives in Huī Xing or Frihet have any access to orbital scanner arrays or information on ships in-system."

All twelve of Seventh Fleet's captains were in on the call, though Mira was the only one physically present in the conference room attached to Admiral Alstairs' office.

"We do know, from agents in the Commonwealth Navy's logistics division, that Walkingstick assigned fifteen ships to the security of those five systems," Costa continued. "Most are last-generation ships, with two Volcanos, a Saint, and a Hercules to stiffen their strength."

"The Hercules is gone," Roberts noted. "That reduces the really nasty surprises they can throw at us."

"So, you're saying our original briefing was based on taking the number of ship's Walkingstick's people have and dividing by five?" Mira asked dryly. "That seems a little...crude."

"It was an accurate an assumption as we had to work with at the time," Costa replied calmly. "Without the ability to predict whether or not they were using a nodal force or where that force would be positioned, planning around that assumption would be dangerous."

"And sending us in assuming they had a maximum of three ships per system *wasn't*?" Alstairs demanded. "We are supposed to receive the full intelligence, Captain, not your assumptions presented as *facts*."

The hologram of the swarthy Renaissance Trade Factor officer shrugged.

"*I* did not draft that report," he said flatly. "You are correct, Rear Admiral. More information *should* have been given, and a false impression of certainty was provided. Those responsible have been advised of their error and additional layers of review added. The error will not be repeated."

"It better not," the Admiral told him. "What *can* you tell us?"

"We are certain on the number of hulls assigned to this sector," Costa replied. "Given Commonwealth losses to date, that means you are facing at most twelve capital ships. We have limited information on what has been provided in terms of fixed defenses, but we do not *think* that you will face anything heavier than Zahn's defenses outside of Via Somnia itself."

"Since they clearly *have* a nodal fleet, do we know *where* it is?" Mira demanded.

"Via Somnia seems likely," the intelligence officer said. "If they took the logistics facilities the Alliance assembled at Huī Xing, they could also have based the fleet there. I would say it is at least seventy percent likely that the nodal force will not be waiting for you at Frihet."

"What about Via Somnia itself?" Alstairs asked.

"We believe the defenses we saw at Zahn, Cora and Hammerveldt were drawn from a set of freighters we had assessed as being sent to Via Somnia," Costa explained. "Nonetheless, defenses at Via Somnia remain likely in excess of two thousand starfighters and roughly a quarter of that in orbital missile satellites. Neutralizing the local fleet would be wise before engaging the defenses at the naval base."

That was *Alstairs'* decision, but no one bothered to correct the intelligence officer. He wasn't, technically, assigned to Seventh Fleet—Battle Group Seventeen's assigned intelligence officer had been killed in the attempted mutiny aboard *Avalon*—but he was the closest thing they had, which gave him the right to make recommendations.

"Do we have any data on whether we're likely to see that sprint mode again?" Mira asked.

"It's not an official program," Costa said slowly. "But, given how effective it was, I suspect you will see it again. I wouldn't expect to see it in fleet actions, but as an extra boost to system defenses, it could give us some serious headaches."

"What about duplicating it ourselves?" Roberts said.

Costa shook his head.

"That's out of my realm of expertise," he admitted. "My understanding is that the Federation's JD-Tech is studying the possibility of adding the functionality to our own Jackhammers, but I have no details."

"Thank you, Captain Costa," Alstairs noted. "If we come up with anything else on Via Somnia or the ships in this sector, I want to be notified immediately, understood?"

"Of course, Rear Admiral," he confirmed. "We got lucky—our error could have caused far more damage. I *refuse* to allow that to happen again, ma'am."

CHAPTER 21

Frihet System
03:30 March 24, 2736 Earth Standard Meridian Date/Time
DSC-078 Avalon, *Bridge*

Every neural implant on *Avalon*'s bridge was displaying the timer. With five minutes before emergence, the last few members of the bridge crew were filtering into the room in response to the blaring battle stations alarm.

"Pendez?" Kyle said questioningly.

"We are on schedule and on target," she told him, her eyes glazed over as she controlled the immense carrier through her implants. "All ships in Battle Group *Avalon* also report on schedule and on target," she continued. "As do Battle Group *Zheng He* and Battle Group *Camerone*. We are four minutes, twenty-two seconds from emergence...now."

"Thank you," he told her, then opened a channel to engineering. "Commander Wong, what's our status?"

"All systems are go," Senior Fleet Commander Alistair Wong reported. The shaven-headed engineer was technically senior to the ship's executive officer, though the arcane rules of chain of command actually put him under Anderson if something horrible happened to Kyle. "We have spun up all of the zero point cells, positron capacitors are at sufficient levels for instant engagement with all weapons systems. Please try not to break my ship, Captain."

"I believe it's *my* ship, Commander," Kyle pointed out.

"That's what the Captain *always* thinks—and he's always wrong," the engineer groused.

"Tell it to the Navy, Wong," the Captain told him. The engineer chuckled but didn't stop him cutting the channel as he flipped his attention to the starfighters, opening a channel to Michael Stanford's command starfighter.

"CAG, are you ready to fly?"

"Got the Chiefs around the birds, kicking tires and poking engines," the Vice Commodore replied.

"Michael, your Falcons don't *have* tires," Kyle replied. "And poking antimatter engines is a *really* bad idea."

"Sir, with all due respect, I do *not* question my Chief Petty Officers when they tell me what they're doing," Stanford replied virtuously. "SFG Zero Zero One is cleared and ready for action," he concluded. "I've checked in with the other CAGs as well. All Battle Group Seven-Two starfighter groups are cleared and ready for action. Give us a target and we will rip it to shreds."

"Thank you, CAG," Kyle told him, turning his attention back to his bridge. "Commander Xue?"

"Yes, sir?"

"Tactical status?"

"All sensors, computers and weapons are online and reporting correctly," the dark-haired officer replied. "I have a twelve-Q-probe spread ready to launch as soon as we emerge."

"Good. Carry on."

The cycle through his officers complete, Kyle glanced back at the timer. Two minutes.

He brought up the tactical plot showing Frihet. There wasn't much on the plot just yet, only the system's eleven planets—most importantly, the fifth planet, Fyr, home to roughly two and a third billion people. Another thirty-odd million were scattered around the star system in various orbitals and asteroid habitats—highlighted on the plot as best Intelligence could locate them—but control of an inhabited system inevitably went to the people who held the habitable planet.

Icons on the plot marked where the three Battle Groups of Seventh Fleet were intended to emerge—outside the point where Fyr's gravity well would throw off their Alcubierre drives, within roughly a light-minute of each other. Any capital ships would be in Fyr orbit, best placed to defend the planet.

"Alcubierre-Stetson emergence in thirty seconds," Pendez announced.

"All right," Kyle replied, turning his attention back to his people and scanning the bridge around him. Everyone looked ready. The other ship captains reported ready.

"Let's make the Commonwealth wish they'd never come to Frihet, shall we?"

#

In a flash of blue Cherenkov radiation, *Avalon* reappeared in the normal universe. Fractions of a second later, the light from her compatriots' emergences—all fifteen thousand kilometers away to provide a safety margin—reached her, the icons of the two cruisers and a battleship materializing on Kyle's plot as the computers confirmed their presence.

New green icons flashed onto the plot moments later as Q-Com-equipped probes blasted away from each of the four ships at a thousand gravities, sweeping deep into the system and relaying instant data back to their motherships.

"What are we seeing, Lieutenant Commander?" he asked softly. He would only see icons on his plot once Xue's team had reviewed the data—with copious amounts of help from the ship's AIs—and assessed the reality of what they were seeing.

"Old light still," she pointed out unnecessarily—they'd come out of FTL twenty-four million kilometers from the planet. It would be thirty-seven minutes before their first probes blasted past the planet at twenty thousand plus kilometers a second to give them their first close look at Fyr, and over fifty-two minutes before any of the probes permanently settled in orbit.

"But," she continued, "we've got some clarity on what's in orbit. Looks like they set up a full defense network." Four large red icons lit up in orbit, followed by hundreds of smaller ones. "I've got four *Zion*-class platforms and two hundred missile launch platforms."

That was the same defenses Zahn had been equipped with, plus a few extra missile satellites. Seventh Fleet could take that in their sleep...

"Damn," Xue cut off his thought. Two *more* large red icons lit up in orbit, followed by a swarm of smaller icons. "I've got two capital ships in orbit. Still resolving volume, but energy signatures suggest they're both twenty million tons. I'm also reading a fifty-fighter combat space patrol."

"Damn," Kyle echoed. That meant either both Volcanos or one of the Volcanos and the Saint from the ships Intelligence had identified. "Let me know as you break down size and details."

The *Saint* would be a handful, but in many ways, it would be more of a headache if it was the two heavy carriers. Six hundred starfighters was more than any of Seventh Fleet's three subgroups carried—and starfighters were fast enough that they might manage to pin one battle group down.

"Any word on the rest of the Fleet?" he asked calmly.

"Just got Q-Com confirmation," Anderson interjected. "Dropping them onto the plot now."

Eight more green icons flashed onto the screen, split into the two other subgroups of Seventh Fleet—both exactly on target.

"Orders, sir?" Pendez asked.

"For now, keep an eye on the bogies in orbit and try to tell me if we have a battleship and carrier or two carriers on our hands," Kyle told his people. "Maria, set our course towards Fyr—but take it nice and slow.

"I'm going to raise the Flag and see what the *Admiral* wants to do."

03:45 March 24, 2736 ESMDT
BC-129 Camerone, *Bridge*

As light propagated in and Q-probes shot out across the system, it was something of a relief for Mira to sink into the all-Captains link and apply multiple brains to the problem.

"Should we jump back into Alcubierre, concentrate our forces?" Force Commander Aleppo asked. "If that's a pair of Volcanos, we could be in serious trouble."

"Any of the battle groups *should* be able to handle even six hundred starfighters," Lord Captain Anders pointed out. "If they sent all six hundred starfighters straight at one of the Battle Groups, they'd be knowingly sacrificing the carriers for only an even chance of doing damage to us."

"It's a chance to do damage they won't otherwise have," Force Commander Roberts pointed out. "Even if that's a Saint, the pair of them could be a handful of any of our subgroups. I suggest we consolidate our forces and avoid the risk."

"*You* want to avoid the risk?" Anders asked.

"Despite what everyone seems to think, I tend to reserve suicidal options for when we have no *choice*," Mira's boyfriend pointed out. "I don't see a point in taking a risk we don't *need* to."

"There's another risk you are all missing," Rear Admiral Alstairs told them. "And an opportunity—if we keep our forces divided, we can all but guarantee that those ships will not escape. It *is* a risk," she admitted. "But to take down two thirds of the remaining modern units in the sector? I think it's worth it.

"We will expand our coverage," she continued, "and remain outside the gravity zones to open the possibility of an FTL intercept if needed. They don't have the forces to stop us retaking Fyr, people, so let's see what additional advantage we can take today."

"Yes, ma'am," Roberts and Anders conceded in unison.

"Captain," Commander Rose interrupted the conversation to get Mira's attention. "It's definitely two Volcanos—they've just launched their birds and are assembling a full sixty-squadron strike."

Sixty Commonwealth squadrons was the full six-hundred-fighter capacity of two Volcano carriers plus the four Zion platforms—the Terrans used a ten-starfighter squadron instead of the eight-ship formation the Alliance powers used.

"Thank you, Commander," Mira told her, then returned to the all-Captains channel. "My tactical officer tells me they're pulling together their birds for an all-or-nothing strike—*I'd* guess to cover the carriers' retreat."

"Rough on the starfighters," Roberts noted. "But Terran starfighter crews are the same hotdog breed as ours. They'd carry out the mission."

"Get our starfighters in space," Alstairs ordered. "Let's keep our options as wide open as we can."

04:00 March 24, 2736 ESMDT
SFG-001 Actual—Falcon-C type command starfighter

The efforts of several million Federation stellars' worth of mass manipulators did their best to reduce the impact of firing Michael's starfighter out the launch tube at four thousand gravities. It still felt like being stepped on by a giant and took the breath of his entire three-person crew away.

But he had all two hundred and forty of his fighters into space in a little over a minute. *Courageous* and *Indomitable* had fewer fighters to launch, getting all of their birds into space in the same time frame.

"Intercept those starfighters," Roberts ordered harshly in his ear. "They've gone all-or-nothing, Michael—there are six hundred ships headed for Seven-Three, and Aleppo has less than two hundred to meet them with."

Michael ran the numbers through his implant. It was going to be tight for his people—and there was no way Seven-One's fighters could get there in time.

"Understood," he replied crisply to Roberts, then pulled all of the CAGs onto a network, running numbers through his implant and his starfighters' computers as he assembled his orders.

"SFG Zero Zero One, *Courageous* Wing, *Indomitable* Wing, I'm downloading a course to you now," he snapped crisply. "We need to get on that intercept *now*. Even at our best acceleration, we're only going to intercept them a few minutes before they hit Seven-Three."

Even as he gave the order, he was twisting his own starfighter and bringing up the engines. A Falcon was an expensive, finely tuned machine—it leapt from a standing start to five hundred gravities of acceleration instantly.

The three hundred and thirty-six starfighters of Battle Group Seven-Two, *Avalon*, joined him instantly. They were cutting the line, accelerating to a point between *Zheng He* and the Terran Scimitars. With the geometry as it was, their missile range would be almost three million kilometers—and they'd launch while the *Scimitars* were four million kilometers clear of *Zheng He* and her escorts and...

"Force Commander Aleppo," he said quietly, opening a channel to *Zheng He*'s captain. "I need you to give me more distance. Play for time—right now, they'll hit you before we take them out."

"If we evade, we cannot prevent the carriers escaping," Aleppo replied. "That is not the mission."

"I have a plan for those carriers," Michael replied. "You won't be intercepting much of *anyone* if your battleship takes a few dozen Javelins to the nose!"

There was a pause, then Rear Admiral Alstairs came onto the channel.

"He's right, Force Commander," Seventh Fleet's CO told them. "Keep them cut off if you can, but I am *not* prepared to lose ships today, understand me?"

"Yes, ma'am," the Trade Factor captain conceded. "We are evading."

Michael breathed a sigh of relief as *Zheng He* and her companions started moving *away* from the starfighters at two hundred and thirty gravities—and reworked his numbers.

Now they had time. The extra time was enough that he could even coordinate Battle Group Seven-One's fighters in for a combined strike... but he had a better idea for Seven-One's birds.

"Vice Commodore Bachchan," he addressed the commander of *Grizzly*'s flight group—the senior CAG in Battle Group Seven-One. "I want you to take your birds and *catch those carriers*. They're maneuvering to try and evade *Zheng He* and they'll maneuver to evade you, but you've got *twice* their acceleration and they sent everybody out to try and buy themselves time.

"Let's make sure that purchase doesn't clear, get me?"

"Yes, sir," Vice Commodore Gopinatha Bachchan—promoted in the last two months like the rest of *Grizzly*'s senior officers and hence junior to *Avalon*'s CAG despite their sharing a rank—replied. "Our Imperial friends have a few extra missiles to introduce them to."

"Thank you, Vice Commodore," Michael told her, then turned his attention to the CAG from the *other Ursine*-class carrier in Seventh Fleet—the one with six hundred fighters bearing down on it.

"Vice Commodore Ozolinsh," he addressed Gabrielle Ozolinsh, *Polar Bear*'s CAG. "I'm flipping you a course. Double-check my math, but I have you holding position for thirty-five minutes before accelerating to meet the Terrans at max accel."

A moment passed, then Ozolinsh spoke.

"I get the same numbers," she said calmly. "That will give us combined time-on-target salvos if we start the adjusted course at the right moment."

"Ladies, gentlemen," Michael addressed all his flight crews. "This system's name means Freedom. Let's give it back to these people."

#

The Terrans appeared to have guessed his plans, Michael noted. Once all three fighter formations were in space—Seven-Two's birds accelerating hard for an intercept, Seven-One's chasing the carriers, Seven-Three's holding position while their motherships ran—there wasn't any hiding his maneuvers.

Hundreds of antimatter drives firing at five hundred gravities made one *hell* of an energy signature, and the Terrans had probably already seeded the system with Q-probes. If the Commonwealth officers had any clever ideas, he'd be seeing them shortly.

Minutes ticked away. His own fighter wing was still over forty minutes from intercept, and the Terrans were easily an hour away from *Zheng He* and her battle group now.

Seven-One's fighters were a few more minutes behind the *Volcanos* as the two big carriers ran. Admiral Alstairs' warships were behind them, barely maintaining the distance but opening up with long-range missile salvos. Those first salvos would close with the carriers well before his own ships caught up with the Scimitars. *Zheng He*'s battle group was losing ground against the carriers but still cutting off their easiest escape. Aleppo's people were launching as well—and their missiles were going to be the first of Seventh Fleet's weapons to arrive on target.

Their positions had pushed the Commonwealth carriers onto a non-optimal vector, leaving them needing to travel almost seventy light-seconds to clear the gravity wells around them. Seven-One's starfighters would only get one good missile salvo in, but the capital ship missiles would have almost thirty minutes to pound them—not that Battle Group *Camerone* had the *magazines* for that kind of sustained fire.

He watched the icons move around on the tactical plot in his implants. If something came up, he could maneuver the fleet starfighter in moments—but with the enemy still millions of kilometers away, that was unlikely.

The Commonwealth fighter force was still on course. Michael doubted whoever was in command thought that Vice Commodore Ozolinsh's fighters were going to stay in place. There was no chance of the Terrans defeating his people in detail. They did have *more* starfighters than Michael and Ozolinsh did combined, but the Commonwealth had received a number of salutary lessons in what happened when sixth-generation fighters met seventh-generation craft in anything resembling even numbers.

If they wanted to be *stupid*, *Avalon*'s CAG didn't mind—but he wondered what he was missing.

04:10 March 24, 2736 ESMDT
BC-129 Camerone, *Bridge*

Mira watched the ammunition counters for her battlecruiser's ammunition stocks evaporate like water on a hot summer day. Every twenty-two seconds, Battle Group Seven-One's ships sent another thirty-four missiles after the carriers.

They had already launched over twenty salvos, and she glanced at her link to Admiral Alstairs.

"Ma'am," she said quietly over their direct channel. "The Imperials have fired off almost half of their magazines."

Seventh Fleet could replenish those magazines. *Camerone* carried the mass manipulators—the only truly difficult-to-manufacture part—for five times the number of missiles her magazines could hold. Her fabricator shops could turn the appropriate raw materials into as many new missile chassis as she needed, and her zero point cells could charge a functionally infinite number of positron warheads.

All of that took *time*—enough time that the capacity was rarely used to any significant degree. Rebuilding half of their magazines could take a week—a week Operation Rising Star didn't have built into its timetables.

"Cease fire after twenty-five salvos," Alstairs ordered on a wider channel after several moments' thought. "You're right," she noted on her private channel with Mira. "I forgot that the Imperial ships had smaller magazines. Thank you."

"Think the missiles will achieve anything?" Mira asked the Admiral quietly.

"We'll find out in about thirty minutes," she replied. "Keep your people on those Q-probes—final telemetry can make all the difference."

"Yes, ma'am," *Camerone*'s Captain replied, without noting that the Admiral was giving *ship* captain orders, not fleet commander orders. Alstairs knew that already.

Mira was watching the ten salvos that *Zheng He*'s battle group had launched first. Between those and Seven-One's missiles, the Volcanos would be under fire for over fifteen minutes—followed up shortly afterwards by their starfighters' missiles.

The Volcanos were big, modern warships—the best the Commonwealth had. Mira figured they had better than even chances of making it out, but they were going to have to *work* for it.

"There go Ozolinsh's fighters," Keira Rose noted aloud. "Twelve minutes to missile launch range for both fighter groups."

"What are the orbital platforms doing?" Mira asked. In all of the confusion, she'd almost forgotten about the two hundred platforms—*six hundred* missile launchers—in orbit.

"Nothing..." Rose said slowly. "They launched fighters and then... nothing."

"That makes no sense," Mira replied. "Admiral, are you seeing anything on the orbital platforms?"

"No," Alstairs replied instantly. "They're silent. What are the Q-probes showing?"

"Pulling it up now," Rose told them. "*Starless Void*."

"What?" Mira demanded.

"The fighter platforms are venting," the tactical officer reported. "I'm seeing...I'd say at least ten to twelve different breaches on each Zion—looks like multiple internal explosions."

"Sabotage," *Camerone*'s captain realized. "No wonder those carriers are running. Bombs must have started going off as soon as we showed on the system sensor net. They are having a *bad* day."

"My heart bleeds," Rose told her. "First of Seven-Three's missiles should be hitting their defenses...now."

"Show me," Mira ordered.

There were enough Q-probes scattered around the system now to give them nearly real-time data on their salvos as they charged in. As the missiles closed in on the two carriers, it was quickly apparent why they hadn't been launching missiles back at the Alliance ships.

A Volcano's twelve missile launchers wouldn't do much against the defenses of a four-ship Battle Group.

Twenty-four missiles detonating in the middle of even a fifty-six missile salvo, however, made one *hell* of a dent. Half of the salvo vanished in those balls of fire—and then a *second* set of twenty-four missiles slammed into the remainder.

Only two missiles made it through the missile screen the carriers had thrown up, and they didn't stand a chance against the prepared defenses of two modern carriers.

The second salvo died similarly, none of them making it through the missile screen.

When the *third* salvo of fifty-six missiles died in its entirety to the same trick, Mira wondered what was going on and checked the telemetry. Force Commander Aleppo was *specifically* maneuvering her missiles to hit the screen the Terrans had set up. The fourth salvo followed suit, and Mira saw the Trade Factor officer's plan.

The *fifth* salvo dove straight into the middle of the massive hole the suicidal sacrifice of their compatriots had opened. Shielded by the radiation of the earlier explosions and their own jammers, they sliced through the missile screen without losing a single weapon.

The Volcanos' defenses opened fire, sweeping space with lasers and positron beams. They stopped every missile—barely. The closest was less than a kilometer from the nearest carrier before it died, and the *Volcano* looked the worse for wear after the impact.

Their missiles screen swept back in and wiped the sixth and seventh salvos. The eighth died well clear of the carriers, but the ninth crept a bit closer, creating a radiation wave that covered the arrival of the last salvo from *Zheng He*'s battle group.

Over five *hundred* missiles had detonated around the Commonwealth ships now, and the radiation storm filling the space behind them was immense. High-powered radar swept through that storm, picking out missiles and allowing lasers and positron beams to wipe them from space.

For a moment, Mira thought it would be enough for them. Almost six hundred missiles thrown, in exchange for one near miss.

Then four missiles detonated simultaneously—not destroyed by the defenses but self-destructed by Lora Aleppo herself. Eight missiles shot through the new radiation cloud, shielded almost all the way to the enemy.

Five still died too far away to do damage. The defensive systems of a twenty-million-ton carrier were smart, responsive, and powerful. Even almost blinded, they killed five of those last eight missiles.

Two detonated at almost point-blank range, stripping sensors and defensive lasers from the hulls of both carriers.

The last hit the closer carrier a third of the way along its length and detonated, a one-gigaton flash of white light that *visibly* moved a sixty-million-cubic-meter ship already traveling at two percent of the speed of light.

When the light faded, the Volcano was incredibly still there. A massive gaping wound had opened in the big ship's side, but she was still accelerating—still running.

"Rose?" Mira said quietly.

"Fifty seconds, ma'am," her tactical officer replied, her voice equally quiet. "Then it's my turn."

"We've opened the way for you," Aleppo told Mira over the channel. "Give 'em hell."

"With pleasure, ma'am," *Camerone*'s Captain replied, then passed on the sentiment to Rose.

The tactical officer smiled coldly.

"Don't worry, ma'am—I intend to put Vice Commodore Bachchan out of a target."

Then both women's attention was focused on the missiles. While the bandwidth to and from the Q-probes wasn't sufficient for Rose to send the missiles fully updated telemetry, it *was* enough for her to feed them new orders—orders the Jackhammers' AIs tried doggedly to carry out.

Rose expended Battle Group *Camerone*'s first three salvos exactly the same way Aleppo had, intentionally blasting the missile screen out of the way. Her fourth salvo charged into the teeth of the Volcanos' defenses, spread wide, then detonated on their own as the carriers' defenses lashed out.

The fifth dove through that cloud, crossing almost a third of the Volcanos' defensive range in the cover of their sisters' deaths, and charged straight at the carriers. Once again, the empty space around the two Commonwealth heavy carriers lit up with fire.

The one hit *Zheng He* had landed had clearly hurt its victim. The defensive fire was far weaker and sparser than it had been—but Rose had only thirty-four missiles a salvo, not fifty-six.

Her fifth salvo died far closer to the carriers than the Terrans could have liked. Blast waves and radiation swept over the carriers, more defenses and targeting scanners failing—and Battle Group Seven-One's *sixth* salvo was right on its heels.

Three missiles made it through everything the Commonwealth ships threw at them, and the damaged carrier vanished in a tripled ball of flame. Cheers echoed around *Camerone*'s bridge and Mira bared her teeth in excitement, watching as Rose neatly guided their *seventh* salvo in.

The excitement faded into an awed respect as the big Volcano pirouetted, dodged, drew their missiles in, and lashed out with every weapon at their disposal—and *stopped* thirty-four missiles. And then, to Mira's shock, did it *again*.

"Clever boy," she heard Rose murmur. "But you're not clever *enough*."

Missiles came apart in balls of fire as Fleet Commander Keira Rose fed new orders to the nanocircuitry brains of her tenth missile salvo. Some were killed by the enemy; some were self-destructed, slamming hammers of fire tracing a swirling path through space all the way to the Terran carrier.

Captain Mira Solace had access to Rose's consoles, the reporting communications from the missiles, and the Q-probes Rose was transmitting her orders through—and Mira had *no* idea how many missiles the tactical officer delivered to the target at last.

It was enough. The swirling path of fire intersected the big carrier—and the Volcano came apart in shocking white fire.

"Target destroyed," Rose announced.

04:25 March 24, 2736 ESMDT
SFG-001 Actual—Falcon-C type command starfighter

The destruction of the two Terran carriers barely registered on Michael's mental radar. He was focused on the fighter formation his two-pronged strike was converging on. Range counters were dropping fast, and a second number representing the range of his formation's Starfires, given the current relative velocity, was rising.

Those two numbers were about a minute from intersecting. He had the same pair of numbers for Ozolinsh's starfighters as well—*Polar Bear*'s CAG had nailed her acceleration window perfectly. All five hundred plus fighters in the two formations would reach missile range effectively simultaneously.

The Terrans had continued on their pursuit course of Battle Group Seven-Three, straight into the teeth of Ozolinsh's Falcons and without even trying to evade Michael's Falcons and Templars. Their commander had to have *something* in mind, but *Avalon*'s CAG wasn't seeing it—there was no way the Scimitars would win against almost-even numbers of seventh-generation fighters.

The greater acceleration of the Alliance fighters gave the Terrans the edge in range by a few seconds—and in the moment that they fired, Michael finally saw what the battle-hardened Terran commander had seen from the beginning.

Six hundred Scimitars put twenty-four hundred Javelin fighter missiles into space—and *every single one of them* was targeted on Ozolinsh's formation. The hundred and seventy-six starfighters from *Polar Bear* and *Culloden* couldn't survive a salvo of that magnitude.

They could have survived the half-salvo or the proportionate-to-their-numbers salvo that Michael had been expecting. But he barely had time to register his mistake before his own ships had to launch.

Over twelve hundred missiles launched from his own formation and seven hundred from Ozolinsh's, a total over nineteen hundred weapons targeted on six hundred targets. He wasn't going to get a clean sweep with that number, but he was going to gut their formation, leave them vulnerable for the follow-up salvos.

"Stanford," Ozolinsh cut into his channel, her voice harsh. "I'm launching my follow-up salvos, then I am ordering my people to ditch their ships. Sixty seconds should get us clear of the blast zone, but we *cannot* stop that salvo—maybe if your missiles could intercept, but they can't.

"We're handing off telemetry control to your gunners," she continued. "Get me a list of people. I'm sorry, sir."

"It's the right call, Gabrielle. Do it," Michael ordered.

As they were speaking, the Terrans launched a second salvo—still at Ozolinsh's people. They weren't leaving any chance of those starfighters surviving. Her plan *should* save most of her people, but Michael still felt his guts twist as he looked at the tsunami that was going to wipe a fifth of Seventh Fleet's starfighter strength from the universe.

It took him fractions of a second to pull a list of the three hundred plus gunners in Seven-Two's fighters, sort it by their official skill ratings in their last formal test, and then send Ozolinsh the top hundred and seventy-six names.

In the same instant, his starfighters fired again, another nineteen hundred missiles blasting into space, heading for the *Scimitars*.

Forty-five seconds after that, the third Terran salvo launched into space—and this time, the Terrans were targeting Michael's people. He had almost twice as many starfighters as Ozolinsh—what was a *smart* action on her part could easily be called cowardice on his.

"All squadrons," he said aloud, his voice surprisingly calm. "Use your final missile salvo for missile defense. We're going to make it through this."

Even as he spoke, he watched the telemetry from Battle Group Seven-Three's fighters—as the emergency pods blasted free of their spacecraft, engines blasting them away from their motherships at four hundred gravities. They'd be clear of the blast zones, barely.

The first salvos arrived before a fourth salvo could be launched. Michael's gaze was fixed on Ozolinsh's starfighters. Without a human aboard, the computers could only do so much—Federation AI was *smart*, but it wasn't *intuitive*. It couldn't be *random*.

It couldn't make guesses. That was *why* there were humans aboard a starfighter.

And why without humans aboard, *Polar Bear* and *Culloden*'s fighters were doomed.

They did better than he expected. Eighty to ninety percent of missile defense was effectively done by the computers regardless. The networked AIs coolly assessed the incoming salvo, allocated lasers and positron lances, and maneuvered the fighters with mechanical precision for the shots they needed to take.

The computers took out over a thousand missiles—and almost fourteen hundred made it through. Some starfighters were hit by single missiles, others by as many as fifteen. It didn't matter—in one Void-cursed sequence of explosions, all one hundred and seventy-six starfighters ceased to exist.

The Scimitars had more fighters, with gunners backing the computers and engineers running the ECM. They *also*, however, had over three hundred modern fighters slamming their ECM into the teeth of their scanners and defenses, the Falcons' and Templars' mind-bogglingly powerful transmitters making hash of scanners now less than a hundred thousand kilometers distant.

Michael's starfighters followed their missiles in, the time lapse between salvo launches eaten by the rapidly shrinking distance. Lances targeted Terran missiles and Terran starfighters indiscriminately in a point-blank cataclysm of fire the Templars' and Falcons' heavier lances ripped open from twice the Scimitars' range.

The Vice Commodore's focus was on—could *only* be on, at this point—his own starfighter's maneuvers as he danced the Falcon through the deadly maelstrom he and his enemies had conjured.

Three seconds after the first salvos struck home, Michael's starfighters interpenetrated with the handful of surviving Terran ships, both sides slicing beams of positrons through space with wild abandon.

Nine seconds after that, the Alliance fighters were out of range of the expanding debris cloud that *had* been six hundred *Scimitar*-class fighters.

Forty-three Falcons and twenty-four Templars didn't make it that far.

Michael swallowed, trying to process the sheer chaos of the last minute, then swallowed again as he swept the tactical plot for emergency beacons.

"Everyone slow to zero relative velocity," he ordered slowly. "SFG Zero Zero One Actual to *Avalon*—we need search-and-rescue out here *now*. For ours and theirs," he noted finally.

There weren't many of the latter. Automatic safeties kicked in where they could, but the power of spaceborne weaponry meant there was very little time to do so unless, like Ozolinsh's people, the crews bailed early.

Say what you like about the Commonwealth—and Michael often did—their soldiers had courage.

CHAPTER 22

Frihet System
05:10 March 24, 2736 Earth Standard Meridian Date/Time
AT-032 Chimera *Landing Group, Assault Shuttle Four*

The approach from *Chimera* to the Zion platforms was nerve-wracking. Intimidating, massive, and tough as modern personal battle armor was, it would do *nothing* for the Marines if the assault shuttle took a positron-lance hit from the fighter launch bases. .

But those bases, damaged as they were, absolutely *had* to be secured before the starships could enter orbit. If someone was alive and sitting on the control systems for even a handful of the missile satellites, firing them off at point-blank range would be a quick way to destroy a couple hundred trillion stellars of starships.

"We're heading in for a nice, gentle contact," Edvard's pilot informed him. "ETA sixty seconds. Be aware, we have no atmosphere at the contact point, so keep your suits sealed."

Edvard passed that on to his people with a quick text update. The armor *should* take care of that on its own—the AIs in the armor suits weren't geniuses, but they were effective in their limited areas—but it was better to be safe.

"Do we have any update from Seventh Fleet on what they're seeing in the station, sir?" he asked Major Brahm. Last he'd heard, the Navy had been maneuvering Q-probes in to close range to give them live data on what, if anything, had survived the apparent sabotage.

"We do," the Battalion XO confirmed. "There are pockets of what appear to be power and atmosphere, but most of the station is a dead hulk. I'm dropping you your objective markers—you're landing closest to the main command center, which looks like it still has power and atmosphere. One of the blast sites is on your way; we want you to check it out before you hit the command center. We don't know enough about what happened here."

"Understood, sir," Edvard replied. "We'll play tourist on our way over."

Brahm made a repressive clucking sound but didn't directly respond.

"Be careful," he said after a moment. "Just because the place looks dead doesn't mean there aren't Marines playing dead—hell, in that kind of environment, a Navy puke with the right control panel could wipe half your company."

"Wilco, Major," Bravo Company's commander told him. "Making contact now; will report when we reach the blast site."

Brahm signed off with a click, almost lost in the vibration and thump of the assault shuttle contacting the station.

A flash and a bang announced the application of the shuttle's breaching system—followed by the access hatch springing open to reveal the gaping hole into the ship.

"Go! Go! Go!" Edvard snapped over the channel, waiting for his Alpha Platoon to enter the station before following them in. Procedure dictated he couldn't go first, but he'd let the Starless Void eat him before his headquarters section went *last*.

He drifted across the gap easily, then triggered the electromagnets in his boots—without power feeding to the exotic-matter coils of the station's mass manipulators, there was insufficient gravity to walk in, and what gravity there *was* wasn't aligned with silly things like floors.

"Waypoints on your implants, people," he told his Alpha Platoon troopers. "Move out!"

Battle-armored troopers obeyed with a will—the lack of gravity and manipulation of armor thrusters allowing them to progress through the station in massive leaps, their weapons tracking corners and crannies as they moved.

Two hundred meters and two levels passed surprisingly quickly, and Lieutenant Major Edvard Hansen arrived at the shattered piece of the station where *some* kind of explosive had gone off, to find his people already establishing a perimeter—and stringing a line to enable the company to cross the gaping void the blast had left.

"What have we got?" he asked Alpha Platoon's heavy weapons sergeant.

The demolitions expert shook his head, eyeing the roughly spherical section they were standing on the edge of.

"Radiation count is high but fading fast," he noted. "Schematics say that one of the main network hubs was there." The sergeant waved an armored hand in the direction of the upper section of the void. "Sending all of the data back to *Chimera* for analysis to get a hard answer, but if you want my gut feeling..."

"I asked for a reason, Sergeant," Edvard pointed out.

"You're looking at a laser-initiated micro-fusion device," the sergeant said flatly. "No radioactive materials, no exotic matter coils. Small, easy to conceal, difficult as all hell to *manufacture*, low yield—but still a nuke. These stations have a lot of internal reinforcing." He gestured at the hundred-and-fifty-meter void they stood next to. "*That* was a ten-kiloton charge at least. Could be as high as twenty-five, given that they vaporized an armored network hub."

Edvard whistled in his helmet, making sure no one could hear him, then reopened the channel.

"That's *damned* impressive. Where would they have *got* those?"

"Fyr Special Ops," the noncom replied instantly. "Scary, scary, *scary* fuckers. With nukes."

"It seems they opened the doors for us," Edvard agreed. "I'm not complaining. But...yeah. Scary."

#

"*Chimera*'s first-cut analysis confirms Sergeant Sato's assessment," Brahm told Edvard. "That one was an MFC. It looks like the saboteurs—personally, I agree that it's likely they were Fyr Spec Ops—didn't have very *many* of those. A few key points on each platform got micro-fusion charges; most of the rest were 'just' high-yield chemical explosives.

"We're finding a lot of bodies," the Major continued. "You're on track to get to the command center before anyone else reaches survivors on this station. See if they're willing to play nice—at this point, I'd honestly rather not have to shoot anybody. They've had a bad-enough day."

"Roger, Major," Edvard replied. "Knock first. I'll be in touch."

This close to the command center, the station was in an incredible amount of disarray. They hadn't crossed any more nuke sites, but a lot of smaller charges had been used to cripple internal systems and cut the command center off from the rest of the platform. The floor was impassable as often as not, though thankfully usually either a wall or a roof was available for Bravo Company to traverse.

It took longer to cross the hundred meters from the nuke site to the main command center than it had taken to reach the blast site itself. Eventually, Edvard's people reached their objective, and he carefully made his way forward to join his Alpha Platoon Lieutenant at the door.

"It's an emergency airlock," the Lieutenant told him. "We can blast through, but they'll lose atmo *instantly*. Close-range scanners figure between forty and fifty people—probably the command center night shift."

"We've got supplies for just that," Edvard noted. They'd carried the pieces of an emergency replacement airlock and emergency survival bubbles from the shuttle. "That said, let's see if they'll talk. Can we splice me into the local intercom?"

"Give me a minute," one of his headquarters section replied, the trooper producing a complex-looking electronic toolkit from a panel on her suit. She wired it into the shattered exterior panel and worked on it in silence for a little over two minutes—and then a new icon popped up in Edvard's implant.

"You're linked in, sir," she told him. "Can't guarantee they'll listen."

"That's my job, Lance-Corporal," he replied. "Well done."

Inside his helmet, Edvard sharply shook his head to kick his brain into gear, then thought-clicked the icon.

"Hello? Is anyone in there?"

There was no response for several seconds, then a voice came back—an older male with a distinctly crisp Terran accent.

"This is Captain Xolani Bhuku," he answered Edvard. "Commanding Officer Zion K Three Oh Four. Are you the rescue party?"

"Not exactly," Edvard replied. "This is Lieutenant Major Edvard Hansen of the Castle Federation Marine Corps. I'm afraid I'm going to have to ask for your surrender."

Bhuku laughed, a deep infectious chuckle that almost made Edvard smile back despite the circumstances.

"Son, you may be officially a boarding party, but as far as anyone left alive on this dead hulk is concerned, you're the rescue party," he told Edvard. "I will gladly surrender whatever remains in my authority in exchange for making certain my people are extracted alive."

"It's always nice to talk to someone reasonable," Edvard replied. "I accept your surrender, Captain Bhuku. I've got enough survival bubbles out here for about a hundred people. Shall we see about getting you off this station?"

"Lieutenant Major, right now I am looking *forward* to your POW camp. Let's see what we can do."

08:30 March 24, 2736 ESMDT
DSC-078 Avalon, *Captain's Breakout Room*

"We are now fully in control of Fyr orbit," Rear Admiral Alstairs announced to her captains and CAGs.

Nobody quite cheered—but Kyle could pick up the general feeling of relief even through the holograms he was seeing of the rest of Seventh Fleet's captains.

"Brigadier Hammond's people have done a superb job of securing the stations. Brigadier, if you can fill the Captains in on what you found?" Alstairs asked.

Hammond took half a second to glance around the captains, the stocky bald man apparently reminding himself of who the captains were before speaking. As the senior of the three Marine Brigadiers, he was equal or senior to everyone on the conference except Alstairs herself and the two breveted Force Commanders.

"All four Zions were very neatly, professionally, and *completely* disabled," he said crisply. "We have confirmed the use of two laser-initiated micro-fusion bombs on each platform, plus several dozen more conventional explosives. All appear to have been smuggled aboard the stations and detonated upon confirmation of the arrival of Alliance forces."

"Do we know who?" Kyle asked.

"We suspect Fyr Army Special Operations," Hammond said calmly. "I am preparing my men to deploy to the surface and have reached out on certain frequencies the Fyrans provided us prior to the invasion. My understanding is that we have received several data packets in return—targeting locations for drops and kinetic bombardments."

"I have summoned the planetary forces to surrender," Alstairs noted. "They have half an hour to comply. If they haven't by then, the Brigadiers have a go for their landings."

"What is the status of our fighter wings?" Force Commander Aleppo asked quietly. "I know my own are...gone. But..."

"Our casualties were lighter than we had any right to expect," Stanford replied. "Ozolinsh's people were clear before the missiles impacted, and the Terrans self-destructed the second salvo to avoid risking damage to the ejected pods."

"She still lost fifteen people," *Avalon*'s CAG—Seventh Fleet's senior starfighter officer—said quietly. "My own losses were heavier. With the violence of the engagement, we had a low ejection percentage. Out of sixty-seven lost ships, only nine pods were launched. With injuries and radiation damage aboard the pods, we lost a hundred and eighty people."

"Vice Commodore Ozolinsh's actions were unacceptable," Lord Captain Anders snapped. "To abandon her starfighters in the face of the enemy like is pure cowardice!"

Kyle kicked Stanford under the table before his CAG could reply, leaning forward himself to speak more calmly than he suspected Stanford could.

"What would you have had her do, Lord Captain?" he asked bluntly. "My personal assessment is that the presence of human pilots and gunners would have enabled her to destroy perhaps another five hundred missiles—still leaving three or more weapons for every single ship she had. Once their missiles were away, there was no point in sacrificing her flight crews against a salvo they could not stop.

"*Polar Bear* and *Culloden*'s starfighters were doomed as soon as the Terrans decided to concentrate their fire on only one fighter formation," he continued. "That Vice Commodore Ozolinsh held her people on long enough to launch not just one salvo but *all* of their missiles in the teeth of their annihilation speaks to a rare level of courage."

He carefully did *not* look at Stanford—or Ozolinsh—as he continued.

"That said, I agree that the Vice Commodore's actions need to be assessed," he said very calmly. "Admiral, I do not believe we have a choice but to field a Board of Inquiry."

"In theory and per the letter of the Federation Articles of Military Justice, you are correct, Force Commander," Alstairs told him. *She* did look directly at Gabrielle Ozolinsh, a sallow-faced black-haired woman who looked even more exhausted that the rest of Seventh Fleet's senior officers. "However...faced with the constraints of Operation Rising Star, the strict letter of the law will not serve us today.

"Vice Commodore Ozolinsh, how long will it take you to get your fighter wings back to combat-readiness?" she asked sharply.

"We can pull replacement fighters from the logistics ships, though that will reduce the value of the fighter platforms we were reserving to protect Via Somnia," Ozolinsh said slowly. "To get the starfighters set up, re-linked to my pilots, and run both the ships and my people through at least basic exercises to make sure we are combat-ready... three days. We'll still be short four ships for lost crew. I *could* replace those crews, but it would take even longer."

"Vice Commodore Stanford, your wings' status?" Alstairs asked crisply.

"We have sufficient spare starfighters aboard the freighters to provide new ships for our surviving flight crews," Stanford said slowly, slightly calmer now. "But neither I nor my Royal compatriots"—he nodded to the two Phoenix CAGs— "are in a position to replace our lost crews. Accounting for that, we will be combat-functional within thirty-six hours."

The Admiral turned back to Ozolinsh.

"Vice Commodore, I don't think we have *time* for the Board that, yes, should be convened on your actions," she said bluntly. "The Ops plan for Rising Star calls for us to move on Huī Xing and Via Somnia in four days. Are you prepared to continue doing your duty, being aware that a Board may still need to be convened once Rising Star is complete?"

Implicit in that, of course, was that her actions in the *rest* of Rising Star would heavily slant the results of that board. It wasn't quite a complete approval of her actions—but it was a safe way out for everyone involved, inside the spirit if not the exact letter of the Articles.

"I am, Admiral Alstairs," Ozolinsh confirmed slowly.

"Is that sufficient for you, Force Commander Roberts?"

"Yes, ma'am," Kyle agreed instantly. By putting forward the demand for a Board himself, he'd given the *Federation* control over whether Ozolinsh would be punished—and rendered Lord Captain Anders' opinion of the decision mostly irrelevant.

Surprisingly, though, the Imperial Captain nodded his own acceptance of the decision and leaned back in his chair.

"It appears Fyr Special Operations has helped open the door to their homeworld," Admiral Alstairs told them all. "Brigadier? Are the Marines ready to act on the intelligence they're providing?"

"Yes, ma'am," he said calmly. "*Chimera* and *Manticore* currently have drones sweeping the target locations they provided to confirm their data, and *Pegasus* is preparing the bombardment. We have received no response from the Terran surface commander. We are ready to go as soon as the deadline expires."

"Good luck, Brigadier," she said quietly.

"Watch your fucking flight zones!"

Edvard Hansen winced as the bellow came over the shuttle channel. As a company commander, he was an eavesdropper on the channel for the landing group. He wasn't sure who had shouted—he suspected it might even have been *his* pilot—but he definitely sympathized.

In that moment, a pillar of white light lit up the sky barely a hundred and fifty meters from his shuttle, as another of *Pegasus*'s "rods from God" blasted past. That was *six* by the Lieutenant Major's count—six *within visual range* of his shuttle.

"Please tell me this is worth it," he snapped at the pilot.

"Unless you *want* a close personal introduction to a terawatt-range air defense laser, it's *definitely* worth it," the pilot replied. "Now, *sir*, shut *up* and let me *fly*."

As a *seventh* kinetic projectile blasted past—this one *much* closer! —Edvard obeyed the junior officer.

The problem that the 103rd and the other two brigades were facing was simple: the Terran Commonwealth Marine Corps had dug in *hard* around Landning City. Dozens of mobile and immobile space defense units, prefabricated fortifications, the works.

Edvard's impression was that they'd been holding the capital city hostage as a lever to try to keep a planet of notoriously stubborn Viking descendants from exploding on them. It also, apparently, had given the TCMC General in charge of the planet a feeling of invulnerability—if the Alliance took the time to bombard the space defense units, he could relocate his HQ and ground positions, giving them a giant headache when the Marines landed.

Unless, of course, the Castle Federation Marine Corps decided to land *while* bombarding the space defense units. It was perfectly safe—assuming the shuttles didn't diverge from their planned courses and none of the gunners firing one-tenth-kiloton kinetic weapons *slipped*.

"We're dropping you in forty-five seconds," the pilot announced. "Did one of you people *volunteer* to go into the heaviest fire on the planet?"

Edvard smiled without responding, sending nonverbal orders for his people to check their systems.

As it happened, he *had* volunteered to be one of the companies hitting the main command center—but he wasn't going to admit that to the pilot.

#

The shuttle never even touched the ground. It came blasting over the reinforced concrete walls of the fortress above the Terrans' command center at three times the speed of sound, dropping a swarm of smart munitions and spraying seventy-millimeter cannon fire across the open interior.

The interior *had* been a vehicle park, with a dozen or so formal-looking vehicles on one end and six medium tanks on the other. One of the dozens of tenth-kiloton weapons dropped by *Pegasus* had been aimed at the tanks, however, and the interior was mostly *crater* at this point.

"Drop!" Edvard ordered as they hit the *seconds*-long window, and his people obeyed — the speakers on their suits amplifying and projecting their wolf howls as they plummeted from the passing shuttle and slammed into the broken mud and concrete.

The sensors in his battle armor were already sweeping for targets—not least because he knew how *Castle* Marines would have handled the situation. Terran Marines, it turned out, ran on a very similar playbook.

Bravo Company had barely hit the ground when the shuttle passed over the other side of the compound's wall—and chameleon-coated battle armor suits boiled out of the exits of the underground facility.

Edvard had been expecting it. His heavy-weapons troopers opened fire even before the doors finished opening, bolts of superheated plasma blowing entrances wide open before the Terran Marines could exit them. Miniguns, barely portable even in suits of battle armor, began to chatter, spraying the emerging Terrans with dozens of penetrators.

Then the rest of his people joined in. There were eight separate entrances to the facility, and the Spec Ops data package the Alliance had received had told them where all eight were. Each of his two hundred troopers had an entrance tagged as their zone of responsibility—and their fire added to the plasma rifles and miniguns.

It wasn't entirely one-sided. Like the Castle Marines, the Terrans knew the playbook. They *hadn't* known the invaders would know exactly where they would emerge from. Edvard watched his people get thrown back, though even tungsten penetrators weren't a guaranteed kill against full powered battle armor, and charged forward where the Terrans were breaking out.

He fired on the run, his rifle spitting penetrators even as he activated the auto-tracking micro-missile launchers built into the armored suits' shoulders. Micro-missiles couldn't do *much*—dozens of them were detonating across the battlefield every second, mostly unable to penetrate battle armor—but they helped pause the assault.

He reached the gap, stepping into a hole where several of Bravo Platoon's troopers had gone down, and joined the firing. The Terrans seemed to *keep* coming. The only intelligence Edvard *didn't* have was how many troops were in the fortress under his feet—and he was starting to think he'd poked a hornet's nest.

Then he ran out of ammo. Given the weight that an armor suit could carry and the low volume of the tungsten penetrators his battle rifle used, the weapon took stupendously sized magazines—but *could* run out.

The reload process was simple. He mentally ordered the weapon to eject the empty magazine, ordered his suit to open the panel containing a replacement, and slammed it in. It took barely a second—a second after which he realized he was now staring down the barrel of a Terran Marine's almost-identical weapon.

Before the Marine could pull the trigger, his entire torso *exploded* and Edvard's suit started flashing up a threat warning. *Someone*, not in the fortress but with a clear line of sight, had a mass-manipulated gauss sniper rifle—and the Alliance hadn't *dropped* any of the sniper weapons with their Marines.

Fyr Special Ops had apparently decided not to leave their world's liberation *entirely* to the Castle Marines.

More of the characteristic supersonic explosions rippled across the compound, easily a platoon's worth of snipers on a nearby hilltop backing up his Marines as they faced what had to be an entire *brigade* trying to break out.

It lasted perhaps two minutes—until all eight entrances were filled with shattered armor and broken bodies.

Then he started picking up an omnidirectional, unencrypted radio transmission.

"This is Lieutenant General Michail Popov to all Terran Commonwealth Marine forces and Castle Marine forces," the transmission said calmly. "Commonwealth forces—lay down your arms. Alliance forces—we surrender."

CHAPTER 23

Frihet System
08:00 March 25, 2736 Earth Standard Meridian Date/Time
DSC-078 Avalon, *Captain's Office*

They'd been in the Frihet system for twenty-nine hours, and Kyle had managed to sneak a three-hour catnap at roughly the twenty-four-hour mark. He'd been tied up in some of the coordination with the apparently still-*very*-intact Frihet government, but he'd intentionally not included his CAG in the conference to let the man rest as he flew back to *Avalon*.

From the bags under Michael Stanford's eyes and his general shattered expression, that had been wasted effort. There was no way *Avalon*'s CAG had slept since the strike had launched yesterday morning. He slumped in the chair across the desk in Kyle's office like a student called in front of the principal.

"I fucked up, sir," Stanford said harshly. "Dammit, I should have seen that *coming*—it *made sense*."

"Arguable, yes, and yes," Kyle replied. "Yes, you should have seen it coming—but what would you have done differently?"

That, thankfully, looked like it scored a hit.

"If you were wondering," the Force Commander—who had, a long time before, been *Stanford's* CAG—continued, "I *did* see it coming. And the reason I didn't tell you is because I thought you had as well—because I wouldn't have been doing anything different. It was a risk you had to take or *Zheng He* and her sisters were going to end up on the receiving end of that same firepower."

"There had to have been *something* I could have done to save Ozolinsh's ships," Stanford replied. "Hell, I lost almost two *hundred* of my own people."

"In hindsight," Kyle said quietly, "knowing that the orbital platforms were out of the fight as soon as they launched their starfighters, you could have adjusted your vectors to bring your fighter wing into range at the same time as Battle Group Seven-Three. Adding the starship's defensive fire to that of Vice Commodore Ozolinsh's ships *might* have protected them long enough to drag the Terrans into a lance-range dogfight.

"Might.

"*But* that would also have allowed those starfighters to fire *on* Battle Group Seven-Three—and honestly, those salvos would probably have cost us starships as well as starfighters had we taken that risk. Pulling Seven-Three out of the fight wasn't your call," Kyle noted. "It was your *recommendation*—but it was Admiral Alstairs' call. She made it."

"The starfighter deployments were my call, though," Stanford said hoarsely. "Sending Seven-One's fighters after the carriers was redundant..."

"But still the right call," Kyle replied. "You couldn't *count* on capital ship missile fire taking out the carriers—it's not something that we see often at that kind of range. Not to mention, they couldn't have intervened against the fighter strike.

"Damn it, Michael," he told his subordinate, "the *physics* only gave you one option. You played it—and you backed Ozolinsh when she saw a way to save her *people* if not her *ships*."

"I still lost so many people."

"I know," Kyle admitted. "And it *sucks*, Michael—we both knew those people. Losing them hurts. That your squadron and wing leaders survived helps keep the Group together as a fighting unit, but losing sixty-seven fighters and a hundred and eighty people is never easy. We tell our people that starfighters exist to die so starships don't, and it's true—but the cold calculus of war is no comfort to lost friends and those Gods-damned letters home."

"I've never...lost this many people before," Stanford pointed out.

"There are no charmed ships and no charmed fighter groups," his captain replied quietly. "Sooner or later, we all run out of luck."

The CAG shook his head as if trying to clear cobwebs.

"It felt bad enough after Tranquility, but that wasn't nearly as many," he said quietly. The fighter group they'd taken into the Battle of Tranquility had had fewer starfighters at the start than SFG-001 had lost in this battle. "What happens now?"

"First, Vice Commodore, you need to remember that you do *not* need to write those letters yourself," Kyle pointed out. "The Phoenix flight crews' families will be informed by their officers. Your own people's families should be informed by their Wing Commanders. You should be *involved*, but you are sure as hell not writing one hundred and eighty letters yourself. Understand me?"

"Fair," Stanford allowed. "Doesn't make me any less responsible for their deaths."

"No, it doesn't," *Avalon*'s captain said gently. "But second-guessing yourself won't change what happened either. Go get some *sleep*, Michael. You need it."

"What about you?" the CAG asked, glancing around the office. Kyle was suddenly very aware of the uniform jacket haphazardly tossed over a bookcase, the pile of dirty coffee cups on one corner of his desk, and the *very* visible packet of stimulant pills on his desk.

"Anderson is asleep right now," Kyle pointed out. "He'll be awake in about two hours, then I'm going to go pass out for as long as I can. I have a meeting planetside this evening—I get the impression I don't want to deal with Frihet's people while half-asleep."

18:00 March 25, 2736 ESMDT
Landning City

The shuttle landing pad on the outskirts of Fyr's capital city was crowded. Kyle watched through his implants as his pilot neatly slotted *Avalon*'s Shuttle One in next to the pair of shuttles carrying Rear Admiral Alstairs, Captain Solace, and the Admiral's staff.

Most of the shuttles were local, suborbital craft delivering personnel from around the planet. The fourth Alliance shuttle was from *Zheng He*, carrying Force Commander Aleppo.

Kyle wasn't sure when his and Aleppo's temporary ranks would be canceled, but they were still the titles they'd been invited to the surface under. Alstairs might have brought enough people to justify the second shuttle, but his only companion was Lieutenant Commander Jessica Xue. His XO was in command and his CAG was—thankfully—asleep, so the tactical officer drew the straw of playing Kyle's "staff" for this affair.

Stepping out of the shuttle onto the surprisingly cool surface of the pad—there had to be some *impressive* heat exchangers and cooling systems under its surface—*Avalon's* commander watched a local ground-car zoom across the landing pad and come to a perfect stop several feet from him.

A dark-haired young woman in a crisply pressed Frihet Defense Force uniform sprang out of the passenger side, quickly opening the rear door for Kyle and his tactical officer.

"Welcome to Fyr and Landning City, Force Commander Roberts, Lieutenant Commander Xue," she said brightly. "I'm Lieutenant Yvonne Svenson, Frihet Defense Force. I've been assigned as your attaché for the duration of your stay on Fyr."

"Thank you, Lieutenant," Kyle replied, gesturing Xue into the vehicle as he looked around the pad. "Your people seem... Well, you seem to be back on your feet surprisingly quickly."

Svenson looked askance for a moment and then shrugged.

"Appearances are everything," she said quietly. "Most of the government and military managed to go underground before the orbital platforms fell. Now we're coming back *out* of hiding, hence"— she gestured at the suborbital shuttles—"we'll put our best foot forward with the Alliance," she said brightly. "Shall we?"

#

The car didn't, to Kyle's mild surprise, take them to the big Government Plaza near the center of the city. Instead, Svenson took them to a nondescript office tower, only about sixty stories tall, in Landning City's main commercial district. Taller towers surrounded the building and nothing about the skyscraper itself stood out.

The street in front of it, however, had been blockaded. A quartet of light tanks sat ominously just outside the main entrance to the tower, their cannon backing up a cordon of Frihet Defense Force troopers manning security checkpoints.

The actual entrance itself was guarded by a squad of Federation Marines and a matching team of what Kyle suspected were Fyr Special Ops troopers—lithe men and women in light powered armor, carrying immense gauss rifles.

"This is one of our emergency continuity centers," Svenson told them. "We can't take the car any closer—come with me, please."

Getting out the car, the big Force Commander took in the defenses with a slightly more cautious eye. Any kind of orbital strike would take out the tower and its defenders with ease, but a ground force would have to get past the Fyr Army infantry, then the tanks, then the Marines and Special Ops troops. Kyle wasn't a Marine, but he suspected that hypothetical attackers would have a very bad day.

Svenson led them through the defenses at a careful, occasionally hesitant pace. It was clear she was familiar with the plan for how the defenders were going to set up but hadn't actually *been* through these defenses.

Like the car and Svenson herself, everything there had clearly been prepared to leap into action as soon as the planet was liberated. Frihet had been *taken*, but it had clearly not been *defeated*. They might not have been able to free themselves with Commonwealth warships in orbit, but given their destruction of the fighter platforms, Kyle suspected the Terrans would have had a nasty surprise if they'd pulled their ships out.

The Fyr Lieutenant's presence alone cleared them through all of the checkpoints up to the front door. There, however, one of the Spec Ops troopers suddenly materialized in front of them.

"I need to scan your implant IDs," she said sharply. "No one enters the Center without full identification validation."

Kyle glanced over at the Federation Marines standing by the door. It was hard to tell, as the troopers all had their helmets on, but he sensed a degree of discomfort in their body language—but they weren't objecting.

He sighed and opened a *very* secured section of his implant memory containing only his ID to prevent the Spec Ops trooper from accessing any of the confidential data locked up in his silicon. Opening a channel, he flipped that piece of data to the Fyr soldier.

The entire process was contained entirely in everyone's implants with no verbalization. To anyone else, Kyle, Xue, and the Fyr woman just stood there blinking at each other for a moment before she nodded and stepped back.

"Validated. Thank you Force Commander, Lieutenant Commander. Welcome to Continuity Center Bravo. You're expected."

#

Svenson led them into an elevator that swept them up to the top floor of the building with alacrity. The elevator opened onto a lobby and conference room setup that wouldn't have looked out of place as the main meeting area of a mid-sized planetary corporation, except for the presence of more Frihet Defense Force troopers providing security, including a set of half a dozen in full powered battle armor.

Admiral Alstairs and the other Federation officers, including Mira, were waiting in the lobby, the Rear Admiral imperiously gesturing for Kyle to join her as she spotted him.

"Carry on, Force Commander," Svenson told him. "You're in conference room seven, over there"—she pointed—"when your Admiral is ready."

Kyle joined Alstairs as instructed, nodding to Force Commander Aleppo and the two XOs while exchanging smiles with Mira.

"We're waiting on the Brigadiers," the Admiral told Kyle as he and Xue joined the cluster of officers. "Hammond and the others will be arriving shortly; they've been directly coordinating with the commander of Fyr Special Ops." She glanced around the room with its uniformed security and power-armored soldiers and lowered her voice.

"They're playing a game of perceptions, more for their people than us, but don't be fooled," she told Kyle quietly. "These people *are* really FDF, but they've got basically everyone in uniform out in the streets of Landning right now, being visible on the news and to the people of the planet's largest city. My best guess is that they've got the Spec Ops forces and maybe a division of regular troops. Most of the rest..." She shrugged. "I'd bet they have means to track down everyone who survived, but I doubt their continuity plans called for everyone to disappear."

"They want to convince everyone that things are okay and the government is in control," Kyle said aloud.

"Exactly," Alstairs agreed. "Brigadiers!" she loudly greeted the two men and a woman who exited the elevator in perfect step with each other. "Good, we're all here. Let's go," she ordered.

The Castle Federation Admiral led her people to the conference room Svenson had pointed out to Kyle upon arriving, where she paused for a moment to allow the security guard to announce they were coming in.

Then the Alliance officers entered the conference room. Like the lobby outside, it looked like any large conference room in a midsized corporate headquarters, but in here, at least, the décor was a bit clearer on just what the space actually was.

Stands in each corner held the blue-on-white sun flag of Fyr, while the back wall had been painted with a three-meter-wide version of the flag above the words, in a decorative script, FYR GOVERNMENT CONTINUITY CENTER BRAVO

A dozen men and women in Frihet Defense Force uniforms filled part of the conference table, while another dozen in the plain suits that were practically the uniform of governments the galaxy over occupied the far third.

The closest third of the table was empty, and the Alliance officers quickly found chairs and waited by them for a moment as the woman at the far end of the table slowly rose to her feet. The woman was old and had been badly injured in some previous conflict—probably the last war with the Commonwealth. Both of her eyes and her right arm were obvious, if very functional, cybernetic prosthetics.

Age and injury might have slowed her, but her voice was calm and collected when she spoke.

"Admiral Alstairs, you and Seventh Fleet's officers are most welcome here," she told them. "I am Premier Rosalyn Ahlgren, the elected head of Fyr's government."

As soon as he heard the name, Kyle recognized her. *Captain* 'Rosie' Ahlgren had earned those cybernetics the hard way—having her ship shot to pieces around her while she held a Commonwealth formation in place long enough for reinforcements to arrive. She'd saved the Zahn system from invasion and lost an arm and both eyes doing it.

She was one of the entire Alliance's heroes from the last war. Kyle wasn't surprised she had ended up in charge of her planet.

"Please, all of you, sit," Ahlgren told them. "It's been a busy twenty-four hours for all of us. Our own plans, as ably executed by General Andrews"—she gestured to one of the uniformed women—"were predicated on us acting once the carriers withdrew in another week or so and the orbital defenses were the only Commonwealth forces in system. The good General, as we all saw, adapted to the new circumstances."

"I must," Andrews—a smallish woman with a shaven head—said, "thank you for your timely intervention. Without your ships and Marines..." She shrugged. "I gave us no more than a fifty percent chance of success. A risk we were willing to take, of course, but..."

"The bigger risk we faced was that the Commonwealth would retake our system," one of the suited, unidentified, politicians added. "With the size of your force, Admiral, I believe that will not be an immediate concern."

"Unfortunately, mister..." Alstairs trailed off.

"Lund," he replied shortly. "Matteus Lund—Minister of Security."

"Unfortunately, Minister Lund," the Admiral repeated, "Seventh Fleet's liberation of Frihet is part of a larger operation. We will not be able to remain in the system for long before it will be necessary for us to launch further offenses."

"But without your fleet, we are defenseless!" Lund squeaked. "We *need* you—we signed with the Alliance because we were to be protected!"

"And we understood the necessity of war meant that sometimes that protection would be longer-term," Ahlgren said, cutting him off. "We do have certain resources that were preserved under the continuity-of-government plans, Admiral Alstairs, but Matteus is functionally correct. None of the resources available to us would suffice to stand off even a mildly determined attack."

"I did not," Alstairs said sharply as the Premier finished speaking, "say we would be leaving you defenseless. Our logistics ships are carrying a full set of orbital defense platforms earmarked for the Frihet system, as well as starfighters and a training cadre for the platforms and fighters. If you have personnel to man the stations, we can have them operational inside forty-eight hours."

In truth, the platforms designated for Frihet had been aboard the transport lost at Zahn. Since Kyle had set up captured *Commonwealth* platforms to defend Cora, however, they were only short *four* platforms instead of eight.

Each of the four logistics ships they'd started with had contained eight *Citadel*-class fighter launch and missile control platforms, the seven hundred and sixty-eight Falcons to fill the Citadels' bays, another hundred or so *Falcons* as spares for Seventh Fleet, and four hundred Atlatl-VI missile satellites.

With one ship lost and two ships having offloaded half their cargo, they still had the platforms for four standard system-defense suites. The problem was that Operation Rising star called for *three* of those suites to be deployed in Via Somnia, and they would also need to see to the Huī Xing system's security.

"That suite consists of four fighter platforms, just under four hundred starfighters to go in them, and two hundred missile satellites. I intend to have the full suite emplaced in Fyr orbit by this time tomorrow," Alstairs noted. "Actual operational status will depend on your personnel availability."

"We have people we can deploy," Ahlgren said calmly. "We can also support them with our flotilla of sublight missile boats—they should be receiving the orders to leave their hiding place in the gas giant shortly. They're out of missiles, but if you can provide us reloads from those freighters..."

There was a *long* untold story there from the sounds of it, and Kyle was curious—it was rare for sublight guardships like the missile boats Ahlgren was describing to survive the fall of a system. Preserving that flotilla was impressive. So, for that matter, was managing to hide *inside* a gas giant.

"We have more than enough munitions to do so," Alstairs promised. "We will need to be on our way inside three days, Premier Ahlgren, but we will do all that we can first."

CHAPTER 24

Frihet System
22:00 March 25, 2736 Earth Standard Meridian Date/Time
Landning City, Capital Star Hotel

The Alliance officers eventually reconvened in a private meeting room on the eightieth floor of Landning City's best hotel. Mira had arranged security by the simple expedient of booking the top five floors of the massive hotel and telling the management to lock the elevator down at the eightieth floor.

Now that floor swarmed with Marines and was being rapidly, if temporarily, converted into a planetary command center. There were still plenty of rooms in the four floors above them—far more, to be honest, then the Alliance presence required, even with the Marines.

"Your impressions, people," Alstairs asked as they settled in at the table in the genteel conference room. The table was a local wood, as were the comfortable chairs. One wall of the room was windows looking out over the city, and the others were painted in calm forest greens.

"They had a solid continuity plan and kept their government together," Kyle rumbled. "But they're still damned short on resources after a multiple-month occupation."

"They're putting on a good face," Mira agreed with her paramour. "But their reaction when we told them we couldn't stay says everything— they *need* our help."

"And we really can't stay," the Admiral confirmed grimly. "None of the systems we've liberated are in great shape. They *all* need our help— but the best thing we can do for them is neutralize Via Somnia. Once the naval base there is down, these systems will be safer than they were before the war started."

"There's still some kind of fleet around here," Mira pointed out to her admiral. "They weren't here, which means there is a ten-starship formation either in Via Somnia or Huī Xing. If we run into that on top of the defenses we know are already at Somnia, our next operation could go very bad."

"Liberating Huī Xing and taking Via Somnia are the only remaining original objectives of Operation Rising Star," Alstairs noted. "To maintain the security of these systems, the neutralization of the nodal fleet is also a requirement, one I'm now including as an operational objective of Rising Star.

"The question, ladies, gentlemen"—she glanced around at her flag captain and Force Commanders—"is how to best achieve those three objectives. I don't expect answers right now," she continued. "We've been going nonstop since we arrived in-system. I suggest we all get some rest and discuss in the morning. Captain Solace has arranged these ground-side facilities for us; I suggest we make use of them."

As the officers filtered out, Mira met Kyle's gaze and smiled at him, indicating for the big Force Commander to follow her.

"I *may*," she told him as they detached from the other officers, "have forgotten to book you a room. I'm afraid you're going to have to bunk with me, Force Commander Roberts."

He sighed and shook his head at her.

"The sacrifices we make to save funds in the Alliance's service," he replied virtuously.

#

At this point, Fleet Captain Mira Solace was very used to waking up at whatever time she decided before she went to sleep. The morning meeting was set late enough, however, that she actually allowed herself to sleep in—waking up to the sight of Frihet's dawn streaming through the hotel window.

Kyle Roberts stood in the window, looking out onto Landning City, and Mira simply lay in the bed, a rumpled disaster after the prior evening's extended activities, and watched him. *This* had not been where she'd expected to end up when she'd been pulled from her nice, comfortable, *safe* posting aboard *Sunset*.

But then, she also hadn't expected to make Captain anytime soon, either. She'd first hit it off with the big carrier captain and then been promoted herself. The opportunity had seemed too good to pass up.

Now she worried. The current split of Seventh Fleet meant Kyle could easily end up in another star system, fighting—possibly dying— far away from her. Their positions and ranks made them luckier than many in the fleet—they were physically close enough that they could steal time together, and senior enough to be *able* to do so.

It was hard to feel guilty about that while her lover was standing naked in the window, haloed by the light of the planet's slowly rising sun.

"You're awake," he said brightly without turning around. "It's still a couple of hours till the conference. I've checked in with *Avalon*; all's quiet in orbit."

Kicking off the blankets, Mira joined him at the window.

"Looking at anything in particular?" she asked.

"Just...the city," he replied, gesturing outward. The Capital Star Hotel was far from the tallest building in Landning City, though it was far enough out from the main downtown to tower over its immediate surroundings.

Landning was a pretty typical colonial capital. It had a central core of skyscrapers, some towering as much as half a kilometer into the sky, where the planet's big corporations and local branches of multistellars were headquartered. That core was surrounded by a vast expanse of suburbs, linked by carefully coordinated ground and air traffic. Sections of relatively small apartment buildings—mostly under fifty stories here—were scattered at points throughout those suburbs. Her implant said the city was roughly fifteen percent of the planet's population.

There was surprisingly little visible damage from the fighting. Even looking beyond the city, the craters and smoke plumes where the space defense units had dug in were barely visible from here. The Terran Marines had, to their credit, made a *point* of surrendering before any of the fighting got into the city.

"It all looks so peaceful from up here," Kyle eventually said. His voice was less cheerful than she was used to from him, and she looked at him carefully from the corner of her eye. "If we screw this up, the Terrans will come back, and a lot of people could still die."

"That's the risk the whole operation is dealing with," she agreed. "Five systems liberated from the Commonwealth, but...only fixed defenses, no starships, and ten warships out there somewhere." Mira shivered. "We think we're saving these people, but we could be setting them up for a world of hurt."

Kyle shifted, wrapping her in his arms and warming her shivers with his body heat.

"I know," he agreed. "It's war, it's strategically necessary, and I *hate* it."

For all of his bulk, Mira was much the same height as Kyle, and she easily wrapped her arms around him in turn.

"What do we do?" she asked quietly. Her question had more meaning than she realized. She wasn't even entirely sure there *was* a "we" yet. She enjoyed Kyle's company, respected him, but even she wasn't sure what the long-term potential for them as a couple was yet—and that was assuming the war *let* them have any potential.

"Our jobs," Kyle told her. "Too many people look to one or both of us for us to forget that," he continued. "But..." He pressed her fingers to his lips. "We *are* allowed to be human, Mira. We can have doubts; we can steal this time to be *us*."

His eyes met hers and Mira realized he'd heard *both* her questions. He didn't know either, but he saw the potential for an "us" too.

That was...all anyone could ask for sometimes.

GLYNN STEWART

CHAPTER 25

Frihet System
09:25 March 26, 2736 Earth Standard Meridian Date/Time
DSC-078 Avalon, *CAG's Office*

"You should *see* what Zahn has given us for flight crews," the man on the other end of the Q-Com link told Michael Stanford. "Half of them are amazing—older officers, vets of the last war to a man and woman. The other half…" Flight Commander Antonio Zupan shuddered. "They're so green, I think they're drinking chlorophyll."

Zupan, a whipcord-thin man with tanned-dark skin and black hair, had been promoted off *Avalon* when they'd brought Battle Group Seventeen's fighter wings up to strength. His promotion had landed him an assignment to one of the cadres being delivered to the systems Rising Star liberated.

Despite his junior rank and recent promotion, the man was the second-ranked Castle Federation Space Force officer in the Zahn system, tasked with taking the crews that the planetary defense force provided and training them to fly the three hundred and eighty-four Falcons the Federation had given Zahn.

"You were no better once," Michael told him. "Hell, *you* were a rabble-rousing fight-starter once, and I don't think any of your greenhorns have grown into that level of iniquity yet!"

"I think you promoted me to *make* me behave," Zupan accused. "And I'm still a rabble-rouser, for that matter. This lot will make good crews, given time. We've got *maybe* twenty squadrons of mostly qualified crews. The other thirty squadrons? They can get the birds into space, but I need more time."

Four *Citadel*-class platforms based eight Federation fighter wings—forty-eight squadrons. Michael was actually surprised that Zahn had come up with enough people *qualified* to serve as fighter crew in the time they'd had—starfighter crew members required a ninety-ninth percentile ability to run data through their implants.

"Do they all meet the bandwidth requirement?" he asked, wondering if they'd simply let the recruiting standard slip.

"I wondered the same thing, Vice Commodore," Zupan replied. "I checked them all—they managed to find twelve hundred souls with enough bandwidth in two days. I suspect someone, somewhere, already had a little list."

"That helps, though it may have other issues," Michael warned.

"If any of these kids were drafted, they aren't whining about it," the trainer told him. "They saw the Commonwealth occupation firsthand. They'll fight."

"Just make sure they *can*."

"That's what they sent me..." Zupan trailed off, staring at something Michael couldn't see. "Fuck. FUCK. No!"

"Flight Commander!" *Avalon*'s CAG snapped.

"Going to have to cut this short," the trainer replied shortly. "The Commonwealth is here."

09:45 March 26, 2736 ESMDT
Landning City, Capital Star Hotel

There was something inherently *wrong* to Kyle about sitting in a comfortable hotel conference room, well rested and well fed, while watching a data stream announcing that your subordinates almost a dozen light-years away were going to die.

The scheduled conference had been canceled. None of the Marines or junior officers had joined them, but the captains of the warships in orbit were being linked in to the room where Kyle sat with the other Force Commander, the Admiral, and Mira.

The holograms helped fill a room that would otherwise have felt empty with only the four of them, and helped shield against the data feed now coming in from Zahn.

Eight capital ships accelerated towards the planet at an even two hundred gravities, spearheaded by the massive bulk of a *Saint*-class battleship. Arrayed around the twenty-million-ton, sixty-million-cubic-meter battleship were two *Resolute*-class battleships, two *Assassin*-class battlecruisers and three *Lexington*-class fleet carriers.

It was a stupendous amount of firepower, a force that would have crushed any of the three Battle Groups Seventh Fleet had been divided into for the last portion of the operation.

Against the four launch platforms, three hundred and eighty-four starfighters and two hundred missiles satellites in Zahn orbit, it may as well have been the Sol Home Fleet.

As Kyle watched, the carriers started to fall back with the cruisers as escorts. A small group of starfighters remained with the carriers, but five hundred Scimitars advanced toward the planet alongside the battleships.

"They don't stand a chance," Anders said aloud, putting into words what every senior officer in Seventh Fleet was thinking. "Damn it all."

No one in Zahn was bothering to update Seventh Fleet on their plans, but access to the full telemetry from the Citadels told the story. All of the Falcons were in space, carefully establishing the swirling, semi-random formation of space combat.

Then, *almost* as one—too many of the pilots were green for smooth simultaneity—the starfighters lunged out at their enemies. Moments later, seventy-eight new icons lit up on the screen as the Terran battleships opened fire.

"Thirty-six minutes to fighter missile range," Kyle noted softly. "The Atlatls will need to open up in just under eleven minutes for a massed time-on-target strike."

A mass strike from the six hundred launchers those two hundred platforms carried, combined with the sixteen hundred fighter missiles from the starfighters, had a decent chance of hurting those battleships... except for the close-in fighter escort.

With five hundred fighters playing missile defense for the Terrans and the defending starfighter pilots being so green...Kyle wasn't sure how it would end. But from ten light-years away, all that Seventh Fleet's office could do was watch.

But watch they did. Minutes ticked by, and Zahn's defenders launched their missiles a few seconds later than Kyle predicted. It shouldn't make too much of a difference, but the slight coordination failure worried him.

And the others. He felt Mira sneak her hand under the table into his and squeezed gently. There was *nothing* they could do—nothing but watch and hope that this commander had learned the lesson that Dimitri Tobin had sacrificed his career to teach the Commonwealth.

Atrocities would *not* be tolerated. If this fleet fired on Zahn, Operation Rising Star would be put on hold while Seventh Fleet hunted down the bastards who'd killed a world. *Avalon* had done it once. Kyle would gladly do it again.

More missiles blasted out from each side, the Atlatls going to rapid-fire at the command of the Citadel platforms, while the battleships maintained an even metronome of one salvo a minute for fifteen minutes.

The Atlatls, like the Terran defenders of the system before them, emptied their magazines before the Terran missiles reached them. Like Admiral Alstairs, however, the Terrans had realized this and ignored the platforms. Their missiles targeted the Citadels and hammered home with devastating force.

Seven minutes before the starfighters reached their range, the first Stormwinds reached the Citadel defensive platforms. Defensive fire filled the space above Zahn, and the Stormwinds responded with jamming and evasive maneuvers.

It wasn't enough. The cadre of Federation officers and spacers left behind hadn't had enough time to train their new crews. They stopped the first salvo, but not the second or the third. The fourth salvo finished the job, missiles slamming into already-crippled hulks and vaporizing them in blasts of antimatter fire.

Now Mira was gripping Kyle's hand with horrified strength, and he knew he was clinging to her too as he watched the fighter strike lunge forward. With an experienced fighter group, the gunners could have fully taken over control of the capital ship missiles, augmenting the strikes and delivering a hammerblow.

It was rapidly clear Zahn's defenders had done no such thing. The missiles charged in on their own highly capable brains alone. The fighters crossed the invisible line in space marking their own weapons range and opened fire.

Kyle winced. Half of the defenders had fired in perfect unison, linking up with the new timing of the first Atlatl missile salvo. The other half...scattered their missiles over a five-second window. In this kind of battle, five seconds was everything.

The *Terran* fighters, on the other hand, launched in perfect synchronicity, sending two thousand missiles back into the defenders' teeth. The Falcons fired again, launching their remaining two salvos while they still had a chance.

The Terrans...didn't bother.

Fourteen seconds before the missiles hit, the Falcons entered the range of the battleships' defensive lances and the dying began. Positron beams tore through space, ripping apart missiles and fighters with equal abandon. The defending starfighters launched themselves forward, interposing their own positron lances and lasers between the incoming missiles and the battleships—but leaving the Falcons themselves to the battleships.

Kyle couldn't close his eyes. He watched as the mix of veterans and half-trained crews, including men and women who'd served under his own command, drove into that maelstrom—their focus on the battleships.

The last Falcon died two full seconds before reaching lance range of the battleship or seeing a missile strike home. Lasers and lances alike turned on the inbound missiles, a devastating harvest of explosions ripping through space as the battleships tangled with the thousands of weapons targeted on them.

The Scimitars ripped the heart out of the missile salvos. They didn't do it easily or cheaply—dozens of the starfighters died to direct hits and near misses—but they gutted the salvos, leaving them easy victims for the close-in defenses of three modern battleships.

As the last missiles came apart in balls of antimatter fire, Kyle finally closed his eyes, trying to clear his mind of what he'd seen. In sixty minutes, Seventh Fleet's liberation of Zahn had been transformed into dust and death, with almost five thousand starfighter and platform crew killed in that vain attempt to achieve *anything*.

"What are they doing?" he heard Mira ask, and slowly opened his eyes, studying the data feed.

"They're breaking off," Anders said slowly. "Why? That makes no sense."

Everyone in the room studied the screen for a long silent moment before the Admiral saw what they should have noticed from the beginning.

"No transports," she said slowly. "They didn't come equipped to reconquer—just to shatter whatever defenses we'd put in place. Opening a path and making an example..."

"Delivering a warning," Kyle said harshly. "Arrogant bastards."

CHAPTER 26

Frihet System
20:00 March 26, 2736 Earth Standard Meridian Date/Time
DSC-078 Avalon, *Shuttle Bay*

Kyle stepped off the shuttle into the landing bay of his carrier, feeling like a zombie. Last night, everything had seemed to be coming together. Operation Rising Star had swept four of its six targets, crushing the Commonwealth everywhere along the way. Even the warning that there *were* more warships in the sector hadn't really sunk in at a gut-level, not after an unbroken string of victories.

Now thousands of Alliance spacers and flight crews were dead. One of the planets they'd liberated had been left wide open, with no defenses once the Commonwealth managed to scare up an assault division to retake them—the number of Terran POWs left behind on Zahn meant they wouldn't even need that many troops.

James Anderson and Michael Stanford were both waiting for their Captain outside the safety zone of the shuttle bay. The pale, redheaded executive officer just looked tired, greeting Kyle with a firm nod.

Avalon's CAG looked like Kyle felt. Despite the fact that the fighter pilot *had* to have rested last night, there were bags under his eyes and new lines under blond hair that looked noticeably more silver than it had a few weeks before.

"Gentlemen," Kyle greeted them. "What's our status?"

Anderson visibly shook himself before speaking.

"*Avalon* is fully restocked and prepared to move on your command," the exec replied. "Michael is better able to speak to the fighter group, but we are above ninety-nine percent readiness in all other aspects. Crew could use a day or two of liberty if we have the time to spare."

"We don't," Kyle told him. He didn't elaborate for now. "Michael?"

"We've replaced the lost fighters from the logistics ships and I've reorganized my squadrons," the CAG said quietly. "I have two hundred starfighters ready to deploy from *Avalon*'s group. *Courageous* and *Indomitable* are both down ten ships apiece." He shrugged. "Not sure if we're keeping the Battle Group together, so I've been keeping in touch with them."

"The Admiral will be briefing us all shortly," the Captain told him. "Thank you, gentlemen," he continued, leading them out of the shuttle bay. "The attack at Zahn was a shock to all of our systems, but we will need to adapt and recover."

"Zupan was one of mine," Stanford said quietly. "One of *ours*. He fought at Barsoom. Damn it, Kyle—he deserved better than to be run out on a branch and cut off like that."

"I know," Kyle replied, glancing around the corridor to be sure none of the crew were listening to the CAG tear into the operations plan. "I don't even disagree," he said heavily. "It's been the big known weakness of the plan for Rising Star since the beginning, gentlemen."

"So, what do we *do*?" Stanford demanded. "We've got a dozen squadrons of our own people playing cadre—with barely enough time to get the people they're training used to sitting in a damn starfighter, let alone flying one! If that fleet sweeps through Hammerveldt and Cora, all we'll have achieved is a lot of new corpses."

"We don't know where they'll go, Michael," Kyle pointed out. "But... we have a plan."

"*What* plan?"

"We make them come to us."

21:00 March 26, 2736 ESMDT
DSC-078 Avalon, *Captain's Breakout Room*

Once again, the holographic conferencing program vastly expanded the tiny conference room attached to Kyle's office. The small room was undecorated except for a copy of *Avalon*'s commissioning seal—a gold circle around a hand rising from waves, with the hull number DSC-0078 at the top and the ship's name at the bottom—painted onto one wall.

That seal was currently hidden by the projectors, which were creating the image of a room large enough to hold every Captain, XO and CAG in the entirety of Seventh Fleet, plus Rear Admiral Miriam Alstairs and her chief of staff.

Even knowing only three of those thirty-five people were actually *in* his conference room, knowing the true dimensions of the room left Kyle feeling mildly crowded at the size of the briefing.

And this time it was definitely a briefing, not a meeting. Kyle could guess what was coming, as the two Force Commanders had spent most of the day after the attack on Zahn discussing their options, but even *he* didn't know what Alstairs' ensuing discussions with High Command had turned up.

"Ladies, gentlemen, herms," Alstairs said calmly. "We are all aware of the attack on Zahn, and it does change our operational objectives and constraints. The presence of a significant Commonwealth Navy force in the region is a clear and present threat both to our direct objectives and to the safety of the worlds we are here to liberate.

"I have consulted with many of you over yesterday and today both directly and in groups, and have spent the last few hours in direct conference with Fleet Admiral Blake and Sky Marshal von Stenger. We believe we have assembled a strategy that will enable us to complete Rising Star's operational objectives."

A three-dimensional map of the region appeared in the center of the briefing room, the six inhabited stars highlighted amidst the dozen or so uninhabited systems in a spherical region of space almost thirty light-years across, from Cora—closest to Alliance space—to Via Somnia—*inside* Commonwealth space.

"We have now liberated these four systems," Alstairs noted, with Seventh Fleet's previous targets flashing in the screen. "The Commonwealth force hit Zahn, here." Zahn flashed red. "They trashed the orbital defenses, vaporized what orbital industry was still left, and then moved on. At this point, Zahn has been left with no significant strategic value to either side," she said grimly, "which I'm sure was their intent."

Distance markers flashed up on the screens, as even trained eyes could misread scale and distance looking at three-dimensional models like this.

"This puts them ten light-years from Frihet, eight light-years from Hammerveldt, ten light-years from Cora—and also twenty-one from Via Somnia and eighteen from Huī Xing.

"*We* are thirteen light-years from Via Somnia, and nine from Huī Xing," she continued. "An assault group from here can be at Huī Xing in six days—Via Somnia in a little over seven. That force may be making payback strikes right now, but if they face a clear and present danger to their logistics base, they will *have* to move to defend it.

"And that, people, is our opportunity," Alstairs finished flatly. "Over the next twelve hours, the Fifty-Eighth and One Twenty-Fifth Brigades will be transferring from their assault transports to the ships of Seventh Fleet.

"The transports themselves, along with our empty logistics freighter and the freighter carrying the defensive suites for Huī Xing, will be assigned to Battle Group Seven-Two under Force Commander Roberts," she continued. "The transports have significant ECM capabilities of their own, and the freighters will have several ECM drones mounted to their hulls, allowing all five ships to pretend to be warships."

Kyle nodded as the concept sunk in. He'd wondered how they could pull the enemy fleet away from Via Somnia without actually sending the lion's share of Seventh Fleet to Huī Xing. Using the support ships as decoys would definitely work.

"Seven-Two is weak on starfighters," he admitted. "If we're pretending to be the entire Fleet..."

"We will reinforce your wings," Alstairs confirmed. "While we don't have any additional Templar ships or crews, my understanding is that the *Fearless*-class cruisers are able to service Falcons?"

Her questioning glance went to Captains Olivier and Albert, who both nodded.

"We'll need to fabricate some adaptors, but I'd rather that than going in understrength," Olivier told the Admiral. "I'm not sure we can support the Arrows, unfortunately."

"We'll spread the draw as wide as possible across the Federation ships," Alstairs assured the other CAGs. "We will need full squadrons—three from each carrier, one from each cruiser."

The other Federation ship and fighter group commanders winced but nodded.

"I want those transfers complete by ten hundred hours tomorrow," the Rear Admiral said grimly. "Same time as the Marines. Force Commander Aleppo?"

"I'm handing back the fancy chevron, aren't I?" the Trade Factor officer replied cheerfully. The only rank insignia for the inherently temporary rank of Force Commander was a small chevron above the original collar insignia.

"Sorry, Lora," Alstairs confirmed. "We'll be rolling Seven-Three back into the main fleet. You've done a good job, but we'll need the firepower to take on Via Somnia."

"It wasn't something I would ever get to keep," Aleppo told her.

"The plan, as it stands," the Admiral told everyone, "is that we move out at eleven hundred hours tomorrow morning. Battle Group Seven-Two hits Huī Xing *hard*. Punch out their defenses and any ships they have left. Be...paranoid. Make them think they can intercept you, that it will be a fair fight."

"I can do that," Kyle said after a moment. "What about the logistics depot?"

"If it's still there, I leave it to your discretion," Alstairs told him. "If the Terrans are clearly using it, you are authorized to destroy it by long-range bombardment. We'll discuss the exact details of your mission before you leave."

"Understand, ma'am," Kyle agreed. He wondered why *he* was the one keeping the chevron—Aleppo was the senior Captain and he had figured that if one of them had to give up the Force Commander rank, it would be him.

"With the Marines aboard, the rest of Seventh Fleet will proceed to the Via Somnia system," Alstairs continued. "I will note that only four light-years separate Via Somnia and Huī Xing. Either Battle Group can move to relieve the other if needed."

Assuming the group in need of relief could survive four days, at least. The light-year-per-day-squared acceleration of the Alcubierre-Stetson drive, with its need to decelerate to the same velocity you started with, made longer-distance trips more efficient than short-range jumps.

"While Battle Group Seven-Two attracts the attention of the Commonwealth nodal fleet, Seventh Fleet will assault Via Somnia," Alstairs concluded. "With the warships drawn out of position, we should mostly be facing fixed defenses that can be engaged from long range. Once the defenses have been neutralized, we will deliver the Marines to board the remaining facilities. Once Via Somnia is ours, we will set up the defensive suites we brought with us.

"At that point, Seven-Two will fall back to Via Somnia, presumably bringing the Commonwealth fleet with them. Expecting to arrive in a system under their control, they will instead find the rest of Seventh Fleet and our fixed defenses waiting for them.

"Once they arrive, they can run or they can fight against overwhelming odds. Either way, this sector will be secure."

#

"I'm sure you have questions, Kyle," Admiral Alstairs told him as he settled into his office chair, the main briefing over and a private channel now open between them. "Shoot."

"More than a few," he admitted, his usual cheerfulness beginning to return after the shock of the loss at Zahn. "Not that I'm objecting to the chance to crack some Terran skulls, but why me? I would figure Aleppo was a better choice for an independent command if you only needed one of us."

"It's not a question of seniority, Kyle," she pointed out. "It's a question of skillset and temperament. Lora is a very competent officer, perfectly capable of planning and leading an attack on Huī Xing and fighting any enemy on equal ground.

"But I'm not sending you to fight an equal enemy, Force Commander," she said flatly. "I'm sending you to play matador to a fleet with twice your hulls, twice your cubage, and a clearly competent commander. Encountering that force, what would Aleppo do, Roberts?"

"Withdraw," he responded immediately. "It's the only sensible tactical choice."

"Exactly," Alstairs told him. "But the right *tactical* choice won't meet the *operational* objectives. I need that fleet in Huī Xing. I need them to *stay* in Huī Xing until we are in possession of Via Somnia and in a position to kick their ass when you bring them to me.

"Aleppo doesn't have the twisty brain necessary to play cat and mouse with a superior fleet for a goddamn week, Kyle, and that's what I need *you* to do. Plus, the Commonwealth knows your reputation by now. If I can't send enough actual *ships* to make them think you're a real threat, I can send the Stellar Fox."

"I hate that nickname," Kyle observed. "I'm considering a campaign of beating up journalists in dark alleys when I get home to convince them to stop using it."

The Admiral laughed, shaking her head at him.

"That may be, Roberts, but it's a name the Terrans know," she told him. "A name whose presence makes Battle Group *Avalon* a threat they have to respect. Combined with the ECM to make them think your Battle Group is a *fleet*, you should be able to attract their attention before we hit Via Somnia.

"I intend to hold Seventh Fleet outside Via Somnia until they have arrived at Huī Xing," she admitted. "We need a week to get the defenses online—I need you to hold their nodal fleet for three days, Kyle. Don't let them trap you in the gravity well. Drag them out, dance around them—keep them guessing."

She shook her head, her eyes grim.

"Bluntly, Kyle, being in control of Via Somnia and having the defenses in place is *critical*," she told him. "Which brings me to the other reason I chose you over Aleppo: she's a brave woman, a strong woman—but I don't think she has the steel in her spine to lose starships and still fight a holding action."

He swallowed. Starships were *massive* investments in money, technology and lives. Losing them was a high price to pay, especially given the losses the Alliance had already taken in the war. The massive industrial might of the Commonwealth could replace the ships the Terrans had already lost in this campaign more readily than the Alliance could replace *Avalon* alone.

"I need you to press them that hard," Alstairs said quietly. "I'd *rather* you came home with everyone—all your ships, all your fighters, all your people. But if it comes down to a close action or that fleet arriving at Via Somnia before we're ready for them, I need you prepared to spend *starships* to hold them. Do you understand me, Force Commander Roberts?"

He swallowed. He was mentally prepared to lose starfighters—it hurt, but it was what they *existed* for—and hated it. To be willing to send cruisers, battleships, even *Avalon* herself to near-certain death to buy time?

"Ma'am, I'm not certain *I* have that 'steel in my spine'," he admitted. "I swore to lead these people, not sacrifice them."

"I know," his Admiral told him. "I judge that you have that steel, Kyle. But I don't want you to fight them, not unless you have to. Keep them guessing, keep them dancing. Outside the gravity well, you can play Alcubierre cat and mouse with them.

"But I need seven days, Force Commander, whatever the cost."

"Then I guess I will need to hold the Terrans for you," Kyle said simply.

CHAPTER 27

Frihet System
11:00 March 27, 2736 Earth Standard Meridian Date/Time
DSC-078 Avalon, Bridge

Force Commander Kyle Roberts watched Frihet and the rest of Seventh Fleet disappear behind him with mixed feelings. Battle Group Seven-Two's "reinforcements" were a giant bluff, which left him with the same four warships and one understrength Marine brigade to play matador to a fleet of over twice his strength.

His introspection didn't leak out to his crew. He was *sprawled* in his command chair with a giant grin on his face, projecting a confidence he mostly *did* feel. If *Avalon* was being sent to *fight* the Commonwealth's local fleet, it would be a suicide mission. But since his job was to simply keep them in one place, he figured he could do it.

"What's our ETA to Alcubierre distance, Commander?" he asked Pendez.

"Two hours, Force Commander," she told him. "Then six days, one hour, thirty-five minutes to Huī Xing. We will arrive approximately twelve hundred thirty hours on April second."

"Any commentary from the other navigators?" Kyle said. With three more ships tacked onto his order of battle, even if none of them were actual warships, he was now asking the Fleet Commander to coordinate courses for nine starships.

It was a task well outside of her normal responsibilities—and one to which she was rising with an aplomb he was carefully noting for his personnel evaluation on Fleet Commander Maria Pendez. The evaluation in which he intended to recommend she get the third gold circle of a *Senior* Fleet Commander and move to an XO role somewhere.

"Commentary?" she replied. "Yeah, we got commentary. *Useful* or *meaningful* feedback? Not a drop."

"Fair enough," he chuckled. "Any concerns of your own?"

"We're not pushing the engines or doing anything twisty," Pendez told him. "It's a pretty straightforward trip: accelerate, flip, decelerate and drop in well outside the limit. I could plot this course in my sleep."

"Please don't," Kyle told her. "I'm going to check in with the flagship. Prod my implant if you see anything."

With that, he was effectively surrendering the watch to her. As the carrier's navigator, Pendez stood only a few of the formal watches—a gap in her experience he was quietly making up to allow for the XO slot she didn't know was in her future.

"Have fun, sir," his navigator told him with a meaningful wink.

A mental command dropped a privacy screen around his command chair, blocking off sound from the rest of the bridge. His implant was still open to accept messages, but his people couldn't overhear his conversations now.

Kyle opened a channel to *Camerone*. He didn't even have to ask for Mira, as the Captain had obviously been waiting for him to reach out.

"We're on our way," he told her with a smile. "Arrival on the second, a little after twelve hundred hours."

The flagship's captain nodded.

"I'll pass the timing on to the Admiral," she replied. "Any concerns I should pass on as well?"

"She and I went over everything last night," Kyle said. "I know what needs to be done."

There was silence on the transmission for a moment, the professional part of the conversation over but neither *quite* willing to leave it at that.

"Be careful," she finally said. "It looks like a suicide mission to me."

"It isn't," he reassured her. "I don't think the Admiral is any more interested in sending my people to their deaths than I am. The plan is solid. It's not risk-free," he admitted with a chuckle, "but I'm hardly charging their fleet, all guns blazing."

"I'm not sure I put charging them, guns blazing, past you, Kyle," his girlfriend noted. "Be *careful*."

"I'd only charge them if it would serve a purpose," he replied. "I will be careful, Mira. I promise. *You* be careful. Via Somnia is an important naval base, a launching point for this entire invasion. It won't be a pushover."

"We're not expecting it to be," she replied. "That's why most of the fleet is going there and not to Huī Xing. We'll be fine."

"So will we," Kyle told her cheerfully. "I've got Michael and all his people to keep me safe. We'll toast to victory in Via Somnia—I will see you there."

"You're ever the optimist," Solace replied with a chuckle of her own. "As you say, then—we'll toast Seventh Fleet in the ruins of Terra's dreams of conquest!"

12:00 March 27, 2736 ESMDT
DSC-078 Avalon*, CAG's Office*

Michael's office was crowded with all five of his Wing Commanders gathered in it, but sometimes that was a necessary price to pay. Rokos had produced a bottle of expensive Castle-made whiskey from somewhere and was passing around small glasses.

"To Flight Commander Antonio Zupan," the CAG told his officers as he raised his own glass. "May he ever fly amidst the Eternal Stars."

Michael himself was Christian—Third Reformation Anglican—but the Stellar Spiritualists were the majority aboard *Avalon*, as they were in the Castle Federation itself. Zupan himself had been as devout a follower as that semi-agnostic religion had.

"May he ever fly," his Wing Commanders chorused back, and Michael drank. The alcohol burned its way down his throat with a surprisingly smooth fire. It was apparently worth whatever Rokos had paid for it.

The room was silent for a moment in memory. Even in peacetime, the starfighter corps lost people. That was what happened when you flew the most fragile armed spacecraft in the galaxy. At war, though, the Castle Federation Space Force had already grown very used to the loss of men and women they'd served alongside.

"I want," Michael told them as the moment faded, "to set up an intense series of exercises over the next few days. We have entire new *squadrons* to integrate into our tactics and to make sure everyone is comfortable at each other's backs."

"And if we work them and us as hard as we can, it's hard to fall into a funk," Rokos pointed out. "If we keep running, we don't stop and think."

"I wasn't going to *admit* that part of my thought process," the CAG told the others with a laugh. "But Russell's right. We need to keep busy—and our crews need to keep busy. *But* we also need to be as sharp as possible.

"You've seen the mission brief. We're going to need to be on the very top of our game if we want to pull off this stunt the old man has signed us up for without losing too many of our people. Remember, people," Michael said quietly, "while it's going to be easy enough for us to evade the Terran capital ships, dodging their *starfighters* is going to be harder. It's going to be our job to remind the Terrans why they don't *want* to catch Alliance starfighters."

The chorus of growls that responded made him smile coldly.

13:00 March 27, 2736 ESMDT
BC-129 Camerone, *Bridge*

Mira watched through the scanners as the matched gravitational singularities of Battle Group Seven-Two flared to life, whisking the nine starships away toward Huī Xing.

The rest of Seventh Fleet was setting out a bit more slowly, since their role in Admiral Alstairs' plan called for them to hit Via Somnia *after* the Terrans caught up to Kyle. Hanging her boyfriend out as bait rankled more than a little, though it was at least half watching him and *Avalon* go off into danger without her.

"How are we doing, Commander?" she asked her XO.

Notley shrugged, the older officer's eyes also fixated on the big display where *Avalon* and her sisters had vanished.

"*Camerone* is ready for action," he said simply. "Wing Commander Volte is...unenthused with the loss of a squadron, but his people understand that Seven-Two needed the help. We've replenished our missile stocks and Engineering is in the process of carrying out a full survey of our systems.

"Analysis also confirmed our missiles got in one of the killing blows here, so Engineering is *also* reportedly trying to find somewhere to paint a Volcano silhouette."

Mira snorted, amused. It was hard, given the sheer number of munitions flying around, to validate a specific vessel as being responsible for a kill in a fleet action. While the Federation didn't adhere to the tradition of painting kill silhouettes, enough of the Alliance members *did* that it was a running joke.

"I thought the traditional place was on a primary zero point cell?" she suggested sweetly. "Where no one will ever see it."

Notley laughed.

"You *think* you're joking," he pointed out. "That's exactly where we *did* paint them on a few ships last time around—where the Captain wouldn't look."

"I promise not to look closely at any strange markings I find on the cells when I inspect Engineering next," Mira told him. "No concerns? Any issues with the Marines aboard?"

They had, after all, crammed an entire thousand-Marine-strong battalion aboard the cruiser.

"None," he replied crisply. "Colonel Xavier's people are being *very* cooperative. I leave the rest of the Fleet to the Admiral's staff, though."

"And they are in equivalent shape, if not *quite* as good as *Camerone*," Alstairs said loudly. Mira wasn't sure *quite* when the Admiral had slipped onto the bridge, but she'd done it without anyone noticing. The practice of long years in command of the battlecruiser herself, Mira supposed.

"You've done a good job with my old ship, captain," the Admiral noted, "but the rest of the Fleet is almost managing to keep up. We're almost ready to go."

"Six hours," Mira said quietly. "Is that enough time for Frihet?"

The three senior officers were clustered around her command chair. The acoustics of the bridge were carefully designed—loud announcements would carry to the entire room, but quiet conversation wouldn't.

"No," Alstairs admitted. "I've had to assign more pilots to their cadre from the crews that are supposed to be taking over at Via Somnia than I'd like. We underestimated how quickly the Terrans would hit these systems; we *should* have been providing full sets of fighter crews, not just training cadre."

"Did we have them?" Mira asked. Across dozens of systems and billions of souls, there were hundreds of millions of people with the ninety-ninth percentile implant interface capability needed to fly a fighter—but that didn't mean they had millions of trained fighter crews.

"No," the Admiral told her. "We didn't. That's why we went with this plan in the first place—the security of the systems we were going to liberate was always the Achilles heel of this plan. We *need* to take out Via Somnia to make Rising Star a success; otherwise, all of this"—she made an encompassing gesture of the bridge—"has been for nothing. I won't let this much death and blood be for nothing; do you understand me, Captain?"

"I do, ma'am," *Camerone*'s Captain said quietly, looking at the operational display and the countdown timer. "I just wonder how much *more* we're going to lose before it's over."

"We're fighting a half-awake giant," Seventh Fleet's admiral said grimly. "It's going to take time to bring the Alliance's systems to full war status—but if the *Commonwealth* ever does the same, we're doomed. I don't know if this is ever going to be 'over', Captain Solace. Nor do I know how much we'll lose.

"All I know is that I plan to fight every step of the damned way," Alstairs told them. "And that this war can't be fought entirely on our soil—something it has been to date. Something that changes the instant we leave FTL in Via Somnia."

CHAPTER 28

Deep Space, En Route to Huī Xing System
14:10 March 30, 2736 Earth Standard Meridian Date/Time
AT-032 Chimera

"Move out!" Lieutenant Major Edvard Hansen, Bravo Company Commander, 3rd Battalion, 103rd Marine Brigade, ordered his people crisply as they entered what *had* been Second Battalion's quarters. "And remember—keep it quiet, keep it low. The Colonel is buying the drinks for the company that performs best."

With three transports and three battalions, Brigadier Hammond had made the snap decision to split his brigade up as the other Marines moved onto Seventh Fleet's warships. It reduced their points of failure and also left the Marines rattling around their assault transports like loose change.

Colonel Silje had decided to take advantage of the extra space by using an entire battalion's quarters and exercise area as the "target" for a practice space-borne assault. Having *three* of said quarters allowed him to set up two company level exercises—and Bravo Company had been assigned to "clear" Second Battalion's quarters of resistance.

They opened the dance by pushing through with Bravo Platoon leading the way, sweeping the main "lobby" area and checking for ambushes by Delta Company's troopers.

There was no battle armor for this affair, just light body armor and training lasers. The lasers, unlike their *actual* weapons, were line-of-sight—but the network of everyone's implants would calculate whether a battle rifle round would have hit.

Delta chose to concede the main entrance, allowing Edvard's company to move in and leaving him with choices as to how to proceed. Between the entertainment section with the mess, the training gym with the simulators, and the actual battalion quarters, there were three different spaces, each of which could hold the entirety of Delta Company easily.

But there was also a *time* component to the game, and splitting up would let them hit all three simultaneously. It was a risky venture, one that could lose him the game if he guessed wrong...but he *knew* his people were better.

"Split up," he ordered his platoon lieutenants. "Alpha Platoon, take the mess. Bravo, you get the training sector. Charlie, hit the quarters. Keep linked in, call for the HQ section if you need backup. Go! Hit them hard."

Without the battle armor suits to absorb the sounds, they couldn't wolf-howl. His officers fist-bumped instead before splitting off to launch their sweeps.

Only Bravo's headquarters section was left in the lobby when Delta launched their ambush. All the exits from the lobby area slammed shut to a command override, trapping Edvard's headquarters section in the open space.

"Cover!" he snapped, diving for one of the handful of couches in the lobby. There *wasn't* much cover; Delta had planned it *well*.

"They're coming through the roof!" Ramirez bellowed.

"Aim high, take them as they come," Edvard replied, suiting actions to words and firing blindly into the air he swept the room for targets.

Lieutenant Major Fenton might be in trouble later, he noted in the back of his mind. Delta had actually *cut* holes in the roof, accessing the emergency spaces above the quarters. Edvard wasn't sure how many people they'd crammed up there, but it gave them an element of surprise that *should* have been enough to take down his command squad.

The moment's extra notice from the doors slamming shut, however, was enough for him and Ramirez to be looking for the ambush. The Gunnery Sergeant launched the first virtual grenade, but Edvard was only moments behind him—and three of his troopers had the same thought.

A dozen or so Delta troopers made it to the ground. The rest were still in the ceiling when the computers assessed the result of five hypervelocity fragmentation grenades going off in an enclosed space.

None of the rest of the platoon made it down. The dozen on the ground still mostly had surprise, simulated gunfire spraying over Edvard's people and taking half of his headquarters section down—including Gunny Ramirez.

Twenty seconds after the doors slammed shut, it was over. Delta Company's Bravo Platoon was out of action, and Bravo Company's headquarters section was down eleven effectives.

"Watch the ceilings," he ordered his lieutenants. "Fenton's down a platoon to that trick, but he might still try it again."

One of his people got to work on opening the doors, while Edvard's "dead" carefully started helping Delta Company's "dead" get safely down from the emergency spaces.

The Lieutenant Major watched with a grin on his face, already plotting how to modify the trick for when it was *his* turn to defend against Fenton's company.

#

It was a sheepish crowd that gathered in Third Battalion's officers' briefing room at the close of the day. Edvard was trying not to grin *too* obnoxiously—Bravo Company had made a clean sweep of its assault, taking down Delta Company with only fifty-two casualties of their own.

His defense hadn't been *quite* as clean, turning into a point-blank slug-fest with over a hundred losses in Bravo Company—but had left Fenton's people retreating with over *ninety percent* losses. That made his people the only one of the five companies to win on both assault and defense.

Of course, *then* he'd taken Bravo Company against *Alpha* Company's defenses and been reamed. None of the company commanders gathering around Colonel Silje and Major Brahm had won all of their exercises.

"Let's start with what I hope everyone has realized," Colonel Amanda Silje informed her officers. "Lieutenant Major Hansen's Bravo Company gets drinks on me tonight. Not only did they win two out of their three exercises, which Alpha Company *also* managed, but Lieutenant Major Hansen *also* carried an assault with under fifty percent casualties."

She shook her head.

"Out of six exercises, it appears Delta Company carried *no* victories at all, but we only had two victories by our attackers," she noted. "Alpha carried their attack on Charlie, but at over seventy percent casualties, I can't call that a shining example of Marine courage and strategy.

"We have been and will be launching boarding actions in the face of Terran Commonwealth Marines, people," Silje said sharply. "They are every bit as good, every bit as determined, and every bit as well equipped as we are. To date, we've either had orbital bombardment or surprise on our side, or been boarding stations already battered to hell. We can't rely on that—the day *will* come when we will be hitting Terran Marines who've had ample time to prepare. Marines who'll know we're coming.

"If today was any example, we'll lose over half the battalion when that day comes, and that is *not* acceptable," she snapped. "We have two more days before we hit Huī Xing, people. We're going to run through the same exercises tomorrow. Then the next day, we're going to run two-company assaults. When we reach the target, I want to *know* I'm not going to be writing five hundred letters home!"

"I thought the op plan didn't call for us to be assaulting anything?" Lieutenant Major Fenton, a tall and gangling blond man, asked. "Last I saw was the Battle Group was going to be bouncing around the outside of the system, playing bait—there's not much out there to land Marines on, ma'am."

"We are Castle's *damned* Marines, son," Silje told Fenton, the self-applied nickname for the Corps rolling off fiercely. "We do not prepare for the *ops plan*. We prepare for *war*. Most importantly, we do not *relax* because the ops plan doesn't call for us!"

Fenton looked suitably abashed, though Edvard wasn't entirely unsympathetic. It was easy to plan for the theory that the Marines wouldn't be needed and treat the exercises as a game.

"The plan may change," the Colonel noted. "A battleship could get crippled without being destroyed. A target may present itself outside the gravity well. Any of these things could result in Force Commander Roberts needing the Federation's Marines. We will not be found wanting when the Federation calls, will we?"

Edvard wasn't sure who started the wolf howl in reply, but even a handful of Marines could fill the briefing room if they needed to.

22:15 March 31, 2736 ESMDT
DSC-078 Avalon, *CAG's Office*

It was late in the ship's day when Michael Stanford dropped into his chair, a summary of the day's exercises running through his implant as he opened the beer he'd snagged from the mess on the way over.

The new starfighter flight crews were working out better than he'd allowed himself to hope. That he'd been able to poach complete squadrons helped, a lot. He'd merged them under his Epsilon Wing's Wing Commander Lei Nguyen.

He'd actually had *more* problems with the reorganized squadrons for his other two hundred crews. Only a handful of his squadrons had lost more than one starfighter at Frihet, but he'd been forced to dissolve most of those more-understrength squadrons to fill in the rest of his formations.

The members of the dissolved squadrons were less than happy, especially as that had left three Flight Commanders leading sections instead of squadrons. He'd personally talked to all three of them, but their discontent was showing in their flying.

It took him a moment to notice the flashing icon of a personal message. His implant was set up to only notify him of those at certain times and places—his office after about twenty hundred hours was on that list.

He hit a mental command, opening the message from Kelly.

"Hey, lover," she greeted him. "Busy tonight, but I wanted to send you a quick note. Scuttlebutt is drying up *hard* around Fourth and Seventh Fleet's ops, which makes me worry. When things are this quiet, I always wonder if it means something's gone wrong.

"*Last* time scuttlebutt went silent on *Avalon*, rumor says an Admiral ended up in a cell," she said quietly. "I'm hoping things are running a bit smoother this time! Hope to be able to talk to you live soon. Love you!"

With a smile of his own, he leaned back in his chair and activated the tiny camera hidden in his wall for just this person.

"Hi, Kelly," he greeted her. "You know I can't tell you anything about Seventh Fleet's ops. I'm surprised the rumor mill has much of *anything* about the Alliance's offensives, though I'll confess I've learned to never underestimate it.

"It's been...rough," he admitted. "I think I can say that much. But things are holding together. The Commonwealth knows we're coming now, though. The next few ops are going to be hard. But...we've got Roberts—the Stellar Fox himself—and the Terrans don't.

"I don't put much stock in the exaggerations the media sells as news," he told his girlfriend, "but I *watched* Kyle earn that name. Things may not go *our* way, but I'm betting Kyle makes sure they don't go the Commonwealth's way, either.

"How can they, after all?" he finished with a grin. "*I'm* here to execute whatever crazy plan he comes up with!"

#

Michael wasn't entirely surprised to find the flight deck wasn't empty when he wandered through it, making one final check before he slept. There were always some of his people, often under Olivia Kalers' own guidance, checking over starfighters and equipment, even in the inviolable sanctuary of warped space.

He *was* surprised to find it empty other than Force Commander Kyle Roberts.

Avalon's Captain, a vastly larger man than Michael's own slight frame, was studying the plaque where the names of the flight crews who'd died aboard *this Avalon* had been carved. There were other places those names were recorded—notably, they'd been carved onto the obelisk in the atrium that had been transferred from every vessel that had ever born the name *Avalon* in the Federation's service—but this was the one the Space Force kept for their own.

There wasn't much difference between Navy and Space Force uniforms in the Federation's military. Both wore the same self-sealing shipsuit, a one-piece garment that passed for slacks and a turtleneck at a moderate distance, with a uniform jacket. Roberts' shipsuit was piped in gold versus Michael's blue—but the Force Commander had worn the same blue once upon a time.

"Kyle," Michael announced his arrival. "Wasn't expecting to find you here."

"It's one of the quieter places on the ship at this time of night," Roberts replied. "Always used to come down and look at the plaque when I was CAG. Old *Avalon* didn't have anyone who'd died under my command until I wasn't CAG anymore. *Alamo* did."

Michael nodded. Roberts had first made his reputation salvaging a boarding operation gone *very* wrong on the pirated transport liner *Ansem Gulf*. He'd seen half of his Wing shot apart around him before he'd taken command—and lost people after that as well.

He'd seen more combat action before the war than Michael had—but now, Michael had lost more starfighters and flight crew under his direct command than Roberts had as CAG.

All of *Michael's* losses were still *Roberts'* losses, though.

"I should have seen a better solution," the Force Commander said quietly. "I didn't expect it to go so wrong."

"You told me yourself: there *was* no better solution," Michael pointed out. "We can't carry every victory without losses. We won't have a clever trick for every engagement, every clash. I'd rather bring all my people home," he admitted, "but the only way to do that is not to fight."

"That's not what the Federation pays us for," Roberts agreed. "I just feel I owed them something...*more*."

"I know," the CAG agreed. "Like we should have done better. Our jobs."

Roberts shook his head, glancing back at the smaller starfighter pilot with a smile.

"Shouldn't be dumping this on you," he admitted. "Bad for morale for people to see the Force Commander get all weepy."

"You may be my boss," Michael told him, "but you're also my *friend*. I heard nothing, saw nothing. Only the Stellar Fox preparing for war."

Roberts laughed.

"Don't be ridiculous," he replied. "I'm no legend. Just lucky."

"I'll take that luck, then," the CAG answered. "I don't care if you're lucky or good, Kyle; you've brought us this far and I don't expect that to change. We chose our path when we put on these uniforms. I won't pretend I like losing good people. I don't. But..."

"I will not leave these worlds under the heel of Terra," Roberts promised him. "I won't sacrifice our people in vain, either, but I will *not* bow to the Commonwealth's Unity."

"That's the point, isn't it? They believe this is right." Michael gestured around them. "That the cost of war is worth it, because Unity is better for us."

"Our Senate and our allies disagree," the Force Commander told him. "As do I. They'll choke on their Unity before this is done."

"I'd drink to that," Michael agreed, "but I finished my beer in my office."

"You've seen my stash," *Avalon*'s captain replied. "My office?"

CHAPTER 29

Huī Xing System
12:10 April 2, 2736 Earth Standard Meridian Date/Time
DSC-078 Avalon, *Bridge*

Battle Group Avalon erupted into normal space once again, the unavoidable blue corona of the starships' emergence announcing their presence to any with the eyes to see.

Inevitably, *someone* had to have those eyes—and the Alliance crews needed to know who.

Kyle waited patiently as Xue and Anderson ran over the data, correlating with the feeds from the other eight ships in the battle group. The logistics freighters' sensors weren't worth much, but even they were another pair of data points to feed into the analysis.

"Where exactly are we?" he asked Pendez.

"Where I told you we'd be," his navigator replied. "Exactly twenty-nine million kilometers away from Xin—roughly one point six light-minutes, as requested. Battle Group is closing positions to formation Alpha-One as previously instructed."

He nodded his thanks. Alpha-One was a very simple formation—an oblong box with the four warships at the front and the five transports behind.

"What is Xin's gravity well?" he asked.

"Twenty million kilometers," Pendez replied crisply. "She's a big, heavy rock—I'd hate to live there. You want to watch this, though," she noted, marking a second, larger sphere in Kyle's implant map. "Goudeshijie"—roughly, "Dog World" in English—"is Huī Xing's fifth planet, and she's aligned with Xin right now. Since Goudeshijie is a super-Jupiter with a full astronomical unit of gravity well deep enough to stop us going to Alcubierre, the unsafe zones intersect right now."

"We're staying well away from Goudeshijie's gravity well, right?" he asked.

"You said to stay where we could jump clear, so yes," she told him. "You just need to be aware that we don't have the freedom to maneuver we normally would near a habitable world."

He nodded. Habitable worlds were usually well clear of other gravity wells significant enough to prevent Alcubierre-Stetson drive use. The super-Jupiter barely seven and a half light-minutes away had to be an incredible sight from the surface—assuming you got past the over-half-again Earth gravity long enough to look *up*, anyway.

"All right, sir," Anderson addressed him over the link from Secondary Control. Kyle stood and crossed to the tactical section. Presumably, their analysis was done. The pale, redheaded XO met his gaze over Xue's screen and nodded calmly before continuing.

"We have good news, bad news, and 'well, shit' news," he said bluntly.

"Lay it out, Commander," Kyle ordered.

"The *bad* news is that the logistics depot in orbit is intact and clearly in use by the Commonwealth," Anderson said bluntly. "I'm also reading eight *Zion*-class platforms intermingled with the storage stations and a pair of *Assassin*-class battlecruisers.

"The *good* news is that they didn't put in heavy fixed defenses because the nodal fleet is supposed to *be* here. There are fighter bases and the two battlecruisers, but no missile satellites we're picking up."

That *was* good news. Eight Zions and two Assassins was still four hundred and sixty starfighters—a hundred and twenty or so more than his Battle Group carried—but the Assassins were outclassed by his own warships and the Scimitars were outclassed by his starfighters. The defenders were out of their league and almost certainly calling for help right now.

Exactly according to plan.

"What's the 'well, shit' news?" he asked.

"Taking the platforms intact means they took prisoners here," Xue answered for the tactical department. "Their victories across the sector meant they've taken a *lot* of prisoners, and we haven't seen many on the worlds we've taken so far...

"But there's a cluster of ten storage platforms in a polar orbit flashing a Tau Ceti Accords prisoner-of-war camp identifier code. They're *Commonwealth* stations, added to the logistics depot after the system fell," she noted. "Assuming they're complying with the Accords, they probably have about ten thousand prisoners on each platform."

The Tau Ceti Accords were the modern "rules of war," a replacement for the Geneva Conventions heavily supported by the Commonwealth. It would be...very out of character for Terrans to break those rules.

Potentially a *hundred thousand* prisoners of war. The crews of twenty starships. Thirty thousand starfighters. A dozen logistics depots like the one the Alliance had set up here at Huĭ Xing.

A hundred thousand people captured and imprisoned by Terra, in need of rescue. Deep inside a gravity well that his entering could put his entire battle group in danger.

"Well, shit."

#

"Take us onto our planned course," Kyle ordered Pendez. "Let's see if we can lure those cruisers out."

He also needed time to think, and the long, arcing course around Xin would buy him that. They were inside capital missile range, but it would be literally *days* before even the Terran starfighters could bring Seven-Two into range unless Kyle maneuvered to meet them.

Doing so would risk bringing him into the gravity well, entirely against his orders.

On the other hand, his three-day timer didn't start until the Terrans' nodal fleet had arrived. Allowing the two battlecruisers still in Xin orbit to meet up with the other eight warships swanning around somewhere was dangerous, both for Kyle and for Seventh Fleet's plan to lure the Terrans into a trap.

"Xue." He called his tactical officer over. "I want you to set up a three-salvo time-on-target strike on those battlecruisers. They'll see it coming, but I want them jumpy. I need them to come out after us."

Running the numbers in his implant, he could tell that it would take two thirds of the Jackhammer missiles' hour-long flight endurance to reach the Terran ships. The hundred and eleven missiles he was planning on hitting them with would be a serious threat to the two cruisers—except that the Zions' fighters would make short work of them.

The point was to force the cruisers to come out with the starfighters. If they remained in orbit, he could throw ever-heavier salvos until either Seven-Two ran out of ammunition or the Terrans ran out of starfighters.

Since both he and the Terran commander knew the latter would probably happen first, the only way the Commonwealth ships had a chance of surviving this encounter was to close with Seven-Two. If they eliminated *Sledgehammer* with missiles or starfighters, the two battlecruisers would at least have a chance of getting into their own positron lance range of Kyle's ships.

In roughly four days, if he didn't turn to face them.

He watched the missiles blast into space, the accelerations of the first two salvos adjusted ever so slightly to account for their longer flight times. The cruisers were still waiting in orbit, but the fighters were starting to deploy as their Q-probes drew closer, compressing the time delay before Kyle saw their actions.

"Anderson," he said softly over the channel to secondary control. "Do we have any data on where their fleet is?"

Presumably, the nodal fleet had been notified by Q-Com now. How quickly they could get to him—how large his safety margin was—depended on *where* they were right now.

"They left Zahn on the twenty-seventh," his XO replied. "About twelve hours before we left Frihet. All we can say for sure is we know that they didn't go to Hammerveldt—they'd be there by now." He paused. "Best guess is they headed for Cora," he said grimly. "They would only have just known we'd taken Frihet, and may well have known Cora was the most heavily defended."

Kyle nodded. If nothing else, they would know that he had taken the logistics ship somewhat intact. The Captain would have informed them via Q-Com that he was being boarded. It would be a safe assumption that a significant portion of the defenses aboard the ship now defended Cora—though the Terrans probably wouldn't know that his Marines had irreparably broken the Alcubierre drive taking the ship.

"What's intel's opinion on that?" he asked, his gaze back on the icons of the prisoner of war stations.

"That's *their* guess," his executive officer told him dryly. "After the cluster that was their original estimates, they're giving us probabilities now. They figure a sixty percent chance the Terrans are on their way to Cora, q thirty-five percent they're headed to Frihet, and a five percent chance they *are* heading to Hammerveldt and either dropped out early or stepped down their acceleration for some reason we don't know."

"So, no matter what, the closest intel thinks they are is nine days behind us?" Kyle murmured, a smile settling onto his face.

"I'm *told* there is no logical reason for them to do anything except complete their retaliation sweep in one pass," Anderson replied.

"It's what *I* would do," the Force Commander noted cheerfully, "but *I* have a reputation for mindless aggression and shock-and-awe tactics to maintain."

Anderson eyed him askance from the image fed to Kyle's implant.

"Why do I get the feeling we're about to *add* to that reputation?" he asked.

"Because, Fleet Commander Anderson, like any good XO, you're learning to anticipate your Captain," Kyle told him. "If we have nine days, we have time. Tell me: the platforms they've used for the prisoner camps—can our logistics ships hold them?"

Anderson ran the numbers, his eyes acquiring the slightly glazed look of a man consulting his implants, before he blinked and met his Force Commander's eyes.

"They're bigger than the fighter platforms," he said carefully, "but yes. Without having them to hand to test, I can't be certain, but I think we can fit four in each transport—*if* we abandon the fighter platforms and missile satellites."

"And the Marine transports can easily take twenty thousand bodies if we pack them in," Kyle noted. "Commander, I have *no* intention of leaving those POWs behind."

"Sir, I have to point out that there *is* the chance that the nodal fleet left Zahn for here," Anderson told him. "Intel has regarded it as null probability, but that would give us two days at most."

"Then we'd better get on it to be safe, hadn't we?"

13:00 April 2, 2736 ESMDT
SFG-001 Actual—Falcon-C type command starfighter

"They're coming out after us, and I've changed my mind about stringing them along," Roberts' voice announced brightly in Michael's ear.

The CAG sighed. Somehow, he wasn't surprised that the Force Commander had decided *not* to stick to the nice, safe plan that avoided combat.

"We did have a plan, boss," he pointed out. He didn't expect it to change anything. *He'd* seen the Tau Ceti Accords transponders as well. Hell, he wasn't sure he *wanted* to change Roberts' mind.

"We did," Roberts acknowledged. "But that plan didn't call for leaving a *hundred thousand* Alliance prisoners in a Commonwealth POW camp, did it?"

"No, it did not," Michael confirmed. Even as he was "arguing" with his senior officer, he'd been collating information on the status of his wings—all in space, following the battle group along at a sedate one hundred gravities. "What would you like us to do, sir?"

"Fifteen minutes to missile contact," the Force Commander noted. "They've wrapped enough starfighters around themselves as they've come after us that I don't expect much from that, but it should ablate their starfighter strength. Their missiles will hit you not long after, and they'll keep throwing them at us until they run out. Twenty-eight missile salvos aren't much of a threat, but for your own safety, you'll want to shoot down any that get near you.

"We'll be launching new salvos of our own shortly to cover your way in," Roberts continued. "I want you on your way ASAP—we'll be right behind you." He paused. "We'll be firing ten salvos of missiles, but I can't risk more than that. Diving in this deep, we face the risk of having to fight our way out, and I don't know if we'll have time to replenish our magazines."

For every actual missile stored in Battle Group Seven-Two's magazines, they had the parts they couldn't manufacture on site— mostly the mass manipulators—for another five. Given access to the average nickel-iron asteroid, *Avalon* alone could replenish the entire Battle Group's munitions in about three days.

"It's down to the starfighters this time," Roberts warned him. "I don't expect our missiles to do more than take out some of *their* starfighters."

"It's always down to the starfighters," Michael pointed out. "That's why we build carriers. A few hundred Scimitars and a pair of last-gen ships? We'll handle them for you, boss."

Avalon's Captain laughed.

"The Navy is humble enough that I forget that all starfighter crews are as arrogant as I was," he replied. "We're not certain, but it looks like both of those cruisers have had their deflectors upgraded. You'll have less than half the lance range you used to have against them."

"We'll deal," Michael replied. Missiles might be the main killer of a starfighter strike, but positron lances...positron lances were the finishers. If the battlecruisers survived his missile salvo and he had to close to sixty thousand kilometers to use his lances, that was going to hurt.

"We're turning and opening fire in sixty seconds," Roberts told him. "Are you ready to deploy?"

Vice Commodore Michael Stanford was a starfighter pilot, with an implant interface bandwidth capable of piloting a starfighter, coordinating a three-hundred-plus ship formation, and writing fiction simultaneously. He'd spent the entire conversation with Kyle Roberts passing orders and checking over his own ship.

"We are ready to deploy."

#

It didn't take the Terrans long to respond to Seven-Two turning toward them. Within a minute of Michael's fighters launching away from the Battle Group, the Terran starfighters did the same thing. Four hundred plus Scimitars could stop the hundred-missile stacked salvos *Avalon* and her companions had launched at the battlecruisers, but they wouldn't suffice against the over *twelve* hundred missiles the starfighters could launch.

Coming out to meet him made *them* the targets of those missiles. The risk on the starfighters went up dramatically, but the risk to the star*ships* went down equally dramatically. It was an exchange every starfighter pilot, gunner, and engineer knew instinctually, one they effectively agreed to when they put on the uniform of any starfighter force in the galaxy.

Michael mentally saluted their courage and then started assessing times and distances. There were still a little over ten minutes until the first missile salvo would intersect the starfighters—he dropped a mental note to Lieutenant Commander Xue to issue new targeting orders to those missiles. They were unlikely to get past the starfighter screen in the first place, but they could take out a few of the Scimitars if they tried.

More missiles were flying past his starfighters as they closed with the enemy. At minimum cycle time, it took less than four minutes for the ten salvos Roberts had promised to be launched—and not a lot more time for them to pass the starfighter formation. A Jackhammer capital ship missile had twice the acceleration of a Falcon or Templar.

The deadliest part of the entire engagement would be when the starfighters reached their own missile range of the Scimitars. The Commonwealth's Scimitars had inferior positron lances, inferior engines and inferior ECM...but their Javelins were just as deadly as the

Alliance's Starfires, and they would be launching almost five hundred more of them at Michael's people.

His fighter groups could *probably* handle it and come out mostly intact, but he'd be happier if the capital ship missiles took out, oh, half of the Terran ships.

The new salvos would start hitting roughly fifteen minutes after the original salvo intercepted the fighters, four minutes before the two starfighter formations ranged on each other. His squadrons would be launching, in fact, just as the last fifty-seven missile salvo from Battle Group Seven-Two struck home.

He opened a channel to his Wing Commanders, pulling in the two Phoenix Sub-Colonels as well.

"I'm not seeing a lot of clever options beyond riding the Navy's fire straight down the bastards' throats," he told them. "I'm open to ideas to keep us alive past the next, oh, twenty-five minutes."

"I had a thought," Wing Commander Rokos replied after a long moment. "I don't know if it's a *clever* thought," the big pilot continued, "but...we have all of this ECM. We can fool their missiles, lure them away, confuse the hell out of them. So, why don't we just, well, make a hole and lead the missiles into it?"

Michael thought about it.

"It's not a trick we could do twice," Sub-Colonel Sherry Wills said slowly. "They'll angle Q-probes in for closer looks in the future."

"But the nearest Q-probes right now are half a million klicks away," Wing Commander Nguyen pointed out. "If we start gaming the ECM *now* and open that hole..."

"Worst-case scenario, it doesn't *help*," Wills noted. "We couldn't spread out enough to remove mutual support or it won't look realistic to them."

"All right, Russell," Michael finally answered. "Let's try your donut hole. You have about six minutes to run your numbers by me."

That gave the Wing Commander until the first missile salvo hit to have an actual plan.

#

It took Rokos less than *three* minutes to have the numbers together—and the numbers looked good.

By reducing the safety distances between the starfighters by roughly five percent, the Wing Commander's design opened up a five-thousand-kilometer-wide hole through the heart of the Alliance fighter formation. Using the ECM drones and projectors available to the Alliance, they promptly filled that gap with phantoms—what *appeared* to be starfighters but were, at most, expendable remotes.

And then a careful tuning of the jammers and projectors across the formation would make those remotes ever so slightly an easier target than the rest of the formation. That was where the *art* versus the *science* of electronic warfare came into play—too much easier a target, and the humans in the loop on the other side would realize something was strange. Not *enough* easier a target, and the effort would be wasted.

Studying the plan, Michael wasn't surprised to see that Rokos appeared to have got it *just* right. The Wing Commander had always seemed to have just the right touch with the Falcons' ECM systems. Even knowing what they'd set out to do, Michael was barely able to pick out the gap they were trying to lure the Commonwealth missiles into.

Only time would tell, though—and that was passing quickly.

"Flip it to everyone," he ordered the Wing Commander. "Execute immediately—let's pull a curtain over ourselves."

For a moment, even *his* screens dissolved into static as the squadrons around him brought their jamming online. Then the datalinks from the starfighters reconnected, feeding him the locations of his own ships. The networked computers of his squadrons and their motherships resolved the locations of the starfighters and the drones, showing the ships falling into their designated locations in Rokos's plan.

No starfighter was ever on a constant course; even this far away from the enemy, their formation was a chaotic swirl of spirals and side-jets, designed to throw off missiles and beams at long ranges. The main positron lances of a battlecruiser like the Assassin, after all, could punch through a Falcon's deflectors at six light-seconds.

They couldn't *hit* a starfighter at that range—unless the starfighters were being fat and lazy. So, pilots didn't *ever* let themselves get complacent.

As the Alliance missiles came crashing down on the Terran formation, it was promptly clear that those pilots had learned the same lessons as Michael's people. All the Scimitars were moving, dodging around the missiles' paths and producing firing angles for their positron lances and defense lasers.

Against a similar number of fighter missiles, it would have been more than enough—but capital ship missiles were *smart*. The Jackhammers threw out decoys of their own, filled the area around themselves with jamming—and waited until the *last* possible moment to redirect from being targeted on the two battlecruisers to targeting the starfighters.

Smart and tricky missiles or not, the Terrans did a good job of protecting themselves, but capital ship missiles saw through the Scimitars' ECM with ease and drove straight for the starfighters. Only active defenses meant anything—and the Jackhammers had ECM of their own.

Twenty starfighters—two entire squadrons, as the Terrans organized their ships—vanished in balls of antimatter fire. The remaining starfighters were haloed for thirty or forty seconds in the radioactive debris cloud from the deaths of a hundred-plus missiles and twenty starfighters, and then space was calm again.

That was worse than Michael had hoped—and suggested that the ten salvos of fifty-seven missiles apiece now fifteen minutes away from the Terrans might be even less effective than expected.

#

The next missile salvo lived down to Michael's expectations. This time, the Terrans were expecting it to go for the starfighters, and it showed—the Scimitars opened up on the missiles from slightly farther out, accepting lower hit probabilities to allow a greater number of shots per target.

With more than ten starfighters firing on each missile, the odds were against the Alliance Jackhammers. The missiles barely survived long enough to cut the firing window on the second salvo by a few precious seconds.

The second salvo also died well clear of the starfighters but cut a few more seconds off the response time to the third salvo. *Those* missiles got close enough that the explosions of their deaths helped cover the arrival of the *fourth* salvo until it was almost too late.

To Michael's surprise, the Terrans *still* stopped every missile in the fourth before any of the starfighters were hit—but some of the missiles were detonating within mere kilometers of their targets. Several of the Scimitars fell out of formation, no longer accelerating—"soft" kills from the radiation.

There was a small but noticeable drop in the intensity of their sensor output as well. Sensor and jammer emitters had been burnt away by the near misses, rendering the remaining fighters less effective.

The Terran missile salvos had arced farther away from Michael's people, sacrificing flight time to reduce the threat of the starfighters. As opportunities presented themselves, his people were firing on them with lances and lasers, but they were barely taking a tithe of the Terran missiles. Those, Michael concluded grimly, were going to be up to Roberts.

The Alliance's fifth salvo died a bit farther clear of the Scimitars than the fourth, sparing the Terrans further immediate losses, but the sixth and seventh salvos were another series of near misses, sending starfighters spinning off into space—either their crews or their computers dead.

One missile actually *hit* from the eighth salvo, a starfighter vanishing in a one-gigaton ball of antimatter fire. The ninth closed on their heels and Michael smiled coldly. They wouldn't do *much*—but it was almost time for *his* people.

"All right people," Michael said on his all-ships channel. "The Navy is plowing the road for us. Let's follow it and send these bastards to Hell and Starless Void!"

The last seventy-four missiles slammed into the Scimitars' teeth, near misses and direct hits knocking another dozen fighters out of the fight. All told, the thirteen salvos of Navy missiles had destroyed or disabled almost fifty starfighters.

That helped even the odds. Michael was perfectly happy to throw his three hundred and thirty-six seventh-generation starfighters against three hundred and eight *sixth*-generation birds.

The timer hit zero and his people opened fire. Included in Rokos's "donut" strategy was a crisscrossing pattern of missile flights, burying the exact origin of the almost thirteen hundred missiles in a confusing blur of jamming and antimatter rocket trails.

The Scimitars launched moments before his people did, the entire *sky* seeming to disappear in the light of almost sixteen hundred missile trails. Thirty seconds later, both starfighter formations launched again.

That was all Michael could fire—he still needed missiles to engage the battlecruisers. The Terrans apparently had the same logic, as *they* stopped firing after two salvos as well.

"For what we are about to receive, may the Stars make us forever grateful," *someone* prayed on the open channel.

"Save the prayers for later," Michael ordered. "For now—target those missiles. Stay *alive!*"

Every stratagem was already in place. Either their attacks and defenses would work to get them to lance range, or they'd all die. There was nothing the Vice Commodore could do at this point to change the fate of his people.

He could only change the fate of his own starfighter.

The defensive lasers were his gunner's problem. His ECM was his flight engineer's problem, under the plans and strategies already laid out in Rokos's donut strategy. As the pilot, he controlled the ship's position, orientation, and fifty-kiloton-per-second positron lance. The three of them worked together, linked through their neural implants to a level of communication that made them *all* part of the ship itself.

Michael danced the eight-thousand-ton tin can of his starfighter through space, slashing at missiles with his lance—focused in the moment on the survival of his own ship.

Starfighter missiles were orders of magnitude less capable than capital ship missiles—and also orders of magnitude *smaller*. A Jackhammer or Stormwind was two thirds the size and half the mass of a Falcon. A Starfire or Javelin was a thirtieth. What they gave up in capability was worth it for starfighters to be able to launch them in mass salvos.

Four capital ship missiles per starfighter would be instant death to the entire formation. Four starfighter missiles per ship was merely... difficult.

Between his maneuvers, the lance, and the lasers, Michael's own command starfighter took out five missiles. Others didn't do as well. His implant informed him that over seventy percent of the fifteen-hundred-plus missiles fired at his people had been destroyed—but that left over four hundred in terminal mode.

Time ran out and Michael nearly bit his tongue as he watched *hundreds* of missiles slam into the donut hole in the center of their formation, either destroying easily replaceable drones or flashing clean through into deep space, stuttering into darkness as their engines failed.

Only his implants allowed him to assess the losses in the fractions of a second available to him. Thirty-two of his starfighters were gone—in exchange for over *two hundred* of the Scimitars.

Then they were in lance range, the second salvo of missiles howling down on both sides as they flashed towards and interpenetrated. Michael twisted his starfighter across the stars, triggering the positron lance as it crossed targets—watching as the smaller Scimitars were ripped apart under the beams of antimatter, and praying that his people were luckier.

Nine seconds after entering range, the Alliance spacecraft flashed through the debris that *had* been the Terrans' fighter formation. They were clear, and Michael breathed. *He'd* survived, but...

"Check in," he ordered aloud. They had less than three minutes to missile range of the battlecruisers—he had to know what he had left.

The answer rapidly filled his mental screens as each of his Wing Commanders checked in. He winced at the lack of update for *Avalon*'s Epsilon Wing, reaching out for the answer he knew had to be the case.

Wing Commander Lei Nguyen was gone, her command starfighter debris somewhere behind him and the brave young woman who'd served with him since *Avalon* commissioned ashes within it.

The rest of his Wing Commanders were still with him—as were a surprising number of their fighters. The second Terran missile salvo had fared even worse than the first, and the shorter lance range of the Scimitars had spared his people the worst of the dogfight.

He'd lost eighty-six ships and an unknown number of people, faces and names that would haunt his dreams—but for now, he had two hundred and fifty seventh-generation starfighters to command and a pair of battlecruisers to kill.

13:37 April 2, 2736 ESMDT
DSC-078 Avalon, *Bridge*

Kyle watched the debris and static fade from the inevitable storm of radiation and jamming that ensued when starfighters clashed. Q-Com links to the command starfighters told him the status of his people—the starfighters lost, the complete destruction of the Terran starfighters.

The Q-probes around the fight also showed the capital ship missiles launched by the two Commonwealth battlecruisers. While the salvos were of a mere twenty-eight missiles each, the cruisers appeared to have *emptied* their magazines at him. Twenty salvos were still flashing through space, even though ten salvos had smashed themselves on Battle Group Seven-Two's defenses already.

There was still a chance of a lucky shot, but Captain Ainsley had moved *Sledgehammer* out in front, putting the battleship's heavier defenses between the missiles and the biggest target: *Avalon*. With four capital ships' defenses firing on the missile salvos of *two* capital ships, Battle Group Seven-Two seemed safe enough for now.

"Get me a radio channel relayed through the Q-probes at those battlecruisers," Kyle ordered. A moment later, an icon on his screen informed him they were transmitting—though, of course, whether the Terrans were *listening* was an entirely different issue.

"Commonwealth warships," he said calmly, "you are outnumbered and outgunned. We both know what the result of my starfighter strike on your ships will be. I am prepared to accept your surrender and allow your personnel to be interned on Huī Xing.

"This isn't your system," he concluded. "Why die defending it?"

He waited.

"They've received it," Xue told him. "No response."

"Damn," Kyle said mildly. He glanced at the timer. Michael had less than thirty seconds until the geometry of the engagement put his missiles in range.

"Inform the Vice Commodore the Terrans have refused to surrender. He is to destroy those cruisers by whatever means necessary. Once the starfighters have cleared the way, inform Brigadier Hammond he is to secure the orbitals as soon as possible.

"I want to have those prisoners on their way out of this system *yesterday*."

13:39 April 2, 2736 ESMDT
SFG-001 Actual—Falcon-C type command starfighter

Michael shook his head as he acknowledged the message from *Avalon*. Roberts had intimidated *one* second-rate ship into surrender at the start of the war, and so he thought any outclassed Terran force would consider it?

Avalon's CAG had many and lengthy opinions of the Terran Commonwealth Navy and the Terran Commonwealth Starfighter Corps—and of the cause they had lent themselves to the service of—but he did not doubt their courage or their determination.

Which was unfortunate since, like his Force Commander, he would have preferred *not* to kill the ten thousand or so people on the battlecruisers in front of him.

There was no place for regrets in the battle space.

The range dropped below three million kilometers, and his squadrons' relative velocity to the battlecruisers was over eighteen thousand kilometers a second and rising. They would be in range... now.

"Fire!" he snapped.

The order was probably redundant, and most of their salvo was in space before he'd finished speaking. The battlecruisers had no missiles left now. Their big positron lances would start firing any second, but *they* had only a limited chance of hitting his starfighters.

The secondary anti-fighter lances would be in range six seconds before his own people were and five seconds before his missiles hit. Even if he could guarantee his missiles would kill the cruisers, he couldn't pull his people aside at a rate that would keep them out of the range of those seventy-kiloton-a-second guns.

His ships' deflectors were *much* weaker than those mounted on the battlecruisers, but the starfighters only needed to deflect the electromagnetically charged positron beams a few dozen meters. The battlecruisers' deflectors needed to deflect the starfighters' beams *hundreds* of meters to guarantee a miss.

It was a question of whether his people could dodge and swerve well enough to survive those six seconds—the deadliest seconds a starfighter could face. As Wills had predicted, the Commonwealth had brought their Q-probes in closer to make sure they weren't fooled into firing into an area with no starfighters at all.

No tricks left—only the twisted, worming spiral of a starfighter assault.

Michael led his people into it with the grim determination of experience. Too many fights against too many ships, trying to dodge and twist without falling into a pattern a computer—or a gunner with a hunch—would identify.

Seconds ticked by in eternities. Positron lances tore at his fighter wings while defensive laser batteries slashed at his missiles, destroying the one-gigaton weapons by the hundreds.

One of the battlecruisers was a few kilometers ahead of the other, a miniscule difference in space, fractions of a second to the missiles' flight time—fractions of a second that the defenses didn't have. At least a dozen Starfires slammed into that battlecruiser, vaporizing it in a single burst of fury.

The second cruiser had those fractions of a second more. One, maybe two, missiles impacted. A damaging blow—probably crippling, possibly fatal to any but the most armored of ships.

It didn't matter. Michael Stanford's fighters swept over the surviving battlecruiser and *hundreds* of fifty-kiloton-a-second lance strikes ripped the ship to pieces.

CHAPTER 30

Huī Xing System
18:00 April 2, 2736 Earth Standard Meridian Date/Time
AT-032 Chimera *Landing Group, Assault Shuttle Four*

"This is Force Commander Kyle Roberts aboard *Avalon*, commanding Alliance Battle Group Seven-Two, to the Commonwealth forces in the Huī Xing system. This system is now in Alliance control. It is within my capacity to destroy your positions from orbit and vaporize the space stations that remain from beyond your range. I call on you to surrender to prevent further loss of life."

Edvard Hansen listened to the Force Commander's voice through his implants and shrugged at the Gunny.

"Think anyone will *actually* surrender?" he asked Ramirez quietly. It would, if nothing else, make Bravo Company's upcoming assault on one of the prisoner-of-war holding stations easier if they didn't have to *assault* it.

"Doubt it," his senior NCO told him. "They know their fleet is on its way. *I'd* try and hold 'til it got here."

"Yeah," Edvard agreed. "Me too. A man can hope, though."

His implant showed him the five assault shuttles carrying Third Battalion arrayed around *Chimera* itself. This wasn't a high-speed assault, the shuttles screaming ahead of the assault transport at five hundred gravities.

The space around the prisoner-of-war holding stations had been seeded with short-range defensive satellites. Designed to shoot down missiles and debris, they were normally a commitment to the *protection* of the prisoners, but they'd also do a solid number on assault shuttles.

Chimera and *Manticore*, on the other hand, had the meters-thick ferro-carbon ceramic of warships. They led the way into the defensive satellites, their armor shrugging aside the lasers even as *their* lasers and light positron lances swept the satellites away.

Ten assault shuttles—one per holding station—followed them. Edvard, like the other company commanders, kept a careful eye on the assault transports' computers' assessment of the safety of the zone around the holding camps.

None of the shuttles waited for the area to be perfectly clear. As soon as the threat level dropped below an estimated forty percent chance of a hit, all ten ships lunged to the attack simultaneously.

"Let's go get our people," Edvard told his company as the shuttle engines blazed to life beneath him.

The howled response vibrated the shuttle as much as her rockets did.

#

Assault Shuttle *Chimera*-Four was one of the unlucky ones. Edvard found himself locking his armor's magnetics to the side of the little ship as she rocked under repeated laser hits.

The assault shuttle wasn't *unarmored*, per se. Her defenses paled into insignificance against her mothership but were more than capable of standing off a few laser strikes. Flying into an unreduced set of defensive laser satellites would have seen her ripped to shreds by hundreds or even thousands of hits.

The remaining satellites simply made the ride a little more jarring. The shuttle shed the handful of strikes, then slammed Bravo Company into the prisoner holding station the Brigadier's staff had designated "Target Seven."

"They'll be waiting for us," Edvard snapped to his people. "*Move!*"

This time, Delta Platoon had the point of the spear. Armored Federation Marines hit the hole the shuttle had blown through the side of the station with commendable speed, spreading out to cover their brand-new entrance before the Terran Marines responded.

Unfortunately, they weren't the only Marines reacting with commendable speed. Charlie Platoon had only barely begun to move into the corridors of the station when Delta came under fire. Suit-carried battle rifles spat tungsten penetrator rounds *both* ways down the corridor as the Terrans responded to the intrusion.

Edvard regarded the feeds from his Marines for a fraction of a second before making a decision he hated.

"Grenades and advance!" he snapped. "We need a hole, people; *push them!*"

He had to *hope* that any prisoners were deeper into the station, outside the effective range of the hyper-velocity fragmentation grenades. Certainly, the interior bulkheads didn't have the strength to withstand the weapons.

Delta's men were linked to each other through their implants, running a live tactical net that allowed them to see what the others saw and practically read each other's thoughts. Fighting with it was a learned skill, a *hard* skill—but it also meant that when Delta's lieutenant interpreted Edvard's orders as "one man in five grenades the Terrans," there was no confusion as to *which* Marines got to play with explosives.

The Terrans were coming at them from both sides of the corridors, and Delta Platoon sent five grenades flying at each position. Fired from shoulder-mounted launchers, the weapons went farther and faster than they could be thrown—and detonated in the air based on sensors scanning the area around them.

It was hard to be sure how many of the Terrans went down from the grenades, but the weapons opened up enough of a gap—a moment of shock on the part of the Commonwealth Marines, if nothing else—for Delta to charge.

Edvard could only watch through the tactical network as his people went gun-to-gun and bayonet-to-bayonet with the Terran force trying to contain their intrusion. His headquarters section was behind Charlie Platoon in the queue, and even with Delta expanding the beachhead, only one of Charlie's squads was in.

As his people pushed the Terrans back, more of his troops filtered in, turning the momentum. Terran and Federation Marines alike went down, stabbed by monofilament bayonets or shot down by tungsten penetrators.

Then, suddenly, it was over. The survivors of the Terran force withdrew in good order, their own grenades taking down half a dozen of Edvard's troopers who tried to follow.

"They've got to have a fallback position," Ramirez warned the Lieutenant Major. "They probably had platoons spread out through the exterior, but now they can lure us into their main force."

"I know," Edvard said shortly. "Get me floor plans," he snapped. "I want to know where they'll think they can catch us—and I want another route if you can give it to me!"

#

Edvard looked over the plans his headquarters section's information specialist had pulled from the station's computer before the Terrans had locked out this area's computers. Unfortunately, the Commonwealth hadn't just thrown the prisoners into cargo containers in a storage or transfer station. The facility he'd boarded was clearly specifically designed for the purpose to which it had now been turned.

It was the standard disk shape of a major space station on the outside, five hundred meters across and three hundred meters thick. The top eighty meters, and thirty meters in from the exterior on all sides, contained the quarters for the guard contingent, the technical support systems, the power generators, and all the general functional systems of a space station.

Then there was a thirty-meter-wide void inside the station, surrounding a one-hundred-and-thirty-meter-thick disk three hundred and eighty meters across. This was the actual prison, accessed only via two heavily armored columns attaching one side of the prison to the main habitation section of the prison.

Edvard's people were on the far side of the station from those access points, leaving him with the unpleasant option of slogging his way through the series of ambushes and traps the Terrans were even now preparing, to reach either of the ways into the prison.

The command center for the station was in an even more awkward position, in the interior of the station and directly between the two big connectors. Edvard doubted his people could reach the armored capsule at *all*, let alone without crippling losses.

"This place is set up to make our job hell, boss," Ramirez muttered. The Gunny was reviewing the same data. "There's only about four routes we can take to the other side of the station, only the *two* routes to the prison itself, and the command center looks like it's a damned fortress."

"My dear Gunny, I do believe you're thinking far too linearly," the Lieutenant Major said dryly.

"Oh? Do *you* see another solution to this mess?" the Gunny demanded.

"No," Edvard admitted. And it wasn't looking pretty—they'd hit each prison facility with a single company, which, it turned out, meant the defenders actually had him *outnumbered*. On the other hand, the separation of the prison facility meant that the assault transports could hammer the exterior portions of the station with kinetic weapons without worrying about hurting *their* people.

Except, of course, for potentially killing the air, power, lights and other such minor necessities that kept them alive.

"I do," another voice interjected, and Edvard looked over at his Delta Platoon commander. Senior Lieutenant Cruz Machado was the second-ranked of his platoon commanders, one of only two Senior Lieutenants in the company. He was also, unlike the Sherwood-born Lieutenant Major Hansen and Castle-born Gunnery Sergeant Ramirez, spacer-born. A child of one of the massive space stations in the Elpída system that fueled that system's gas-extractor economies, he'd grown *up* on a platform like this.

"The place was designed by planet-born," Machado pointed out. "Everybody's thinking in terms of corridors and defenses and ambushes, but they built the biggest corridor on the station leading straight to the command center."

Linked into the tactical net, Machado drew a simple curving line—it started with a straight line from their current location to the vacuum "moat" guarding the prison, and then arced its course *around* the prison—through the gravity-less vacuum—to intersect with the command center.

"Unless they're *idiots*, they have defenses in the moat," the Senior Lieutenant pointed out. "But we can move the whole company to have line of sight on whatever they throw up. *We're* vulnerable—but so are they."

"And if we take the command center, suddenly those two companies of Terran Marines are on the wrong side of the defenses protecting, oh, the consoles that control *gravity*," Edvard said aloud, awed at how simple the point was when you thought about it from the right direction—a direction very few of the planet-born would think from.

"If this works, Machado, I'm recommending you for your gold circle," he told the platoon commander. "You may have just saved a *lot* of lives."

#

"Fire in the hole!"

The unnecessarily bellowed warning across the company tactical net cut off what Brigadier Hammond was saying, but the tiny image of the 103rd Brigade's commanding General simply gestured for Edvard to attend to his own business.

Explosives flashed, the sound rapidly fading to silence as the air blasted out into the vacuum "inside" the space station. Bravo Platoon was out the hole in moments, weapons tracking the empty darkness as they left the station's artificial gravity field.

"Clear," a voice reported over the network. "About what we expected—no light, no grav, no bad guys."

"Use your armor lights," Edvard ordered. "We've got over half a klick to jet, folks; let's get moving."

A few moments later, he followed his Marines into the void. It was darker than almost anything he'd ever seen, with even the light of the stars cut off by the bulk of the space station that surrounded them.

"Starless Void," he heard Ramirez mutter. "That is *creepy.*"

The Lieutenant Major couldn't disagree. There was a reason a Void without Stars or light was the closest thing the Stellar Spiritualists had to Hell.

"I don't plan on dying in here, Gunny," he replied crisply, talking over a bone-deep fear he couldn't show his subordinates. "Let's move."

Jets on their armored suits responded with practiced ease, moving the Marines through that void. Edvard quickly attached himself to Delta Platoon, dropping a private link to Machado.

"The other companies are skirmishing and holding the line," he told the platoon leader quietly. "If this works, they're going to try and duplicate it."

He *heard* the younger man swallow.

"No pressure, huh?"

"Welcome to the hot seat, son," Edvard told him dryly.

"*Incoming,*" one of the lead Marines snapped. "Jamming and evading—we have seeking missiles launched from the command center's chunk of the hull!"

"Take them out—*hard!*" the company commander snapped, jetting forward with his people.

Smart battle rifles identified the automated turrets and opened fire. Self-propelled armor-piercing rockets flashed across the void, the rocket flashes lighting up the dark spaces. Grenades followed, detonations rippling along the chunk of hull Edvard's computer identified as the command center itself.

All of it occurred in eerie silence, the armor and the weapons identifying the environment and using appropriate munitions. One of Edvard's people flashed red in his tactical display—a victim of the Terran defenses.

And then there was darkness again.

"Targets down," Bravo Platoon's Lieutenant reported. "All turrets disabled. We've done a number on the hull, but it looks the armor shell held. Demolitions forward!"

Edvard landed just behind the demolitions expert, magnetic boots latching his armor suit to the torn-up metal. It looked like the command center had been encased in warship-grade ferro-carbon ceramics.

"Can we pierce this?" he asked the demolitions Sergeant, actually worried for the first time since Machado had given him the plan.

"Oh, Voids yes," the Sergeant replied. "Flashing you an approval request. Gonna need a *lot* of safety radius. Everybody back!"

Edvard knew better than to doubt the expert. He approved the request without even a cursory glance, then jetted off from the metal surface again. It took several moments to clear the flashing orange sphere the sergeant had dropped onto the tactical net.

"Everyone clear?" the Sergeant demanded. She waited for a moment to check, then continued. "Fire in the hole!"

That was the moment when Edvard realized he'd approved the use of positron charges. Pure white fire lit up the interior of the station in a tight circle, forcing his armor to black out his vision to avoid damage to his eyes.

"Go!" he snapped, resolving to have a *word* with the Sergeant later.

He was one of the first through the hole, diving into the command nexus of the space station. The exterior hatches were slamming shut to contain atmosphere loss and people were diving for cover. Shipsuits were sealing, protecting them from the loss of atmosphere—but some of the people were Marines.

They went for guns.

The tactical net tagged them, lighting up the soldiers with weapons in bright red. Edvard tracked across the room with his battle rifle, the smart weapon linking with his implant and firing as it aligned on each of the armed Marines.

They needed the command center intact, and that tactical data was loaded into the weapon. Low-velocity stun rounds spat from the barrel, self-calibrating shock weapons that punched through lightly armored shipsuits to deliver incapacitating charges.

"Surrender!" he bellowed. "Drop your weapons."

There was enough air to carry the order, and the chaos slowed—and stopped. The handful of red icons dimmed as they dropped their weapons and rose above consoles, hands above their heads.

"Get me an emergency airlock on that hole," he ordered to his people. "Then get the information team in here. I want control of this station *now*."

CHAPTER 31

Huī Xing System
01:30 April 3, 2736 Earth Standard Meridian Date/Time
Prison Platform Huī Xing—Lambda

Edvard inched down the corridor connecting to the prison platform very, *very* carefully. The Marines aboard had surrendered once his people had started turning their local gravity up on them—stations like this one were designed with the ability to produce fifteen gees for a limited period for a *reason*. Even powered armor couldn't do much more than keep the wearer alive in those conditions.

That didn't mean there weren't any traps or tricks hidden in the accessway to the prison camp. His information people assured him they were in control of the automated systems, but he *knew* Marines.

Finally, the point woman in Alpha Platoon—no one would have let him take this trip *alone*, even if he was that stupid—signaled the all clear, and he walked forward to join her at the hatch sealing off the prison camp itself. With only two accesses that didn't lead straight to vacuum, the designers of the platform had lavished those connections with security and defenses.

"Open it up, Ramirez," he ordered the Gunny—currently in charge, despite his protests, of the station's command center.

"Is it too late to remind you that point is *not* the company's commander's job?" his senior noncom asked.

"Point may not be, but coordinating with the prisoners themselves is," Edvard replied. "You're sure there are no guards inside?"

"They do random sweeps, but otherwise, the guards only enter the actual prison camp to deliver food or if there's an emergency," Ramirez told him. "I guess with the prisoners cut off from everything by thirty meters of hard vacuum, they figure they can mostly leave them to their own devices. Though, believe me, everything—and I do mean *everything*—is monitored."

"Any sign they know we're coming?"

"None. How would they?" the Gunny asked. "Opening the hatch now," he continued. "Good luck, sir."

"Thanks, Gunny," Edvard muttered, standing back while the massive metal hatch slowly and noisily retracted.

Alpha Platoon's point squad swept in, weapons at the ready as they surveyed the immediate perimeter. Another all clear signal, and the Lieutenant Major followed his people into the actual prison camp part of the station.

It was better than he'd been expecting. The access tunnel opened into an open area roughly a hundred meters long by fifty wide, with actual greenery in it. Mostly the space was a gathering and sports area, but there were little clusters of bushes providing natural oxygen.

Utilitarian-looking corridors stretched off from that meeting area, presumably leading to mess halls, gyms, and sleeping rooms. He understood most of the facilities to be cramped but serviceable—there were *ten thousand* people in the disk he stood in, after all.

Only a few dozen people were in the area, though, keeping an apparently lazy eye on his armored Marines.

"Wait, you're not Terrans," someone suddenly exclaimed. "Who *are* you?"

"I am Lieutenant Major Edvard Hansen of the Castle Federation Marine Corps," Edvard introduced himself to the speaker, a hard-bodied woman he was *certain* was a Marine or Special Ops trooper from somewhere. "My understanding is that you are permitted to organize yourselves—I need to speak to the senior officer. This facility is now under Alliance control."

She blinked at him like he was speaking a strange language, then a giant grin split her face.

"Of course, sir," she replied, coming to perfect attention and saluting crisply. "Sergeant Major Amanda Harding, Hessian Space Marines, sir! The Brigadier is going to be happy to see *you*."

"Lead the way, Sergeant Major," he told her. "I look forward to meeting them too."

02:00 April 3, 2736 ESMDT
DSC-078 Avalon, *Bridge*

In just over fourteen hours, Battle Group Seven-Two had entered the Huī Xing system, destroyed two Commonwealth battlecruisers, and secured ten prison platforms. Apparently, a platoon commander had spotted a weakness in the space stations, one that wasn't present unless you'd already boarded them but which made taking control of the facilities surprisingly straightforward.

That control had forced the Terrans to surrender, which meant that Force Commander Kyle Roberts now had the best part of a Commonwealth Marine *Division* he needed to find somewhere to put. So far, they were being transferred into empty cargo containers in civilian transfer stations.

Unlike the Terrans, he didn't have custom-built platforms to load them into—and he was taking the *Terrans'* custom-built platforms with him.

"How long are we looking at to load the platforms into the freighters?" he asked. This deep inside Xin's gravity well, it would take his fleet over an hour to reach space where they could bring up their Alcubierre-Stetson drives and escape. Given that his orders had been to stay *outside* the gravity well, that was making him twitchy.

"They're still assessing *how* they're going to fit them in," Anderson told him quietly. "It's going to take them twelve hours just to offload what they're already carrying. I'm assuming we want the satellites dropped into orbit in autonomous mode?"

"Yeah," Kyle agreed. "We're going to have to run, but let's not leave Xin entirely in their hands."

"Best guess, yeah..." His XO added numbers in his head. "Twelve hours to offload the fighter platforms and missile satellites. We'll have to use starfighters to position them, but I think the CAG's people should be down for that.

"After that, seven hours per platform to load into the transport," the other man continued. "If everything goes *exactly* to schedule, we'll be clear to move at eleven hundred hours tomorrow."

"What about the prisoners we're moving onto the Marine ships?" Kyle asked.

"That's why we'll need the fighters to place the missile platforms," Anderson replied grimly. "I'm commandeering *every* shuttle in the battle group to move people from Platforms Nine and Ten," — Kyle's implant cooperatively highlighted the two space stations in questions— "over to the three assault transports. *That* is going to take twenty-six hours. They'll be done before the other eight platforms are loaded into the transports."

Kyle had updated timers on his mental displays as Anderson spoke, and sighed. "If we're wrong about where they left Zahn for, we're going to cut this damned tight," he warned his XO. "A seven-day variance in possible enemy arrival times makes me itch."

"Intel says the near-term arrival is a low-order probability," his XO replied.

"Yes, and Intel told us that they'd divided their fleet into nicely digestible three-ship packets,' *Avalon*'s Captain pointed out. "We need to plan for worst-case. Get with Commander Pendez," he ordered. "I want full high-speed evasion courses worked out for all likely arrival vectors of their fleet.

"I'll freely admit I've stuck our heads in the bear trap, James. Make sure we know our way out."

A moment later, the current com officer flashed Kyle a warning note. The Force Commander looked away from Anderson to meet the young woman's gaze and nodded to her.

"What is it?" he asked.

"We're being pinged by someone on the planet," she told him. "It's from a relay transmitter in one of the mountain ranges—I could trace the original source if you want."

"That won't be necessary, Lieutenant," Kyle said. "It appears the resistance is reaching out to us. I'll take it in my office."

It wouldn't do to disappoint a planetary government-in-hiding in public, after all.

#

Kyle dropped into his chair, took half a moment to make sure he was in front of the big commissioning seal on the wall behind him, and then accepted the transmission.

"This is Force Commander Kyle Roberts, Castle Federation Space Navy. To whom am I speaking?" he asked calmly.

It took a moment for his response to filter through whatever relays the Xin had set up and garner a reply of its own. Several seconds after his transmission went out, his implant informed him a proper communication channel had been established, and the image of a tall Asian woman appeared on his wallscreen.

"I am Deputy Premier Wen Lau of the Republic of Huī Xing," she told him. "We have noted the destruction of Commonwealth *space* forces in this system, and I am forced to ask what your intentions with regards to *Xin* are."

There was still an occupation garrison, a full division strong, scattered across Xin's surface.

"The occupation force has not responded to my summons for them to surrender," Kyle told her. "I do not have the capability at this time to launch a ground assault—we are expecting a significant Commonwealth force to arrive in system in under forty-eight hours."

"Twenty-Third Fleet, yes," Wen Lau confirmed. Kyle made a mental note of the Terran force's name—it would help to have a *name* rather than constantly referring to it as "the nodal fleet." "Do you intend to do *nothing*, then, Force Commander? Why are you even here?"

"The exact details of my mission are classified," Kyle warned her. Tightbeam transmissions with relays were as secure as anything short of a Q-Com link could be, but he had no idea how large Wen's staff was. *She* was on his list of contacts on Xin, but even that didn't mean she hadn't been compromised herself.

"We are in the process of rescuing the prisoners held in orbit," he continued. "I *hope* that by not engaging the surface forces, I can minimize the chance of retaliation once the—Twenty-Third Fleet, you said?—returns."

She blinked, a momentary gesture that made Kyle think he'd hit a nerve, then continued in a steady voice.

"I see your logic, Force Commander. Do you have any listing of the prisoners?" she asked, the steadiness wavering. "My...wife was a guardship commander in our system fleet. I do not even know if she survived."

"We are extracting that from the Terrans' computers as we speak," he told her. "I will have my people forward it to you as soon as we have a complete list of Huī Xing prisoners. If your wife is alive, we will take her safely from this system with the rest of the prisoners.

"However, I have no choice but to ask you to refrain from action on the surface. If we keep our activities in orbit and you do not attack the garrison on the surface, you should be safe from Commonwealth retaliation."

The Deputy Premier sighed and bowed her head.

"I understand," she confessed. "I will pass your suggestions on to the Premier with my agreement. We will keep our heads down—I can only hope you will be back soon."

"I can make no promises," Kyle told her. "All I can say is 'That's classified.'"

And hopefully, she would understand that meant they would be back sooner rather than later. If Via Somnia fell, Huī Xing would soon be free.

"Just what did you *feed* your boyfriend before we sent him off to be the distraction?" Rear Admiral Alstairs asked Mira sourly. "I was under the impression his reputation was *inflated.*"

Mira sighed, glancing at the wallscreen in Alstairs' office that showed the tactical situation in Huī Xing. The most notable aspects of that display were the faded red intersecting spheres around Xin and Goudeshijie marking the gravity well in which Battle Group Seven-Two couldn't go faster than light—and the green icons of said Battle Group deep inside those spheres.

"Would you have done differently?" she asked quietly, tapping the *other* set of green icons—the ten red-ringed green disks representing the holding facilities. "They're still getting a final count on how many people are aboard those stations, but Kyle's last update had it at over ninety *thousand* prisoners.

"Would you really have wanted us to stand by and leave those people in imprisonment?"

Alstairs sighed, her gaze following Mira's tap.

"No," she admitted. "But I don't *trust* intel's assessment of where this Twenty-Third Fleet was headed—if I did, we'd be hitting Via Somnia as soon as we could get there, not stopping a light-month out to wait and see what happens in Huī Xing."

"I doubt Kyle does either," Mira reminded the Admiral. "If they have nine days—eight now, at best—there's be no need for the level of rush his people are doing. With a week, Seven-Two could secure the surface and help the local government dig in, give the Terrans even more reasons to bypass Huī Xing and meet us at Via Somnia."

The Admiral gave a command through her implant, and the display zoomed in on Seven-Two's icons. Shuttles were *swarming* over two of the platforms, even as the larger parasite tugs worked to move the fighter platforms the Alliance had gone to so much expense to deliver out of the logistics platforms.

"I already gave him permission to blow the Citadels," she admitted. "If the Terrans take a week to show up, we're going to look damned foolish. They're cheaper than starships, but..."

"And if the Terrans show up tomorrow, ditching those stations may be the only thing that allows Kyle to pull off the largest prisoner rescue in the last eighty or ninety years," Mira pointed out. "I think everyone will call that worth it."

"I hope so," Alstairs told her. "This is one of those cases where I'm glad I sent Kyle, *because* he didn't follow his orders to the letter, and furious he didn't follow his orders," she admitted with a chuckle. "But if this goes wrong, history will remember him as the man who disobeyed orders and got his battle group destroyed."

"I hope it doesn't come to that," Mira said with a shiver. Her relationship with Kyle was still...formative. They hadn't had much time together since she'd left *Avalon* for *Camerone*, and before then, they'd both been trying hard to deny their interest in each other.

She needed the big man to survive long enough for them to sort out just *what* they had between them.

"So do I," the Admiral agreed. "My reasons are notably less personal," she continued dryly, "but I'd like very much if this plan works out with both Battle Group Avalon *and* Kyle Roberts intact."

CHAPTER 32

Huī Xing System
15:00 April 3, 2736 Earth Standard Meridian Date/Time
DSC-078 Avalon, *Captain's Office*

"So, with a day to think on it, would you do anything differently?" Mira asked Kyle quietly.

He shook his head, smiling at her.

"No," he told her. "The risk might be making my shoulders itch, but I couldn't stand by and leave those prisoners behind."

"Have you even *spoken* to any of them?" his lover asked.

He laughed.

"Now that you mention it, no," he admitted. "I've had a few messages relayed through the Marines, but I haven't spoken to any of them directly. Ninety-six thousand people," he said in an awed voice with a shrug. "But I can't go over there, and it's not like we can divert a shuttle to bring anyone over here just to satisfy my curiosity. I have a job to do."

She shook her head at him.

"If this goes wrong, there are people who will hang you out to dry for disobeying orders," she warned him. "And you aren't even going to meet the people you've risked it all to save?"

"I don't need to," he told her, smiling as he thought about it. "They're soldiers and spacers, just like those I've fought alongside and served alongside for years. They stood to defend their worlds, and the Gods dealt them a shitty hand.

"I could no more leave them behind than I could leave *you* behind," he concluded. "They are my brothers- and sisters-in-arms, just as much as if they'd served on *Avalon*. We *owe* them this."

"You're not wrong," she admitted. "But...be safe? All duty aside, you big lug, *I* want you to make it back. Still so much we need to learn."

"I know," he agreed softly. "I need to meet your sister. You need to meet my son. We need to, well"—he laughed—"get to know each other better. See how things end."

"I don't care how they end, so long as it's not soon," Mira told him. "The beginning is going swimmingly—don't you *dare* get yourself killed before we even begin to find out what the middle looks like!"

"Believe me, my dear," Kyle replied brightly, "I do not intend to do *any* such thing."

The problem, as both of them knew without him saying a word, was that *intentions* weren't going to matter much if the Commonwealth's timing was right.

18:00 April 3, 2736 ESMDT
DSC-078 Avalon, *Observation Deck*

Kyle wasn't *quite* hiding as he sat in *Avalon*'s quietest observation deck, watching the firefly lights of dozens—*hundreds*—of spacecraft swarming through Xin orbit. He could pick out the patterns in swarm that would be invisible to a layman. This swarm of lights along these lines was the Marine assault shuttles transporting the prisoners—still!—to the cargo transfer stations being used as prison camps, while *that* swarm of lights was starfighters moving missile satellites into position, and *those* lights were the constant stream of small craft moving the rescued prisoners to the three Marine assault transports.

Hundreds of smaller spacecraft and over a hundred thousand souls, all moving in accordance with his commands and his will. It was a heady feeling.

It was a sickening feeling.

His choices had brought them here, and if he had guessed *wrong,* a lot of those people were going to die. The Terrans *probably* wouldn't intentionally target the transports, but even a single rogue missile could destroy a logistics transport with forty thousand rescuees aboard. The assault transports looked more like warships and were more likely to be attacked, but they at least had warship-grade *defenses.*

"Let me guess: you're hiding in here to worry so you can put on a bright, cheerful face when you have to talk to everybody else?" Michael Stanford asked from behind him.

Kyle laughed, turning around to find his CAG crossing the observation deck toward him.

"I don't 'worry,' Vice Commodore Stanford," he told the other man. "I consider strategies and operational consequences."

"Like I said, worrying," Stanford confirmed. He tossed Kyle a beer.

Kyle looked at it and recognized it as one of his small-brewery beers picked up on Frihet.

"Did you raid my stash?" he asked.

"Nah, just your office fridge when I went looking for you there first," the CAG replied. "If it helps your 'consideration of strategies and operational consequences', we'll have the last of the satellites emplaced inside an hour. All they're going to do is open fire on the first big non-Alliance ship they see, so the planet is effectively blockaded until they're gone or we shut them down."

"We passed that on to the locals," Kyle noted. "They can warn off everybody—including the Terrans, for that matter. It serves everyone's purposes that way."

It had turned out that Wen Min, Wen Lau's wife, *had* survived the First Battle of Huī Xing and *was* one of the prisoners they had rescued. The Huī Xing government-in-hiding's cooperativeness had gone from "present but grudging" to "significant" almost instantly, once they'd provided the list of prisoners.

"Everything else is running on schedule," the Force Commander told Stanford. He might have been "hiding" on the observation deck, but it wasn't entirely hyperbole to say he could command the carrier from *anywhere* aboard.

"I'd like it to be running *faster*," Kyle continued. "I *want* to be outside the gravity well ten minutes ago—but I'm also *not* abandoning the transports until we can get them clear."

"Are we sending them straight back, then?" Stanford asked.

"All the way to Alizon," Kyle confirmed. "It's a thirty-light-year straight trip—eleven days, give or take a few hours. I'm pretty sure there is at least *one* person on the surface with a telescope and a Commonwealth Q-Com, so, sadly, the attempt to make us look bigger is probably a bust.

"Since that's the case, and since I wouldn't want to risk the transports in combat now we've stuffed them full of rescuees, the best thing we can do is get them out of the line of fire," he concluded. "And as soon as they're loaded, that's *exactly* what I plan on doing."

"Doesn't that risk the mission, though?" Stanford asked quietly. "Are four ships really going to be enough bait to bring the entire Twenty-Third Fleet here?"

"They'll all come here," Kyle noted. "They'll keep their fleet together because throwing equal numbers at us is *stupid*. We have better starfighters and, well..." He shrugged. "They know my name. I may *hate* that Gods-cursed nickname, but it's filtered back to the Commonwealth.

"Since I'm now a bona fide hero"—he puffed out his chest and gesticulated broadly—"according to our press and theirs, that makes me a target all on my own. While losing me wouldn't impact our actual war effort significantly, there would probably be an impact to civilian morale."

"Not just civilian, and not just according to the press," his CAG pointed out. "Also, speaking as one of the people who's supposed to die before anyone gets to your carrier, I fully intend for you to live through this."

"So do I," Kyle agreed. "But if they look like they're not going to play, or like they're going to send ships to reinforce Via Somnia, we're going to have keep their attention in the oldest way possible."

He *saw* his starfighter commander wince.

"And how exactly is that?" Stanford asked levelly.

"Oh, that's easy," the Force Commander told him with a wide grin. "We punch them in the nose and insult their mothers."

10:30 April 4, 2736 ESMDT
DSC-078 Avalon, *Bridge*

The loading was proceeding ahead of schedule, though not nearly as much as Kyle had hoped. They were already into the potential arrival window for the Commonwealth Twenty-Third Fleet, and there was still another ten minutes of work to do.

"Sir, *Sunshine* is reporting that one of the prisoners on their platforms wants to speak to you," his com officer reported. "Apparently an Imperial Vice Admiral—says it's a matter of 'honor'."

Kyle winced. There were, in fact, *seven* flag officers among the prisoners of higher rank than him. Most were the senior officers of junior members of the Alliance, people who weren't going to jog the elbows of the man trying to get them out alive.

There was also a Castle Federation Space Force Rear Admiral, the original commander of the Huī Xing defenses, who neither Kyle nor Stanford had heard a peep from, and Coraline Imperial Navy Vice Admiral Wilhelm Reuter—who, it seemed, was not so sensible.

"Forward it to me," Kyle ordered with a sigh, then dropped the privacy screen around his command chair.

"Vice Admiral Reuter," he greeted the older man who appeared on the screen. "How can I help you?"

Reuter reminded him a *lot* of his last Captain. Like Malcolm Blair, Reuters was gaunt, his hair pure white with age. Also like Blair, one of his eyes had been replaced with an emergency prosthesis during the war and never updated.

"You already have, Force Commander Roberts," the Imperial replied. His voice wavered with age—Reuter looked well into his second century—but his tone was firm. "You have saved my life and the lives of those I am sworn to command and protect. I wanted to thank you directly before you sent us all off to safety."

"Did the Terrans mistreat you at all, sir?"

"No," Reuter allowed. "We were treated in full compliance with the Tau Ceti Accords. But a life in imprisonment is not the life my people should live. They have families they should return to, and can no more do that as prisoners than if they were dead."

The old man shook his head.

"I should have run," he admitted. "Three old cruisers against a Terran Battle Group was suicide. But Hammerveldt's defenses were weak. We had to fight. We failed Hammerveldt, regardless. I must thank you and your Admiral for succeeding where I failed."

"We did our duty, sir," Kyle replied, a little embarrassed. He was *far* too aware of how fragile the defenses they'd left behind them were to feel they had truly "saved" the system.

"Perhaps in Hammerveldt, Force Commander Roberts," Reuter told him with a small smile. "But I know there's an entire Terran fleet in this sector. Many would have used their presence as an excuse to avoid the risks you took in rescuing us prisoners."

"I could not leave a hundred thousand spacers and soldiers of the Alliance in Terran hands," he replied. "It would not be right."

"Your actions speak of honor and integrity," the Imperial Admiral told him. "And my honor requires such be repaid in kind. This will be the end of my career, Force Commander. I intend to return to Coral and take up residence in my estates, but I am and remain an Elector of the Imperium."

The Imperator of the Coraline Imperium was elected for life—but only the noble caste known as Electors held the franchise for that election—and only if they'd performed military or diplomatic service. The *rest* of the Imperial government had a broader franchise, but only Electors got to vote for the Imperator.

"I owe you a debt of honor that cannot be repaid," Reuter concluded. "My life and the lives of those I commanded, returned to us from our imprisonment. If ever I or mine can serve you or yours with treasure or with blood, you have but to call. The Reuter family *will* answer."

An attention icon flashed on Kyle's implants—a message noting that the loading was finally complete.

"I would refrain from swearing life debts, Admiral, until we escape this system," Kyle noted dryly. "We should be on our way momentarily. If you'll excuse me?"

"Of course, Force Commander. Do not forget what I have said," Reuter told him. His voice might have shown his age, but his certainty shone through regardless. "Odin guide thee."

"Thank you, Admiral. May all the Gods watch over you."

Dropping the channel and the privacy screen, Kyle turned back to his bridge.

"That was weird," he muttered. "Is everyone ready to go?" he asked.

"Still confirming," Anderson told him. "A few minutes at most." The XO paused, then stepped closer to Kyle and continued more quietly. "I think I know why the Admiral wanted to talk to you."

"Oh?"

"Electors have to have served in the military to claim their vote when the Imperator dies," the younger man explained. "So, they *all* go to war. Reuter's *granddaughter* was an Ensign aboard one of the ships under his command. She lived—and now gets to go home because of us. Because of *you*."

Kyle thought about that for a moment. If someone managed to liberate Jacob from a prison—however comfortable said prison—what would *he* be willing to do for them?

Debts of honor, indeed.

#

"Everyone reports ready to go," Anderson informed him after a few more minutes of rushed preparation. "All of the platforms we're taking are locked down and under the control of the senior prisoner aboard. The rest of the prisoners are aboard the Marine transports and pointedly *not* complaining about the cramped quarters."

Kyle's XO shook his head.

"We have confirmed that we have ninety-eight thousand, five hundred and seventy-one Alliance prisoners of war aboard the transports," he noted. "For those keeping track, that makes this the seventeenth-largest prisoner rescue of all time."

"Damn, I was hoping to be higher in the record books than *that*," Kyle replied. "If we're ready, then let's move. Estimated time to clear the gravity well?"

"The transports can only pull two hundred gravities," Anderson pointed out. "Seventy-one minutes to Alcubierre activation, sir."

"Understood," the Force Commander turned his attention to Pendez, who was watching calmly, waiting for her orders. "Take us, Commander Pendez. Two hundred gravities for now."

"Yes, sir."

Kyle had the impression that *everyone* in Battle Group Seven-Two was feeling the same itch between the shoulder blades he was. Even the most efficient formation—which his Battle Group was well on its way to becoming—generally had a noticeable gap between the flagship starting to accelerate and the rest of the formation responding to the order. That was why combat instructions tended to have activation times sent along with them, usually in the underlying data channels that accompanied most military communications.

The gap this time was under half a second. His nine ships were underway in *moments*, trekking away from Xin in the opposite direction from where they expected Twenty-Third Fleet to arrive.

If they appeared before Seven-Two was clear of the gravity well at this point, Kyle expected to be able to outrun them anyway. He still watched the screens feeding to his implant carefully—they were *almost* clear, but *almost* wasn't safe yet.

Each minute they accelerated away from Xin, he relaxed a tiny bit more.

And then everything went to Hades.

"Alcubierre emergence!" Xue shouted, flashing an alert to everyone's screens and implants. "We have multiple Alcubierre emergences—*dead ahead*."

Someone had been playing clever games, Kyle realized. Once he was underway, his course had been transmitted to the incoming Terran fleet, who had adjusted *their* course to emerge from FTL and cut him off.

"What have we got?" he demanded. Depending on their strength, he *might* be able to fight through them. If nothing else, they'd dropped out too early—he could still run the *other* way and escape them.

"I've got five ships," Xue reported. "Lead is registering at twenty million tons, cubage uncertain—she's probably our missing Saint. Rest are twelve million tons by their engine signatures—last-generation ships, Assassins and Lexingtons, likely."

Kyle nodded slowly. Depending on the ratio of battlecruisers to carriers, he *might* be able to take out the blocking force—but it wasn't likely, and he'd risk stray weapons fire hitting the transports packed with rescued prisoners. It wasn't a risk he could afford.

"Turn us around," he ordered. "One-hundred-twenty-degree flip, take us up from the ecliptic and away from them. They dropped in too early; we should be able to evade them." He considered. "Show me their Alcubierre reach," he finished grimly.

He was in the gravity well, limited to the acceleration he could produce with antimatter rockets. They were *outside* the well and could use their Alcubierre drives to skip around the exterior.

"We'll need to angle further way from them," Pendez noted as she dropped their reach onto his implants. They couldn't reach *all* the way around Xin before he could evade them, but with the *hundred and thirty thousand*–gravity acceleration of their A-S drives, they could cut him off from most of his exit points.

"Do it," he ordered grimly. If the other three ships of the Terran Twenty-Third Fleet had gone to Via Somnia, that was going to create a headache for Alstairs—but would work well for him.

Hell, if the other three ships—none of them modern—were here and tried to stop him, he could punch them out with starfighters and keep going. The trap had *almost* worked.

"I have another emergence!" Xue announced, as if Kyle's thoughts had conjured them. She swallowed and turned to look back at him.

"Sir, I have five more ships," she said quietly. "Two are in the twenty-million-ton range. Those were not in our intel estimate."

She hadn't told him where they'd emerged—he could see it for himself. The second half of the Terrans' trap, dramatically more powerful than he'd estimated, had dropped out of FTL exactly opposite the first half. Between them, they covered both Xin and Goudeshijie's gravity wells.

Battle Group Avalon was well and truly trapped.

CHAPTER 33

Huī Xing System
11:00 April 4, 2736 Earth Standard Meridian Date/Time
DSC-078 Avalon, *Bridge*

The bridge was silent for a long moment, which Kyle used to think furiously. Pulling a datapad from the arm of his command chair, he started rapidly entering commands both through the physical medium and his implants, trying desperately to find a solution.

There was no way out. But while the *ultimate* objective had to be escape, there were other objectives he could fulfill without getting away—and still putting the commander of the Terran fleet between a rock and a hard place.

"Commander Pendez," he snapped. "Set a course for Goudeshijie orbit. Maintain two hundred gravities."

"That won't get us out of the gravity well, sir," she told him. "Goudeshijie's well and…"

"Xin's are currently merged, yes," Kyle told her. "I know. That gives us room to play, Maria. They want to keep us in this system, but they can't enter the gravity well themselves without risking our escape. So, let's get *deep* in the gravity well—if they want to play, let's make them dance.

"Xue," he turned to his tactical officer, "I want Q-probes close enough to read the names on their cursed hulls. If they turn into the gravity well, I want to know before they do. Clear?!"

"Yes, sir!" Xue replied.

Through his implants and screens, Kyle saw the big carrier turn, and the rest of Battle Group Seven-Two followed her. Goudeshijie was over a full astronomical unit, just under nine light-minutes, from Xin, but the gas giant's immense gravity well merged with Xin's, giving Kyle a *huge* amount of space to play in.

The Terrans' ability to use their Alcubierre drives outside the gravity wells meant he couldn't escape them—but he *could* force them to come to him if they wanted a fight.

"Michael," he subvocalized through his implants to his CAG. "I need you to get a full combat patrol up, but cycle your pilots. We're going to need a missile defense net for *days* if I make this work."

"What happens if they come in after us?" the CAG asked.

"If nothing else, that will let us get the transports free," Kyle pointed out. "And either way, we'll buy the time that Admiral Alstairs needed. If they go after her in Via Somnia, they can't leave enough ships here to fight us and still have a fleet that can challenge her.

"They have to choose—us or her. If they choose her, we'll follow them and ram a fighter strike up their ass while they're occupied. If they choose us..." *Avalon*'s Captain smiled grimly, knowing the channel would carry the emotion to Stanford, "Via Somnia falls."

"I'll have your missile defense in the air in sixty seconds," Stanford said finally. "Anything *else* you'd like, sir?"

"If you're sitting on a superweapon capable of taking out twice our numbers and tonnage that you haven't told me about, now would be the time," Kyle said brightly. "Otherwise, keep your people on their toes. I can play this game longer than they can possibly like—and sooner or later, they're going to send every starfighter they've got at us."

"We'll be ready," his CAG promised.

"I know."

Dropping the channel, Kyle turned his attention back to his bridge. Consoles and screens surrounded him, linking with his implants to provide a fully encompassing view of the system outside *Avalon*.

The computers tagged Force Alpha and Force Bravo on his retinas, happily showing him their real-space and Alcubierre interception cones. Like his freighters, the older ships in the Terran fleet were limited to two hundred gravities—but that was enough to keep pace with his Battle Group as they arced outside the gravity well.

For now, they were content to keep him trapped. He wondered how long that would last.

Deep Space, One Light Month from Via Somnia System
11:15 April 4, 2736 ESMDT
BC-129 Camerone, *Bridge*

Mira studied the data being relayed to *Camerone* carefully, hoping to see *some* solution for Kyle's predicament that wasn't immediately obvious. Something that someone not involved could see, a way out for her lover and a hundred-thousand-plus fellow soldiers.

She hadn't seen one by the time she got a ping from the Admiral.

"Ma'am?" she replied.

"I'm in conference with Roberts in two minutes," Alstairs told her calmly. "I want you on for your perspective."

"Yes, ma'am," Mira confirmed. She paused. "I'll have my head on straight," she promised.

"If I thought differently, I'd have stepped on your relationship instead of encouraging it, Captain," Seventh Fleet's commanding officer told her bluntly. "Have your bridge crew ready to move. We'll be on our way to Via Somnia in ten minutes."

Camerone's Captain swallowed and nodded.

"Yes, ma'am."

Mira passed on the preparatory orders to her bridge crew quickly, then dropped the privacy screen around her command chair. She took a moment to compose herself, breathing deeply to push back her moment of panic at seeing Kyle surrounded.

Finally, she linked into the Q-Com channel. A virtual conference table opened in her mind, with Kyle and Rear Admiral Alstairs joining her.

None of the three were actually in a conference room. She and Kyle were on their bridges. Alstairs was on the flag deck. But a conference room was the default setting for this kind of implant-driven meeting, so a conference room was what they all saw.

"What is your status, Force Commander Roberts?" Alstairs asked.

"We are running for Goudeshijie," he replied cheerfully. "If they want to dance in the dog world's rings, I'll happily indulge them—if nothing else, if their two battle groups enter the gravity well, I'm reasonably sure I can sneak the transports out."

"And if they continue to simply block your escape?"

"Then you'll get your seven days, Admiral," Kyle said flatly. "Once you hit Via Somnia, they're going to have to choose—Seventh Fleet or Battle Group Seven-Two. They've got ten ships to our twelve; their best chance is to knock out me and then go after you. Believe me, Admiral, I can stretch out this dance as easily in Goudeshijie's gravity well as I could outside the gravity wells entirely.

"I can give you your week."

"Roberts," Alstairs said quietly, "that's not a game you can play forever. I'm not prepared to sacrifice your battle group for that week."

"Via Somnia is the objective here," he pointed out. "*They* know that as well as you and I do. Leave them the hard strategic decisions, ma'am. I can play this game for long enough."

"It will take four days for us to relieve you, Kyle," Mira said quietly. "You won't have time to realize if things are going downhill."

"That's the risk we have to take," he replied. "This sector isn't safe unless Via Somnia falls. The bastards already jumped us with two more modern warships than we expected. If you neutralize the naval base, this Twenty-Third Fleet *has* to fall back—I can get the prisoners to safety and we can catch the bastards between your and ships and mine at Via Somnia."

"And if they believe Via Somnia can hold and press you harder?" Alstairs asked. "Or if they decide to destroy you and *then* come after us?"

"Then I will give the bastards a fight they won't soon forget," Kyle told them grimly. "I don't plan on dying here, Admiral. They'll make a mistake sooner or later."

"Very well, Force Commander," the Admiral replied. "We will proceed as originally planned."

Alstairs dropped out of the channel, leaving Mira and Kyle looking at each other's virtual avatars.

"Do *not* die on me," she told him fiercely.

"I'll be fine," he said breezily. "They have to *catch* me first, and I've got an entire gas giant's gravity well to play in."

Mira shook her head slowly. "Give them hell," she told him.

CHAPTER 34

Huī Xing System
18:00 April 4, 2736 Earth Standard Meridian Date/Time
DSC-078 Avalon, *Bridge*

Avalon settled into the rings of Goudeshijie with careful precision. The Battle Group had slowed, but not to a velocity where the gas giant could actually hold them in orbit. An orbit was too predictable, a path that would allow the Terran ships still drifting outside the gravity well to fire missile salvos.

"I'm surprised we made it this far without them shooting at us," Xue said quietly. "Or sending fighters in, for that matter."

"With our fighters out, they know they couldn't get any birds through our defenses," Kyle pointed out. "Long-range missile fire also makes accurate targeting a problem—they'd risk hitting the transports carrying the prisoners, and it appears that our Terran friends don't want to risk that."

"So, what, they're just going to orbit out there until we run out of food and have to surrender?" his tactical officer asked.

"Given that we barely have enough food aboard the transports to make it to Alizon as it is, it's not the worst plan they could have," Kyle replied. "The platforms had a thirty-four day stock of food. Removing the guards from the calculation doesn't add *that* much extra to the allowance. Keep us trapped for a few days and the options for the transports start shrinking fast. Keep us trapped for a few weeks and *our* food supplies start being a problem."

The warships could recycle a *lot* of things. Food was...technically one of them, but the efficiency was low, and once they started on the ship-produced nutrient bars, everyone *knew* what they were eating. The transports full of rescued prisoners would run out of food much faster than the Battle Group's warships—but the Battle Group would go onto nutrient bars before the transports ran out of real food.

Morale would suffer. Demoralized crews would be less efficient. Right now, if Kyle didn't have the transports to protect, shooting his way through one of the Terran task forces would be a reasonable option—he wouldn't get *everyone* out, but he'd probably get at least two of his four warships clear. A demoralized Battle Group's odds would go down—not from any active desire on the part of his people not to escape, but from the inevitably slowed reactions of terrified, underfed spacers.

He wasn't that desperate yet. For now, all he needed to do was bide his time—if Alstairs and Mira could take Via Somnia, the enemy would be forced to withdraw. He could achieve his mission without firing a shot.

"Sir, we're receiving a wide-beam transmission from the Commonwealth forces," his com officer told him. "It's addressed to you—personally."

"We didn't exactly hide who was in command," Kyle reminded his XO. "Put it through."

It popped up on the screens of his command chair, and Kyle found himself looking at a recording of the flag bridge of a Commonwealth warship.

He couldn't actually guess which ship it was—like the Federation, the Commonwealth standardized both the command and flag bridges of warships. It was one of the three modern ships—one each, apparently, of the *Saint, Volcano* and *Hercules* classes—but he couldn't narrow it down more than that.

In the center of the recording, with the screens around him blocked out by automatic censoring software, sat a slim pale-skinned blond man in the black-and-red sashed uniform of the Commonwealth Navy, three gold stars at his neck marking him as a Vice Admiral. This had to be the commander of the fleet trapping him.

"Force Commander Kyle Roberts, I am Vice Admiral Kaj Ness of the Terran Commonwealth Navy's Twenty-Third Fleet, charged with the security of Sector Charlie of the Rimward Marches. A Sector, I hardly need to tell you, that you have rampaged through, destroying ships and killing men and women I have served with for longer than you have been *alive*."

Ness inhaled sharply, bringing his hands together and then releasing them as he exhaled.

"Nonetheless, Force Commander, I am prepared to be merciful. You can hide like a rabbit in the rocks if you wish, but we both know you only delay the inevitable. Surrender, and I promise that you and your people will be treated gently.

"If this comes to a battle, you will not win. You will only die and take all of those under your command with you."

The message ended and Kyle smiled.

"Record for response," he ordered, then leaned back to face the camera in his chair.

"Vice Admiral Ness, I appreciate the kind offer you have extended, but I must decline," he told the Terran calmly. "I am a soldier of the Federation, sir, and I have not yet begun to fight." A mental command ended the recorded and transmitted the message.

The bridge was very quiet, and Kyle looked at the channel from secondary control to see Anderson watching him.

"So, what happens now, sir?" his XO asked quietly.

"We wait," Kyle replied. "We see what our Admiral Ness does once he knows Via Somnia is under attack." He paused, considering. "Oh, he'll also probably fire missiles relatively quickly. They'll take over an hour and a half to *get* to us, but they're going to do *something*."

#

"Missile launch, sir," Xue reported about five minutes later. "You were right."

Kyle sighed. He'd hoped he wouldn't be—long-range missile fire was notoriously inaccurate, putting the transports packed full of rescued prisoners at risk.

"What do we have?" he asked.

"Looks like two salvos from each task force," she told him. "They also seem to be moving their Q-probes in closer to refine their targeting—I don't have clear hits, but the ghost zones are getting smaller."

Like Battle Group Seven-Two, Twenty-Third Fleet had Q-probes in close to provide near-real-time data back to Admiral Ness on their enemy's actions. The quantum entanglement com–equipped probes were the stealthiest things in anyone's arsenal—as much as anything with an antimatter rocket capable of a thousand gravities could be *stealthy*.

Their sensors and computers could tell Xue and Kyle that there were Q-probes out there. They could even make a guess at how *many*— but they couldn't tell them the exact location or velocity. Only an area where the probe could be—hence "ghost zones'." Speed and engine size decreased the size of the ghost zone rapidly, rendering the technology useless for just about any *other* purpose, but it let both Ness and Kyle have eyes on the other that were less than a second out of date as opposed to over eight minutes.

Speaking of the Q-probes...

"Do we have probes detached to follow the missiles?" he asked.

"Yes, sir."

Kyle nodded and leaned back in his chair, studying the two salvos. Both salvos were roughly sixty missiles, which matched up with what the Q-probes were telling him. Admiral Ness had to be cursing whichever Terran Navy bean-counter had assigned his fleet so many of the *Lexington*-class carriers.

The *Lexington* was a last-generation ship with a hundred and fifty starfighters aboard, a perfect unit for a nodal force defending multiple systems—but it had *no* missile launchers. Admiral Ness had three of them, two with his Saint flagship and one with the other task force.

He also had three modern ships and four last-generation battlecruisers, which made up much of the difference. There were a lot of games Kyle could play with eight light-minutes of maneuvering room to prevent Ness's people from consolidating their fighter strength, but fewer he could with missiles.

"Inform Vice Commodore Stanford we will have missiles inbound in one hundred minutes," he said aloud. "Keep everyone in the Battle Group informed on the status of the salvos. I presume we're looking at time-on-target impacts?"

"I can't be certain yet," Xue warned, "but it appears so. I believe we'll have all two hundred and thirty-six missiles arriving simultaneously on two vectors."

"Thank you, Lieutenant Commander," Kyle told her. "Keep me informed."

There wasn't much to do now but wait and watch. The missiles simply added a new timer to the series of countdowns running in his implant. How long until Seventh Fleet arrived in Via Somnia. The estimated time for Seventh Fleet to destroy Via Somnia's defenses and plant the defenses they'd brought with them.

The estimate for how long until the ships under his command ran out of food.

The timer for incoming missiles was in appropriate company.

#

Both salvos cut their engines roughly eighty-eight million kilometers away from Battle Group Seven-Two, doing just over ten percent of lightspeed. The Q-probes kept pace with the missiles, allowing Kyle's people to dial them in for long-range defensive fire—but nothing in their arsenal except their own missiles reached that far.

"Should we at least fire back?" Anderson asked over the intercom, the XO clearly perturbed by simply *waiting* for the missiles to arrive.

"No, I want to hang on to our missiles," Kyle replied. "That said, now that they're flying dumb, it's time for us to do *something*. Transmit these course directions to the Battle Group."

He'd spent the hour the missiles were accelerating toward him preparing his plan. The freighters now lunged away from the capital ships at two hundred gravities, tucking toward Goudeshijie's largest moon. In the forty minutes the missiles were ballistic, they'd be able to put the midsized lifeless rock between them and the weapons.

The capital ships went one way, turning to close the distance with the sixty-missile salvo inbound from one task force, while most of Stanford's starfighters went the other. With pure ballistic courses, many of their weapons could start killing missiles at about ten light-seconds—about twenty-five seconds before the missiles would bring up their drives for their terminal attack.

Moving after they went ballistic wouldn't *confuse* the missiles necessarily—they were smart weapons, being fed data from their motherships with plenty of time to adapt, but it opened up Kyle's options and narrowed the missiles'.

Minutes ticked by, with the timer to impact in Kyle's implants seemingly running down slower and slower as he tried not to hold his breath.

Finally, his ships reached their range of the missiles and opened fire. Defensive lasers and positron lances slashed across space, hundreds of invisible beams drawn onto the displays by the computers to allow humans to follow them.

Of the hundred and twenty missiles charging at his ships, only seventy-three lived long enough to bring up their drives for their terminal assault. His starfighters, facing fewer missiles but with fewer weapons truly designed for the task, still faced eighty.

Kyle watched in silence as the missiles closed. At this point, he'd given his orders. All he could do was leave the defense of his ships to the tactical officers and fighter crews.

The advantage to ballistic salvos was that if your target didn't see them enter ballistic mode, they had no idea where the missiles were. The *dis*advantage was that if your target had Q-probes on top of the missiles for their entire ballistic component, they knew *exactly* where your missiles were.

Even a thousand gravities of acceleration couldn't do much to change the cone of probabilities for a missile moving at over thirty-four thousand kilometers a second. Missiles died in their dozens, Battle Group Seven-Two's capital ships having them *far* too dialed in for them to evade.

The last of the salvo they'd charged died over a quarter million kilometers clear of the capital ships, and then the ships turned on the missiles they'd left behind.

Those missiles had waited to turn on their drives, the intelligence that made capital ship missiles so much deadlier than starfighter missiles recognizing that they wouldn't hit if they activated on schedule. They dove through the starfighter screen trying to stop them, chasing real targets—targets worth their time.

They were twenty-eight seconds into their terminal burn before Kyle realized that they weren't going for his *warships*. He doubted it was intentional—Ness has not struck him as the type to *intentionally* target the transports loaded with unarmed rescued prisoners—but the missiles' silicon and molecular circuitry brains had fallen victim to the dangers of long-range missile fire.

"Take us at them, full acceleration," he snapped. "Those missiles *cannot* get through!"

The fighters turned, chasing after the missiles burning at twice their acceleration. The starships turned, desperately trying to close the distance to save the freighters. The freighters themselves moved, trying to buy precious seconds for the intercept.

Sixty missiles had survived so far. Dozens more died as the weapons of four capital ships were unleashed on them.

Nine, confused by the starfighters' massive ECM projections, missed the necessary adjustments and slammed into the moon. Between antimatter explosions and kinetic force, the entire unimaginably massive planetoid visibly *moved*, jumping dozens of kilometers as a gaping crater was ripped into its side.

Eight missiles made it past everything, skipped around the planet, and charged straight for the transports. Three Marine Assault Transports stood in their way—the only ships with real missile defenses and carrying fewer people, the massive assault ships made *themselves* a target to guard the transports with their forty thousand civilians apiece.

The assault transports had the defenses, if not the weapons, of a battlecruiser. They could stand off eight missiles—given time and space to play with. They had a hundred thousand kilometers and three seconds.

Kyle couldn't watch. He closed his eyes—only to open them again as his bridge erupted in cheers.

Chimera had nailed the last missile seventeen hundred meters clear of her hull. A blast wave of radiation and heat smashed into the assault transport—but her armor held.

The transports had survived.

#

It was easily several minutes before anyone on *Avalon*'s bridge could breathe properly. The warships moved to cover the transports again, and damage reports flowed in.

The Battle Group had survived surprisingly well, Kyle noted. *Chimera* had lost a chunk of her missile defenses and sensors but was otherwise fully functional. They hadn't even lost a single starfighter, which was unusual when using them as an antimissile screen.

"Sir, we're receiving a transmission relayed through the Q-probes from Admiral Ness."

"Put it on the main screen," Kyle ordered. "Let everyone see what the man has to say."

Vice Admiral Kaj Ness looked uncomfortable to Kyle's eyes, though he wasn't sure what exactly gave him that impression. Once again, the Admiral sat in the middle of his flag bridge and faced the camera levelly.

"Force Commander Roberts, I apologize for the unnecessary attack on the transports carrying the rescued prisoners of war," Ness said calmly. "While we both know it was an accident, it was also an inherent risk of long-range missile fire. I take full responsibility and appreciate the efficacy of your people's defense."

What Ness *didn't* mention was that the Tau Ceti Accords would have made the destruction of a transport with thousands of rescued prisoners aboard a war crime. Kyle suspected that he had a *reputation* with the Commonwealth where it came to war criminals.

"As long as this standoff continues, that risk continues," Ness continued flatly. "I can and will keep you trapped in this system until starvation forces you to fight or surrender. You lack the firepower to successfully break out.

"Trapping you here puts those same prisoners at risk, however, so I am prepared to offer a compromise. If you surrender and offer the parole of yourself and all the personnel aboard your ships, and the rescued POWs, that you will not serve against the Commonwealth, I will permit you to transfer your warship personnel to the transports and leave this system unmolested.

"I make this offer out of a desire to avoid unnecessary loss of life on either side and a personal respect for your prior actions," Ness concluded. "I await your response."

Avalon's bridge was silent. Kyle glanced around, but none of his staff would meet his eyes. It was a generous offer—one that would risk Vice Admiral Ness's career to execute.

It was also one that would require Kyle to either hand *Avalon* blithely over to the Commonwealth or destroy one of the most powerful and modern warships in the Alliance's order of battle himself. Either way, it required him to surrender without a fight.

"Well," he said quietly. "That's quite the offer."

The image of Anderson being relayed from the secondary control center acquired a dark blue box in Kyle's mind, noting that the XO had taken the channel completely private. No one would hear or see what the two men who ran *Avalon* discussed.

"Accepting would *destroy* your career, sir," Anderson murmured.

"And guarantee a hundred and thirty thousand lives," Kyle replied.

"If you can trust him."

"I think we can trust him."

"So?"

"So, what?"

"Do you really have it in you to surrender without a fight?" Anderson asked flatly.

Force Commander Kyle Roberts, the "Stellar Fox", captain of the supercarrier *Avalon* and commander of Battle Group Seven-Two, laughed aloud. His bridge crew looked at him, and suddenly, they *were* meeting his eyes—and their gazes were determined.

"Record for transmission," Kyle ordered, then leaned into the camera.

"Vice Admiral Ness," he said flatly. "You threaten the men and women I have rescued from your prisons to force my surrender. You blithely expect that I will yield to you without a fight—that I will yield *Avalon* to you without a fight!

"You know who I am, Admiral. Remember it—so when you reach the River Styx, you can tell Charon who sent you!"

He paused and gestured for it to be sent.

"Now, while he chews on that," Kyle told his bridge crew, "let's see if we can get our transports out of this system."

CHAPTER 35

Kyle tossed the tiny black pill into his mouth far more casually than the overpowered amphetamine deserved, washing it down with a mouthful of water. He'd ordered the Battle Group to stand down from general quarters, letting at least some of the crew rest while he plotted.

They'd have hours to respond to anything Admiral Ness did in response to Kyle's rejection of his offer. His people could get some sleep—even if *he* wasn't going anywhere.

He'd been running scenarios on his implant and command chair computers for an hour, though, and he wasn't coming up with any clean solutions. The two Terran task forces could cover any path he took to escape Goudeshijie's gravity well, though there were routes he could take to force them to use their Alcubierre drives to intercept him.

Once in warped space, they'd have a lot fewer options to change course, but that didn't help him much. Either of those forces could destroy the freighters single-handedly and would have better-than-even odds of taking on the entire Battle Group.

Though...in Ness's position, Kyle would concentrate his forces in the face of a breakout attempt. Once Battle Group Seven-Two had built up enough of a vector toward a given side of the well, he could risk uncovering part of the well to concentrate his forces and reduce his losses.

A single ship left behind could take out all seven freighters in a single salvo, though. Unless...

Kyle activated a ping on his two main subordinates' implants. "Anderson, Stanford, I need you both on a private channel now."

"Here," Stanford replied immediately. Apparently, his CAG was still aboard his starfighter, probably taking the same pills Kyle was.

"Give me a moment," Anderson replied. A few seconds passed, then the XO was back on the line, sounding slightly more awake. "If you send me to sleep, you could give me more than an hour," he pointed out grouchily.

"You can sleep for a week once we're out of here," Kyle told him. "Gentlemen, I need ideas, options, plans—we need a way to make Admiral Ness think we have the freighters with us while leaving them behind."

"Why?" Anderson asked.

"I think I see," Stanford interrupted. "They'll still have a *four-hour* flight out, sir."

"Three and a half," the XO corrected in a distracted tone.

"Which is plenty of time to turn around if it looks like Ness is throwing too much in their way," Kyle pointed out. "The logistics transports also have the capacity to retrieve starfighters—they can't *launch* them quickly, but they can pick up everybody and take them with them if we send a wing out to escort them.

"And I'll stack any of your wings up against an Assassin any day of the week," he told Stanford. "But the key is to make Ness think we're going for a full breakout with the transports in our wake—and the bastard has Q-probes stuck to us like burrs."

"Okay..." Anderson said slowly. "I'm not saying that's impossible, boss, only that it's spectacularly difficult."

"If it wasn't, we wouldn't need *Avalon*," Kyle replied. "I'm well aware I'm asking for minor miracles, but there are a hundred thousand lives on the line."

"Can I add 'miracle-worker' to my business bio, then?" the XO asked, his voice suddenly awake and excited. "Because I have an idea."

There was a program, inside the tactical network interface that allowed Vice Commodore Michael Stanford to command the three-hundred-plus starfighters they'd started with, that simulated drawing straws. A group of individuals—in this case, the two Phoenix CAGs and all five of Michael's Wing Commanders—were entered, and the program presented each of them with a virtual straw.

"Why is it *always* me?" Rokos demanded after the selection ended, Bravo Wing's burly commander looking at the other wing leaders grumpily.

"Normally, it's because I *pick* you," Michael pointed out. "Apparently, the computer noticed a pattern." He shook his head at the grumpy officer. "Yours is the most important job," he continued. "If everything else goes wrong, you'll be the only chance those freighters have of getting out alive."

"Right, so we're the meat shield."

"I don't care *what* name you stick on it," the Vice Commodore told him. "You draw the short straw, you get the escort duty. Everyone else—sorry, you're giving up starfighters to bring Bravo Wing up to full strength. You've got thirty seconds to identify them.

"Keep those people alive, Russell," he finished, a bit more seriously as his other Wing Commanders assigned crews and fighters to bring Bravo Wing up to a full forty-eight-fighter strength. "I'm trusting you."

"We'll make it happen," Rokos promised. "Bravo Wing, breaking formation."

Michael's implants showed him the world around him as if he *was* his starfighter, and then overlaid icons and data to track the two hundred and fifty starfighters, four capital ships, three assault transports, and two logistics freighters of Battle Group Seven-Two.

Forty-eight of the starfighter icons now dropped away from the main formation, cutting a carefully calculated course that dropped them behind Goudeshijie's moon. There was a blip on his scanners, even *his* computers thinking that the assault transports and logistics freighters were duplicated for a moment.

"Seven-Two starfighter wings, form on me," he ordered. Turning his own fighter, he aligned it with the Saint and its attendant task force orbiting Goudeshijie a full astronomical unit away. A few moments later, his implants confirmed that the remaining two hundred and two starfighters of Seven-Two's fighter strength were aligned on him.

"Force Commander," he sent to Roberts. "Starfighters are prepared to move."

"Carry on, CAG," Roberts ordered. "We'll be right behind you."

"Seven-Two starfighters," Stanford addressed his people. "Two hundred gees for ten minutes, then drop to one hundred until we've matched velocity with the battle group. Engage in t minus ten seconds."

Seconds later, his entire force leapt forward into space, charging directly at the largest ship in the enemy fleet. If that wasn't enough to make Admiral Ness blink, moments after that, all four capital ships moved out, followed by the five transports a few moments later at one hundred and fifty gravities. A slow acceleration, one that conserved fuel and looked like blood in the water to the enemy.

Adjusting accelerations would align them all in a neat formation with the transports protected well before they reached any range at which Twenty-Third Fleet could engage them. The fighters led the way but were still in range of the weapons of the capital ships. It combined all of Battle Group Seven-Two into a single hammer, designed to blast its way through Force Alpha and cover the escape of the transports behind it.

"Just don't look behind the moon, Mister Ness," Michael muttered.

#

Once the Battle Group had assumed its final formation, Michael started to feel like they were almost *walking*. It was an exaggeration: one hundred and fifty gravities was over double what any civilian ship could accelerate at, but it was a gentle acceleration for the starships, let alone the fighters that normally ran at five hundred gravities.

"So, boss," Arnolds asked quietly, "what happens if Force Bravo *doesn't* take the bait?"

"Most likely?" Michael considered his gunner's question. "Most likely we hit Force Alpha with the hammer we're waving under Admiral Ness's nose, punch our way through, and go back to the original plan of dancing around the outer system with, well, whatever's left of the Battle Group."

"That seems...dangerous."

"It's a head-on suicide charge, a true ship-to-ship action," the CAG agreed. "But it actually offers us the best chance of getting *some* of the Battle Group out—but you're right. We wouldn't get everyone out."

The gunner swallowed.

"But we'd probably reduce Force Alpha to debris and cripples," Michael continued after a moment of silence. "They have the edge in hulls, but we have better starfighters—and we have the Stellar Fox. The Terrans will blink."

"Think they're that scared of the old man?" she half-whispered.

"*I* would be," Michael replied. "If there's any officer in this galaxy I'd believe was actually about to ram this hammer of starships and fighters down Admiral Ness's throat, it would be Kyle Roberts. It might not be the *smartest* thing to do, and it would expensive as all hell, but it would *work*."

He smiled as an icon on his implants flashed and vanished—the Q-probes watching Force Bravo reporting that the second Terran Task Force had brought up their Alcubierre drives and disappeared into warped space.

"And there we go," he concluded. "There's the blink."

The warped space bubble that the Terrans had entered wasn't automatically faster than light. It had to accelerate up to that at its mind-boggling light-year-a-day squared acceleration. Bound to, roughly, straight lines that couldn't cross Goudeshijie's gravity well, the flight would take a full half-hour.

Not a big deal when it came to intercepting Battle Group Seven-Two. Force Bravo might be blind in their bubbles of warped space, but

Force Alpha and the Q-probes would keep them readily updated on the Alliance force's position.

"Q-probes are moving for clearer lines of sight on us," Xue reported, *Avalon*'s tactical officer updating the CAG along with all of the ship captains. "The ghost zones are moving around Goudeshijie toward us. They haven't opened much of a blind spot, but it is there. Let's keep it flashy and keep the eyes on us, people."

Michael nodded, sending out mental notes for his starfighters to spread out, their high power-to-weight ratios making their antimatter engines the most visible despite their small size. Enough movement and bright lights on his people's part would be *very* flashy—and also help disguise that he was missing an entire wing of starfighters.

23:45 April 4, 2736 ESMDT
DSC-078 Avalon, *Bridge*

Kyle honestly hadn't expected to make it this far. In two hours and forty-five minutes, the Battle Group had crossed seventy-two million kilometers and was still almost eighty million kilometers away from Twenty-Third Fleet.

Vice Admiral Ness had clearly decided that this was Kyle's push and concentrated his two forces. With ten capital ships and eight hundred starfighters, there was no question what would happen when Battle Group Seven-Two slammed into the Terran fleet. Twenty-Third Fleet wouldn't come away unscathed, but Kyle's battle group would be obliterated.

No one was going to question if he broke off, but given that on one memorable occasion, Kyle had *rammed* a battleship—entirely by accident, to be fair—he suspected that Ness was starting to believe Battle Group Avalon might carry through the attack.

"Wait, I'm getting activity in the fleet," Xue reported. "Lots of movement suddenly—and *damn*."

One of the ten icons on Kyle's display disappeared, a notation warning him the ship had warped space.

"Which one was that and where did they go?" he demanded.

"Bogey Eight is an Assassin," Xue replied quickly. "She moved back on a reciprocal course—she's got to be headed to block the transports. Didn't even take her fighters with her—just the one battlecruiser."

"Gods curse it," Kyle swore, checking his own screens. "Keep the ECM up and warn Rokos," he ordered.

His mental screens split into two: one showed his own Battle Group, with all five of *Avalon*'s one-hundred-thousand-ton space tugs adjusting their mass manipulators to match the fuel burn of the much bigger transports. The other showed the five transports on the opposite of Goudeshijie, using the gas giant's heat to help hide their own energy signatures as they burned directly away from the now-concentrated Terran fleet.

"If they keep following the same course that Force Bravo used to join Force Alpha, Bogey Eight will be in position to intercept the transports fifteen minutes before they exit the gravity well," Xue told him grimly. "They can no longer break off."

"Are we sure they saw through us?" Kyle asked.

"They could be responding to a blip the Q-probes picked up," his tactical officer allowed. "They've got a blind spot the transports are flying right down the middle of, but 'blind' is relative."

"Hold the ECM on the tugs until Bogey Eight arrives on target," he ordered after a moment's thought. "As for us..." He sighed.

"Orders to the Battle Group," he said formally. "Flip and burn—take us to two hundred and fifty gravities on everything, including the tugs, on a zero-zero course to return to Goudeshijie orbit."

"What if Ness takes that an excuse to send more of his ships after the transports?" Anderson asked from his battle station halfway down the ship from the bridge.

"Then we flip again and see if we can make the bastard sweat," Kyle replied. "For now, let's make damned sure we stay out of lance range of the rest of his warships."

"What about the transports?" Xue asked.

"That's down to Wing Commander Rokos now," *Avalon*'s Captain said grimly. "He and I have played battlecruiser versus fighter wing before. I hope he has better luck with the game than I did."

His fingers twitched as he resisted the urge to rub his temples—specifically, the spot where he still got headaches from the remnants of his old implants. The ones that had been burnt out when Kyle Roberts had nearly died leading a single wing of starfighters against a Commonwealth battlecruiser.

From almost ten light-minutes away, however, there was nothing he could do for Bravo Wing's commander but wish him luck—and make sure no *more* capital ships got in his way.

#

The wonders of modern technology had given Kyle Roberts a front-row seat to the death ride of the navy of an entire star system before... twice. Watching the transports continue to flee the system knowing that a Commonwealth battlecruiser was about to appear in their path felt similar—if nothing else, there were more people aboard those five freighters than there had been in either of those fleets.

Unlike those death rides, however, the odds were a lot more even this time. Given the chance to hit the battlecruiser without any supporting starfighters getting in the way, Rokos's forty-eight starfighters were about an even match for the bigger ship in terms of firepower, if not endurance or survivability.

With the starfighters tucked in tight to the five starships and matching their acceleration to the bigger vessels' maneuvers, it was possible—even *likely*—that the Terrans hadn't picked up Bravo Wing. If they had, Bogey Eight would have brought her own starfighters with her.

"I don't think they see us, Force Commander," Rokos said over the Q-Com, mirroring Kyle's own thoughts. "Can someone double-check my math? I make it that if we do nothing until the cruiser emerges from A-S, there is no way anyone else can intercept us."

"I have the same, Wing Commander," Kyle told him. "There's only about ten more minutes in which anyone else can intercept you. I don't like to micromanage, but if you could stay hidden under the Marines' skirts for at least that long, I think everyone can appreciate it."

Rokos laughed.

"Just for admitting Marines wear skirts, sir, I think I can do that," he replied cheerfully. "I'll get them home—skirts and all."

"Good luck, Wing Commander," Kyle told him softly.

Avalon's bridge was silent as the minutes continued to tick by. Their own headlong rush toward the edge of the gravity well was slowing, their engines laboring to bring their speed down by almost two and a half kilometers a second every second.

A word of command could flip that acceleration around and send them driving for the Commonwealth's Twenty-Third Fleet. It would be a suicide run—but one that could buy the transports time to escape. With less than thirty thousand people on his four warships and one hundred and twenty thousand on the freighters, it was an order Kyle was prepared to give.

Not one he intended to give or wanted to. But an order he was *prepared* to give—if only because every minute he accelerated *away* from Vice Admiral Ness was a minute he could accelerate *at* Vice Admiral Ness without actually committing to the suicide run.

"Five minutes to Bogey Eight emergence," Xue told him quietly. "Transports are now twenty minutes from exiting Goudeshijie's gravity well. It is no longer possible for any more of Twenty-Third Fleet's ships to intercept the freighters."

"All right," he said brightly. "Let's show Admiral Ness the game. Drop the ECM, have the tugs go to regular power and reboard *Avalon*."

The icons displayed in his implant data streams changed. The ECM that had been pretending that the hundred-thousand-ton service tugs were sixty-million-cubic-meter freighters vanished like a popped soap bubble. The energy signatures blazing from the tugs suddenly toned down, no longer wantonly wasting fuel pretending to be bigger ships.

"Tug pilots report they'll be aboard in ten minutes," his com officer reported. "No expected issues."

"Any reaction from our Terran friend?"

"No missiles so far," Anderson said dryly. "Some shuffling of ships— but it looks he can do the math on intercepting the transports as well as we can. I bet fifty stellars he's going to wait and see how Bogey Eight does before he decides."

"If we're betting on our chances of incipient death, can the stakes be higher than an expensive coffee?" Kyle asked cheerfully.

"I would tend to think they are by default," Xue pointed out, her voice level enough that it took even Kyle a moment to realize she was joining in the banter.

He eyed the bridge crew out of the corner of his eye. There were smiles and concealed chuckles at their senior officer's antics, which was *exactly* what he was aiming for.

"So, it's down to Rokos," he said more seriously. "Let's see what happens."

#

Exactly on schedule, Bogey Eight erupted back into normal space. The warped space bubble dispersed in a blast of radiation, lacking much of the normal blue sheen of Cherenkov radiation, as they'd only barely broken the speed of light on their trip around the gas giant.

They'd nailed their jump perfectly. Regardless of how accurate their data on the transports' course had been, they had emerged *exactly* in the escapees' path.

As soon as Bogey Eight was back in regular space and locatable, Bravo Wing sprang into action. In one pre-coordinated movement, the transports flipped and started accelerating away from the battlecruiser— buying the starfighters time to deal with it—and Rokos's wing lunged for the battlecruiser at five hundred gravities.

Bogey Eight's captain didn't even flinch. The battlecruiser turned into the teeth of the starfighters and charged at the freighters. Seconds ticked by and neither side flinched, then missiles started to blast away from the cruiser.

Kyle found himself muttering blessings in Greek under his breath, imploring the old gods to let the transports be able to handle those missiles.

They *should*—the three assault transports were well protected and they had range to play with this time—but there was no way Rokos's people could take more than a passing tithe of the weapons. It would mostly be down to the Marine ships to defend the freighters.

Then the missiles reached Rokos's fighters and Kyle realized they hadn't been *aimed* at the transports at all. That would, after all, have been a war crime, and Ness still didn't strike him as the type.

The weapons charged into the fighter wing, dodging and weaving as lasers and positron lances took out their sisters. Kyle realized he was holding his breath, watching the starfighters—and the men and women he commanded—die.

Four capital ship missile salvos slammed home before Bravo Wing reached their own missile range of the cruiser. Fifteen of the Falcons died in balls of white antimatter fire, but thirty-three survived to open fire themselves.

A hundred and thirty-two Starfires blasted into space, a tsunami of fire versus the salvos of fourteen missiles still closing on Bravo Wing.

More capital ship missiles slammed home, and only a hundred and twenty missiles launched in the second salvo. The third was barely a hundred as the battlecruiser's positron lances began to rip holes in Bravo Wing's formation.

As the first salvo struck home, Rokos led his last twenty-two starfighters spiralling into their own lance range of the Assassin. Antimatter fire flared, positron beams flashed in both directions—and seventeen starfighters exited the inferno they'd created.

The twelve-million-ton battlecruiser didn't.

"Rokos, report," Kyle snapped. Silence responded. The Q-probes' resolution wasn't good enough to tell him *which* seventeen fighters had survived. He waited a long moment.

"Bravo Wing, report," he ordered.

"This is Rokos," the Wing Commander finally replied. "Sorry, we were putting out a fire. Literally. My bird took a near miss.

"We are clear. Target destroyed and the Marines are launching assault shuttles for pod pickup. I have fifteen of our emergency pods and two hundred and ten Terran escape pods on my scopes; we should have everyone picked up and aboard the freighters before they're far enough out to go FTL."

"Thank you, Wing Commander," Kyle replied. He wasn't just thanking him for the report, and everyone knew it.

"All in a day's work, Force Commander," Rokos told him. "Transports will be clear of Huī Xing en route to Alizon in ten minutes. Sorry to be leaving you behind, sir."

"All in a day's work, Wing Commander," Kyle repeated back to him. "We'll deal with Vice Admiral Ness. Get out of here, Rokos, and take those people with you."

"Yes, sir," the Wing Commander replied crisply. "Good luck, sir."

CHAPTER 36

"What are they *doing*?" Kyle asked aloud, watching the Terrans' Twenty-Third Fleet simply sit and wait.

A quick calculation in his head confirmed that they would come to zero velocity and start heading *away* from the Terrans over thirty-four million kilometers inside the gravity well—and about the same distance from the Commonwealth fleet.

But even with the destruction of Bogey Eight and the escape of the transports, the Terrans seemed content to simply sit and watch him decelerate. He'd expected missiles, a fighter swarm—for that matter, if Vice Admiral Ness wanted to bring his battleship into play, now was the best time he'd have. Right now, Battle Group Seven-Two's velocity was *toward* the Terran Fleet. The Battle Group was burning fuel wildly to reduce that velocity, but until they were building velocity away the Terrans, it would far easier for the Terrans to force a starship engagement they'd handily win.

"Remember that expensive coffee?" Anderson replied. "I'd bet it that Ness is under hard orders from Walkingstick not to risk his fleet—he won't enter the gravity well himself until he knows where the *rest* of Seventh Fleet is."

"Which leaves him able to go after the Admiral once he does," Kyle said grimly. "On the other hand, I'm pretty sure Ness *really* doesn't like me right now. Xue." He turned to the tactical officer. "Have everyone quietly start deploying missiles. I want a ten-salvo, cascade-activated, time-on-target attack ready to go as soon as we hit zero velocity relative to the Commonwealth ships."

That was a quarter of the Phoenix ships' remaining magazines. A fifth of *Sledgehammer*'s. *Avalon* had the missiles to spend, but her nine launchers weren't going to stack enough of a salvo to yank Vice Admiral Ness's nonexistent beard.

Five hundred and seventy missiles, ten stacked salvos from every ship in Battle Group Seven-Two, had a decent chance of doing real damage. With eight hundred starfighters flying escort on Ness's remaining nine warships, Kyle put his odds of actually taking a *starship* out at only thirty percent or so. Ten salvos was the most their fire control could handle, however, and they'd take out starfighters if nothing else.

Kyle would back Stanford's starfighter pilots against any the Commonwealth had one to one, and their Falcon and Templar starfighters were worth half again their numbers in the Terran Scimitars. Sadly, Twenty-Third Fleet had almost *four times* the number of starfighters Battle Group Seven-Two had left—eight hundred to barely more than two hundred.

Sending Bravo Wing to escort the freighters had turned the balance of starfighter power even further in the Terrans' favor—but it had also got the transports *out*, which was worth it.

"Once we hit zero-v," Kyle told Xue, "I want to shove those missiles down the Terrans' throats and run for Goudeshijie as fast as we can. Let's see if we can make this jackass chase us."

His tactical officer nodded, surprisingly calm for just having been asked to poke a much larger fleet in the eye.

"We'll hit him, sir," she promised. "But what he'll do..."

"We can't predict that," Kyle agreed. "All we can do is poke him and see what happens."

GLYNN STEWART

"Emergence from warped space in ten. Nine. Eight."

Fleet Commander James Coles' countdown echoed through *Camerone*'s bridge while Mira waited impatiently to see what waited for them at Via Somnia. They'd picked up a lot of data waiting a light-month away from the system, but resolving, for example, whether a specific space station was a transfer station or a fighter base was all but impossible at that range.

"Emergence," Coles announced.

Camerone erupted into open space, surrounded by her sister ships. Eight Alliance capital ships arrived in the Via Somnia system, their arrival heralded by bursts of blue Cherenkov radiation.

The main target in the system was the Via Somnia Commonwealth Navy Base, a massive complex orbiting the third planet of the system—a dead rock three times the size of Earth with a gravity well that impeded Alcubierre drives for two light-minutes.

Mira waited patiently for her tactical officer and Alstairs' staff to grind the data, comparing what they were seeing now to what they'd picked from a light-month out and what Alliance Intelligence had predicted.

"I'm not seeing any capital ships in the system," Fleet Commander Rose, her tactical officer, reported after a few moments. "I *do* see four logistics freighters docked with the naval base, but no warships at all."

"Anything here has been sent to Huī Xing," Notley told Mira grimly. "That's worrying, ma'am."

"Other than giving our friend Ness the forces to keep Kyle pinned, why?" she asked, eyeing the screens.

"Because it means that the *Terrans* weren't worried about leaving the naval base—which represents a cool ten trillion Commonwealth dollars, the price of a couple of warships—with *no* warship defenders," her XO reminded her, and she remembered—once again—that Notley had more time in combat than the rest of her bridge crew combined.

"Void," she cursed softly. "Xue, what are you seeing?" she demanded.

"Not good," the tactical officer replied. "We're still validating, but I'm throwing our certainties on screen as they firm up. Big icons are fighter bases. Small icons are missile satellites. Middle icons are positron lance platforms."

The red icons started dropping onto the main screen and Mira's implants. The lance platforms were a new wrinkle on Mira, though she was familiar with the concept—fixed platforms with the big versions of the modified zero point cells used as main capital ship weapons, usually megaton-range beams. An outer shell of at least two hundred of the things covered the approaches to the naval base.

The missile platforms made the section of the display showing the Naval base look *diseased*. Hundreds—possibly *thousands*—of the miniscule three-launcher, twelve-missile automated platforms were scattered through the space around the repair and logistics stations.

The last piece of the cake was the fighter platforms. Rose and the other tactical officers were still narrowing down the split between fighter bases and the stations making up the base itself—but they'd already confirmed twenty *Zion*-class platforms—over *twice* as many starfighters as Seventh Fleet had brought with them.

The fixed defenses of the Via Somnia Naval Base had Seventh Fleet well and truly matched—if not outgunned.

"Oh, *Starless* Void."

#

"Options, people," Rear Admiral Miriam Alstairs snapped.

All eight ship captains and the two carrier CAGs were linked in to a holoconference. While they conferred, Seventh Fleet orbited outside the gravity well of Via Somnia III, looking intimidating but not really *doing* much.

"We *can* take them," Mira said slowly. "We can carry out long-range missile bombardment from here—that'll force *them* to launch the satellites' missiles while they're least effective. We'll still have to take on their starfighters, and those lance platforms are going to be a Void-accursed nightmare."

"We can't protect the fleet from a thousand starfighters," Vice Commodore Ozolinsh told them bluntly. "We'll cut them down, hard, but you'll still have several hundred starfighters close enough to launch missiles."

"We can take that," Lord Captain Anders reminded the CAG flatly. "We can take that," he repeated, "but we'll lose ships. Take damage. As Captain Solace says, though, we can take this system."

"And will what's left of Seventh Fleet afterward be able to engage the Terrans' Twenty-Third Fleet when they come after us?" Lora Aleppo asked, the Trade Factor officer glaring at Anders.

"That would depend on how much damage Force Commander Roberts was able to do," Anders pointed out.

"Much as I dislike the cost involved, Roberts is more than capable of hammering Vice Admiral Ness's fleet down to a manageable size," Alstairs replied. "The mission objective remains Via Somnia..."

Anders held up a hand, forestalling the Admiral.

"What is it, Lord Captain?"

"Ma'am, Captain Solace is trying very hard *not* to be biased in her paramour's favor," the Coraline Lord Captain said flatly.

Mira flushed and started to glare at the man—he wasn't *wrong*, but it wasn't polite to point it out. Yes, she and Kyle were lovers, but she *wasn't* letting it influence her recommendation—otherwise, she'd be taking them to Huī Xing at maximum speed!

"This is leading her to make a *mistake*," Anders continued, and Mira stopped glaring, wondering where the Imperial officer was going. "Force Commander Roberts and I are not friends. Most of the rest of you are on far better terms with our 'hero' than I am, and you are all bending over backward to *not* allow that to influence your decision.

"And so you are all *wrong*," he snapped. "As Walkingstick has shown us again and again in this war, there is no true target but the enemy *fleet*. If we neutralize Twenty-Third Fleet, Via Somnia is ours to take. If we sacrifice Captain Roberts and his ships to capture this system, we will have thrown away a third of this fleet for *nothing*."

To say that Kyle and Anders were not friends was an understatement, Mira considered. Kyle had forced the man to replace a CAG who'd screwed up badly—but had also been a longstanding friend and protégé of Anders's.

"The Fleet Base is irrelevant without a fleet to support and is sufficiently defended to make taking it expensive," Anders noted. "I *must* recommend that we immediately proceed to the Huī Xing system and engage Twenty-Third Fleet in combination with Battle Group Seven-Two. Anything else risks leaving a significant Commonwealth strike force operating in this area—one we are unlikely to be able to neutralize if we take losses securing Via Somnia."

Mira found herself staring at Anders in shock, and she wasn't the only one. He was right—it hadn't just been her assuming she wanted to rescue Kyle only because he was her lover. Everyone else had tried to put their feelings aside—and missed the blatant strategic point.

Walkingstick had spent the entire war to date trying to grind down the Alliance's fleet strength, making neutralizing capital ships a priority over taking or even holding systems. *Twenty-Third Fleet* was the only real target on the board.

The conference was silent for a long moment, and then Alstairs broke the silence.

"Thank you, Lord Captain Anders," she said formally. "I believe you are correct that we had all missed that perspective. An additional point that has not been made is that the addition of *Avalon*'s battle group to our own order of battle would make taking this system significantly easier.

"However, from Force Commander Roberts' last set of transmissions, it appears that Vice Admiral Ness is under orders to avoid risking his fleet by entering the gravity well. If he remains outside the gravity well, he may be able to escape before we can destroy his fleet."

Mira chuckled, then smiled when everyone looked at her.

"The answer is also in Kyle's transmissions," she pointed out. "We have a stockpile of ECM drones—for that matter, our logistics freighters have piles of missile satellites.

"We can set them all up, attached to a few shuttles or tugs on autopilot, and give the appearance of our fleet hanging out back here, maintaining a long-term missile bombardment. With no humans in the loop, the accuracy will *suck*, but it will give the Commonwealth every sign they need to think we're settling in for a siege of Via Somnia."

CHAPTER 37

Huī Xing System
01:25 April 5, 2736 Earth Standard Meridian Date/Time
DSC-078 Avalon, *Bridge*

Help was on the way.

Said help was *four days* away, but it was coming—and that meant Force Commander Kyle Roberts' people had been spared from what had been appearing to be an inevitable death. He wouldn't have told any of his people that he didn't think they could win, but he'd used up the only tricks he had to get the rescued prisoners out.

The only thing *he'd* had left was to drag things out and see how many of Twenty-Third Fleet's ships he could make Vice Admiral Ness spend to kill them.

With the rest of Seventh Fleet on the way, however, his main task had become to keep his people alive. It would be *helpful* if he could lure Twenty-Third Fleet into the gravity well—though he'd rather do so closer to Admiral Alstairs' arrival if he had the choice—but not a necessity.

"We are approaching zero velocity," Pendez reported. "We'll start building our vector *away* from our lovely Terran friends in about a minute."

"That is going to be *so* nice," the XO murmured. "Something about *not* suicidally charging into the teeth of the enemy is going to feel so relaxing."

"Are the missiles set up?" Kyle asked Xue.

"Ready to go," she confirmed. "Roughly nine minutes from engine activation to mass impact."

"Good. Fire at the best timing—use your judgment," he ordered.

"Wait!" she short-stopped him. "Aspect change—hold on a moment."

The tactical officer blanked out, focusing on her implants as she studied the new data from her Q-probes.

"Three ships just went to Alcubierre," she finally reported. "Looks like the Hercules and two Assassins—on their way to take up the old blocking position. They left their starfighters behind, though."

"That helps," Kyle replied with a smile. The starfighters were the single biggest obstacle to landing hits with the salvo they'd prepared, but removing three capital ships from the defensive suite *definitely* made an impact. "Are we still in the zone for time-on-target?"

"Yes, sir," Xue told him instantly. "Forty-five seconds till optimal activation."

"Good. Fire at will."

Seconds later, ever so infinitesimally, Battle Group Seven-Two, *Avalon*, stopped moving toward the Commonwealth Twenty-Third Fleet and started moving away from it.

"I have starfighter movement!" Xue announced. "Damn—every one of those starfighters is coming right at us!"

A quick study of Kyle's data feeds confirmed the tactical officer's assessment—all eight hundred of the starfighters from Twenty-Third Fleet's ships were now chasing after Kyle's Battle Group at four hundred and fifty gravities.

That was only a two-hundred-gravity edge over the fuel-wasting pace that Seven-Two was maintaining—but that was a pace Kyle hadn't planned on keeping up.

"I guess we're staying at two hundred and fifty gees," he noted aloud. There was no way he could slow down now, not with enough fighters to eat his command and spit out the pieces trailing in his wake. "Commander?"

"Missiles activating now," she said flatly.

"Keep me in the loop," Kyle ordered, then flipped his attention to his CAG. "Michael, we have a fucking *swarm* of Scimitars heading our way. I hope you have *some* kind of clever idea."

"I don't have much except smashing right into them and holding them in the gap between our lance range and theirs until one of us is dead," Stanford admitted. "We're moving out. See you on the other side, Kyle."

Avalon's Captain swallowed. He'd been a CAG once—he knew what kind of fight Stanford and his people were charging into—a close-range mutual suicide duel. But Stanford was right—it was the only hope *Avalon* and her battle group had.

And starfighters existed to die so starships didn't. They could lose their entire fighter strength and lose fewer people and resources than if they lost a single one of their four starships.

Kyle didn't have to *like* it.

"Missiles in range of their fighters," Xue reported, interrupting his thoughts. "They're engaging."

His attention turned back to his attempt to poke the Terrans. Five hundred and seventy Jackhammer capital ship missiles flashed through the same space occupied by the Scimitar attack formation, allowing the eight hundred starfighters to lash out at them with positron lances and lasers.

Part of him wished he'd set those missiles to target the fighters—he wouldn't have taken out many of them, but every fighter that died before they clashed with Stanford increased the chance for his people to live.

Instead, the missiles took out a dozen starfighters, almost by accident, and the starfighters took out over three hundred missiles in turn. Two hundred and sixty-three weapons charged into terminal mode on the Commonwealth Twenty-Third Fleet, and Kyle felt his hands clench into fists.

Six ships remained in the blocking force closest to him—a single Assassin battlecruiser, the Saint battleship, a Volcano carrier and the three Lexingtons. Their combined defenses were formidable, but his missiles were coming in with a high base velocity and their ECM running at full power.

The Saint swung forward, the big battleship putting her massive defenses and armor between the missiles and her more vulnerable sisters. The missiles swooped in, detonating in their dozens as the Terran defenses took their toll of shattered weapons and shining white antimatter explosions.

A near miss rocked the massive battleship, and a muttered curse of hope escaped Kyle's lips. As the light faded, it was clear the ship had survived, her weapons shattering the missiles that made it past her.

The networked intelligence of capital ship missiles was astonishingly smart and amazingly suicidal. Nine missiles somehow made it through everything and passed the battleship toward their programmed targets. Their networked mind concluded that it couldn't get any of the missiles through as it was—and self-detonated eight of the warheads in a rapid sequence.

The ninth warhead slammed dead center into the single Assassin left on this side of Goudeshijie—and vaporized the older, lightly armored warship in a blaze of annihilating matter.

02:40 April 5, 2736 ESMDT
SFG-001 Actual—Falcon-C type command starfighter

Michael watched the oncoming swarm of starfighters and capital ship missiles with a calm that surprised him. His implant had run the numbers on the missiles Twenty-Third Fleet had fired as his fighters maneuvered to set up their position—the Terrans had launched five salvos and the first would reach his starfighters about thirty seconds before they could launch *their* missiles on the Scimitars.

The Terrans clearly saw their fighter strike as the best chance to knock Battle Group Seven-Two out of the fight and were doubling down. The Saint and Volcano were the only units in the current battle group with missile launchers, but they were also big ships with magazines to spend. Two hundred and ten capital ship missiles were going to hit Michael's starfighters while his people were engaged with the Terran ships.

Already outnumbered almost four-to-one, Vice Commodore Michael Stanford was forced to the conclusion that there was no way he could actually *stop* the Terran fighter strike. His people could hurt it—possibly even cripple it—but he couldn't stop at least some of those ships from reaching the Battle Group.

"All starfighters," he said calmly, activating a channel that reached out to all two hundred and two of the Falcons and Templars currently accelerating *away* from the Terrans, reducing their closing velocity to give them as much time outside the enemy lance range as possible.

"You know what we're facing," he told them. "You know the mission, you've received your formation slots, and you what we have to do.

"But I remind you that these people are coming to kill us. They're coming to kill our friends. Perhaps most importantly, they're coming to kill our *carriers*, so if you like your bunk, I suggest we stop them," he continued with a chuckle.

A timer continued to tick down. The first missiles would hit his people in less than two minutes. Shortly after that, roughly eighty-four minutes after the starfighters had left the Battle Group behind, his people would be launching the first of their own missiles.

"It has been an honor and a privilege to command you all," Michael finally finished after a long pause. "Today, we will do the Alliance proud. When this is over, the drinks are on me."

When this was over, many—if not most—of his people were going to be dead.

#

The missiles came first, a harbinger of the destruction following them. Forty-two of the massive weapons came crashing in on the Alliance starfighters with relative velocities well over ten percent of lightspeed. Michael coordinated the defense as best as he could, running four different assistant AIs as he assigned single missiles as targets for an entire squadron's worth of defensive lasers and positron lances.

The first wave died easily, the sole focus of twenty-five fighter squadrons' firepower. But then their attention needed to be split—Michael handed off control of the defensive suite to his starfighter's engineer while he and Arnolds started setting up the first mass missile strike.

Unlike the Terrans, he didn't need to preserve missiles to attack the starships. Unfortunately, the Templars only had three launchers to the Scimitars' or his Falcons' four, and his two hundred and two starfighters would only launch seven hundred and sixty-four missiles. Worse, in many ways, the Terran ships had one more missile per launcher than any of his ships.

But the Stormwinds had been meant to reduce his numbers before his people launched—and they'd failed.

Still over a million kilometers away from the Terran starfighters, Michael gave the mental command—and his ship shuddered as all four of her missile launchers fired.

A new timer popped up into his implants—the fighter's computers informing him how long it was going to take to rearm the launchers. Another timer told him that the next capital ship salvo was going to hit before his people could launch *their* next salvo.

This time, he had to leave it in the hands of the starfighters' flight engineers. A high-level set of eyes helped, and even with Q-Coms, the carrier's staff were too far away, but the engineers could do the job no matter what.

The clean sweep the first time had been a combination of luck, skill, and a lack of distractions. Now the fighter gunners were concerned with defensive ECM against both the capital ship missiles *and* the Scimitars' missiles. The pilots were in defensive mode against everything, focused on dodging more than bringing lances to bear against the heavy missiles. The engineers, tasked with running the defensive lasers, were also focused on balancing the power requirements of the starfighters' dozens of systems as they closed into combat range.

This time, explosions pocked the space amidst Michael's fighters. Most of the missiles still died well short of his fighters, but two were close enough near misses that starfighters spun out of formation, both ships spinning helplessly for a moment before ejecting their emergency pods and self-destructing.

Their crews could be retrieved later, but the starfighters were entirely out of the fight. Two down, and Michael was grimly certain they wouldn't be the last.

His starfighter shuddered again as the second salvo blasted into space. The command starfighter itself didn't have the munitions for a fourth salvo—each of his Wing Commanders flew similar ships, which would rob his last salvo of another dozen missiles.

The third missile salvo from the capital ships robbed it of more. Again, most of the missiles died clear of the starfighters, but two more ships drifted away, disabled by from near misses—and three missiles made it through everything the fighters could throw at them to hit their targets, annihilating starfighters in one-gigaton balls of antimatter fire.

Seven fighters down before his people had even reached lance range, and Michael watched the distances drop rapidly. Once his ships were in lance range, they'd have to cease accelerating away from the Terran ships and turn to face them.

His people would have less than twenty seconds to kill as many of the Scimitars as possible. Once they were in the range of the Terran fighters' dual twenty-five-kiloton-a-second positron lances, the balance of the engagement was going to swing dramatically in the Scimitars' favor.

His final missile salvo had no response from the Terrans. The Scimitars were preserving their missiles to kill Battle Group Seven-Two's carriers. They'd already thrown two salvos of over three thousand Javelin fighter missiles apiece at him. The geometry meant they'd been launched later and were arriving more slowly, but clearly, whoever was leading the Commonwealth fighter strike thought the sheer numbers would be enough.

Despite everything, every so often, Michael ran into a Terran starfighter commander who just didn't seem to *learn* the lessons the Alliance's seventh-generation starfighters kept teaching the Terrans' sixth-generation ships.

Along the way, his people had been slowly assuming the donut formation that Rokos had suggested earlier in the same star system. His sensors suggested that none of the Q-probes were close enough to pick out the ECM drones.

The dispersal of the starfighters hadn't been enough to fool the capital ship missiles, but against *fighter* missiles, it had already proven effective. Massive waves of ECM, jamming, and false images were already rippling off Michael's command as the Terran fighters slowly overhauled his own formation.

The Terran missiles would reach his ships nine seconds after his people were in lance range. That all on its own limited the effect those thousands of weapons would have on this clash.

His own two thousand-plus missiles would arrive in rapidly shortening intervals, but even as he studied their salvos, his first salvo entered range of the Terran ships. Defensive lasers, electronic countermeasures, and positron lances lashed out into space, eight hundred starfighters' defenses lashing out at a mere seven-hundred-odd missiles.

Those missiles' motherships were right behind them, and their *jamming* reached out at the speed of light. The Falcons' and Templars' ECM suites were vastly more powerful than the Scimitars' defenses—and overwhelmed them even from two hundred thousand kilometers away.

And then, just as the missiles hit terminal acquisition, the starfighters reached lance range. Hundreds of positron lances flashed across space, beams of pure antimatter seeking out the Terran starfighters.

Staying on a single course was anathema to a starfighter pilot, the randomness necessary to reduce hit probabilities drilled into them until it was second nature. Many of the positron lances missed, second-long flashes of white energy in the empty void around Goudeshijie.

Others hit. Dozens of the Terran starfighters went up in flames, emergency pods ejecting as the positron beams ripped the ships to shreds.

In the wake of the positron lances, the first missile salvo struck home. The Terran defense had gutted the salvo, a mere tithe of the original thousand-plus missiles surviving to claim victims.

More lance fire followed. Michael spun his own starfighter through a deadly pirouetting spiral that tracked the nose of the ship—and its deadly positron lance—across a field of the Terran starfighters. As the computer-predicted future positions of starfighters crossed the beam's path, the weapon fired. Again and again, he and his people fired.

Then the *Terran* missiles arrived. Only the defensive laser suites were available to protect the Alliance ships—the lances *had* to kill starfighters or the whole fight was for nothing.

The donut hole, with the vast amounts of ECM poured into the fake center of their formation, absorbed over fifteen hundred of the Javelins. That still left over sixteen hundred missiles charging at Michael's people—a vast amount of overkill, compared to the salvo they'd leveled at the larger Terran force.

Michael focused on *his* task. There was little he could do to turn the tide of the grander battle beyond surviving and killing starfighters. His implant kept him informed of the defensive sweep and of the total kills inflicted on the Terran fleet.

He felt the failure of his peoples' defenses like a punch to the gut. In a single series of fiery bootsteps through his formation, the Javelins blew seventy of his starfighters to pieces. Over a *third* of his remaining strength disappeared in a single instant.

His own second salvo then returned the favor. Seven hundred and sixty-plus weapons slammed into the Terrans' defenses, dancing around and through his people's repeated lance strikes. With the lance fire incoming and their formations ripped to pieces, there was no way the Terrans could stop them all.

Eighty starfighters blew apart in an instant, bringing the Terran losses to well over four hundred. Over half of their force was gone, and Michael finally started to believe his people might make it through.

Then the *second* Terran salvo arrived. Without their motherships to feed them data, many of them were flying stupid—but a salvo of Stormwinds came with them, their networked intelligence replacing the starfighter controls.

They'd adapted for the hole in his formation and hit the top half of the Alliance fighter strike—and when the explosions faded, almost half of Michael's remaining strength was gone.

Less than a hundred Alliance starfighters survived, plunging toward the Terran formation. Even Michael, linked to his computers and riding the flame of his fighter's engine, couldn't keep track of everything. He dodged missiles, he struck, he dodged again as the Terran lances opened fire, and then killed another starfighter. Only the moment mattered— only killing the Scimitars in front of him could save *Avalon*.

He never saw the positron lance that blew his starfighter to ashes.

Kyle stared forward into space, trying and failing to process the information his implant was giving him. Stanford couldn't be dead. He *couldn't*.

But the data feeds coming into his head from *Avalon's* computers, a consolidated mix of data from the Q-probes near the battle and the starfighters themselves, refused to magically change. A tiny red notation on the starfighter labeled SFG-001 ACTUAL noted it as destroyed with no escape pod launch detected.

Some of the starfighters had made it through the clash. They were now over a million kilometers behind the Terran ships, not accelerating at all. The tiny handful of surviving ships looked as shell-shocked on the display at Kyle felt.

"Seven-Two starfighters, report," he ordered. "Whoever is in command, report!"

A few seconds passed, then a female voice with a Phoenix accent answered him.

"This is Sub-Colonel Sherry Wills of *Indomitable's* Infernals," she responded, her voice shaky. "I think I'm the last O-5 left outside the pods. I have…" She paused, then resumed after audibly swallowing. "… twenty-four effectives with no munitions.

"We have between one hundred and one hundred and ten emergency pods on our screens," Wills continued. "I can confirm that Vice Commodore Stanford's pod did not deploy. The Battle Group CAG is KIA."

Killed In Action.

The woman on the scene confirmed what the sensors told Kyle—his friend was dead. With two hundred and fifty Terran starfighters still bearing down on his position, there was *nothing* he could do to mourn either.

Kyle swallowed hard and focused.

"Can you keep pace with the pods?" he asked. The emergency pods had no engines of their own; they'd continue on at the velocity their fighters had had when they'd launched. Fortunately, that vector was towards Goudeshijie, which meant *Avalon could* recover them if she survived the minutes to come.

"We can," Wills confirmed.

"You're out of this fight for now," Kyle told her. "Keep an eye on our people; we'll be coming to get them soon enough."

"Thank you, sir," she replied. "Make it...make it worth it, sir. I just lost a lot of friends."

"So did I," Kyle murmured. "We'll still be here when the dust settles, Sub-Colonel. I promise you that."

The undertones that accompanied implant communication gave him the impression of a firm nod, then Wills cut the channel to focus on keeping twenty-four starfighter crews from going mad from grief.

"Battle Group orders," he said aloud, activating a channel to his captains. "We're going to see one giant pile of crap land us in about three minutes," he told them simply. "I want all of us going to maximum-cycle fire on our missile launchers *now*."

"We can't sustain that for long," Captain Olivier of *Courageous* pointed out. "We're down almost half our magazines already."

"We can sustain it for three minutes and maybe cut a chunk of this fighter strike off before they eat us alive," he reminded her. "We'll move to formation Alpha-Foxtrot Two."

"Sir," Captain Ainsley of *Sledgehammer* suggested. "I recommend Sierra-Foxtrot Five instead."

The two formations were basically identical. Both were staggered formations that put the battleship *Sledgehammer* and the supercarrier *Avalon* in front of the battlecruisers, where their more intensive defensives could protect the two Phoenix ships.

The difference was that Alpha-Foxtrot put *Avalon* in the most exposed position, where Sierra-Foxtrot put *Sledgehammer* in that position.

"Neither *Indomitable* nor *Courageous* can take more than one hit and keep fighting," Ainsley continued. "And if *Avalon* takes crippling damage, we may not be able to retrieve our fighters. We all know it's the battleship's job to stand in front and take the beating so everyone else doesn't. Let us do our job, sir."

Kyle started to object but stopped himself. Ainsley was right. Kyle's desire to keep everyone else out of harm's way was a dangerous feeling in a battle group commander. The battleship *needed* to be in front. *Kyle* was just afraid to put them there.

For the first time since Alstairs had made him Force Commander, Kyle felt truly out of his depth. He took a deep breath and nodded.

"You're right," he admitted. "Sierra-Foxtrot Five, people. Remember—let's stay *alive*."

#

At the speed Battle Group Seven-Two was moving, a few careful half-second long lapses in acceleration were enough for the battleship and the big modern carrier to drop behind the other ships. A matter of seconds to stabilize their positions and begin sending fifty-seven missile salvos dropping into their wake at the rapidly closing starfighters.

The missiles wouldn't hit before the starfighters launched their own weapons, but they would hit long before any of the starfighters closed to lance range—pathetically short for the Scimitars' underpowered weapons.

Stanford's people had inflicted massive losses along the way. The two hundred and fifty ships still bearing down on him were less than a third of the force they'd started with—but would still manage to put two thousand missiles on target. More capital ship missile salvos had been launched to coincide with their expected arrival—combined with the thousand starfighter missiles in each batch, Kyle's people were in real danger.

Just past oh three hundred hours Earth Standard Time, the Scimitars finally swept into missile range and promptly fired. Exactly one thousand starfighter missiles blasted into space, a wall of crimson icons bearing far too rapidly down on Battle Group Seven-Two for Kyle's comfort.

"Maintain missile fire, but use our missiles to support missile defense," he ordered. "Hammer them, people."

Nine seconds before the starfighters could launch their *second* salvo, the Alliance missiles arrived. Against the full force, fifty-seven missiles wouldn't have been much of a threat. Against the much-reduced remnant he currently faced, many of whom had lost sensors and laser clusters to near misses, they took out a full dozen starfighters.

That left the second salvo from the starfighters at a "mere" nine hundred and fifty-two weapons.

His missile salvos continued to strike home as Kyle watched their tsunami come crashing towards his command. Six salvos were in space, and five slammed home before the fighter missiles reached his ships. Even the secondary lances aboard *Avalon* and *Sledgehammer*, though not the Phoenix cruisers, reached the starfighters before their missiles reached his people.

The Terran ships started to go up like moths, dying in their *dozens* as they closed with his ships—but the deaths of the starfighters that launched them didn't slow the missiles already in space.

ECM sang songs of confusion and lies to lure missiles aside, and starfighter missiles were dumb. Lasers flashed out in deadly sequence, and the armor on starfighter missiles was nonexistent. Massive capital ships maneuvered to throw targeting solutions off, and threw their every defense into the missiles' teeth.

The Alliance's defensive missiles killed hundreds. Hundreds more went astray and hundreds more again died to the lasers. Kyle found himself holding his breath as the missiles came crashing down.

Of the thousand missiles in the first salvo, *one* got through—slamming dead center into *Sledgehammer*, the gigaton-plus blow sending the battleship lurching away.

"Report!" Kyle snapped.

"Still here," Ainsley replied instantly, *Sledgehammer*'s Captain's voice strained. "We'll stick it out!"

The second salvo followed only a few seconds after he'd finished speaking. These missiles had been launched that much closer with that much more base velocity. Again, missiles went astray by the hundreds, and died by the hundreds more—but the interceptions had started later, and this time, the starfighters were right on their heels.

Another missile hit *Sledgehammer*, near the stern. The battleship lurched—and then stopped accelerating as her engines failed.

Like sharks scenting blood, the missiles swarmed the old battleship even as her every weapon strained to defend herself.

It wasn't enough.

Even as the starfighters came swarming through the haze of explosions and death to bring their lances into range, the missiles that had come before slammed into *Sledgehammer* again and again. *Hammer*-class battleships were tough—but no armor known or defense built could withstand *that* many hits from antimatter warheads.

Sledgehammer died—but she took the last of the missiles with her. Kyle had a moment of hope that Captain Ainsley's sacrifice had saved the battle group.

Then the last hundred Scimitars came bursting through the debris field of *Sledgehammer*'s death, finally in the lance range they'd bled so hard to reach.

At this range, the secondary lances of the three capital ships could barely miss the starfighters if they tried, but the Scimitars' lances fired back. *Avalon* bucked under Kyle's feet, her immense size no defense against the beams of pure antimatter that flayed her hull. Lances and missile launchers exploded, automatic failsafes blasting failing zero point cells and antimatter capacitors free of the big ship's hull.

Linked in through his implants, Kyle felt every wound his ship took as his own, and turned her remaining weapons on her tormentors. Secondary positron lances, primary positron lances, close-range missiles and even anti-missile lasers blazed after the Terran ships.

The Scimitars were in range for barely four seconds. Three survived to run.

The flashing red on his implant displays and the pseudo-pain Kyle felt told him all he needed to know. The Terran strike hadn't *killed* Battle Group Seven-Two—but it was entirely possible they'd crippled it.

CHAPTER 38

Huī Xing System
03:10 April 5, 2736 Earth Standard Meridian Date/Time
DSC-078 Avalon, *Bridge*

As the pseudo-pain his implant fed him to warn him about damage to the ship faded, Kyle became aware of very real pain. Between cascade failures forcing the mass manipulators to hand gravity generation around and the impacts themselves, the bridge crew had been thrown around emphatically.

His shoulder hurt where his safety straps had held him in, and his neck felt...sprained. Interrogating his implants, they promptly informed him he'd partly dislocated his left shoulder and had moderate soft tissue damage in his neck.

The latter his own nanites could deal with. The former was going to need about thirty seconds of a medic's time at some point.

A point that would need to be later. All three ships left in his battle group had dropped to one hundred and fifty gravities—an almost automatic safety measure after taking this level of damage. His starfighters and the emergency pods from their dead comrades continued to hurtle towards Goudeshijie at thousands of kilometers a second.

There was work to do.

"Wong, report," Kyle ordered, opening a channel to his chief engineer. "What's our status?"

"Extra crispy," Senior Fleet Commander Alistair Wong replied flatly. "Sending in survey crews now, but the good news is that the core power modules are fine. We have main power; we have main engines. What we *don't* have is full mass manipulator capacity. I wouldn't suggest pushing her past two hundred gees."

"Can we retrieve fighters?"

"Yes," Wong confirmed. "Kalers says the deck is undamaged. What we *don't* have anymore are half our launch tubes. The starboard broadside is *gone*, Kyle. No lances. No missiles. No fighter launch tubes."

Casualty reports were already filtering into Kyle's implants. Not even counting the loss of fighter crews, it was looking at over five hundred wounded or dead. *Avalon* had been hit hard.

"Keep me informed," Kyle told Wong. He flipped open another channel. "Kalers, can we deploy retrieval ships?"

Keeping *himself* busy kept him focused. He had every intent of applying the same methodology to his crew.

"We can," his deck chief replied after a moment. "They're defenseless if the Terrans start shooting, though."

"We have to take the risk," he told her grimly. "I don't *think* they'll shoot at search-and-rescue ships, but we need to catch our pods before they fly past—or *into*—Goudeshijie and are lost."

"Understood, sir," she confirmed. "I'll have them in space shortly."

"Thank you, Chief."

Kyle checked his channel to Anderson, making sure that his XO was tied into all of his communications. If something happened to the bridge, James Anderson would have to fight *Avalon* from secondary control.

"Anything to add, XO?" he asked the Fleet Commander.

"I'm coordinating damage control with Wong and Surgeon-Commander Cunningham," Anderson told him. "If anything, he's understating how bad the upper and lower starboard chunks of the ship are looking. The outer hull is just...gone, Kyle. We'll need *hours* to replace Stetson emitters before we can go FTL, and that's all we're going to manage without a shipyard."

"But our port weapons are intact?"

"For the good it will do us with only twenty-four starfighters, yeah."

"Twelve seven-hundred-kiloton lances and four launchers will do us some good, at least," Kyle noted. "I'm pulling the captains in for a conference. Don't need you to contribute, but stay on the channel."

"Yes, sir."

Dropping Anderson to a secondary channel, Kyle activated his privacy screen and opened up a conference link via the Q-Com to bring in the captains of the other two surviving ships of Battle Group Seven-Two. As Gervaise Albert and Christine Olivier appeared in his mental interface, he felt the twist of a mental knife at the *absences* of Michael Stanford and Urien Ainsley.

Both men had died to keep the rest of the battle group safe, and thousands of their subordinates had died with them. Kyle's body count there in Huī Xing was getting far higher than he liked.

"*Avalon* is badly damaged but combat-capable," he told them without preamble. "We can retrieve and launch fighters, but we're down both starboard broadsides and cannot maintain an acceleration above two hundred gravities."

The two Phoenix women looked at each other, then Albert sighed and spoke.

"*Indomitable* is no longer capable of retrieving starfighters," she admitted. She flashed a damage control report to the conference, and Kyle sucked in a breath as he saw the extent of the damage. A *Fearless*-class battle cruiser was a fourteen-hundred-meter-long even-sided diamond, with her carrier launch deck and most of her weapons on the front half of the diamond.

The forward two hundred meters of *Indomitable* were simply gone. Deep chasms of red cut deeper into the battlecruiser's hull where positron beams had ripped through external armor and just kept going.

"We're barely holding together at one-fifty gravities and have lost the forward Class One Manipulator," Albert continued. "*Indomitable* is not capable of entering Alcubierre drive. My forward positron lances are gone or nonfunctional, but we maintain seventy-five percent of our missile launchers."

Kyle nodded—that meant that the effectively crippled *Indomitable* still had three times the launchers *Avalon* did...and not much else.

"Understood, Captain," he said quietly. "And *Courageous*?"

Olivier shook her head.

"We're in better shape, but not by much," she admitted. "We took most of our hits to the bottom of the ship. We're down...well, we're down our launch deck and half of our weapons, but we still have all of our upper side's lances and launchers." She sighed. "Our engines are in about the same state, Force Commander. We *do* still have all of our Class One Mass Manipulators, though, so once we've replaced our Stetson stabilizers, we can make FTL."

If, of course, Battle Group Seven-Two ever escaped Goudeshijie's gravity well, something Kyle was no longer counting on.

"Maintain a zero-zero course for the gas giant," he ordered. "We'll keep at one hundred and fifty gravities. Remember, people, the cavalry is coming. We just need to stay alive."

"Hundred and fifty gravities of accel is blood in the water, sir," Olivier said grimly. "What happens if the Terrans come in after us?"

"Most likely?" Kyle replied. "We run. We keep running. We dance the bastards in circles around Goudeshijie and Xin until either they make a mistake or Seventh Fleet arrives. We just lost thousands of good people. I will run like a scared rabbit if that's what it takes to keep the rest alive."

#

At the speed they'd already been traveling and with their reduced acceleration capacity, turnover—flipping the ships to slow their velocity toward the gas giant—was less than five minutes later. The actual flight into Goudeshijie orbit would take a little under three hours in total from there, but once there, they'd be shielded by the Dog World's rings and moons.

Kyle studied the gas giant's orbitals. He could use the rings and the half-dozen moons to help protect his crippled fleet from the Terrans, but all that would really do was buy time. Even long-range missile fire could get around a moon to hit him. If Ness chose to close the range and engage with lance fire, Kyle didn't have the fighters to stop him. The Terrans' Saint flagship alone could rip what was left of Kyle's Battle Group to pieces.

Hiding in Goudeshijie's rings was a horrible option, one that would buy him at most one of the four days he needed. There were games he could play, but once the Terrans brought a starship or two down the gravity well, his options would rapidly narrow down to two: fight an overwhelming force with crippled ships, or surrender.

A review of his ships' ammunition levels didn't help. Given time, *Avalon* alone could replenish all three ships to full stocks. Twenty-Third Fleet wouldn't give them that time, which meant those depleted magazines *also* narrowed his options. *Avalon* still had seventy missiles left for each of her four remaining launchers—plus another three hundred-plus in the magazines for the five launchers she'd lost, if they could move them—but the two Phoenix battlecruisers were down to twenty missiles per launcher *after* moving the weapons.

Time passed, and red markers on his damage control display faded to orange as Wong's people and robots swarmed over the damage. Eventually, fatigue forced Kyle to take another stimulant. They would do him no favors in the long run, but he *couldn't* be away from the bridge now.

Few of the damage markers returned to green. Orange simply meant that the damage was contained, no air leaks or exposed power conduits that would transfer damage to the rest of the ship. His starboard broadsides were going to require yard work—*months* of yard work.

A slow net of green was expanding around the outside of the ship as Wong's people replaced Stetson stabilizer emitters. Without them, *Avalon* couldn't safely go FTL, even if Kyle managed to find a miracle that would *let* them.

They were still an hour and a half away from Goudeshijie when the transmission from the Terrans caught up with them. Kyle gestured for the com officer to relay it to him, and the now-familiar blond face of Vice Admiral Kaj Ness appeared in his implant feeds.

The Vice Admiral looked disturbingly calm and cheerful for a man Kyle suspected had been awake as long as he had. If the loss of his ships and starfighters had hit him as hard as Kyle's losses had, he didn't show it—but then, Kyle wouldn't have either, in the other man's position.

"Force Commander Roberts," Ness said calmly. "You have fought bravely—brilliantly, even—but we both know this battle is decided. Goudeshijie's moons cannot save you. Continuing to fight will only cost lives under your command. Please. Let this end."

Kyle felt his bridge crew's eyes on him again, and he looked up at them and shook his head gently.

"The good Vice Admiral wants us to surrender," he told them gently. "Not yet. Maybe before we're done. But not yet!"

"Any response, sir?"

Kyle shook his head and turned back to the main screen showing the massive gas giant.

"No."

#

Forty minutes later, Vice Admiral Ness's response to Kyle's lack of reply became clear.

"They'll rendezvous about two million klicks out from Goudeshijie, and then swing into the gas giant," Xue concluded, tracing the course of the Hercules battlecruiser detached from the new Force Bravo and the Saint battleship detached from Force Alpha.

"Left the battlecruisers and carriers guarding the gravity well," Anderson noted from secondary control. "I guess they figure even a bunch of old carriers with no missile launchers can deal with us in our current state."

"What do we do now, Roberts?" Captain Olivier asked over the Q-Com link. "We can't fight them. Two modern capital ships versus three crippled ones? It's a done deal."

"If we opened up with missiles as they close, we can drop our entire arsenal on them before they reach us," Captain Albert noted. "We should be able to take out at least one of them, right?"

"We're down to twenty-six launchers," Kyle pointed out. "If we threw *everything* at them, we can control about four hundred missiles still. We could do that...twice. At any useful range, they'd be able to use stacked salvos of their own missiles as counters, maneuver to evade, and generally do everything to make their defenses as effective as possible.

"We *might* get one of them—in exchange for being helpless when the other catches up with us," he said grimly.

"I don't see any other option, sir," Xue said quietly. "If we do stack the salvos, we can hammer each of them—we should at least do *damage,* if not take them out."

"I'd give a lot right now for those missiles and satellites we left in Xin orbit," Olivier told them. "Bastard would hesitate if he was staring down two hundred Atlatls and six hundred missile launchers."

Kyle paused, silent in thought for a moment as he ran the course in his head. The Terran ships would arrive *here, then.* They had an eighty-gravity advantage over his ships' current capabilities. It didn't work. If the Terrans turned to intercept his people, they'd catch them over two hours short of Xin.

If the Terrans made it all the way to Goudeshijie before they realized what he'd *done,* however...

"Anderson," he turned to his exec. "How many of those ECM emitter drones do we have left?"

"Maybe twenty?"

"Kalers—the tugs survived just fine, right? And they can run on computer control, right?"

"Yeah," the deck chief replied. "They've only got a day or so of endurance, though, depending on what you need them to do."

"That's plenty," Kyle told her. "I just need them to not fall into Goudeshijie until the Commonwealth gets here."

Battle Group Seven-Two was forty minutes from Goudeshijie. The two Terran warships were three hours and forty minutes from the gas giant—and if they made a zero-zero intercept with Goudeshijie orbit, they'd be a long way behind him.

"All right, people," he said aloud, gathering his subordinates' attention. "This is what we're going to do."

Mira had forced herself to leave her bridge, but sleep was being elusive. She couldn't justify harassing Kyle—*Avalon* might not be in combat at that exact moment, but they remained in a combat zone. Juggling his elbow at that moment would be a *bad* idea.

They'd left Via Somnia three hours before, three hours out of the four days it would take to reach Huī Xing. The last reports from *Avalon* made for grim reading—almost their entire fighter strength gone. A battleship lost. All three remaining ships badly damaged.

Offset against that was the escape of the Marine brigade and the rescued prisoners. Whether it was worth it was something she figured pundits would argue over for years.

She *did* think it was worth it—but she was surprised to find that she was also *very* sure that opinion would change if Kyle Roberts didn't make it out. Mira had never figured their relationship to be a fling, but she was surprised at how fiercely she stared at the icons on her mental display, wishing that Seventh Fleet could go *faster*.

If they didn't make it in time, she wasn't sure she'd be able to live with herself.

CHAPTER 39

Huī Xing System
06:00 April 5, 2736 Earth Standard Meridian Date/Time
DSC-078 Avalon, *Bridge*

For a few glorious moments, Kyle submerged himself in his implant feed, becoming *Avalon* as the big supercarrier dove *into* Goudeshijie. Bright colors flared around him, the sheer friction of the Alliance ships' entry into the gas giant's atmosphere creating firestorms that filled his view.

The three ships were sixty kilometers deep into Goudeshijie's upper atmosphere, low enough that the firestorm forming around them wouldn't be visible to the Q-probes lurking in orbit. Those probes had their own show to watch—three of *Avalon*'s tugs were skimming the top of the gas giant's atmosphere, pretending to be the much bigger, wounded ships.

Kyle *knew* what was going on and it looked realistic to him when he looked at the feed from their own probes. Even knowing where and what to look for, he couldn't see his actual ships. They were safe from the Terrans for now, which allowed him to enjoy the incredible sight around the starship.

Safe was relative, of course. All three of his ships had gaping holes in their hulls, covered by whatever material they could throw together to keep the friction of the gas giant from ripping bigger holes. It was risky— but it bought them the chance of getting away from the Commonwealth without being spotted.

At a hundred and fifty gravities, they were submerged in the gas giant for almost ten minutes—and Kyle held the feed and watched the storms around his ships for every second of it.

Finally, they erupted from the gas giant—on the far side from where the Terrans thought they were.

"Any Q-probes on the sensors?" he demanded.

"None, sir," Xue replied after several seconds—clearly double-checking her own work. "They've got enough around that they'll pick us up *eventually*, but we're clear for at least an hour, maybe two."

"Hope for two, people," Kyle said quietly. "If we get two, we're all the way to Xin."

Behind them, the tugs and their ECM drones continued their more obvious attempts to hide from the incoming ships—doing just well enough to disguise their true nature.

#

Every minute after the first hour stretched like an eternity. Kyle sent Anderson to go sleep but remained on the bridge himself—the risk his battle group carried was on him and him alone. He couldn't *leave* until he knew his people were safe.

He waited, managing to somehow keep himself still and strapped in on the bridge. They were past ninety minutes, into the zone where his people were *probably* safe, when Surgeon-Commander Adrian Cunningham strode onto the bridge.

"Yes, Commander?" Kyle addressed the ship's doctor.

The tall blond man who was responsible for the health of everyone aboard the supercarrier looked down at the sitting captain and smiled.

"You are aware, sir, that your implant informs me if you've sustained injuries?" he asked sweetly.

Kyle blinked. He'd been immersed in his implants, focusing on conversations and battle displays instead of his dislocated shoulder. With the stims he'd taken and his immersion in his own head, the injury wasn't even registering anymore.

"Since you appear incapable of leaving the bridge and all of our major injuries are dealt with, I decided to come make sure the man responsible for keeping us all *alive* didn't permanently injure himself," Cunningham continued. "Get out of that chair and hold still."

There was only one man on *Avalon* that even the Captain would usually obey. With a sigh, Kyle unstrapped himself and stood—only to nearly collapse again as his left shoulder spasmed in pain he finally noticed.

"Thought so," the Surgeon Commander said brightly. He produced a stark white device, split it in half, and placed each half of one side of Kyle's shoulder. "This will hurt," he noted, then gave an apparent implant command to the devices.

Kyle gave a loud, wordless grunt as the device *jerked* against his shoulder. He *felt* the dislocated joint snap into place—and then pain instantly ceased as the device pumped nanites into his body.

"There you go," the doctor noted, removing the device and dropping it into a case. "Now, those extra machines will work with your base suite and repair the damage around the shoulder and you won't, say, pass out from pain in the middle of a battle."

Cunningham studied Kyle's face for a minute, and he returned the doctor's look with a questioning glance.

"How many stims?" he asked simply.

"Three," Kyle replied. "Due for the fourth in an hour."

"No," the doctor said flatly. "Even if we've messed this up and the Commonwealth can intercept us, they're still at least two hours away. I am *ordering* you out of here and into a bed. I don't care if that 'bed' is the couch in your office—you need to *sleep* or you're no good to anyone."

"You're not allowed to order me around in a combat zone," Kyle pointed out. He was *not* leaving his bridge.

"Captain, we are not being fired on. The nearest enemy ship is over a light-minute away now. You have very competent crew, who *you* have ordered to rest properly, who can wake you up if you're needed. You're right that I can't actually *order* you, sir, but *please*—I want to live through this too," Cunningham pleaded. "We need you at your best."

The doctor...had a point.

"Fine," Kyle allowed. He turned to look at Xue's assistant—he'd sent the tactical officer off to sleep as well. "Let me know the *instant* they appear to have detected us," he ordered. "Let's be honest; I'm probably going back to sleep afterward, but I need to know."

"Yes, sir!" the young man replied crisply.

"Bed, Captain," Cunningham said sharply. "Now."

#

It was over an hour later when Kyle was awakened from his nap on the couch in his office by an implant alert.

"Sir, we've definitely been pinged by the Q-probes," the junior tactical officer told him. "Looks like we stirred up a hornet's nest out there."

"Show me the feed," Kyle ordered as he sat up on the couch, focusing on the tactical plot dropping in through his implant datalink. The Lieutenant Commander had the plot updated by the time Kyle had finished asking.

The two capital ships heading in toward Goudeshijie hadn't changed their course—they were past turnover; the fastest route for them to exit the gravity well now was right back the way they'd come. Both of them had changed vectors a little bit—their courses had been to rendezvous with each other, so the course each was now on was a *slightly* faster route out of the gravity well.

The real sign they'd been detected, though, was that the two blocking forces the Twenty-Third Fleet had left outside the gravity well were now blasting after Kyle's people, paralleling their course as best they could while following the arc of the well. They didn't appear to be on a true intercept course, just making sure that there was no way Kyle's three limping warships could escape them.

"Can any of them intercept us before we reach Xin?" he asked.

"They *could*," the younger man replied after a moment. "But they couldn't coordinate it, and it would be at a *very* high relative velocity."

Kyle nodded. A high relative velocity would be to *his* advantage at this point—Battle Group *Avalon*'s biggest vulnerability at this point was that the heavy lances on the Hercules and the Saint outranged anything his people had left. If the Terrans came whipping past at sixty or a hundred thousand kilometers a second, they'd cross that range advantage in seconds.

"If any of them look like they *are* vectoring to intercept, wake me up immediately," he told the younger man. "If not, my implant will wake me when we reach Xin orbit."

"We may be clear the whole way, sir," the junior tactical officer told him.

Kyle nodded and dropped the channel. Clear all the way to Xin helped. Surviving three and a half days once they were there...*that* was an entirely different headache.

12:00 April 5, 2736 ESMDT
DSC-078 Avalon, Captain's Breakout Room

Settled into Xin's orbit under the protective umbrella of two hundred Atlatl-VI missile satellites, Kyle called a meeting of his chief subordinates. With Wong, Anderson and Wills joining him in his breakout room, he had Captains Olivier and Albert linked via radio— and Captain Sansone Costa of Renaissance Trade Factor Intelligence linked in via Q-Com.

"There's not a lot I can tell you about Vice Admiral Kaj Ness," Costa told them once they'd gathered. "I've forwarded what files we have on him and his senior officers. It's slim reading—he commanded part of Walkingstick's main strike force when they hit the fleet at Midori. From what we can tell, he followed the Marshal from the Coreward frontier after his last campaigns there.

"You already have our files on the capability of his ships," the intelligence officer shrugged. "If anything else comes to mind, I'll pass it on. Is there anything else I can do to help?"

"We're sitting on top of a Commonwealth logistics depot packed full of Stormwinds," Olivier noted. "The things won't fit in our launchers, but we could set them up as temporary mines if we could commandeer them. Do you have any codes or software hacks for that?"

That was actually a good idea, Kyle noted. Not a normally useful one, as it would be difficult to drop the missiles into stable orbits, and *nobody* wanted to risk a gigaton-range antimatter warhead plus fuel falling into their atmosphere. In this case though, it could be handy—except...

Costa shook his head with a chuckle.

"I *wish*, Captain Olivier," he noted. "Remember, the ability to override a missile in flight is a holy grail of intelligence work. The secure encryption on those computer cores is insane. You could swap out the cores, I suppose, but I'm not sure how much work that would be."

"Wong?" Kyle asked, glancing over at his engineer.

"Not...easy," the Senior Fleet Commander noted. "We have the parts to fabricate several thousand missile computer cores, but the Stormwind has a significantly different internal layout than our Jackhammer. We'd have to custom-build the template... We might, if we work at it, manage to get a hundred or so missiles converted a day."

"That's not useless," Kyle observed. "Having an extra few hundred missiles to back up the Atlatls when the Admiral comes in after us could be very handy."

"I'll get my people on it," Wong promised. "But...we're probably going to have problems with the Terrans before we have any significant number of missiles out there."

"The planet was transmitting a warning about the satellites, so Ness knows we've got a stack of defenses with us," Kyle replied. "He's going to be cautious—I suspect we're going to be seeing more missiles coming in, trying to take out the missile satellites. I don't want to launch from the satellites until we have to."

"That's...what I was hoping to have the Stormwinds to use as counters against," Olivier noted. "We're damn short on ammo and we don't have the defenses to stop ninety-missile salvos *without* using missiles to thin them out."

"And while Twenty-Third Fleet's Assassins have undersized magazines, the ones that are left have only fired a few rounds," Anderson added. "All told, Ness has the ammunition left for over twenty-five salvos—and we don't have the defenses to stop that much firepower!"

Normally, *Avalon*'s starfighters would form her first layer of defense against heavy missile salvos. Ninety missiles would be a minor but real threat to his three ships even if they were undamaged, but with three hundred-plus fighters, the ships would have been safe.

Since they didn't *have* those starfighters, though... A thought occurred to Kyle, and he smiled sadly. It was an answer—it was just an answer he wished he didn't have.

"Captain Olivier's idea of pre-deployed missiles is a good one," he noted. "Though we can't convert enough Stormwinds for missile defense purposes, I'm not sure we need to. Sub-Colonel Wills—how many Starfire missiles do we have in our magazines?"

The Phoenix officer was now Battle Group Seven-Two's CAG since she was senior to Wing Commander Cortez, the commander of *Avalon*'s Charlie Wing and the only other O-5 survivor still in Huī Xing. She paused to think for a moment before answering.

"I don't have that number immediately to hand," she admitted. "But all three of the ships with fighters aboard carried ten full reloads. We replenished our reloads from the logistics ship before we originally attempted to leave Huī Xing, so we've only fired off one full set.

"Assuming we didn't lose any to the hits on the cruisers, we should have over eleven thousand Starfires in stock."

"Thank you, Sub-Colonel," Kyle said, still smiling sadly. "We can hold onto ten full reloads for our remaining starfighters and *still* deploy ten *thousand* fighter missiles as an anti-missile screen, people.

"My experience suggests we'll need a five-to-one ratio to guarantee kills," he continued, "but if we go to a four-to-one ratio, we'll still be reasonably assured of over eighty kills on each salvo. Those missiles will *eat* Twenty-Third Fleet's long-range firepower.

"I want to make Vice Admiral Ness spend his missiles carefully and completely before he comes after us, people. Remember that above all else, we need to buy *time*."

CHAPTER 40

Whatever else Vice Admiral Kaj Ness was, he was methodical and thorough. His blocking forces had rushed to make sure that Battle Group Seven-Two was still contained at Xin—but the two warships deep in Goudeshijie's gravity well had taken an extra hour of slow acceleration to locate and destroy the drones they'd left behind – the best way to confirm that was truly all they were.

Then, once the battlecruiser and battleship had finally made their escape from the gas giant's gravity and reached Xin under Alcubierre-Stetson drive, Twenty-Third Fleet had proceeded to *saturate* the planet's local space with Q-probes.

By now, Kyle figured his people had killed somewhere around two hundred of the mind-bogglingly expensive tools, each of which contained a block of entangled particles that had been brought all the way from the Commonwealth's core worlds. For every probe they'd killed, at least two had made close passes successfully or settled into stealthed positions far enough way that they couldn't locate them.

The Terrans knew *exactly* where his ships were, though they were moving enough to be reasonably safe. They knew where his missile satellites were, which was risky for Kyle...but they also knew that he'd deployed *ten thousand* missiles in defensive arrays around his ships and Atlatls.

Kyle wasn't trying to read Ness's mind—but the surprise value of the stunt he'd pulled had bought him an entire day. A day to make repairs, to rest, to give his people time to grieve.

"We have movement," Xue reported.

He linked into her display, assessing what she saw. Twenty-Third Fleet had, once again, assembled into Force Alpha and Force Bravo, opposite each other across Xin's gravity well and able to cut him off wherever he tried to run.

Now, all of the ships in both task forces were changing position, moving the Lexingtons back and lining up everyone else...

"They're clearing the launchers on the ships with missiles," his tactical officer concluded before he could speak. "And...here they come."

Force Alpha had the Saint and the Volcano along with its three missile-launcher-lacking Lexingtons. They launched forty-two missiles.

Force Bravo had seen the Hercules rejoin the two older Assassins. They were the smaller force, but without the carriers, they had more launchers. They sent forty-eight missiles dropping into the gravity well for a total of ninety weapons closing from either side of the planet.

Kyle let *Avalon*'s computers run the numbers on them and studied the missiles carefully. The two task forces had arranged themselves perfectly, both exactly eighteen million kilometers away from his own fleet. They were technically *inside* the gravity well, but that was a vague line at the best of times...

Either way, both missile salvos had a thirty-two-minute flight time.

"Inform Sub-Colonel Wills," he told Xue. With a half-hour flight time for missiles and an almost two-hour trip for the Commonwealth *ships*, he'd seen no reason to keep his starfighters in space. Now, however, he needed them.

Twenty-four starfighters were a frail shield against the vise he'd trapped his battle group in, but every piece was going to count today.

"And, Commander Xue?" he said after a moment.

"Yes, sir?"

"Show our displeasure with the good Admiral. I want a full salvo from the Atlatls."

The black-haired young woman flashed him a bright smile and gave a command through her implants. A few moments later, six hundred green arrows flashed into existence on Kyle's implant feeds—an impressive response to the mere ninety the Terrans had thrown at him.

Of course, he could only do that four times. The Terrans could repeat their performance almost *thirty*.

"Any follow-up salvos?"

"Nothing so far," the Lieutenant Commander reported. "Ninety seconds and counting."

"They're testing us," Kyle assessed. There was no way the Commonwealth commanders thought ninety missiles would get through what he'd set up around Xin. His response had a chance of doing damage, though not as much as he'd like.

"Looks like it, sir," she agreed. "What do we do?"

"Fire off four Starfires per missile once they're in range, and then go to standard missile defense procedure," he ordered calmly. They'd discussed all this, but repetition was a habit for any military.

There wasn't much more he could do for his own missiles. They were targeted on Force Bravo, the smaller of the two forces. It would be... interesting to see what they did.

#

Launched first, the Terran missiles arrived well before the Alliance weapons came near Force Bravo. They passed the three-million-kilometer mark closing at seventeen thousand kilometers a second—and a few seconds later, three hundred and sixty of the thousands of fighter missiles in orbit lit off their drives and charged to meet them.

Sub-Colonel Wills and her fighters were behind them, moving far more slowly but still interposed between the three crippled starships and the missiles sent to kill them.

With Q-probes, starfighters, and starships all around them to provide the vectors, the Starfires made surprisingly effective countermeasures.

Two and a half minutes later, the two salvos intersected in a rapidly spreading sequence of antimatter explosions.

This time, the fighters were almost redundant. A single missile escaped the wall of fire the starfighter missiles had built, and one of the pilots nailed it with her defensive lasers while it was still a hundred thousand kilometers from the starships.

Farther out in deep space, their own missiles closed on Force Bravo. The Commonwealth warships defended themselves with skill and vigor, lasers and positron lances blasting missiles to pieces by the dozens— then by the hundreds.

Kyle had a moment of hope as the missile swarm continued—and then sighed in disappointment as the three Terran ships vanished into Alcubierre drive, the gravity distortion of their engines ripping many of the remaining missiles to shreds and leaving the survivors to fly off into deep space.

The battlecruisers were in warped space for less than a minute, returning to normal space barely a million kilometers from their origin point—still exactly one light-minute from Battle Group Seven-Two, but well out of the ability of the missiles to change course.

"Send the self-destructs to the remaining weapons," he ordered quietly. There was no point leaving antimatter explosives floating around in deep space as a navigation hazard. The missiles would self-destruct automatically about an hour after they exhausted their fuel, but why allow a risk they didn't need?

"Still no follow-up salvo?" he asked after watching the missiles vaporize themselves.

"Nothing," Xue confirmed, sounding confused. "I'm...not sure what the goal is."

"Wear us down," Kyle told her. "Grind away the missiles we've placed— Vice Admiral Ness knows that if he brought his ships in now, I'd fire ten thousand missiles at him. That's not something his ships can survive."

"What do we do?" she asked.

"We take it," Force Commander Kyle Roberts said grimly. "We take his best shot, we get him to exhaust his magazines, and we let him take as long as he likes to do it. I'm hoping for three days."

The Lieutenant Commander looked at him in confusion for a moment, and then he saw the realization dawn in her eyes.

Every hour—every *minute* Vice Admiral Kaj Ness of the Terran Commonwealth spent battering away their defenses was an hour and a minute closer to Seventh Fleet's arrival.

CHAPTER 41

A sharp alert through his implant woke Kyle from another abortive attempt at sleep. Checking the time, he saw this had been the longest that the Terrans *had* let him sleep in the last few days—it had been almost four hours since the last time they'd thrown missiles at his command.

The intervals had been completely random, making it impossible for Kyle to give his people any significant rest. They could—and had— cycled flight crews on their handful of starfighters, but there was only so much cycling he could do of the full bridge crews.

The longest interval between salvos before this one had been two and a half hours. The shortest had been fifteen minutes. Some of the salvos had been doubled or tripled up, sending hundreds of missiles swarming into the teeth of his defenses.

Somehow, all of his warships were still there. They'd lost five more starfighters along the way, leaving him with less than twenty of the fleet little ships, but his Battle Group had survived so far.

Seventh Fleet was mere hours away. The clock was ticking in his favor.

Looking at the tactical feed his implant was drawing his attention to though, he realized that Battle Group Seven-Two's time might have run out.

The Terrans had stacked three salvos on top of each other and hurled two hundred and seventy missiles at him. He'd spent the stockpiled Starfires they'd dropped into orbit freely so far, and now found himself with less than a thousand missiles left to defend his ships.

"Pull the battle group closer together," he ordered as he fully linked into the tactical net. "Set all remaining Starfires to salvo. Wong, how many of those Stormwinds have you refitted?"

"Three hundred and fifty," the Engineer replied immediately. If there was anyone on the ship who'd managed *less* sleep than Kyle, it was the Senior Fleet Commander trying to hold *Avalon* together *and* retrofit hundreds of missiles. "We'll have the components for another fifty in about six hours."

"They're not going to give us six hours," Kyle replied. "Hand over control of whatever you've got to tactical."

"Yes, sir."

"Xue, Anderson, what's our ammo status?"

"We've got one salvo left in the satellites," Anderson reported. "Nine hundred and eighty Starfires floating in orbit. The fighters are fully reloaded. We're down to ten salvos apiece for the cruisers and twenty for *Avalon* herself."

The big carrier had a *lot* of missiles aboard for her relatively small number of launchers. With only four launchers left, Kyle had freely used those munitions to thin out previous salvos. Now he wished he'd held them back.

"Hold the satellites and the Stormwinds," Kyle ordered. "Start salvoing everything our starships have left at those missiles. Hold nothing back—Ness wants to court a lance duel. Let him think he'll have one."

"Opening fire," Xue confirmed.

"I'll be on the bridge in twenty minutes," he told her. That would still be ten minutes before the missiles were in range. A shower might help him wake up. He had a feeling that he wouldn't be getting any more sleep before it was over one way or another.

#

Kyle watched Battle Group Seven-Two's missiles intercept the enemy weapons as he dressed with the quickly precise movements of years of practice.

His people had sent ten salvos of twenty-four missiles and ten more salvoes of four against the incoming fire—a total of two hundred and eighty defending weapons against two hundred and seventy attacking. If each of his missiles would score a clean kill, the whole affair would have been much easier.

Instead, the math was far less even. By the time he stepped onto his bridge, the ten big salvos had struck—and wiped away about a hundred of the incoming weapons. He didn't expect much from the remaining salvos—but those missiles were more useful now than they would be against the Terrans' entire fleet later.

"Starfires firing," Xue reported aloud, glancing over at him as he stepped into his command chair. "Still over one hundred fifty bogies inbound."

He gestured for her to carry on. She was linked into everything. Micromanaging the battle group's defense was *tempting* but unnecessary. Lieutenant Commander Jessica Xue, like most of *Avalon*'s junior-for-their-roles bridge staff, had a promotion waiting for her in his recommendations.

Whether the recommendations of a man who lost a quarter of his command and got the rest crippled would carry much weight, well, he wasn't entirely sure. But he'd do what he could for the people who'd served him well.

The last nine hundred-plus Starfires blasted forward. With the losses the capital ship missiles had inflicted, that was probably overkill—but the last thing Kyle could afford was to lose even a single Atlatl platform or fighter, let alone one of his starships.

Multi-gigaton explosions lit up the sky around *Avalon* and his implants automatically dampened his feeds to avoid blinding him. The link might be directly to his nerves and hence impervious to flash-blindness, but psychosomatic symptoms could still occur from very bright light.

"We have leakers!" Xue announced. "Wills, do you see them?"

"On them," the starfighter pilot announced.

Kyle held his breath as a handful of missiles burst through the wave of fire the defensive missiles had wrought, and charged towards his ships.

Sub-Colonel Wills and *Avalon*'s fighters were there. The survivors of Battle Group Seven-Two's fighter wings were a mixed bag of crews, with some of even the individual flight crews having both Star Kingdom and Federation personnel, but they were also the survivors of everything the Commonwealth had thrown at Kyle's people.

Five missiles were *nothing* to those hard-forged veterans, and the last died twenty thousand kilometers clear of Kyle's ships.

He exhaled his held breath in relief. There'd been moments when he'd been afraid they wouldn't make it. The Commonwealth's Twenty-Third Fleet had thrown an *astonishing* amount of firepower at his battle group. If they hadn't thought to use their excess starfighter missiles as counter-missiles, his people would be floating debris in Xin orbit now.

"Sir, they're moving," Xue reported quietly. "Force Bravo just warped space."

"They're consolidating their force," Kyle replied. "They've got a big enough acceleration edge that we can't actually outrun them, but they'll need all eight ships' defenses to stand off the missiles we have left." He shook his head.

"This is it," he told his people loudly. "Wake everybody up; get everything online. The Terrans are going to come visiting."

As his people leapt back into activity around him, Kyle glared at the timers. Depending on just *what* Vice Admiral Kaj Ness decided to do, it could easily be too soon. Seventh Fleet was still three hours out.

#

Fifteen minutes later, Force Bravo emerged from warped space a million kilometers from Force Alpha. The two halves of Twenty-Third Fleet slowly began maneuvering toward each other, acting like they had all the time in the world.

Kyle really hoped they thought that had all the time in the world. A few hours of sorting out formations and lines of fire would be *perfect* in his books.

"Sir, we're receiving a transmission for you."

"Put it through," Kyle ordered, linking his feed to the communications network to see what Vice Admiral Ness had to say now.

"Force Commander Roberts," Ness greeted him. Unlike Kyle, the Terran Vice Admiral had clearly been resting on a regular schedule for the last three days. He was perfectly turned out and looked wide awake.

"This has gone on far too long. My orders are now clear: you will leave this system a prisoner of the Commonwealth or not at all.

"I am aware that you retain a significant quantity of missiles, but you no longer have the firepower to overwhelm the defenses of my entire fleet, nor the acceleration to escape. I respect your courage and your tenacity, but even you must see this battle is lost.

"If you force me to come dig you out of your hole, thousands of both our people will die," Ness concluded. "Please, Kyle," he pleaded. "Surrender. You can run the numbers on this war as well as this battle; you know how this will end. Unity is inevitable.

"Why die standing in the way of history?"

Kyle was silent for several minutes, letting the activity of his bridge wash over him. He considered lying—a carefully constructed deception could buy him the time he needed for Seventh Fleet to arrive—but rejected it. Kaj Ness was his *enemy*, but he had fought an honorable battle.

It was hardly Ness's fault that his nation was utterly convinced that it was their destiny to unify all mankind. To a man raised on Terra itself, both that that unification would occur and that it would be under Terra's banner would truly seem inevitable and good.

Kyle Roberts, however, was sworn to defend the Castle Federation—a nation that would have to fall for the Commonwealth's unification to come to pass. Even if that placed him in the path of history and inevitability, he would not dishonor that oath.

He activated the recorder in his command chair and faced the camera, intentionally relaxing his pose and putting his best cheery grin on his face.

"Vice Admiral Ness, you may believe your victory is inevitable, but I still have tricks you haven't seen," he promised the other man. "Unlike so many of even your peers, you have walked Terra's soil. You're more familiar with foxes than most—and you should know that they're most dangerous when cornered!

"If you want to drag me before your Marshal in chains, to hand him *Avalon* and the Stellar Fox as trophies, then by all the Gods, *you can come and get me!*"

01:00 April 9, 2736 ESMDT
DSC-078 Avalon, *Bridge*

Mouthing off at the Vice Admiral *probably* hadn't bought them any more time, but it had felt good. Kyle had remained on the bridge since the transmission, checking over every preparation and half-praying that the Terrans would give them enough time.

An hour after the exchange with Ness, he learned the final answer.

Assembled into a single force in a rough wall formation, all eight Terran starships turned as one for Xin orbit and brought their engines online. Two hundred gravities—a fifty-gravity edge over anything Battle Group Seven-Two could achieve and still thirty gravities less than the modern battleship and battlecruiser at the heart of their formation.

The Lexingtons, the Volcano, even the Assassins were only there to thicken the missile defenses against the salvo that Ness knew Kyle was holding in reserve. It was the Saint and the Hercules that were going to kill his fleet.

Seventh Fleet would arrive before the Commonwealth ships reached Battle Group Avalon. They would emerge at the edge of the gravity well, a light-minute behind the Terrans, fifteen minutes before those eight warships reached lance range.

Since missile flight time for Seventh Fleet would be over *thirty* minutes, Twenty-Third Fleet had moved fifteen minutes too soon for Kyle's people to survive this. The *Terrans* wouldn't make it out—not with an entire fleet's worth of missiles and starfighters chasing them across the system, even if Battle Group Seven-Two did no damage to them all—but they'd destroy Kyle's people first.

He'd failed.

Mira finished running the numbers herself and looked at her link to Admiral Alstairs' flag bridge helplessly. They would arrive fifteen minutes before Kyle came under attack—and fifteen minutes too late to do anything.

"I did not come this far and cut things this close to watch Force Commander Roberts die," Alstairs said flatly, loudly enough that everyone on both the bridge and flag bridge heard her.

"Commander Coles," she continued, her voice sharp. "Have you ever threaded the needle before?"

Mira's navigator looked at her, then at the intercom screen to the flag bridge as he swallowed hard.

"No, ma'am," he admitted. "Some of the Marine transports have done it, but they're all on their way back to Alizon now."

"Coordinate with the other navigators, then," the Rear Admiral ordered. "Find someone who has—I want us to drop out *right* behind these bastards."

"Ma'am, that's *sixteen million* kilometers into the gravity well," Coles objected. "I don't know if we can *do* that."

"Commander, Pendez dropped Roberts into goddamn *orbit* at Tranquility," Alstairs told him flatly. "She'd never done a late Alcubierre emergence at that point either. Make. It. Happen."

Mira walked over to the Commander after Alstairs turned her attention away, dropping her hand on the young man's shoulder.

"We know it can be done," she said quietly.

"Everybody forgets that the old *Avalon* had neutronium armor," Coles pointed out. "She could take a *lot* more of a beating than any of the new ships."

"Is it going to rip any of the ships in half?"

"Probably not," he admitted. "Not unless we screw up the math or one of the engineering crews misbalances their singularities. This is *very* tight."

"Then get the math right," Mira told him. "And I'll go step on the engineers. I am *not* getting to Huī Xing in time to watch Kyle die. Understand, Commander?"

"No pressure, huh?" Coles asked bitterly.

"Do you understand, James?" Mira repeated.

"I get it," he told her. "Now if you'll excuse me, I have to calculate a needle for eight starships to thread."

CHAPTER 42

Huī Xing System
01:45 April 9, 2736 Earth Standard Meridian Date/Time
DSC-078 Avalon, *Bridge*

"Salvo all missiles," Kyle ordered.

Watching the Terran warships close for a full fifty minutes had been *painful*, but at this point, the survivability of his own battle group wasn't the primary concern anymore. Launching earlier would allow the ships Ness didn't need to kill *Avalon* to break off and be outside the gravity well once Seventh Fleet arrived.

Now that Twenty-Third Fleet was approaching turnover, there was no way those ships could help protect the fleet from his missiles *and* escape the gravity well before Seventh Fleet arrived. No one on his bridge or even the other warships had questioned the delay either.

Everyone in Battle Group Avalon had accepted their fate. Their deaths were going to bait the trap that handed the Commonwealth one of their worst defeats of the war. If the ships Ness was bringing to Xin were taken or destroyed, *seventeen* Terran capital ships would have been destroyed in Operation Rising Star.

That was over a fifth of the strength the Federation had started the war with. Kyle didn't want to die any more than the next man. He wanted to live. He wanted to see where things went with Mira, to finish rebuilding his relationship with his son, to dance at Lisa Kerensky's wedding to another man.

But he'd sworn an oath. Like the crew of his ships, he faced his fate unhesitatingly, watching his salvo of nine hundred and fifty missiles charge out at the Commonwealth fleet.

Seconds ticked away, turning into minutes. The Terrans hit turnover, slicing away their velocity by almost two kilometers a second every second.

The Terrans' defenses opened up a full minute before impact, lasers and positron beams ripping into space from a million kilometers away. At that range, they scored few hits—but every missile that died was one they didn't need to kill later.

Electronic countermeasures and jamming lit up the space around the Commonwealth fleet to *Avalon*'s sensors, even as streams of energy tore across the same void. Missiles died, their fiery deaths lighting up Kyle's view and releasing expanding balls of radiation that added to the jamming.

His view of the battle was starting to disintegrate under the jamming and radiation, even the Q-probes in the middle of the fight barely able to sustain a clear view of the action. At this point, there was little the launching ship's computers could do for the missiles—it was all down to the networked intelligence of the rapidly shrinking missile host.

"Go go go!" Kyle heard someone whisper on *Avalon*'s bridge. He grinned. The *Captain* couldn't say that, but he could *agree* with the sentiment.

A cascade of fire and radiation reached across a million kilometers of empty space and crashed down on the Commonwealth ships. Desperate last-ditch defenses wove a shroud of explosions around the Twenty-Third Fleet, and it was easily ten seconds—an *eternity* to officers living in their implants and tactical nets—before the Commonwealth ships emerged.

Even as the Q-probes scanned the Terrans, studying and analyzing, there was one obvious sign of the effect of their missiles: eight starships had met the missile storm.

Six had left.

Kyle waited patiently for the identities to be established, for the data to be collated.

"We got the Volcano," Xue reported after a minute. "The Volcano and one of the Assassins. Looks like the other Assassin and the Saint both took hits but are still ticking."

Avalon's Captain shook his head in admiration. Modern ships might not have the incredibly dense neutronium armor of pre–positron lance warships, but their meters-thick ferro-carbon ceramic armor could take a *lot* of punishment.

"Estimated time to lance range?" he finally asked.

"They haven't adjusted their course at all," Xue told him. "They will range on us in thirty minutes."

The satellites had shot their bolt. Every missile he'd suspended in orbit was gone. All that he had left were nineteen starfighters and three crippled starships. Xin didn't even have a *moon* to hide behind.

"Battle Group orders," he said calmly. "Assume formation Alpha Foxtrot One." He paused. This channel only went to the bridges, but he knew whatever he said would rapidly be conveyed throughout all three ships.

"Spacers, fellow soldiers," he told them. "It has been a privilege and an honor. We aren't done yet. Let's...see what happens."

He watched the Commonwealth ships close, counting down the seconds and minutes. There was *nothing* he could do—the only trick he had left was a last-minute suicide charge to try to get his own ships' heavy lances into range. Everything was down to Admiral Alstairs' desperate throw of the dice.

Then his starfighters started moving. *That* was not in his plan.

"Wills, what are you *doing*?" he demanded.

There was no response, and all nineteen of his remaining starfighters were now charging at the Commonwealth fleet. He ran their courses— and was somehow unsurprised to realize they were on kamikaze flights.

"Damn it, Wills, *answer me*," he snarled into the communicator, his hands clenched into fists as he watched the last survivors of his fighter wings charge into the face of the enemy. "We *have* a plan. Please!"

"I'm sorry, sir," the Star Kingdom of Phoenix officer replied softly. "If that doesn't work, we won't have time. This way...well...this way, if nothing else they're looking at us."

"Damn you, Sub-Colonel," he whispered.

"It's the job, sir," she told him. "Starfighters die so our friends live."

Kyle blinked away tears he wouldn't—*couldn't*—show.

"Gods speed you, Sherry," he finally told her.

Silence covered *Avalon*'s bridge as the nineteen tiny ships, less than a thousandth of the size of their enemies, lunged across space. The Terrans recognized the threat instantly, heavy positron lances beginning to flicker out at starfighters they were unlikely to hit.

The secondary lances *should* be enough against nineteen fighters, but clearly Ness wasn't willing to take the chance.

Weapons fire flashed across the stars again and Kyle clenched his fists so hard, he suspected he was drawing blood, counting seconds as his people charged to their deaths.

They might make it work. Even if Alstairs' gamble failed, Wills might manage to save them all. All nineteen fighters survived the heavy lances, dancing around the Terran weapons with the deadly skill of survivors.

And then a massive explosion of Cherenkov radiation blasted out of the space behind Twenty-Third Fleet. A million kilometers behind the Terrans, it wasn't as close as he knew Alstairs had aimed...

But it was close enough. *Zheng He*'s immense positron lances might be weaker than those aboard the Hercules, but they were more powerful than anything *else* in the Terran fleet—and they hit the *Hercules*-class battlecruiser first.

Even before the blast of bright blue radiation had faded, the Commonwealth battlecruiser had come apart under the Trade Factor battleship's pounding. The Saint, Vice Admiral Ness's presumed flagship, survived only seconds more as *Clawhammer* swung into range of her weaker but still powerful heavy lances.

The Assassin and the Lexingtons only had six-hundred-kiloton-a-second lances—hugely underpowered and hence outranged by every ship in Seventh Fleet—*including* the warships in orbit around Xin.

The commanders of those ships reacted faster than Kyle would have thought. The battle had turned from a certain victory for the Terrans to a crushing defeat in under twenty seconds—but by the time Sub-Colonel Wills' fighters started breaking off their suicide runs, the last four Terran warships were signaling their surrenders.

Without missiles or starfighters, faced with a fully supplied Alliance fleet, this truly was a battle they knew they could not win.

CHAPTER 43

Huī Xing System
10:00 April 9, 2736 Earth Standard Meridian Date/Time
BC-129 Camerone, *Admiral's Office*

Captain Kyle Roberts entered Rear Admiral Alstairs' office slowly, offering a crisp salute to the small woman sitting behind the desk, waiting for him. She wordlessly gestured him to the chair in front of her desk, and he obeyed the implicit command.

Before either of them said anything, he placed the small gold chevron of a Force Commander on Alstairs' desk.

"I hope that next time, you give this to someone who does a better job," he said quietly.

Engineers were swarming over the three ships left of his temporary command. *Avalon* would need months of repairs but would fight again. *Courageous* would also need a yard review but would probably be scrapped—the *Fearless*-class cruiser was too old to be worth repairing the amount of damage she'd taken. *Indomitable* was incapable of Alcubierre. Kyle wasn't sure what her final fate would be, but she would never leave the Huī Xing system.

"And what do you think this hypothetical someone would have done that you didn't?" she asked him.

"*Not* got his entire command crippled or destroyed," Kyle said flatly. "I lost functionally all of my fighters and none of my starships are combat-capable. Had I followed the plan, I might not have lost one of my best friends."

"Which would have left one hundred thousand prisoners of war to the whims of fate," the Admiral pointed out. "You knew the risk when you went in. *I* knew the risk when you went in. We won, in the end."

"A Pyrrhic victory," he replied. "Walkingstick can replace the ships he lost better than we can replace what we lost. The mission to take Via Somnia is a failure. All of these worlds are now at risk."

"Command has already promised us a mobile yard ship and a legion of computer and hardware techs," she told him. "They expect to have all four ships we captured here in service in three months. Yes, given the likely fate of *Courageous*, you effectively lost three ships. But we captured four. We gain one, all told—and Walkingstick loses seventeen."

"And the Commonwealth will build sixty warships this year on an effectively *peacetime* footing," Kyle said. "Ness told me to run the numbers on this war. I did. I honestly don't know if we can win."

"Says the man who got trapped by over twice his numbers and almost didn't need my help to carry the day," Alstairs told him with a smile. "You did all right, Captain Roberts. If you'd known *everything*, could you have done better? Of course.

"But we don't know everything when we make our decisions, Captain. And *not* deciding—not *acting*—places our people and the nation we serve at risk." She shook her head. "I've already signed off on transfer orders returning *Avalon* to Castle for repairs. Unfortunately, that means you'll have to face the media and your political enemies with, as you accurately described, a Pyrrhic victory to your name."

Kyle had sent the son of the current Senator for Castle to prison for fraud, rape and treason. Senator Randall, first among equals of the Castle Federation's thirteen-person executive, did *not* like him.

"I do not envy you your reception," the Rear Admiral told him. "With six months in repairs on *Avalon*, you may well find yourself on the beach. Be prepared for that—but remember this, Kyle Roberts:

"The Commonwealth outmasses, outnumbers, and outproduces the Alliance. If we are to be victorious—if we are to maintain our independence in the face of the people who would force all mankind to kneel—we need brave, *smart* officers who will take risks and accept the consequences of those risks.

"We need officers like you," she finished, standing and offering her hand across the desk. "You did just fine—and I think you'll continue to do just fine, Captain Roberts. Don't disappoint me."

#

Mira was waiting for Kyle outside the Admiral's office, and she fell into step behind him as he walked silently, struggling to wrap his brain around his own confused emotions and feelings. Part of him was convinced he'd failed. *Thousands* of people under his command had died, for a victory that would likely have happened without that sacrifice.

But the Admiral seemed to think that it had been worth it—that things might not have ended as well if he had done differently. He knew that it was sometimes hard to see your own successes past the costs—or your own desires past your fears.

Camerone's Captain had walked silently with him but also managed to guide him to her cabin. Opening the door, she led him into her sitting area, gestured to a chair, and then produced two bottles of beer.

"To Michael Stanford," she said quietly, raising the beer to Kyle.

He took his own and returned the toast.

"To Michael. May he ever fly amidst the Eternal Stars," he murmured the pilot's toast. He shook his head. "I knew he had the riskier job, but...somehow, I never expected to lose him. He always seemed...well, invincible."

"All of you starfighter jocks are convinced of your invincibility," Mira told him. "It came over to the Navy with you."

"If I'm invincible, too many of those around me aren't," he replied. "We carried the day...but the cost..."

"What happens now? *Avalon* looked beat to pieces."

"Last time I flew an *Avalon* back to Castle, she was in even worse shape," Kyle replied with a chuckle, amusement at the thought providing a wedge he ruthlessly used to break past his incipient funk. "But we are taking her back to Castle to be repaired. I'll hand her over to the Merlin

Yards, and then we all go into the general pool for new assignments. Her repairs will take six months—the Navy can't have five thousand of her better crewmen and officers sitting on their hands for that long."

"You'll be on Castle for a while, then?"

"Probably," Kyle admitted. "Senator Randall doesn't like me any more now than he did last year. The politics are going to suck, but it comes with the job." He sighed, looking at the ebony-skinned woman sitting across from him. "And you'll be here. *Doing* the job. Risking your life."

"Every uniformed couple ends up facing that sooner or later," she told him. "We can...end this now, if you want," she offered slowly. "Leave it as a wartime fling, maybe look each other up again come peacetime."

"I *don't* want," he told her fiercely, feeling suddenly more certain than he'd been in a while. "We haven't had much time together since you left *Avalon*, but I know what I want, Mira Solace. I want to take the time to see where things go. I want to put the effort in to match up leaves, to meet on planets in the middle—whatever it takes. I want to see if we can make this work." He paused, his certainty draining away, and sighed. "If *you* want."

He realized she was smiling—the bright, brilliant smile that cracked every semblance of the black statue she could be into the beautiful woman he'd fallen for even when she was utterly off-limits to him.

"I want," she replied. "I want to...see what happens."

Niagara System—Commonwealth Space
21:00 April 9, 2736 ESMDT
BB-285 Saint Michael—*Marshal Walkingstick's Office*

Fleet Admiral James Calvin Walkingstick, Marshal of the Rimward Marches in the name of the Terran Commonwealth, sighed and closed the report from Via Somnia. It had taken the Navy Base's defenses *far* too long to realize that Seventh Fleet had left the system—time that had robbed Vice Admiral Ness of the warning that could have saved the man's life.

"Go with God, my friend," he murmured, looking at the viewscreen showing the map of his Marches. The Alliance's counteroffensive had been stunningly successful, though thankfully also stunningly expensive. Seventh Fleet's victory at Huī Xing *hurt*—but Fourth Fleet had run into meat grinder after meat grinder as they pushed his ships out of his second wave of conquests.

Every system he'd seized in the seven months of war was now back in Alliance hands. The price they'd paid in blood and starships to do so, though... He pulled up the latest analysis from his staff. The Alliance had put two thirds of their entire reserve into commission and was still down to two hundred and forty starships from their starting two hundred and eighty-eight active ships.

Walkingstick pulled the long black braid down his back over his shoulder, the massive Admiral using it as a pointer as he ran down the list of his own losses. They were more than merely painful—each ship was three to seven thousand lives lost. He'd been forced to abandon entire divisions of Terran Marines behind enemy lines.

Even with the loss of Twenty-Third Fleet, he'd traded ninety-seven Commonwealth warships for over a hundred Alliance ships. Given the size and strength of the Commonwealth Navy, those were acceptable losses—but his own available force strength was down under sixty warships.

Fortunately, Huī Xing made a very pointed example. He was waiting for the call he knew had to be coming. The quantum entanglement communications network linked him instantly to Earth. He might have been provided immense power in his area of authority, but he still answered to the elected politicians of the Interstellar Congress in the Star Chamber on Terra.

As if his thoughts had *finally* summoned it, his implant buzzed with the notice that a Q-Com request had come in from Sol.

He threw it on the viewscreen, replacing the map of stars with the white hair and pitch-black skin of Senator Michael Burns of Alpha Centauri—the head of the Committee on Unification.

"Marshal Walkingstick," the Senator greeted him. "What the *hell* happened?"

Burns was many things. He was not frail, and his booming voice echoed through Walkingstick's office.

"My people at Via Somnia failed to realize they'd been fooled," Walkingstick said calmly. "Since we believed Seventh Fleet to be pinned there, I authorized Vice Admiral Ness to neutralize Roberts. The man has been a thorn in our side whose removal I believed was worth the risk." He shrugged. "We were wrong as to Seventh Fleet's location, and we lost Huī Xing and Twenty-Third Fleet."

"You came to us with a plan you said would guarantee the conquest of the Rimward Marches," Burns told him. "Now you have lost every system you captured and appear to have embroiled the Commonwealth in a war that risks *our* territorial integrity."

"I made no guarantees," Walkingstick pointed out. "There are no guarantees in war, Senator, and I made no such claims. The situation, however, is not as dire as you may think, and while we may not be on the optimal path, my plans cover this circumstance."

"Explain," Burns ordered.

"The Alliance has completed every ship they had under construction at the start of the war," the Marshal pointed out. "They have recommissioned well over half of their reserve. They have *lost* more ships than they had in the reserve and now face a minimum eighteen-month period before any of their new construction is ready for deployment.

"Given the force available to me, I can continue to slowly grind down their fleet in penny-packet engagements, clearing the way for a final offensive to seize their most important systems before they commission those new ships."

"Neither the Committee nor the Congress is going to be accepting of slow progress at this point, Marshal," Burns warned. "You have lost over half the forces assigned to you."

"And that is why slow progress is all I can make," Walkingstick replied. "If Congress is prepared to provide significant reinforcements, I could end this conflict in a year. If only the currently planned reinforcements are assigned to me, then it will take sixteen months at a minimum and will likely cost far more in terms of ships and lives before we're done."

Burns grunted.

"Send me more ships, Senator, and I will deliver the Rimward Marches," Walkingstick promised. "Do not, and I will still try. But I may not succeed."

"Very well," the big black man snapped. "I will see what I can do."

Walkingstick inclined his head, and Burns cut the channel. With a small smile, the Marshal opened a file on his implant, running through the chains of branches and possibilities that made up the entirety of his true plan. The one the Committee would never see.

It would never do for the Committee to realize how many of those branches and possibilities called for manipulating *them*.

Walkingstick would get his ships. And the Rimward Marches would join the Commonwealth.

Unification, after all, was inevitable.

OTHER BOOKS BY GLYNN STEWART

Castle Federation
Space Carrier Avalon
Stellar Fox
Battle Group Avalon
Q-Ship Chameleon
Rimward Stars(upcoming, see www.faolanspen.com for latest estimated launch date)

Starship's Mage
Starship's Mage: Omnibus
Hand of Mars
Voice of Mars
Alien Arcana
Judgment of Mars (upcoming, see www.faolanspen.com for latest estimated launch date)

Duchy of Terra
The Terran Privateer
Duchess of Terra (upcoming, see www.faolanspen.com for latest estimated launch date)

ONSET
ONSET: To Serve and Protect (upcoming, see www.faolanspen.com for latest estimated launch date)

Stand Alone Novels
Children of Prophecy
City in the Sky